A Christmas Letter

Fiona
HARPER

Donna
ALWARD

Shirley
JUMP

D1513429

MILLS
BOON

First published in Great Britain 2012
Mills & Boon, an imprint of Harlequin (UK) Limited,
Eton House, 18-24 Paradise Road, Richmond, Surrey TW9 1SR

A CHRISTMAS LETTER
© Harlequin Enterprises II B.V./S.à.r.l. 2012

Snowbound in the Earl's Castle © Fiona Harper 2012
Sleigh Ride with the Rancher © Donna Alward 2012
Mistletoe Kisses with the Billionaire © Shirley Jump 2012

ISBN: 978 0 263 90241 9

026-1112

Harlequin (UK) policy is to use papers that are natural, renewable and recyclable products and made from wood grown in sustainable forests. The logging and manufacturing processes conform to the legal environmental regulations of the country of origin.

Printed and bound
by CPI Group (UK) Ltd, Croydon, CR0 4YY

A special letter is about to change
three lives forever!

A Christmas Letter

Three glittering new stories from
Fiona Harper, Donna Alward
and Shirley Jump

Snowbound in
the Earl's Castle

Fiona
HARPER

As a child, **Fiona Harper** was constantly teased for either having her nose in a book, or living in a dream world. Things haven't changed much since then, but at least in writing she's found a use for her runaway imagination. After studying dance at university, Fiona worked as a dancer, teacher and choreographer, before trading in that career for video-editing and production. When she became a mother she cut back on her working hours to spend time with her children, and when her littlest one started pre-school she found a few spare moments to rediscover an old but not forgotten love—writing.

Fiona lives in London, but her other favourite places to be are the Highlands of Scotland and the Kent countryside on a summer's afternoon. She loves cooking good food and anything cinnamon-flavoured. Of course she still can't keep away from a good book or a good movie—especially romances—but only if she's stocked up with tissues, because she knows she will need them by the end, be it happy or sad. Her favourite things in the world are her wonderful husband, who has learned to decipher her incoherent ramblings, and her two daughters.

CHAPTER ONE

THESE were the kind of gates made for keeping people out, Faith thought as she tipped her head back and looked up at twenty feet of twisting and curling black iron. Neither the exquisite craftsmanship nor the sharp wind slicing through the bars did anything to dispel the firm message that outsiders should stay on her side of the gate.

Too bad. She needed to get into the grounds of Hadsborough Castle and she needed to do it today.

She glanced round in frustration to where her Mini sat idling, her suitcase and overnight bag stuffed in the back, and sighed. She'd had other plans for today—ones involving a quaint little holiday cottage on the Kent coast, hot chocolate with marshmallows and a good book. The perfect winter holiday. But that had all changed when she'd found an innocent-looking lilac envelope on her doorstep yesterday morning. The cheerful snowman return address sticker on the back hadn't been fooling anyone. She'd known even before she'd ripped the letter open that its contents would cause trouble, but the exact brand of nuisance had been a total surprise.

She stared out over the top of her Mini to the rolling English countryside beyond. The scene was strangely monochrome. Fog clung to the dips in the fields and everything was tinged with frost. Only the dark silhouettes of trees on top of the hill remained ungilded.

It was strange. She'd grown up in the country back home in Connecticut, but this landscape didn't have the earthy, familiar feel she'd been expecting when she'd driven out of London earlier that morning. Even though she'd adopted this country almost a decade ago, and her sisters now teased her about her so-called British accent, for the first time in ages she was suddenly very aware she was a foreigner. This misty piece of England didn't just feel like another country; it felt like another world.

She turned round and tried a smaller gate beside the main pair, obviously made for foot traffic. No good. Also locked. A painted board at the side of the gate informed her that normal castle opening hours were between ten and four, Tuesday through Saturday. Closed to visitors on Mondays.

But she wasn't a tourist. She had an appointment.

At least she *thought* she had an appointment.

She shook the smaller gate again, and the chain that bound it rattled, laughing back at her.

That was what Gram's letter had said. She pulled the offending article out of her pocket and leafed through the lilac pages, ignoring the smug-looking snowman on the back. She'd bet *he* didn't have a wily old white-haired grandmother who was blackmailing him into taking precious time out of *his* vacation.

She scanned down past the news of Beckett's Run, past Gram's description of how festive her hometown was looking now the residents had started preparing for the annual Christmas Festival.

Ah, here it was.

Faith, honey, I wonder if you'd do me a favor? I have a friend—an old flame, really—who needs help with a stained glass window, and I told him I knew just the girl for the job. Bertie and I were sweethearts after the war. We had a magical summer, but then he went home and

*married a nice English girl and I met your grandfather.
I think it all worked out as it should have in the end.*

*The window is on the estate of Hadsborough Castle
in Kent. What was the name of the man who designed
it? Bertie did say. It'll come to me later...*

*Anyhow, I know you'll be finished with your London
window soon, and you mentioned the next restoration
project wasn't going to start until the New Year, so I
thought you could go down and help him with it. I told
him you'd be there November 30th at 11 a.m.*

And here she was.

Still gripping Gram's letter between thumb and forefinger,
she flipped the pages over so she could pull up the sleeve of
her grey duffle coat to check her watch. It was the thirtieth,
at ten-fifty, so why wasn't anyone here to meet her? To let
her in? She could have been sipping hot chocolate right now
if it hadn't been for Gram's little idea of a detour.

As beautiful as the window at St Bede's in Camden had
looked when the team had finished restoring it, it had been
four months of back-breaking, meticulous labour. She deserved a break, and she was going to have it.

Just as soon as she'd checked out this window.

She turned the last page over and looked below her grandmother's signature. Reading the line again still gave her
goosebumps.

*P.S. I knew it would come to me! Samuel Crowbridge.
That was the designer's name.*

Without that tantalising mention of the well-known British
artist Faith would have blown off this little side trip on the
way to her holiday cottage in a heartbeat.

Well…okay, maybe she'd have come anyway. Gram had
been the one stable figure in her otherwise chaotic child-

hood—more like a surrogate mother than a grandparent. All Faith's happiest memories were rooted in Gram's pretty little house in Beckett's Run. She owed her grandmother big time, and she'd probably have danced on one leg naked in the middle of Trafalgar Square if the old lady had asked her to.

She supposed she should be grateful that the letter hadn't started, *Faith, honey, try not to get arrested, but could you just hop down to Nelson's Column and...?*

The road that passed the castle entrance was quiet, but at that moment she heard the noise of a car engine and turned round. Thankfully, a Land Rover had pulled in beside her and the driver rolled down the passenger window.

'It's closed today,' the man in a chunky-knit sweater said, in a not-unfriendly manner.

Faith nodded. 'I have an appointment to see...' This was the moment she realised Gram had neglected to reveal her old flame's full name. 'Bertie?'

The man in the car frowned slightly. He didn't look convinced.

'It's about the window,' she added, not really expecting it to help. The appointment her grandmother had made for her seemed as flimsy and insubstantial as the disappearing mist. But the man nodded.

'Follow me in,' he said. 'There's a public car park just up the road. You can walk the rest of the way from there.'

'Thanks,' she replied, and got back into her car.

Five minutes later, after a drive through the most stunning parkland, she was standing beside her Mini as the noise of the Land Rover's engine faded. She watched the four-wheel drive disappear round a corner, then followed the path the man had indicated in the opposite direction, up a gentle slope of close-cropped grass. When she got to the top of the hill she stopped dead in her tracks and her mouth fell open.

Beyond an expansive lawn, gauzy mist hung above a dark, mirror-like lake. Above it, almost as if it was floating above the surface of the water, was the most stunning castle she'd ever seen. It was made of large blocks of creamy sandstone, crested with crenellations, and finished off with a turret or two for good measure. Long, narrow windows punctuated its walls.

The castle enclosure stretched from the bank on her right across two small islands. A plain single-track bridge joined the first island to the shore, guarded by a gatehouse. The smaller island was a fortified keep, older than the rest of the castle, and joined to the newer, larger wing by a two-storey arched bridge.

The whole thing looked like something out of a fairytale. Better than anything she'd dreamed up when Gram had tucked her and her sisters in at night on their summer holidays and read to them out of Faith's favourite fabric-covered storybook.

She started to walk, hardly caring that she'd left the Tarmac, and started off across the dew-laden grass, running the risk of getting goose poop on her boots. The edge of the lake was fringed with reeds, and a pair of black swans with scarlet beaks drifted around each other, totally oblivious to her presence.

That bridge from the bank to the gatehouse seemed to be the only way to get to the rest of the castle, so she guessed she might as well start there. Perhaps there would be someone on duty who knew where this window or the mysterious Bertie could be found.

She was nearing the castle, walking close to the low-lying bank, when she saw a dark shape in the mist moving towards her. She stopped and pulled her coat tighter around her. The damp air clung to her cheeks.

She could make out a figure—long, tall and dark. A man, his coat flapping behind him as he strode towards her. She was inevitably reminded of stern Victorian gentlemen in gothic novels. There was something about the purpose in his stride, the way his collar was turned up. But then he came closer and she could see clearly from his thick ribbed sweater and the dark jeans under his overcoat that he was a product of this century after all.

He hadn't noticed her. She knew she ought to say something, call out, but she couldn't seem to breathe, let alone talk.

She had the oddest feeling that she recognised him, although she couldn't have explained just which of his features were familiar. It was all of them. All of *him*. And him being in this place.

Which was crazy, because she'd never been here before in her life—except maybe in her childish daydreams—and she'd certainly remember meeting a man like this…a man whose sudden appearance answered a question she wasn't aware she'd asked.

Finally he spotted her, and his stride faltered for a moment, but then his spine lengthened and he carried on, his focus narrowing to her and only her. The look in his eyes reminded her of a hunting dog that had just picked up a scent.

'Hey!' he called out as came closer.

'Hi…' Faith tried to say, but the damp air muffled the word, and the noise that emerged from her mouth was hardly intelligible.

He was only a few feet away now, and Faith stuffed her gloved hands into her coat pockets as she tipped her head back to look him in the face. My, he was tall. But not burly with it. Long and lean. She could see why she'd had that dumb notion about him now. Black hair, slightly too long to be tidy, flopped over his forehead and curled at his collar. His bone structure and long, straight nose spoke of centuries of breeding and he addressed her now in a manner that left her in no doubt that he was used to having people do as he said.

'The castle and grounds are closed to visitors today. You'll have to turn round and go back the way you came.'

And he stood there, waiting for her to obey him.

Normally Faith didn't have any problem being polite and accommodating, doing what she was asked—it was the path to a quiet and peaceful existence after all—but there was something about his tone, about the way he hadn't even stopped to ask if she had a valid reason for being there, that just riled her up. Maybe it was the suggestion that once again she was somewhere she didn't belong that made her temper rise.

'I'm not trespassing. I'm supposed to—'

Before she could finish her sentence he took another step forward, cupped his hand under her elbow and started to walk her back in the direction she'd just come.

'Hey!' she said, and yanked her elbow out of his grip. 'Hands off, buddy!'

'Should have known it,' he muttered, almost to himself. 'American tourists are always the worst.' Then he spoke louder, and more slowly, as if he were talking to a child. 'Listen, you have to realise this isn't just a visitor attraction like Disneyland. It's a family home, too, and we have just as much right to our privacy as anyone else. Now, if you don't leave quietly I will be forced to call the police.'

Faith was rapidly losing the urge even to be polite to this stuck-up...whoever he was. No matter how dashing he'd looked walking out of the mist.

'No, *you* listen,' she replied firmly. 'I have every right to be here. I have an appointment with Bertie.'

He stopped herding her towards the exit and his eyes narrowed further. She had no doubt that a sharp mind went hand in hand with those aristocratic looks. 'You mean Albert Huntington?'

Faith took a split second longer than she would have liked to reply. 'Yes, of course.' There couldn't be more than one Albert—Bertie—around this place, could there? That had to be him.

Unfortunately Mr Tall, Dark and Full of Himself didn't

miss a trick. He spotted her hesitation and instantly grabbed her arm again, started marching her back towards the gate. 'Nice try, but nobody but the family calls him Bertie—and you're from the wrong continent entirely to be considered a close relation.'

Hah. That was all he knew.

'Actually, my father is as English as you are,' she added icily. 'And my grandmother—' the American one, but she didn't mention that '—is an old friend of his. I'm here to give my professional opinion on a stained glass window!'

He let go of her arm and turned to look her up and down. '*You're* the expert Bertie's asked to look at the window?'

Close enough to the truth. She nodded. 'I believe it might need some kind of repair.'

Okay, she didn't actually know if any restoration work was needed, but why would Gram have sent her here otherwise? It was a pretty good guess, and she really, *really* wanted to sneak a look at that window at least once before this man frogmarched her off the estate. Not one of Crowbridge's other windows—and there hadn't been many—had survived the Blitz. This could be a significant discovery.

He stopped looking irritated and purposeful, closed his eyes and ran a hand through his dark hair before glancing back in the direction of the castle. 'I hoped he'd given up on that idea.' He gave her a weary look. 'I suppose I'd better take you to meet him, then, Miss…?'

'McKinnon. Faith McKinnon,' she said, trying to get her voice to remain even.

'I apologise, Miss McKinnon, if I've been a little abrupt…'

A *little?* And he didn't look that sorry to her. If anything he'd clenched up further. Her younger sister would have described him as having a stick up his—

'I'm sure you can understand how difficult it is to have your home invaded,' he added, but Faith still wasn't quite sure she was off the 'invader' list.

'People think that because we open our home to them for a few days each week it is somehow public property.'

She nodded. She knew all about invading families, about being a cuckoo in the nest, but she wasn't going to tell *this* man that. It certainly wouldn't endear her to him any further.

'Bertie isn't in the best of health at the moment,' he added gravely. 'I've been trying to make sure he doesn't get too upset.' He led the way back through the thinning mist round the edge of the lake. 'Difficult, though,' he added, 'when he's obsessed with this damn window.'

He strode ahead, and Faith followed him up a short incline and onto the first, plainer stone bridge, through a large arch under the gatehouse and onto an oval lawn that filled more than half of the first castle island. She tried not to let her eyes pop out of her head.

Wow.

The castle was even better close up than it had been rising through the mist. A gravel pathway encircled the lawn and led up to a vast front door covered in iron studs.

This Bertie had his office in the castle itself? *Nice.*

As her guide opened the front door and stood aside to let her pass, he surprised her by allowing one side of his mouth to hitch up in the start of a smile as he checked his watch.

'I imagine Bertie will be finished with his morning tea by now. I'll take you through to the drawing room.'

Faith looked at him sharply. 'You mean Bertie *lives* here?'

The almost-smile disappeared. 'Of course he lives here. It's his home.' He shook his head. 'You Americans really do have some funny ideas, you know...'

Faith held her breath. She would have liked to challenge him on that last comment, but two things stopped her. First, it would have given her lack of knowledge about this Bertie away. Second, she was too busy making sense of all the mismatched pieces of information running round her head.

Gram had left a heck of a lot out of her letter, hadn't she?

She cleared her throat. 'Does Bertie have a full title?'

He gave her the patronising kind of look that told her he thought she'd finally started asking sensible questions. 'Albert Charles Baxter Huntington, seventh Duke of Hadsborough.'

Faith blinked slowly, trying to give nothing away.

Act like you knew that.

A duke? Gram had had a fling with a *duke*? She'd thought from the tone of the letter that he'd been a fellow academic or master craftsman working on a project. She hadn't even considered that Bertie might *own* the window. And the building it inhabited. And this castle. And probably most of the land for miles around. Part of her was shocked at her conservative grandmother's secret past. Another part wanted to punch the air and say, *Go, Gram!*

Faith's throat was suddenly very dry. 'And that would make you...?'

He frowned, then held out his hand, doing nothing to erase the horizontal lines that were bunching up his forehead. 'Marcus Huntington—estate manager of Hadsborough Castle...'

Faith looked at his hand and swallowed. Hesitantly, she pulled her hand from her mitten and slid it into his. Since he hadn't been wearing gloves she'd expected his skin to be ice-cold, but his grip was firm and his palm was warm against hers.

She looked down at their joined hands. This felt right. As if she remembered doing this before and had been waiting to do it again. Worse than that, she didn't want to let go. She looked back up at him, hoping she didn't look as panic-stricken as she felt. That was when her heart really started to thump.

He was staring at their hands, too. Then he looked up and his eyes met hers. She saw matching confusion and surprise in his expression.

He cleared his throat. 'Bertie's grandson and heir.'

* * *

Marcus pulled his hand away from hers, ignoring the pleasant ripple of sensation as her fingertips brushed his palm. Not the cliché of an electric shock racing up his arm. No, something far more unsettling—a sense of warmth, a sense of how right her hand felt in his. And that couldn't be, because everything about this situation was wrong. She was not supposed to be here, trespassing on his family's lives and stirring up trouble.

But it hadn't been just the touch. It had started before that, when he'd caught her walking down by the lake. There was something about those small, understated features and those direct, *reasonable* brown eyes that totally caught him off guard.

And if there was one thing he hated it was being off guard.

However, when she'd slid her hand into his, and all the ear-pounding had stopped and his senses had calmed down and come to rest...

If anything that had been worse.

He couldn't let himself fall into that trap again, so it was time to do something about it. Time to find out what Faith McKinnon wanted and deal with her as quickly as possible.

'If you'll follow me...?'

He turned and led the way through a flagstone-paved entrance hall, its arches and whitewashed walls decorated with remnants of long-ago disassembled suits of armour, then showed her into the yellow drawing room—the smallest and warmest reception room on the ground floor of the castle.

Gold-coloured damask covered the walls, fringed with heavy brocade tassels under the plaster coving at the top. There were antique tables covered in trinkets and family photographs, a grand piano, and a large squashy sofa in front of the vast marble fireplace. Off to one side of the hearth, in a high-backed leather armchair, reading his daily newspaper, was his grandfather. He looked so innocent. No one would guess he'd ignited a bit of a family row with this window obsession.

Marcus wasn't exactly sure what the kerfuffle was about—something that had happened decades earlier, in a time when stiff-lipped silence had been the preferred solution to every problem—but his great-aunt Tabitha had warned him that Bertie was about to open a Pandora's box of trouble, and nothing any of them learned about whatever the family had been keeping quiet for more than half a century would make anyone any happier.

Disruption was the last thing he needed—especially as he'd spent the last couple of years getting everything back on an even keel. Bertie might live at Hadsborough now, but in his younger years he'd all but abandoned his duty to explore the world.

Unfortunately he'd passed his *laissez-faire* attitude down to his only son, and before his death Marcus's father had just seen the castle as somewhere impressive to bring his business friends for the odd weekend. He'd also failed to keep hold of three wives, and the resulting divorce settlements had crippled the family finances further. But that was just the tip of the iceberg where his father had been concerned. It had taken centuries to build this family's reputation, and his father had managed to rip it to shreds within twelve months.

So Marcus had left the City and come to Hadsborough to be by his grieving grandfather's side. It was his job to claw it all back now. The Huntington family legacy had been neglected for too many generations. Taken for granted. These things couldn't just be left to run their own course; they needed to be managed. Guarded. Or there would be nothing left—not even a good name—to pass on to his children when they came along.

'Grandfather?'

The old man looked up from his paper, the habitual twinkle in his eye. Marcus nodded towards their guest.

'I found Miss McKinnon, here, wandering in the grounds. I believe *you* are expecting her?'

If his grandfather had heard the extra emphasis in his grandson's words he gave no sign he'd registered it. He carefully folded his paper, placed it on the table next to him, rose unsteadily to his feet and offered his hand to the stranger in their drawing room.

'Miss McKinnon,' he said, smiling. 'Delighted to meet you.'

The old charmer, Marcus thought.

Faith McKinnon smiled politely and shook his hand. 'Hi,' she said. If she was charmed she didn't show it.

'Thank you for coming at such short notice,' his grandfather said as he lowered himself carefully back into his chair. 'If you don't mind me saying, you resemble your grandmother.'

The blank, businesslike expression on Faith McKinnon's face was replaced with one of surprise. 'Really? Th-thank you.'

Marcus frowned. She'd been telling the truth, then. Yet the reliable hairs at the back of his neck had informed him she'd been lying about something.

Why was she puzzled that someone had said she resembled a family member? He glanced at the portrait of the third Duke over the mantelpiece and raised his fingers absentmindedly to touch the bridge of his nose. There was no escaping that distinctive feature in the Huntington family line. They all had it. Genetics had branded them and marked them as individual connections in a long chain. And, as the only direct heir, Marcus was determined not to be the weak link that ended the line.

He turned to his grandfather. 'Miss McKinnon tells me you knew her grandmother?'

Before his grandfather could answer their guest interrupted. 'Call me Faith, please.'

Bertie nodded and smiled back at her. 'Mary and I were

sweethearts for a time when I was in America after the war,' his grandfather said. 'She was an exceptional woman.'

Marcus turned sharply to look at him. Sweethearts? He'd never heard this before—never heard mention of a romance before his grandmother. It made him realise just *how* silent his family stayed on certain matters, that maybe he didn't know everything about his own history.

'Please do sit down, Miss McK…Faith,' his grandfather said.

She chose the edge of the sofa, her knees pressed together and her hands in her lap. Marcus would have been quite content to remain standing, but he felt as if he was towering above the other two, somehow excluded from what they were about to discuss, so he dropped into the armchair opposite his grandfather, crossing one long leg over the other. But he couldn't get comfortable, as he would have done if it had just been him and his grandfather alone as usual.

'So, Grandfather…what has all this got to do with the window?'

At the mention of the window Miss McKinnon's eyes widened and she leaned forward. 'Gram said you need help with it?'

Marcus kept on watching her. Her voice was low and calm, but behind her speech was something else. As if his words had lit a fire inside her. *Interesting.* Just exactly what was she hoping to gain from this situation? He wouldn't have pegged her for a con artist or a gold-digger, but they came in all shapes and sizes. Stepmothers one and two had proved that admirably.

His grandfather nodded. 'It's in a chapel on the estate here. I wouldn't have thought any more of it, except that a few months ago my father's younger brother died, and his widow found some letters my father had written to him in his personal effects. She wondered if I'd like to see them.'

Marcus squinted slightly. Yes, that would make sense. Now

he thought about it, he realised it *had* been around that time that Grandfather had started muttering to himself and begun hiding himself away in the library, poring over old papers.

Bertie stared into the crackling fire in the grate. 'My father died when I was very young, you see, and she thought I might get more of a sense of who he was through them.'

Marcus resisted the urge to scowl. After his recent heart surgery, and with his soaring blood pressure, the doctors had said his grandfather needed rest and quiet. No stress. They had definitely not prescribed getting all stirred up about a family mystery—if indeed there was one. It would be best to leave it all alone, let time settle like silt over those memories until they were buried. There had been enough scandal in the present. They didn't need extra dredged up from the past.

Pursuing this thing with the window was a bad idea on so many levels. That was why he intended to get the facts out of his grandfather quickly and show this Miss McKinnon the blasted window, if that was what she really wanted. Because the sooner she was off the estate and he could get things back to normal the better.

CHAPTER TWO

FAITH frowned. While Bertie—she couldn't quite get used to thinking of this gentle old man as a duke—was charming, she didn't see what his family history had to do with anything.

'I'm sorry…but how does this connect to the window in the chapel?'

At least she knew that much now. A church window. Next task was to gauge how old it was.

Bertie was staring into the fire again. She had the feeling he'd wandered off into his own memories. Perhaps that was nice, if you had a solid and well-adjusted family as he had, but in Faith's view the less time she spent thinking about her family the better. They certainly didn't make her feel all warm and fuzzy and wistful.

When all three McKinnon sisters got together none of them behaved like the mature women they were; they regressed to childhood, resurrecting deeply embedded hurts and resentments, filtering every word through their past history. It was always the same, no matter how hard Gram pleaded, or how hard they tried to make it different each time. And when they added their flaky mother into the mix—well…

Bertie seemed to shake himself out of his reverie. 'The original window was damaged during a storm almost a hundred years ago, and my father commissioned a new one to be made.'

'And it needs restoration?'

The old man shrugged. 'There does seem to be a little ir-regularity down at the bottom.'

So maybe it was all about establishing the history of the window—just what she was interested in herself. 'My grand-mother says you know who did the design?'

Another shrug. 'Samuel Someone-or-other. I forget the last name.' He stopped looking at her and his gaze wandered back to the fire.

'Crowbridge,' she said. 'Samuel Crowbridge.'

And if Gram was right—if Crowbridge really *had* designed Bertie's window—it would be the stained glass version of finding King Tut's tomb. He'd only ventured into making win-dows late in his life, and none of the few examples remained. At least that was what everybody had thought...

She caught Marcus's eye. His expression was unreadable, but he seemed to be watching her very carefully, as if he was expecting her to make a sudden move. Unfortunately, as well as the spike of irritation that shot through her at his superior, *entitled* study of her, there was a fizz of something much more pleasurable in her veins. She looked away.

She turned her attention back to his grandfather. 'Mr... I mean, Your—' She stopped, embarrassed at her lack of knowledge about what to call her host. *Your Dukeness* just didn't sound right in her head.

'Bertie is fine,' the older man said. 'I never did like all that nonsense.'

Marcus shook his head slightly at his grandfather's re-sponse. Faith knew what she wanted to call *him,* whether he had a proper title or not. She sat up straighter. The grandson might have the looks—and some weird *déjà vu* thing going on—but she'd prefer Bertie's company any day. She could to-tally understand why Gram had been so taken with him once.

'Well, *Bertie*—' she shot a look at his grandson '—if you don't want the window repaired or evaluated, I'm not sure why I'm here.' She hoped desperately he'd let her see it any-way—if only for a few moments.

Bertie's eyes began to shine and he leaned forward. 'You, my dear, are going to help me unravel a mystery.'

'A mystery?' she repeated slowly. She tried to sound neutral, but it came out sounding suspicious and cynical.

He nodded. 'My mother left Hadsborough three years after my father died. I was always told that he'd married beneath himself, in both station and character, and that she hadn't wanted to be stuck out in the countryside in a draughty heap of stones with a screaming child.'

Faith felt a familiar tug of sympathy inside her ribcage, but she ignored it, sat up straighter and blinked. She wasn't going to get sucked in. She wasn't going to get involved. She was here for the window and that was all.

'I'm sure you were a cute baby,' was all she said.

Bertie chuckled. 'By all accounts I was a terror. Anyway, I was also told my father realised his mistake soon after the wedding. But people didn't get divorced in those days, you see…'

Faith nodded—even though she didn't really see. Her own mother had never felt tied by any strings of convention. If it had felt good she'd done it—and it had ripped her family apart. Maybe there was something to be said for doing your duty, sitting back and putting up with stuff, just so everyone else didn't have to ride the tidal wave of consequences with you.

'I have a feeling my uncle Reginald didn't approve of my father's choice of bride, so my father doesn't mention her much in these letters, but I get the impression my parents were happy together.'

Faith could feel her curiosity rising. *Don't bite the bait,* she told herself. *Family squabbles are trouble. Best avoided. Best run away from.*

'And does he mention the window in the letters?'

Bertie grinned. 'Oh, yes.' He pulled some yellowing sheets of paper from a leather folder that he'd tucked down the side of his chair and leafed through them. 'He wrote of his plans to rebuild the window to his brother. He seemed very excited about it.' The smile disappeared from his face as he stopped and stared at one short letter. 'He even mentioned it in his final letter.' He looked up. 'He survived the Great War, but died of flu the following year. This letter is the last one he wrote from hospital.'

He reached forward and offered the letter to Faith. Knowing it would probably pain him to get up, she rose and took it from him. She walked towards the fire and tried to make sense of the untidy scrawl. This was obviously the last communication of a man gripped by fever. The content was mostly family-related, which Faith skipped through. It wasn't her business, even if she *was* starting to feel a certain sympathy for Bertie and his tragic father. She knew all about tragic fathers, be they dead or merely missing from one's life.

'Read the last paragraph,' Bertie prompted.

Faith turned the page over and found it.

It was supposed to be a grand surprise, Reggie, but I don't suppose I'll get the chance to do it properly now. Tell Evie there's a message for her. Tell her to look in the window.

Marcus stood up and strode across to where Faith was standing. He held out a hand, almost demanding the letter. She raised an eyebrow and made a point of reading it through one more time before handing it over.

He shook his head as he read. 'Grandfather, you can't put any stock in this. These are clearly the wanderings of a delirious mind.'

Bertie shook his head. 'It's all starting to come together... bits and pieces of conversations I've heard over the years...

strange comments the servants made... I think my father loved my mother a lot more than I've been led to believe, and I want to know why she left—why the family would never talk about her.'

Faith withdrew from the warmth of the fire and sat back down on the edge of the sofa. She was more confused than ever. 'I can understand that, Bertie...'

If anyone could understand it would be her—to have the security of knowing one parent hadn't deserted you and the other hadn't deceived you—she would have given anything to return to that wonderful state of bliss before she'd uncovered her own family's secret.

'But what does it have to do with me?'

He looked at her intently, his face serious. 'You know about stained glass, about its traditions and imagery. I've stared at that damn window for hours in the last couple of weeks and I'll be blasted if I can see anything there.'

He leaned forward and lowered his voice, and Faith couldn't help tilting forward to mirror him.

'I want you to find the clue my father left for my mother, Faith. I want you to find the message in the window.'

Her heart was hammering. She told herself it was from keeping up with Marcus Huntington's blistering pace as he escorted her to the chapel. An outsider like her couldn't be trusted to look at it on her own, of course.

She glanced at the sky above and realised she recognised that particular shade of grey. Snow was on its way. But a bit of snow didn't worry her. Or even a whole bunch of it. Beckett's Run had plenty every year. But Beckett's Run knew how to deal with it. A few flakes and this country ground to a halt. So she wanted to be tucked up in her little holiday cottage with a stiff salty breeze blowing off the North Sea if it really decided to come down. Which meant she needed to get to work fast—something the man striding ahead of her would no doubt appreciate.

The path they'd been following led them through some trees and into a pretty hollow with a clearing. In the centre was a smaller version of a traditional English stone church. The grass under their feet must once have been a lawn, but it now rose knee-high, and the ground was lumpy with thick clumps of rye grass. Shrubs grew wild, bowed down with the weight of their unpruned branches. Some clung to the walls of the chapel to support themselves. Compared to the rest of the estate, this little corner appeared unkempt and uncared for.

Faith wasn't one for believing in fairy stories. Not any more. And she had the feeling that Bertie, lovely as he was, had the capacity to spin a tall tale or two, but there was something about this little hidden part of the estate that made her wonder if the Huntingtons had deliberately neglected it.

She watched Marcus stride up to the heavy oak door ahead of her and shivered. Twenty-eight years old, and she'd never had a reaction to a man like this before. It was downright freaky.

Pure attraction she could have handled, but this was different. There was more to it. Extra layers below the fizzle of awareness. Pity she was too much of a coward to peel back the top layer and see what lay underneath.

Marcus slid a key into the black iron lock and turned it. He pushed the door open and motioned for her to go inside, stepping back out of the way so there was no danger of them passing within even three feet of each other.

It wouldn't do her much good to peel back that layer, anyway. He didn't want her here. The vibe emanated from him in waves, like a silent broadcast,

She turned back to watch him as he pulled the door closed and followed her inside. He caught her eye and immediately looked away.

She wasn't the only coward.

He felt it, too. She knew he did. But he wanted it even less than her physical presence on his territory, and Faith wasn't going to push it. No point trying to wriggle yourself into somewhere you didn't belong.

She followed him inside, blinking a few times to adjust her eyes to the relative gloom. As always when she entered a church her eyes were drawn immediately to the windows at either end. Hardly able to help it, she ignored where her host was trying to lead her and veered off to stare at the multi-paned window at the back of the church near the door.

Soft light filtered through the glass, filling the dusty interior with colour. She held her breath. Both the glass picture high on the wall and the afternoon sun were beautiful in their own right, but when they met...it was magic.

Their entrance had disturbed a hundred million dust motes, and now the specks danced in the light, as if an unseen artist had painstakingly coloured each one a different shade. And not only did the shapes and pictures in the window sing, but some of that colour—that life—pierced the darkness of the sanctuary on beams of light, leaving kaleidoscope shadows where it fell.

She sighed, even though she could tell at a glance that this was not the window Bertie had been talking about. Too old. A nineteenth-century creation featuring Bible characters dressed in medieval garb. Didn't matter. She was still captivated. These grand scenes always reminded her of the coloured plates from her favourite storybook as a child—noble men and beautiful ladies in flowing, heavy robes, bright lush pastures and an achingly blue heaven above.

'It's over here,' a voice said from somewhere close to the altar.

Faith took one last look at the window and turned, screwing her 'don't care' face back in place as she did so, and walked towards where Marcus Huntington was standing, hands in his pockets.

As she walked down the aisle she looked around. It was obvious someone had been trying to tidy the place up, but there was still a long way to go. Nothing a mop and a bucket and some elbow grease wouldn't sort out, though.

'We plan to reopen the chapel this year and have a Carol Service here,' he explained, then stooped into a smaller niche in a side wall, revealing a much smaller stained glass window. He stepped back to give her access, but turned his intense stare her direction. 'So...what do you think?'

Faith took a few paces towards the narrow window. It was maybe a foot wide and six feet high, with typical Gothic revival tracery at the top. Her heart began to pump. Could this really be it?

The glass was all rich colours and delicate paintwork: a fair-haired woman knelt praying at the bottom of the picture, her palms pressed together, face upturned, eyes fixed on the blaze of celestial glory at the top of the window. She was surrounded by flowers and shrubs, and a small dog sat at her feet, gazing at her in much the same way she was gazing at the heavens. It was stunning. And unusual. More like a painting in its composition than a church window.

There was something in the woman's face... Something about her expression of pure joy that made Faith want to lean in and touch her—see if she could absorb some of that emotion by pure osmosis. Truly, the window was enchanting.

She turned round to see what her reluctant host could tell her about it and bumped into something warm and solid. She'd been aware that he'd been standing behind her, but not that he'd stepped in closer.

'S-sorry!' she stuttered, finding herself staring into his chest.

'Well?' he asked, a hint of impatience in his tone.

She knew she really ought to step back, move away, but her gaze had snagged on a feathery piece of cobweb that was stuck in his hair just above his right temple. For some reason she was suddenly much more interested in reaching up and gently brushing it away than turning round and looking at the coloured glass and lead she'd been so desperate to set eyes on.

What was even more worrying was the fact that she'd almost done it anyway—as if she'd known him long enough to share that easy kind of intimacy. It seemed unnatural *not* to.

Breathe, Faith. Turn around. Just because he looks like a modern-day Prince Charming it doesn't mean you should audition for the role of Cinderella. That would be a really dumb idea.

He frowned, followed her gaze, and discovered the cobweb on his own. He brushed it away with long fingers and then did the oddest thing: he chuckled softly. To himself, though. None of the humour was to be shared with her. But it changed his face completely, softening the angular planes, and made him seem younger, less stand-offish. Faith discovered she'd stopped breathing.

No. Don't you do it, Faith McKinnon. Don't you believe where there's no hope. You learned those lessons young. You're not that soft-hearted girl any more, remember?

She didn't smile back at him, but turned abruptly and stared at the window again. He moved away, thank goodness, walked closer to the window to inspect it for himself. They remained silent for a few minutes, both focused intently on the gently lit glass picture in front of them.

Marcus came and stood beside her. 'For a long time all the windows here were boarded up. I don't think I've ever taken a really good look at this before. It's actually quite beautiful.'

Faith nodded, still staring at the golden-haired woman. 'If I lived here I'd come to see it every day.'

He folded his arms and looked around. 'This chapel hasn't been used by the family for decades. No one has been here much since—' He stopped short, as if a jagged thunderbolt of a thought had just hit him, and then turned to look at her. 'Since my grandfather was a small boy.'

She met his gaze. 'You think there's a link? Something to do with what your grandfather said earlier?'

He pressed his lips together. 'There could be any one of a dozen reasons why the family has left this place alone. For a start, I don't think any of my immediate ancestors were very religious.'

He wasn't going to budge an inch, was he? On anything. He was right and everyone else was wrong. That chapped her hide. He reminded her so much of her older sister, always issuing orders as if they were divine decrees.

She folded her arms across her chest. 'You don't believe him, do you?'

He was silent for a few seconds, and then turned his attention back to the stained glass window. 'I believe there was some big family ruckus—probably a storm in a teacup—but as for there being a secret message in the window... It seems a little far-fetched.' He sighed. 'I think it's what my grandfather *wants* to believe.'

Faith chewed the side of her lip. No pressure, then. It was just up to her to confirm or crush an old man's dreams. She stepped forward again and focused once more on the subject of all the controversy.

'See anything out of the ordinary?' he asked.

She tipped her head to the side. 'It's difficult to say. Despite the subject matter, it isn't a very typical design for a church.'

She pulled a sheaf of photographs out of her bag and held them up so she could compare them against the window. They were images of various paintings and sketches of the supposed artist's other lost windows. 'It's similar to Crowbridge's earlier work, which was heavily influenced by the Pre-Raphaelite Brotherhood.'

He nodded. 'This window certainly has a touch of that style.'

Faith's brows rose a notch and she swivelled her eyes to look at him. 'You know something about art?' What a relief to find he knew about something other than ordering people around, making them feel unwanted.

He gave her a derisive look.

She ignored it and cleared her throat. 'But his work changed dramatically after the turn of the last century. This window isn't anything like the paintings he was producing around the time this window was made.'

A lead weight settled inside her stomach. She hadn't realised it, but she'd been dumb enough to let herself get excited about the window, to let herself hope. She turned away from it, wanting to block the image out for a second.

She should have been smarter than to get sucked in to the fantasy like that. But it was this place… Hadsborough was a like a fairytale on steroids. It was hard *not* to fall into that trap. She would just have to do better in the future.

'I can see how an amateur might have made the error,' she said, looking Marcus in the eye, 'but I don't think Samuel Crowbridge made this window.'

'You know your subject, Miss McKinnon.'

'Nice of you to notice,' she replied. Really, the nerve of the man. She didn't need his validation. 'And it's *Faith*.'

He blinked slowly, as if he'd registered her request and would think it over. Faith didn't usually have a short fuse, but something about this man, his superior attitude, just drove her nuts.

'Any sign of this message my grandfather mentioned?'

She shook her head, although she wanted to say, *Yes, it's there in letters three feet high,* just to get up his nose. 'Nothing pops out, but since it's not a traditional church window the normal symbolic conventions may not apply.'

'I need to know for sure,' Marcus said. 'My grandfather will just keep fretting about it unless you give me something more concrete.'

She thought of the charming old man, sitting by the fire, trying to read his newspaper while he waited for her to give him hope where there was none. But Bertie had asked for her professional opinion, hadn't he? And she needed to honour that—stay dispassionate, objective. It wasn't her fault if it had all been a dead end.

Don't get involved...

Right. That was what she was going to do. Not get involved.

It wasn't normally a problem in her line of work. The people intimately connected with the windows she worked on were long dead, shrouded in the mystery of another century. So this window was a little different, had a sad story to go along with it. That shouldn't change anything. It didn't.

'I could do some further research,' she said. 'I should be able to send you a report in a couple of days, but I don't think it's going to turn up anything new.'

He breathed out, looking slightly thankful. 'Maybe that's for the best.' He glanced over his shoulder to the open door. 'Thank you, Miss McKinnon.'

Still with the 'Miss McKinnon'. He used her name like a shield.

She took one last look at the window. It really was beautiful—so unusual. And apart from the bad repair job down at the bottom it was in good condition. It was sad to leave it that way, especially when it wouldn't be a long job—not like the one she'd just finished...

Marcus moved towards the door. 'We'd better go back and talk to the Duke,' he said, not bothering to look over his shoulder.

Right. And then it would be time to get back to where she belonged—her own world, her own life.

CHAPTER THREE

MARCUS stayed silent when they reached the drawing room, while Bertie insisted Faith have another cup of tea before she continued on her journey. She perched on the edge of the sofa again, and began to explain carefully what she'd found.

He noticed that she worked up to breaking the bad news, and he was grateful to her for that. He was pleased she hadn't just blurted it all out as soon as she'd walked into the room. As far as he'd seen Faith McKinnon had a gift for bluntness. It was reassuring to know that a little sensitivity lay underneath.

He brushed beads of moisture from his shoulders as he stood by the fireplace. Fine flakes of snow, almost dust-like, had fallen on them on their walk back from the chapel and now melted from the warmth of the flames. He looked out of the window over the lake. Snow. That was the last thing they needed right now. Hadsborough lay in a dip in the land, and it was always much worse here than in the nearby towns and villages. Still, it was ten years since they'd had anything but a few inches. He was probably worrying for nothing.

He found himself doing that a lot these days. Churning things over in his mind. Wondering in the middle of the night if there was anything he had missed. It was as if he tried to outrun his own personal cloud of doom all day by keeping busy, and then it would settle over him while he slept, poisoning his dreams.

Some nights, in a half dream-state, he'd travel further into the past, endlessly trying to relive moments that would never come again. He'd try to make the right decision this time, hoping he'd prevent the coming tragedy, that he could save his father from both disgrace and the grave, but when the sun rose in the morning all his nocturnal fretting hadn't changed anything.

He should have done more. Foolishly trusting his father, he'd seen it all happening and yet stood by, believing his father's assurances when he should have doubted them. But he wasn't going to make that mistake again; he had his eyes open now.

And not just when it came to family; when it came to *everything*. He should have realised that the woman he'd trusted with everything he'd had left—which hadn't been much—would eventually sit him down and tell him it was all too much for her, that she would leave him on his own to bear all the new responsibility that had come his way while she skipped off to a life of freedom. He'd given himself completely to a woman who hadn't known the meaning of loyalty, who hadn't known how to stand by the people she loved. How had he been so blind?

At least his relationship with Amanda had taught him something important, something the storybooks and the love songs failed to mention—love was always an unequal proposition. One person always gave more, always cared more, was always ready to sacrifice more. And that person was the weaker, more vulnerable side of the equation. One thing he was certain of: he was never going to be that person again.

'I'm sorry I didn't find what you were looking for,' he heard Faith say, and he realised he'd missed some of the conversation.

He lifted his head to look at her. Her face and eyes were totally expressionless. Too expressionless. A casual observer might have thought she didn't care, that she was handing out platitudes, but he recognised that look on her face. It was the one he saw every morning in the mirror when he made sure his own walls were still securely in place. They were more alike than he'd thought.

His grandfather nodded, trying not to look despondent. There was a flinch, a moment of hesitation, and then Faith reached over and covered his hand with hers. And then she smiled. It was the first hint of a smile he'd seen from her all day, and rather than being brassy and bright and false this one was soft and shy. Something inside his chest kicked.

But then the smile was gone, and Faith sat back on the sofa with her mask in place. His grandfather didn't seem to mind. He chatted away about old times while Faith sipped her tea and nodded.

He knew what she'd done—checked into that little place inside her head with its thick, thick walls. He lived out of a similar place himself. But for that soft smile of hers he'd never have guessed those intriguing walls were even there. She hid them well with her on-the-surface frankness and direct words.

She reminded him of Amanda, he realised. Maybe that was why he was reacting so strongly to her. It was another reason he should be doubly wary.

Faith had that same deceptive, ready-for-anything candour that had drawn him to his ex. Remember that word, Marcus. *Deceptive*. Not on purpose, but perhaps that just made the fraud all the more deadly—because it added that hint of honesty that made a man believe in things that just weren't there.

Just as well Faith McKinnon would be off their land and out of their lives before the afternoon was out.

As if she'd read his mind, Faith put down her empty cup. 'Thank you so much for the tea, Bertie,' she said, 'but I have to get going now. I'm renting a cottage down on the coast for the next few weeks.'

'On your own?' His grandfather looked appalled.

Faith nodded. 'It's going to be wonderful.'

It seemed those walls were thicker than even Marcus had guessed.

'I need to go and pick up the keys by three,' Faith said as she collected her bag and other belongings. 'I'll send you the results of my research in a couple of days.'

Bertie raised his eyebrows. 'You might be late picking up those keys,' he said, focusing on the window behind Marcus.

Marcus turned round just as Faith stood up and gasped.

No dusty snow now. Thick feathery flakes were falling hard and fast, so thickly he could hardly see the gatehouse only a hundred feet away.

'I don't think you'll be going anywhere for a while,' his grandfather said, doing his best to look apologetic, but clearly invigorated by the surprise turn in the weather—and events. 'It's far too dangerous to drive in this.'

'What kind of car have you got?' Marcus asked hopefully.

'A Mini.' Faith sighed and took a step closer to the windows. She didn't look as if she believed what she was seeing. 'An old one.'

Well, that was it, then. She'd be hard pressed to make it out of the castle grounds in a car like that, let alone brave the switchback country roads to the motorway.

'It'll probably stop soon,' he said, leaning forward and pressing his nose against the pane. 'Then you can be on your way.'

'In the meantime,' he heard his grandfather say, 'can I interest you in another cup of tea and possibly a toasted crumpet? Shirley makes the most fabulous lemon curd.'

While they drank yet more tea they listened to a weather forecast. Marcus's prediction was soundly contradicted. Heavy snow for the next couple of days. Advice to drive nowhere, anywhere unless it was absolutely necessary.

'Splendid!' Bertie said, clapping his hands. 'We haven't had a good snow in years!'

He was like a big kid again. But then his grandfather had

fond memories of trekking in the Tibetan foothills, and he was going to be able to enjoy this round of snow from the comfort of his fireside chair. Marcus's workload had suddenly doubled, and he was now going to have to tap dance fast to make sure all the Christmas events still went ahead as planned. When had this time of year stopped being fun and started being just another task to be ticked off the list?

He turned away from the window and looked at the other occupant of the yellow drawing room. Faith was back on the sofa again, but this time she wasn't smiling or looking quite so relaxed.

'I can't possibly put you out like this,' she said, looking nervously between grandfather and grandson. 'And I'm used to snow—'

His grandfather straightened in his chair, looking every inch the Duke for once. 'Nonsense! Your grandmother would have my hide if I sent you out in this weather—and, believe me, even after all these years, she is one lady I would not like to get on the wrong side of.'

At the mention of her grandmother Faith's expression changed to one of defeat. 'You have a point there,' she said quietly.

'You can stay here the night and we'll see how the forecast is in the morning.' His grandfather rang the bell at his side again and a few moments later Shirley appeared. 'Miss McKinnon will be staying. Could you make up the turret bedroom?'

'Of course, Your Grace.' Shirley nodded and scurried away.

'But I haven't got any overnight stuff,' Faith said quietly. 'It's all in the back seat of my car.'

Bertie waved a hand. 'Oh, that can be easily sorted. Marcus? Call Parsons on that mobile telephone thing of yours and have someone bring Miss McKinnon's bags in.'

Marcus's eyes narrowed. 'I'll do it,' he almost growled.

His staff had better things to do than to trudge through half a mile of snow with someone's luggage.

'I'll help,' Faith said, standing up.

He shook his head. She'd only complicate matters, and he needed a bit of fresh air and distance from Miss Faith McKinnon.

She frowned, and her body language screamed discomfort. He guessed this didn't sit well with that independent streak of hers. Too bad. At a place like Hadsborough everyone had to work together, like a large extended family. There was no room for loners.

She exhaled. 'In that case the overnight bag in the back will be enough. I don't need the rest.'

'I'll be back shortly,' he said, and exited the room swiftly.

A couple of minutes later he was trudging towards the visitor car park with a scarf knotted round his neck and his collar pulled up. With any luck he'd be repeating this journey in the morning—overnight bag in hand and Faith McKinnon hurrying along behind him.

Faith stood at the turret window that stared out over the lake. A real turret. Like in Rapunzel, her favourite fairy story.

The almost invisible sun was setting behind a wall of soft grey cloud and snowflakes continued to whirl past the mullioned windows, brightening further when they danced close to the panes and caught the glow from the rooms inside. Beyond, the lake was a regal slate-blue, flat as glass, not consenting to be rippled and distorted by the weather. The lawn she'd walked across that morning was now covered in snow—at least a couple of inches already—and bare trees punched through the whiteness as black filigree silhouettes.

How could real people live somewhere so beautiful? It must be a dream.

But the walls seemed solid enough, as did the furniture. Unlike the part of the castle that was open to the public, which was decorated mostly in a medieval style, the rooms in the private wing were more comfortable and modern. They were also filled with antiques and fine furniture, but there was wallpaper on the walls instead of bare stone or tapestries, and there were fitted carpets and central heating. All very elegant.

A smart rap on the door tore her away from the living picture postcard outside her window. She padded across the room in her thick socks and eased the heavy chunk of oak open.

Marcus stood there, fresh flakes of snow half-melted in his hair. Her heart made a painful little bang against her ribcage. *Quit it,* she told it. It had done that all afternoon—every time she caught sight of him.

He was holding her little blue overnight bag. She always packed an emergency bag when she travelled, and it had come in handy more times than she could count when flights had been delayed or travel plans changed. She just hadn't expected to need it in a setting like this.

Or to have a man like this deliver it to her.

He held it out to her and she gripped the padded handles without taking her eyes from his face. He didn't let go. Not straight away. Faith was aware how close their fingers were. It would only take a little twitch and she'd be touching him.

Don't be dumb, Faith. Just because you're staying in a castle for one night it doesn't mean you can live the fairytale. No one's going to climb up to your turret and rescue you. Especially not this man. He'd probably prefer to shove you from it.

She tugged the handles towards her and he let go. A slight expression of surprise lifted his features, as if he'd only just realised he'd hadn't let go when he should have.

'Thank you,' she said, finding her voice hoarse.

'You're welcome,' he replied, but his eyes said she was anything but. 'Dinner is at eight,' he added, glancing at the holdall clenched in her hands. 'We usually change for dinner, but we understand you're at a disadvantage.'

She nodded, not quite sure what to say to that, and Marcus

turned and walked down the long corridor that led to the main staircase. Faith watched him go. Only when he was out of sight did she close the door and dump her bag on the end of the bed.

She unzipped the side pocket, where she always stored her emergency underwear, and then opened the top drawer in an ornate polished wood dresser. Wow. The inside was even lovelier than the outside. Rich, grained walnut, if she wasn't mistaken, with a thick floral lining paper and a silk pouch with dried lavender in it. She took one look at the jumble of bra straps and practical white cotton panties in her hand and dumped them back in her case. Maybe later.

She returned to the window once more.

We usually change for dinner...

A chuckle tickled Faith's lips, but she didn't let it out. *Into what?* she wanted to ask. *Werewolves? Vampires?* Oh, she knew what he meant, but it was another reminder that this was another world. One where people dressed up for dinner and had *luncheon*. Well, she hoped he wasn't expecting ball-gowns or fur stoles from her.

And the tone he'd used... *We understand you're at a disadvantage.*

As if she needed his permission!

In the McKinnon household 'changing for dinner' meant putting your best jeans on—and that was what Faith intended to do.

The brightness behind Faith's lids reminded her of where she was, and why, before she opened her eyes the following morning. She blinked and rolled over to face the window. Snow was piled high on the thin stone ledge. Not good news if she was planning to escape to her little seaside hideaway today.

The bed had been comfy, but she'd had a metaphorical pea under her mattress. Or in her head, to be more accurate—a brooding presence that had been at the fringes of her consciousness all night. As if someone had been looking over her shoulder while she slept.

It was hardly surprising. She'd been aware of his appraising eyes on her all the way through dinner last night, and it had stopped her enjoying what must have been amazing food. Suddenly she'd got all self-conscious about which silver-plated fork to pick up and what she should do with her napkin.

He didn't know what to think of her, did he? Wasn't sure if she was friend or foe.

She'd wanted to jump up and shout, *Neither!* It felt wrong to have been admitted into not only their home but their daily life. *I agree. I shouldn't be here.*

Well, hopefully, if the weather had been kind overnight, she wouldn't be for much longer.

She got out of bed and shuffled over to the window, the comforter wrapped around her, and groaned. It was still snowing hard. Enough for her to know she wasn't going anywhere today, and possibly not tomorrow—not unless the Huntingtons had a snow plough tucked away in one of their garages.

Faith sighed as she watched the scene outside her window. She hadn't seen snow this thick for years—not since she'd last gone home for the Christmas holidays. A little jab of something under her ribcage made her breath catch. Homesickness? Surely not. The bust-ups at Christmas were one of the reasons she'd avoided December in Connecticut ever since.

She glanced at her coat, hanging on the back of the door, remembering how Gram's letter was still stuffed into one of the pockets. She still hadn't read it properly. Now she felt guilty. She stared at her coat. It wasn't that she didn't enjoy Gram's lively and warm narrative, but she knew there was always a price to pay for the pleasure.

Gram's letters always seemed so innocent—full of quirky anecdotes about town life—but in between the news of whose dog had had puppies, complaints about the mayor and Gram's book club gossip was a plea.

Come home.

Faith knew she should, and she planned to some time soon, but she really didn't want to this Christmas. She was too busy, too exhausted. And if both her sisters and her mother turned up there'd be more than enough noise and drama and no one would need Faith there to keep up the numbers. She'd given up trying to be family referee a long time ago, so there was no reason for her to be there.

She walked over to the door and retrieved the crumpled lilac letter. She stared at it for a moment, steeling herself for the inevitable tug on her heartstrings, and then she pulled the pages from the envelope and read.

It was the same old news about the same old town, but it still made her smile.

When she'd finished she reached into her purse and took out the other item that had been in the envelope. Gram had got tired of hinting about her girls coming home and had just gone for the jugular: she'd sent plane tickets to each of the McKinnon sisters, and she'd also requested a 'favour' from each of them. So one sister was travelling from Sydney to Canada, the other had been summoned back to Beckett's Run, and Faith had wound up here, at Hadsborough.

Crafty old woman, Faith thought, frowning. Gram was counting on the fact the sisters wouldn't refuse her—the favour *or* the trip home.

But Faith didn't think she could face it. It would be easier to hide away in her rented cottage until her next job in York. But if she was going to do that she needed time to work up the courage to tell Gram no.

She sighed and pulled yesterday's sweater from her bag. Yesterday's jeans, too. But before she went downstairs she had some internet research to do. Today she was not going to get caught out by Marcus Huntington.

It was still snowing hard when Marcus made the short walk from the estate office in the old stable block back to the castle. He prised his boots from his feet and left them by the kitchen door, then shook the ice off his coat before hanging it on a hook.

He'd almost forgotten about their unexpected guest until he walked into the drawing room and discovered Faith McKinnon sitting on the sofa she'd occupied yesterday. This time, instead of perching on the edge of the seat, she was sitting back against the comfy cushions, her legs crossed, drinking tea out of their Royal Doulton.

When she heard him approach she turned to look at him and put her teacup back on its saucer on the small mahogany table. The warmth that had been in her eyes faded.

'Good morning, Lord Westerham,' she said evenly.

Ah, she'd done her homework, had she? Discovered that as Bertie's heir he had the use of one of his grandfather's lesser titles. Not only that, she'd worked out the proper form of address for a courtesy earl. He wasn't sure if he should be impressed or irritated. It would depend on whether she was trying to be polite or to butter him up. He could accept the former, but he detested the latter, and he didn't know enough about her or her motives to guess which was true.

'I've been talking to the landlord of the Duke's Head in Hadsborough village,' he said, looking at his grandfather. 'He says the snow is drifting and it's already more than a foot deep in some of the lanes.'

'But the snow ploughs will be here soon, right?' Faith stopped abruptly, as if she hadn't meant to blurt that out.

He gave a rueful smile. 'Oh, they'll be here—eventually.'

'And by "eventually" you mean…?'

Bertie reached over and patted her arm. 'They'll concentrate on the motorways and the main roads first,' he said. 'We don't get much traffic in this neck of the woods. But don't you worry… They'll be here in a few days.'

'That's crazy! At home in Beckett's Run the roads would be clear by the next morning.'

Marcus stepped forward. 'Unfortunately this isn't Beckett's Run.'

She looked up at him, the look on her face telling him she was all too clear on that point. He met her gaze—the challenge she gave without even opening her mouth. And that was when it happened again. That strange feeling of everything swirling round them coming to rest. And this time they hadn't even been touching.

Faith was sitting stock still, her face deadpan, but he saw the flash of panic in her eyes before the shutters came down.

'Sorry, my dear,' his grandfather said, looking less than crestfallen at the prospect of having an unexpected house guest. 'It seems as if you're stuck with us for a while yet.'

Faith tore her gaze from Marcus's and fixed them on Bertie. 'In that case,' she said, in a very brisk and business-like fashion, 'is there somewhere I can plug my laptop in? I might as well get on with that research.'

She was meticulous. He'd give her that. Marcus watched as Faith wrote carefully in a large notebook with a pencil. She'd been at it since he'd returned just after lunch, pulling up research on her laptop and then recording it in her notebook in a clear, neat hand. He had the feeling she wasn't the kind to scribble away furiously, no matter how excited she got.

He looked out of the window. The low sun was a pale glowing disc in a gunmetal sky. It had been snowing too hard most of the day for their guest to venture to the chapel, but now the weather had lost its fervour and flakes drifted lazily towards the ground. The forecasts had predicted clear skies tomorrow. He hoped they were right.

'Haven't you got other things you need to do?' Faith asked quietly as she reached for the mouse once again.

He shook his head, and noted the glimmer of irritation that flashed across her features.

'Are you sure?'

She didn't like him hanging around watching her? Too bad. This was his family—his life she was carefully digging into before pulling it apart bit by bit—and today at least he had the luxury of being able to witness each new discovery. He needed to know before his grandfather if she unearthed anything significant.

'You know what? If you're so interested in what I'm doing—' and the look on her face said she didn't believe that for a second '—it would really help if you could check the estate archives for any mention of the window.'

'I already have.'

She raised her eyebrows hopefully but he shook his head.

'You're sure? Finding some documentary evidence one way or the other would help me finish this more quickly.'

The eyebrows lifted again, but this time they had a slightly knowing air. She knew he'd like that suggestion.

He was ashamed to admit it was true. Something about her straightforward 'don't care' attitude set his hair on end and raised his awareness.

He didn't have the luxury of not caring. Once, maybe, he'd thought he'd be able to forge his own path, create his own life, but his father's actions had scuppered those fantasies nicely. Now he had to care, whether he wanted to or not, and it irritated him that he'd been confronted with someone who had perfected that skill so perfectly.

He glanced over at her again. Her dark ponytail hung forward, draping over her shoulder, and she was lost in concentration. It didn't stop him admiring the thick, slightly wavy hair, or her small, fine features.

No, not that kind of awareness, Marcus.

Well, partly that.

Okay, he found her attractive. But that wasn't what he

meant. Ever since she'd arrived and sent Bertie into hyper-drive about this window he'd felt like one of those big black guard dogs the security team used.

He'd spent two years trying to rebuild the family name after the crash of his father's investment company and sub-sequent death, and now he'd discovered he couldn't stand himself down when a potential threat appeared.

The current threat was crouched over her laptop on the an-tique desk, and he had no business noticing its thick ponytail or elegant nose. He didn't want her digging around in the fam-ily's past. Any skeletons lurking around in the Huntingdon closet—and he was sure there were many—should remain undiscovered. Maybe not for ever, but for now. He didn't want to hide from the truth—just to wait until things were more settled.

As for his out-of-leftfield attraction to Faith McKinnon? He sighed. Well, maybe he didn't need to worry about that. The fact that he'd 'changed' after his father's death was one of the things that had sent Amanda running. She'd told him she was fed up with his snapping and snarling. Apparently women didn't find it very appealing. And from the looks Faith McKinnon had been giving him all afternoon she'd joined that lengthy queue. Even if there was something strange hum-ming between them, he was pretty certain she wasn't going to act on it.

And neither was he. So that was all good.

'Oh, my...'

Something about the tone of Faith's breathy exclamation stopped him short. He leaned forward to look at the laptop screen. She was transfixed by an image of an oil painting of a richly robed redhead in a beautiful garden, her arms over-flowing with fruit.

'That looks a bit like the window,' he said.

Faith looked up at him, her eyes shining. 'It looks *a lot* like the window! Do you see that plant with yellow flowers

in the corner?' She used the mouse to zoom in on one section of the high-res photo, showing a low-lying bush. 'It's
quite distinctive,' she said, indicating the papery leaves and,
in the centre of each bloom, an explosion of long yellow fila-
ments with red tips.

Marcus blinked. He was having trouble concentrating on
what she was saying. That shine in her eyes had momentarily
distracted him. All day she'd been like a robot, hardly talking to him, interacting as little as possible, and all of a sudden she was zinging with energy.

He cleared his throat. 'And this means something?'

'Maybe!' She ran her hand over her smoothed-back hair
and stood up, let out a little bemused laugh. 'I don't know...'
Her face fell. 'Darn! I forgot to take a photo of the window
when we were in the chapel yesterday.' She shook her head,
excitement turning to frustration, then marched over to the
window to inspect the weather. 'It's not snowing nearly as
hard now. Do you think we could go back? I need to see it
up close—compare the two side by side.'

Marcus was so taken with this moving, talking Faith that
he forgot to question if he should be pleased about this new
discovery or not. 'I don't see why not.'

She was almost out through the door before he'd finished
speaking, running to get her coat and boots. He followed her
out of the drawing room, only to be almost bowled over when
she dashed back to pick up her laptop.

'Come on,' she said, the hint of a smile tugging at the corners of her mouth. 'It'll be dark soon and I want to find out
for sure.'

He nodded, not quite sure what else he could say, and then
he wrapped up warm and followed Faith McKinnon out into
the snow.

Marcus stood back, arms folded, as Faith walked close to
the window, her laptop balanced on her upturned hands. She

looked from screen to window and back again repeatedly, and then she sat down on the end of the nearest pew and stared straight ahead.

He went and sat beside her. Not too close. She didn't register his presence.

'Are you okay?' His low voice seemed to boom in the empty chapel.

Faith kept looking straight ahead and nodded dreamily. Marcus was just starting to wonder if he should call somebody when she turned to him and gave him the brightest, most beautiful smile he'd ever seen. It was as if up until that moment Faith McKinnon had been broadcasting in black and white and she'd suddenly switched to colour.

'You've found something?' he said.

She nodded again, but this time her head bobbed rapidly and her smile brightened further. 'I think this window might be Samuel Crowbridge's work after all!'

Ah. That. Marcus breathed out. Nothing about a message, then. Good.

She twisted the laptop his way, showing him the zoomed-in picture of the little bunch of yellow flowers. 'They're identical,' she said triumphantly, 'and rather stylised. Rose of Sharon, the article says—although they look nothing like the ones in my grandmother's garden. Anyway, the chances of two different artists representing them this way is highly unlikely.'

He frowned. 'I thought you said Crowbridge had moved on from that style.'

A quick flick of her fingers over the mousepad and he was looking at the full picture once again.

'I know,' she said, 'but I think I may have found the reason he returned to it.' She clicked again and now a webpage appeared, dense with text. The painting was now a long rectangle down one side. 'Crowbridge was commissioned to do three paintings for a rather wealthy patron in the 1850s—

Faith, Hope and Charity—but only completed two out of the three before his patron changed his mind.'

Her lips curved into the most bewitching smile, and he couldn't help but focus on her lips as she continued to explain.

'Apparently they were modelled on his wife and two mistresses, and mistress number two fell out of favour.'

His eyebrows rose a notch, and he found his own lips starting to curve. 'You don't say?' He glanced back at the screen.

'Both paintings have been in a private collection for a long time—hardly ever seen, let alone photographed—but one recently went to auction.' She paused and her lips twitched a little. 'The original...*inspiration* for the trio of paintings came to light, and the family—understandably—decided to part with the picture that *wasn't* of Great-Great-Grandma.'

He nodded at the screen. 'Which virtue is she?'

'Charity,' she said firmly, and then her gaze drifted to the stained glass. 'Oh, how I wish there was a photo of the other one...'

She stood up, set the laptop down on the pew in front and walked over to the window.

Even in the dull light of a winter's afternoon the stained glass picture was beautiful. The pale sun, now on its way to setting, gently warmed the outside of the glass. As Faith drew near patches of pastel colour fell on her face, highlighting her cheekbones. Drawn like a magnet, he stood and walked towards her.

His throat seemed to be full of gravel. He swallowed a couple of times to dislodge it. 'And how does that relate to our window?'

No. Not *our.* At least not in the way he'd meant it when he'd said it. It should be his and Bertie's *our,* not his and Faith's *our.*

He was standing opposite her, with the window on his right, and she turned to face him. The patchwork colours of the window fell on one side of their faces, marking them identically.

'I'm not sure,' she said, and closed her eyes for the briefest of moments, almost as if she was sending up a silent prayer.

Marcus took another step forward.

She opened her eyes and looked at him. Right into him.

'I think Crowbridge may have taken the chance, years later, to finish his trilogy. But not in oils this time—in stained glass.'

'I see.' He looked back, not breaking eye contact, amazed that he could see layer upon layer of things deep in those eyes that had previously been shuttered. 'So this one here would be...?'

'Faith,' she whispered.

No longer did their words seem to echo. They were absorbed by the thick air surrounding the pair of them. Her eyes widened slightly and a soft breath escaped her lips.

Faith. The word reverberated inside his head. But he wasn't looking at the window. In fact he'd forgotten all about it. His gaze moved from her eyes to her nose, and then lower...

'Yes,' he said softly, leaning dangerously closer.

CHAPTER FOUR

SOMEONE was playing drums somewhere. Loudly. They were echoing in Faith's ears.

'Uh—' Her lips parted of their own accord.

Stop it, she shouted to herself silently. *What on earth do you think you're doing? You know this is a really bad idea, and you're not some brainless bimbo who can't think straight when an attractive man is around. At least you've never been up until now.*

Thankfully Marcus came to his senses first, although something inside Faith ripped like Velcro when he abruptly stepped back and turned his focus once again to the kneeling woman in the window, beautiful and serene.

What had happened just then? She blinked a couple of times. Marcus was scowling at her, as usual, and it was as if the last couple of minutes hadn't happened. She folded her arms across her chest and scowled back.

A muscle at the side of his jaw twitched. 'What does this mean? For us?'

Faith's heart stopped. 'For *us?*' she repeated in a whisper.

'For the family,' he said, very matter-of-factly. 'For the Huntingtons.'

Oh, for *them.* Not her. He hadn't been including her. Not that she'd expected him to, of course. Or wanted him to.

'I don't know. Before I can say anything definitive I'll

have to investigate further.' She swallowed. 'I'd need your consent for that.'

He didn't say anything. And he was looking less than impressed at the idea of her poking around his family's home and history.

He was going to say no, wasn't he? She could see it in his face. He was going to tell his grandfather it was too much trouble, too much inconvenience—to protect that lovely old man from the 'upset', as he put it. A flash of anger detonated inside her. Her older sister liked to boss people around that way, make their decisions for them. That kind of behaviour had always driven her crazy. She wasn't going to back down. She didn't care what he thought. The world had a right to know if this was Crowbridge's window.

'There's some minor damage in the corner, and what repair attempts have been made are very poor. If this window turns out to be what I think it might be I could restore it for you. Free of charge. Payment in kind for letting me investigate further. If I'm right, the PR value for the castle—and your family—would be great. And more publicity means more visitors.'

Then she laid down her ace. 'And, of course, your grandfather would know beyond a shadow of a doubt that every inch of the window has been investigated and documented.' She breathed in quickly. 'I'm stuck here for at least a couple of days anyway, and you said you wanted something concrete for Bertie. Well, this kind of work would be about as concrete as you could get.'

He folded his arms. 'What would this *research* involve?'

He said it as if it was a dirty word. Faith's spine straightened. Any beginnings of the truce they'd been beginning to build were gone. Obviously ripped away when he'd had what must have been a *What were you thinking?* moment in the split second before his lips had come close to hers. Just like that they were on opposite sides of the battlefield again.

She lifted her chin, even though inside she was cringing. Why couldn't it have been her who'd pulled away? Now she just felt pathetic and rejected and he had the moral high ground. Of *course* he wouldn't go around kissing an ordinary girl like her. She should have known that. Should have backed off first. But she'd been too excited about the window to care...

Well, she was still excited about the window.

Only now she'd gained a much-needed sense of perspective, too. Good. She'd needed that. Thank you, Marcus Huntington, Earl Westerham, and future eighth Duke of Hadsborough. He had actually done her a favour.

It didn't mean she was going to curtsey or anything.

'Faith tells me she's offered to repair the window free,' his grandfather said over dinner that evening.

Not free, Marcus thought. There was a price. It just didn't involve money.

He picked up his soup spoon. 'Surely proper research will take more than the couple of days you'll be stuck here?' he asked.

A little bit of her bread roll seemed to get stuck in her throat. 'A couple of days will tell me if it's worth pursuing,' she said hoarsely. 'Then, if you give me the go-ahead to repair, I guess it'd take a couple of weeks. I'd finish in time for the Carol Service, I promise you. And I won't intrude on your hospitality any further once the roads are clear. I can commute from the cottage in Whitstable.'

His grandfather made a dismissive noise, letting them know what he thought about that. 'Nonsense. You'll stay here. It's a complete waste of time and petrol to do otherwise.'

Faith opened her mouth and closed it again. Marcus could tell from the determined look on her face she wasn't happy with that idea, but she was sensible enough to leave that battle for another day. There was no talking to his grandfather when he remembered he was a duke after all, and started issuing orders.

It was clear the old man wasn't about to have anyone spoil his fun, and he seemed quite taken with their unexpected guest.

And so are you, seeing as you almost kissed her in the chapel.

Ah, but he'd stopped himself in time. And just as well. Because he wasn't going to choose with his heart again. Love was a see-saw, and Marcus was going to make damn sure he ended up high in the air next time. He would be the one who held the power and could walk away if he wanted to. He'd do what his family had done for generations—choose a sensible girl from a suitable family who would bring some stability and support to the Huntington line.

It was just hard to remember that when Faith McKinnon fixed him with those dark brown eyes of hers and stared at him, peeling him layer by layer, making him feel she could see right inside him. Worse still, he could feel his reluctance to push her away growing. And that was dangerous. Without those walls of his in place he was likely to do something stupid. They were all that stopped him repeating the whole Amanda fiasco.

He reached for the pepper and ground a liberal amount on his soup. 'So you're saying that this research of yours won't disrupt us?'

Her chin tipped up a notch and she looked him in the eye. 'Less than the snow. I promise you that.'

Touché.

While he didn't appreciate her defiance, he admired her pluck. Not many people challenged him outright on anything these days.

'Are you going to take the window away?' his grandfather asked, echoing what Marcus had been hoping.

Faith shook her head. 'I need to be close to the whole window to do my research—not just the bit of it I'm repairing. But I own most of the equipment I'd need, and I can order in supplies quite easily when the snow clears. The first phase will be observation and documentation anyway.' She shot him a hopeful glance. 'I was wondering if you had a space where I can work on the bottom pane? I'd only need a room with a trestle table and decent light.'

Marcus's shoulders stiffened. Unfortunately they had the perfect spot.

Bertie knew it, too. He grinned. 'Of course. Then what?'

'Then I'll snip the old lead away and clean the glass before putting it back together.'

Bertie nodded seriously. 'You will keep your eyes peeled, won't you? For anything unusual?'

She swallowed and glanced quickly at Marcus. He shot her a warning look. She lowered her eyelids slightly at him, before turning her attention back to his grandfather and acting as if their little exchange had never happened.

'Of course I will investigate every area of the window carefully,' she said, her voice losing its characteristic briskness, 'but none of the usual rules apply, and I haven't seen writing of any kind.'

Bertie's face fell. He folded his napkin and placed it on the table.

She reached over and covered her hand with his. 'I promise I will try to keep an open mind,' she added, 'but only if you promise to do the same.'

He nodded, and then smiled at her gently. 'Thank you, Faith. If anyone can unravel this secret it will be you.'

She withdrew her hand and sat back in her chair. 'I'll do my best, Bertie,' she said, shaking her head, 'but you have to face the possibility that what you're looking for may not be there.'

'Holy cow!' Faith said.

'Quite,' was Marcus's dry response.

She'd never seen so much junk in her life. She'd thought Gram's attic was bad. But Gram and Grandpa had only lived in their house fifty years. The Huntingtons had lived at Hadsborough for more than four hundred, and it seemed that no one had ever, *ever* thrown anything away. They'd just stuffed it in the unused vaults under the castle.

They both stood in the doorway and just stared.

Marcus, who had been holding the door open, nudged a little doorstop under it with his foot and walked a couple of paces into the room.

A retired servant, whose sons still worked for the estate, had tipped Marcus off about this place. There had to be at least a couple of centuries worth of debris here, so they were sure to stumble upon something to help her.

She needed to find something that would link Samuel Crowbridge to this window. If she announced her suspicions to the academic community without proof someone could hijack it, find the evidence she lacked, and it wouldn't be her find any more.

'Let's get started, shall we?' she said wearily.

The rooms weren't totally below ground, but with snow piled high against the long, horizontal windows just below the ceiling they might as well have been.

'I was told the cellar wasn't in use,' Marcus said.

'It isn't,' she replied. 'By the looks of it the last of the junk was stuffed in here at least a decade ago.'

His eyebrows rose as the said the word *junk*.

'You know what I mean.'

He strolled over to an old, but definitely not antique filing cabinet and peered inside the bottom drawer. The rusty runners squeaked painfully as he pushed it closed again.

'Stuffed badger,' he said, a faint air of bemusement about him.

'A real one?'

He nodded.

She walked over to the filing cabinet to take a look for herself. It wasn't a very big one, but sure enough a ratty-looking stuffed animal with glass eyes sat morosely at the bottom of the deep drawer, staring at the painted metal sides. She did as Marcus had done and shut the drawer, then she turned to look at him and said, quite seriously, 'Of course it is. That's where I keep mine—amongst the filing. You never know when it's going to come in handy.'

That earned her a smile. Sort of.

Good. If she could get him to lighten up a bit it might help her sanity. For some reason he was on red alert around her, and she sensed it was more than just her intrusion into his family. She had the feeling she was his own personal brand of dynamite.

Which means he should handle you with care...

She slapped the masochistic part of herself that had come up with that dumb thought. He wasn't going to be *handling* her anywhere. At all. Ever. She needed to get that into her thick skull.

Which was easier said than done. Especially as the more he glowered at her the more her pulse skipped. What was wrong with her? Really? Why did something inside her whisper that she should stop running in the opposite direction and just give in?

And when she was aware of him watching her—which was always—her skin tingled and her concentration vanished. She did her best to ignore the prickling sensation up her spine when he was near, but it seemed to be getting stronger all the time.

There it went again—like a pair of fingers walking up her back.

She decided to search the other side of the room from him, just to see if a little extra distance would help.

It didn't.

'Do you think there's any order to this stuff?' she called

out as she lifted the top ledger in a dusty pile and inspected the front page: *Meat ordering: 1962-65*. Fascinating for the right person, probably, but not what she was looking for. She put it down again and inspected the rest of the stack. They were various household accounts from the fifties and six-ties—all decades too late to help her.

'We could spend weeks searching this place,' she said as she came across Marcus again behind a stack of crates. 'Just rummaging could be pointless. What we really need to do is sort it all out, clean the room and put it in some order.'

He nodded. 'But you're supposed to be working on the window. You haven't got time to clean my cellar for me.'

Ah, the ticking clock inside his head—counting down to the moment when she would leave. Even now it made itself apparent.

She nodded up to the snow packed against the windows. After a brief reprieve the snow had returned with a vengeance. 'At the moment I can't even get to the chapel, and I need to find some documentary back-up,' she replied. 'I'm stuck here twenty-four-seven and you haven't got cable. What else am I going to do with my time?'

Marcus just shook his head and wandered off, muttering something about the sheer stupidity of trying to lay cable in a moat and how satellite dishes would spoil the roofline. Faith let her mouth twitch. This getting Marcus to lighten up thing was almost fun, and it had the added bonus that if she managed to keep him from glowering at her she might start acting sensibly for a change.

He was saved from answering her by a rap on the open cel-lar door. A man she didn't recognise poked his head in, and he and Marcus talked in hushed voices. Faith decided not to eavesdrop and took herself to the far side of the cellar and leafed through a stack of old papers. He reappeared a couple of minutes later, looking frustrated.

'Problems?' Faith asked.

He huffed. 'Nothing to do with the window. We host a Christmas Ball every year and ticket sales have ground to a halt. My events manager says the forecast for ongoing snow is to blame.'

'When is it?'

'A week on Saturday.' A grimace of annoyance passed across his features. 'I really don't want to cancel it. We've already laid out a lot of money, and no ball means no revenue and plenty of lost deposits.'

'But you can cover that, right? It's not like you'll be going without your Christmas lunch because of it.'

He gave her a look that told her she didn't know much about anything. 'A place like this *eats* money,' he said carefully. 'I know it might not look like it from the outside, but even Hadsborough feels the pinch of tough economic times.' He shook his head. 'People are worried about getting stuck on the motorway in the snow, or stranded at the station if trains get cancelled.'

She picked up a dusty newspaper and looked at it. 'Can't they just put on some snowboots and walk?'

'Most of the guests aren't local. The ball is a very exclusive event, and people come from all over the south of England.'

He mentioned a ticket price that made her eyes water.

'No wonder people are wary about spending that much and then not even getting here.' She replaced the newspaper on its pile. 'You know what? You should drop the ticket price and get the locals to come—have a party for the villagers. I know it won't raise as much money, but there's a whole heap of other stuff you could do quite cheaply—'

Marcus stood up ramrod-straight. 'Miss McKinnon, I'm very grateful for your…input…but my family has been running this estate for three hundred years. Maybe you should concentrate your opinions on your own area of expertise.'

She blinked. Well, that told *her,* didn't it?

But she found she wasn't going to sigh and ignore it, as

she would have done if one of her sisters had delivered such a stinging put-down. She found she couldn't just walk away from Marcus Huntington when he issued a challenge.

'Actually, when it comes to Christmas I'm something of an expert.'

His face was deadpan. 'You do surprise me. I hadn't pegged you as the reindeer jumper and flashing Santa earrings type.'

'Well, I didn't reckon you'd be quite so up your own butt when I first met you, but it seems you're not the only one who can be wrong.'

His expression was thunderous for a moment, but all of a sudden he threw back his head and laughed. It was a rich, earthy sound, most unlike his clipped speaking voice, and it made him seem like a completely different man. Faith wasn't sure if she wanted to march over there and slap him, or if she should just let go of the tension in her jaw and join him.

'I'm sorry,' he said, when he'd finally regained his composure. 'You're right. I was being horrendously pompous.' And then he spoilt his apology by bursting out laughing again. He dragged his hand over his eyes then looked at her. 'You're very direct, aren't you?'

This time Faith joined him. Just a little chuckle. It was hard not to when she saw the warmth in those normally intense blue eyes.

'So where does all this Christmas expertise come from?' he asked.

'I grew up in a small town that takes the holidays *very* seriously,' she replied. 'Anything that's fixed down—and a few things that aren't—are in danger of being draped with fairy lights and tinsel during the week-long festival each year, running up to Christmas Eve.' She shook her head gently, smiling. 'I pretended I hated it when I was a teenager.' The smile faded away. 'I suppose I kinda miss it.'

Wow. She hadn't expected those words to come out of her

mouth. She suddenly remembered those plane tickets burning a hole in her purse upstairs in the turret.

'When were you last home for Christmas?' he asked.

'Five years ago.'

That was a long time, wasn't it? Suddenly a pang of something hot speared her deep inside. She brushed it away. She didn't *do* homesickness. It was probably something to do with the fact that Marcus had stepped closer, and the fact that he'd stopped glaring at her and was looking down at her with a mixture of understanding and curiosity. Which meant it was her cue to step away.

'Anyway,' she said brightly, shuffling backwards, 'I'm sure there's something you could do here that wouldn't cost the earth and would generate some income.'

Marcus gave her another one of his dry half-smiles. 'As long as it doesn't involve putting a light-up Santa and sleigh on the castle roof I'll keep an open mind.'

She nodded. 'Good. Now, where do you think is the best place to start sorting through this junk?'

'Please, Faith,' he said, but the smile didn't fade completely, making her feel like a co-conspirator rather than an adversary, 'this isn't all junk—some of it is history.'

He'd called her Faith instead of Miss McKinnon. Wonders would never cease.

She smiled. 'Okay… Which bits of this *history* do you think we should put in a garbage sack first?'

Marcus started to open his mouth.

'Kidding!' she added quickly. 'Really, you are too easy sometimes.'

Marcus shook his head and turned away to investigate a pile of tattered copies of *Punch!* Even though his back was turned she could sense he was closer to smiling instead of scowling—which made things more comfortable on quite a few fronts—and they worked side by side for the next half an hour in something approaching comfortable silence.

Then Marcus checked his watch and showed her the time. 'Not long until dinner,' he said.

They both straightened, dusted themselves off and looked at each other.

Clunk. It happened again. That feeling of coming to rest, slotting in. Faith held her breath.

'And we'll carry on tomorrow?' she asked, letting the air out in one go.

He nodded. 'It depends what the weather does, but I can't see those supplies you ordered getting through for another couple of days at least.'

'In that case I have one request,' she said.

Marcus's brows drew together. He didn't much like being told what to do, did he? Didn't like being indebted to anyone in any way. The humour drained from his face, and once again she was reminded of a sleek hunting animal.

The easy banter they'd shared for a few minutes had lulled her into a sense of false security—made her think she could make him less of a threat. She'd been wrong. Just ask its prey how tame the hound was; it knew the wildness that lay underneath the groomed and elegant coat. It didn't attempt to befriend it; it took one look and ran. A lesson she should not forget.

She folded her arms across her chest. 'The badger stays,' she said, doing her best to appear composed and in control under his gaze. It would be a good reminder for her every time she was tempted to do something dumb. A stuffed and glassy-eyed chaperone. One that obviously hadn't run when it should have done.

The intensity of his gaze didn't waver, but his lips curved into a grudging smile and he nodded.

Unfortunately his change of expression didn't help matters one bit. Faith felt that smile down to her toes. Nope. Not safe at all, that smile.

As he opened the filing cabinet drawer and lifted the badger out she drew in a shaky breath.

She needed help. Big time. Because if he kept looking at her like that the woman in Bertie's window wouldn't be the only one on her knees asking for heavenly assistance. Faith would be right there beside her.

CHAPTER FIVE

ONCE again Faith was following Marcus across the castle lawn and off the island. This time, however, their footsteps left six-inch deep impressions in the flawless snow. Here, near the lake, it wasn't that deep, but Marcus had told her it had drifted quite high in some of the dips and dells on the estate.

Out on the road to the main gate a tractor was spreading grit, and up near the old stables a team of men with snow shovels were clearing the paths.

Faith peeked from under the brim of her knitted hat and cast her eyes upwards as her breath made little icy clouds. The sky was the most amazing blend of the palest pastels, from rose-petal pink at the horizon through lilac and lavender to crisp blue high above.

As she walked along a wide path that led away from the castle she could see that the water from the lake flowed underneath their feet and filled a second lake, longer and thinner. On the far side were fields and pockets of woodland, but she couldn't see the nearest bank as it curved round the low hill where the stable block was situated.

In front of the stables the path forked. Faith prepared to leave Marcus, who was on his way to the estate office, and continue her journey to the chapel, but he stopped where the paths divided. 'I'd like to show you something.'

Not exactly a request, but it wasn't an order either. Yesterday she would have said *no way,* suspecting he had a pair of stocks waiting for the interloper, but she couldn't quite wipe the memory of his unguarded laughter from the evening before, so she nodded and followed him under the arch of the redbrick building and into the yard beyond. Single-storey buildings framed the edges of a large cobbled square. Marcus led her to one on the right, unlocked the door and ushered her inside into a large bright space.

'My mother had a fixation with watercolour painting for a while,' he said. 'We had this converted for her.'

Faith took a few steps into the airy studio and stopped. *Wow.* What a view.

The wall opposite the door was all glass, with a stupendous view of the lake. Just outside was a small decked area, and then the land fell away. Beautifully kept terraced gardens, the shape now muffled with great dollops of snow, had been cut into the side of the hill as it dipped towards the lake. Geese floated aimlessly on the water and she watched silently as a low-flying swan made a rather inelegant landing, carving a wake on the lake's surface and causing the other birds to flutter and scurry.

'Will this do for a workspace?'

She looked back at him. Some people would have described his face as blank, but Faith knew better. She could see a difference in his eyes, in the set of his mouth. She knew instantly what this meant. This was his way of calling a truce.

Nothing as simple as a laying down of arms, though. Marcus was like those medieval castles that had rings and rings of walls and defences, and she understood that all he'd done was let her inside the first gate.

And she was quite happy to camp for the remainder of her time at Hadsborough. One notch down from frosty resentment suited her just fine. She'd be safe from those sizzling glares, but not close enough to be tempted by what she saw inside. This would be good. She could handle cordial but distant Marcus.

'So this space will work for you?' he said.

'Yes, thank you,' she replied, giving her best impression of calm and professional. *Fake it,* she told herself. *Pretty soon the rest of you will catch up and it'll become real.*

If only she'd known just how wrong she was—just how the glimmer of humour in his eyes would be her undoing.

'I'm sure you'd tell me if it didn't,' he said.

Faith blinked. Was Marcus—was *the Earl*—teasing her?

The jittery feeling she'd been fighting fairly successfully since the night before returned, but she lifted her chin and looked at him while she locked everything down. Made sure not a hint of a tremor showed on the outside.

'You got that right,' she said, and then she turned and headed back towards the door—away from the beautiful view, away from the beautiful man. Sensible gal.

'Now, I'm off to see that window before we both freeze our butts off.'

She ignored the huff of dry laughter behind her and headed back out into the cold, hoping the chilly air would rob her cheeks of some of their colour.

'That's you? Standing on top of the Great Pyramid?' Faith bent over Bertie's old photo album on the coffee table in front of the fire. Her dark hair swung forward, obscuring her face.

The old man nodded and smiled the smile that she only saw when he was sharing his photo albums with her. One with a tinge of recklessness.

'They used to let you do that in those days.'

'You've been to so many wonderful places,' she said, turning the page and finding more of Bertie and his wife, Clara, in exotic locations. 'My youngest sister likes to travel. Gram says she never could sit still as a child either.'

'Me, too,' Bertie said, sighing and relaxing back into his

wing-backed chair. 'Still wouldn't if I had the choice. Only do it now because I've got to.'

She nodded in mock seriousness. 'But still an adventurer on the inside,'

There was that smile again—the one born of memories of exploration and exploits. 'You betcha, as your grandma used to say.'

Faith's eyes grew wide. 'She did *not!*' Gram had always been a stickler for proper diction and polite manners.

She'd been here five days now. Her preliminary observation and documentation of the window was complete, and tomorrow she would move the bottom of the section to the studio, where she could begin the painstaking work of removing all the old lead, gently cleaning the antique glass and putting it all back together again.

Five days? Had it only been that long? She and Bertie were already firm friends, and she looked forward to their after-dinner chats, when he would regale her with stories from his travels. From the occasional hoist of Marcus's eyebrows as he sat in the other armchair, reading a thriller, she guessed some of the details had become more and more embellished as the years had gone by, but she didn't mind.

'My Lord?' Shirley appeared at the door. 'Telephone call for you.'

Marcus nodded and stood up, excusing himself.

The grandson? Well, he was another kettle of fish. Bertie had welcomed her warmly into his home, but she was still camped inside that first gate of Marcus's defences. She reminded herself that was just what she wanted. Even if it was more like walking a tightrope than camping somewhere safe, at least she *was* walking it. Just.

Marcus returned from his phone call and took up his customary place in the armchair opposite his grandfather. He crossed his legs and picked up his book. 'Parsons says they finished clearing the lanes of snow today. You're free,' he added, with a nod in Faith's direction, 'should you want to fly.'

'Ridiculous,' Bertie said in a dismissive tone. 'I've told you what your grandmother will do to me if I toss you out. You're staying here and that's that.' He closed his newspaper as if that was the end of the subject. 'My grandson tells me you've been badgering him with ideas for the Christmas Ball,' he said, moving on to another topic of conversation.

Faith knew it was useless to argue, so she went with the flow. 'I've suggested lowering the ticket price, relaxing the dress code and inviting people from the village. You wouldn't have to cancel if you did that.'

Marcus looked at her over the top of his paperback. 'The number of people from Hadsborough village who have attended the ball in the past has been very small. I don't think they're interested.'

'I mean something more accessible than an over-priced event that only a handful of rich outsiders can afford. I grew up in a small town, so I understand the mentality. Get them all involved, make them feel it's *their* party, too, and they might just surprise you. Tickets would sell like hot cakes. They must be proud of the castle, of being linked with it—I know I would be if I lived here—so let them show it.'

The grim line of Marcus's mouth told her he wasn't convinced.

Faith shrugged. 'Or you could keep going with your idea and lose money hand over fist. Up to you.'

Bertie chuckled and clapped his hands together. 'She's got you there, my boy!'

Marcus didn't answer straight away. 'I'll think about it,' he muttered, and he picked up his book and obscured his face with it once more.

Marcus whistled as he closed the estate office door behind him. He checked his watch. Four-fifteen. The sun would be setting soon, and he could already feel the impatient frost sharpening the air. It had snowed again over the last couple of days, as the forecast had predicted, but not as hard as it had when Faith had first got here.

Still, on top of the previous snow some of the surrounding lanes were once again blocked, complicating matters. Thank goodness they'd had a couple of clear days that had allowed for deliveries—including Faith's supplies for the window restoration.

He crossed the courtyard and headed for the studio door. After a busy day at the estate office, dealing with all the extra work the weather had thrown up, he'd got into the habit of checking up on Faith near the end of the working day.

When the natural light began to fade she'd sit up from being hunched over the stained glass panel and rub her eyes, as if she was waking from a long and drowsy sleep. Tenacious wasn't the word. If he caught her at just the right time he'd see the warm, vibrant Faith who'd visited the other day in the chapel—the one who only came to life when she was talking about or working on the window.

He knew he probably shouldn't want to catch a glimpse of this other Faith, but she didn't hang around for long. Once the tools were back in their box she disappeared, and temptation was safely out of reach. It wasn't wrong to just *look,* was it? It wasn't as if he was going to do something stupid and *touch.*

He knocked on the door to warn her of his approach, and then opened it without waiting for an answer. He found her just as he'd expected to—perched on a stool next to the trestle table, spine curved forward as she snipped the soft lead away from the antique glass with a pair of cutters.

When she heard his footsteps she put her tools down and then linked her hands above her head in a stretch that elongated her spine. Marcus stopped where he was, suddenly transfixed by the slight swaying movement as she stretched the muscles on first one side of her torso and then the other.

That motion was doing a fabulous job of emphasising her slender waist through her grey polo neck jumper.

Forget stockings and corsets. It seemed that softly clinging knitwear was enough to do it for him these days. Had he been without significant female company for too long? Or was this just a sign that he was getting old, and cardigans and suchlike were going to float his boat from now on? Either way he answered that question it was a pretty sad state of affairs.

Faith stopped stretching and turned round to talk to him, which—thankfully—gave Marcus the use of his vocal cords once again.

'Is it that time already?' She pushed up a sleeve and checked her watch, frowned slightly at it, then got up to head off to the large window that filled the opposite wall. The setting sun was hidden by the castle, but it had turned the lake below them shades of rich pink and tangerine. She sighed as he walked across the space to join her.

'Ready?' he said.

She turned towards him and nodded. 'Sure.'

This, too, had become a habit. Just as his feet had fallen into taking him to the studio at the end of the day, he and Faith had fallen into a routine of meeting up and going down to the cellar when the working day was over. After more than a week of evenings dusting and sorting and tidying they'd made progress.

He knew he could have snapped his fingers and had a whole crew descend on the place and sort it out in a matter of days, but he was quite enjoying sifting through the debris of earlier generations bit by bit. A couple of hours of quiet each evening before dinner, when he was free to do something that interested him rather than something that *had* to be done, was doing him good.

She collected her things, put her coat on and looped a scarf around her neck, before turning the light off and shutting the door. Marcus pulled the key from his pocket and locked it behind them, then they strolled back down the hill towards the castle, its silhouette dark against the sunset.

She filled him in on her progress with the window.

'It's strange,' she said, and frowned. 'It's obvious the bottom of the window has been repaired before. Quite soon after its installation, if I'm right about the age of the materials. I wonder what happened to it.'

He made a noncommittal kind of face. 'Perhaps we'll find an answer if we ever find some purchase records. Someone must have been paid to do the work.'

She nodded thoughtfully. 'Let's hope.'

They made their way down to the cellar and resumed their clear-out operation. Some of the ratty office furniture, which had obviously been dumped here a decade or two ago, when the estate offices had moved to the renovated stable block, had been cleared out, which left them with a little more space. A pile of sturdy lidded plastic crates stood near the door, and anything that might be useful was put safely inside, away from the dust.

They'd also found a lot of 'garbage', as Faith called it, a few treasures and a mountain of paperwork. Most of it, even the grocery ordering lists and letters of recommendation for long-gone parlour maids, they'd decided to keep. It would be the start of a rich family archive, giving glimpses of daily life from the castle over the last fifty years. Faith had suggested having an exhibition, and much to his surprise Marcus had found himself agreeing. In the New Year some time, though, when all this Christmas madness was over.

Faith pulled an old invitation for the Christmas Ball from the nearest pile and lifted it up to show the stuffed badger, who'd been released from his filing cabinet prison and now perched proudly on a wooden plant stand, keeping guard. His beady little orange glass eyes glinted in the light from a single bare bulb overhead.

'What do you think, Basil? Worth keeping?'

Marcus put down the cardboard box full of cups and saucers he'd been moving. 'Basil?'

Faith shrugged. 'Basil the Badger. It seemed to fit.'

Marcus shook his head.

Side by side, they started sorting through piles of assorted papers, books and boxes, stopping every now and then to show each other what they'd found, debating the merits of each find.

It was nice to have someone to discuss things with—even if it was whether to keep a receipt for a peacock feather evening bag or not. It made him realise just how much he'd been on his own since he'd come back to Hadsborough to work. He only discussed the bigger issues with his grandfather, leaving him to rest. The remainder Marcus dealt with by himself.

It had been different in the City. He'd had plenty of friends, an active social life, a woman who'd said she loved him...

Better not to think of her. She was long gone with the rest of them. Everyone he'd counted on had deserted him when he'd needed them most. It seemed the family name had been more of a draw than he'd thought, and once that had been dragged through the mud they'd scattered. Whether it was because he was no longer useful or they thought they'd be painted guilty by association didn't matter.

But now he was back home, with only an elderly relative for company. The staff kept a respectful distance, not only because he was the boss, but because of the family he'd been born into. He realised he hadn't had much time to socialise with people who weren't afraid to meet him as an equal, as a human being instead of a title.

Faith did that. Without being disrespectful or fake. Not many people achieved that balance, and he appreciated it. She wasn't afraid to share her opinions, but she was never argumentative or rude. She just 'called a spade a spade', as his grandmother had used to say. In fact he had some news for her about one of their recent conversations when she'd done just that.

'It's been four days since we cut the ticket prices to the Christmas Ball and sent word around the village,' he said nonchalantly as he dusted off a pile of old seventy-eight records. 'And relaxed the dress code, of course.'

Faith stopped what she was doing and turned round. Her ponytail swung over her shoulder and he got the most intoxicating whiff of camellias and rose petals.

'Yeah? Have sales improved?'

He nodded. 'The locals are snapping them up.'

Her eyebrows rose. 'See? I told you I understood the community spirit you get in a place like this. People just love to feel involved. You're not their lords and masters any more, so it wouldn't hurt to stop hiding away in your castle and mix a little.'

He snorted. 'I do not hide away in my castle.'

She raised her eyebrows. 'Oh, no? When was the last time you went down to the village pub for a drink, then?'

'I could name you a time and a date,' he said, sounding a little smug.

Faith wasn't fooled for a second. 'Sock it to me.'

Marcus closed his eyes and smiled as he looked away for a second. 'Okay, I was seventeen,' he said as he met her impish gaze, 'and I escaped down to the village with a couple of my schoolfriends who were staying over. The village bobby had to bring us back at two in the morning, drunk as skunks. I was grounded for a month. So I remember that occasion very well.'

'It wouldn't hurt you to get outside the boundaries of the estate once in a while, you know.'

He wanted to argue, to say he did—but hadn't he just been thinking about being on his own so much? Had he turned himself into a hermit? Surely not.

'You will come, won't you?' he asked.

'To the village pub? Now, there's an offer a gal can't refuse!' She gave him a wry smile as she took a vinyl record from his hands and inspected it.

'No,' he said, 'to the Christmas Ball.'

She rubbed a bit of dust that he'd missed off the corner of the record sleeve with her fingers. 'It would be lovely, but I...I can't. I'm busy with the window, and a ball's not really my sort of thing.'

'You said you were making good progress,' he replied. He looked around the darkening cellar. The sky through the narrow windows at the top of the room was indigo now. 'An invitation is the least I can give you after all you've done to help resurrect the idea.'

If anything she looked sadder. 'Maybe,' was all she said.

He didn't get it. He thought women liked balls and dressing up and dancing. So why had Faith sounded as if he'd asked her if he could gently roast the family rabbit for dinner? Perhaps he'd better change the subject.

He picked the next record up from the pile. 'What about this Christmas-mad small town you come from? Tell me about your family.'

Faith shrugged and handed him back the first seventy-eight. 'Gram is the only one who lives in Beckett's Run now. One sister lives in Sydney, the other travels all over for work, and my mother just...drifts.'

She wandered off to the other side of the room and started nosing around in a cardboard box over there.

Hmm... One minute she was spouting on about community spirit and getting involved, but the first mention of home and family and she was off like a shot. What was all that about?

He decided it was none of his business. He didn't like people poking around in his family's affairs, and maybe Faith didn't either. Instead of pursuing the matter further he concentrated on the pile of records—a few of which he suspected were collectors' items—and they worked in silence again after that. Not so comfortable this time, however.

He checked his watch again after he'd glanced up to see the sky outside was inky black. Faith saw his movement and stopped what she was doing.

'Time to call it a day,' he said.

She nodded from behind her high stone walls. 'Good. I'm starving.'

He walked over to the plastic crates and put his most recent finds next to the old records in the top one. He snapped the lid back on, then made his way to the door. He tugged the handle, and it turned, but the door itself didn't budge. He tried again. Not even a groan. The heavy oak door was stuck fast. Old Mr Grey had cautioned him to use the doorstop, and up until this evening he had, but Faith had been the last one in and he'd forgotten to share that vital bit of information with her.

And now they were trapped in here. Alone.

CHAPTER SIX

BEHIND him, Faith groaned. 'Really? Stuck in the castle dungeons?'

'They're not dungeons,' he reminded her calmly. 'No leg irons or racks here. It's just a cellar.'

'Can we open a window? Yell for help?'

He marched over to the first high window and tugged at the metal loop. Also stuck. However, he had better luck with the next one along. The window was hinged at the bottom, and he managed to pull it open so there was a gap of four or five inches at the top. A small shower of crunchy snow landed on his arm and he brushed it away before dragging a smallish wooden table over to stand underneath. Once he was sure it would take his weight he stood on it, so his face was near to the opening and shouted.

They waited.

Nothing.

He tried again.

Same result.

'Here… Maybe two voices are better than one.'

Before he realised what she was doing, Faith jumped up and joined him on the table. She wobbled as her back foot joined the other one and instinctively grabbed on to the front of his jumper for support. Marcus looked down at her. Her eyes were wide and her breath was coming in little gasps. His brain told him it was just the shock of almost tumbling down onto the hard stone floor, but his body told him something rather different.

Kiss her, it said.

Faith's mouth had been slightly open, but she closed it now, even as her eyes grew larger.

Nothing happened. Nobody moved. He wasn't even sure either of them breathed. He could read it in her face. She'd had exactly the same thought at the same time, and she was equally frozen, stuck between doing the sensible thing and doing what her instincts were telling her to do.

He wasn't sure who moved first. Maybe they both did at the same time. Her fingers uncurled from the front of his sweater and she dropped her head. He looked away. It seemed neither of them were ready to take that leap.

He turned back to the window and yelled, venting all his frustration through the narrow gap. After a second Faith joined him. When they were out of breath they waited, side by side and silent, for anything—the sound of footsteps, another voice. All they heard was the lap of water against the edge of the path outside and the distant squawk of a goose.

He jumped down from the table, got some distance between them. 'There's nobody out there. Too cold, too dark.'

Faith sat down on the table and then slid onto the floor. She stayed close to it, gripping on to the edge with one hand and tracing the fingers of the other over its grainy surface. 'What about people inside the castle?'

He shook his head. 'The walls are at least a foot thick. I doubt if the sound even left this room.' He checked his watch. 'It's not long until dinner, though. Someone will miss us soon.'

She nodded, but still looked concerned.

Marcus knew she had good reason to. Another hour, at least, and he'd already thought about kissing her once. Thankfully he had a solution to their current predicament that his ancestors wouldn't have had. He pulled his mobile phone from his pocket.

Signals in the area could be patchy, especially near the castle. He checked the display on his phone. One minuscule bar of signal, but maybe that was enough. He tried dialling the estate office, just in case anyone was still there. His phone beeped at him. *Call failed.* The signal indicator on his phone was now a cross instead of any bars. Damn.

'No signal,' he said to Faith. It seemed these thick stone walls could withstand any means of escape.

She jumped up onto the table again. 'Here. Pass it to me.'

Silently he handed his phone over, and she held it up to the window and pressed a button to redial. He held his breath, but a few moments later she shook her head and handed the phone back to him.

'Try sending a text. I've worked in plenty of old buildings, including basements, and sometimes I can get texts even if I can't receive calls.'

He nodded and tapped in a message to Shirley. She always kept her phone in her pocket. In a home like his, sometimes shouting up the stairs wasn't enough. Mobiles were usually pretty reliable—but obviously not when most of the room was underground and surrounded by water.

An icon appeared, telling him it was sending, but a minute later his phone was still chugging away. The blasted thing wouldn't go.

He put the handset up near the window, balancing it on the frame. 'Better chance of getting a signal,' he said. 'Now we just need to wait.'

He stole a look at her. Her mask of composure was back in place. No one would guess that moments ago she'd been flushed and breathless, lips slightly parted… It was as if that moment on top of the table had never happened.

Right there. That was why his warning bells rang—why he shouldn't think about kissing her. It had nothing to do with her nationality or her background, and everything to do with Faith herself.

The woman who lived behind those high walls of hers—Technicolor Faith—would be very easy to fall for. He felt he'd always known her, had been waiting for her to stroll across his lawn and come crashing into his life. He could feel that familiar tug, that naïve, misguided urge to lay everything he had and everything he was at her feet.

But that ability of hers to disconnect, to detach herself emotionally, was what kept him backing off. At least Amanda had tried; Faith McKinnon would always be just a fingertip out of reach.

Coward.

He ignored the voice inside his head, knowing he was right. He wasn't going to be that weak ever again. So he decided he needed to do something to fill the rest of the time rather than just stand close to her, staring at her.

Conversation would be good. It would stop him thinking about doing other things with his lips. But Faith had already resisted his attempt to talk about her family, so he needed another subject. Thankfully, he knew her favourite one. If he could get her talking about the window the hour would fly by.

'You believe Samuel Crowbridge made the window, don't you?' he asked.

She trapped her bottom lip under her teeth and then let it slide slowly out again, exhaling hard, as if she didn't quite want to say what she was about to say. Marcus tried not to watch, tried not to imagine what it would feel like if it were not her teeth but his lips…

'Yes…yes. I do,' she said, and that light he'd been both dreading and waiting for crept into her eyes. 'But believing isn't enough. I need solid proof.'

'For yourself? Or for others?'

She looked perplexed. 'Both. You can't put stock in dreams

and wishes, can you? At some point you have to have hard evidence.'

Marcus frowned. 'Sometimes one doesn't have that luxury,' he said, his tone bare. 'Sometimes you just have to do without.'

That was what he'd done after his father's death. No one had really known the truth of what had happened. He'd tried very hard to believe what people had said—that it had just been an accident—but the collapse of the family firm had started him questioning everything about his father, and he hadn't been able to shake the cynical little voice inside his head.

'Of course hard evidence is preferable, but it's not always there. Sometimes you just have to take a leap and hope you're jumping in the right direction,' he added.

Faith gave him a weary look. 'Unfortunately the academic community don't share your faith in gut instincts.'

'Have you found anything more about the other painting? Hope, wasn't it?'

She shook her head. 'Not much. The family who own it aren't ones for sharing. I can't even find a picture of it. They also own any sketches and documents pertaining to the original commission, so it's unlikely I'll get any confirmation from that source.' She opened the rolltop of an old bureau that had previously been blocked by a hatstand, and coughed as the dust flew into the air. 'That's why finding something here at Hadsborough is so important. It could be my only chance.'

As she searched a small smile curved her lips. He instinctively knew she was thinking about something that amused her.

'What?'

She rolled her eyes. 'A goofy coincidence. It's just that the names of the three paintings are almost a match for me and my two sisters.'

Marcus's eyebrows lifted. 'Faith, Hope and Charity?'

She walked towards him slowly. 'No, my littlest sister would have gone nuts if that was the case. Mom switched Charity to Grace.'

'What are the odds?' he muttered. 'Are you the oldest?'

She shook her head and leaned against the desk next to him. 'Mom never was one for sticking to convention. I'm in the middle. We all used to complain about our names, of course. Can you imagine the teasing we got at school?'

He made a wry face. 'I went to an all-boys boarding school. If that's not an education in just how abominable children can be, I don't know what is.'

She nodded in sympathy. 'Grace complains the most, even though I think she's got the best end of the deal.' She gave him a devilish little grin. 'But when we were younger Hope and I had a way of shutting her up.'

'Oh, yes?'

She nodded, then smiled to herself at the memory. 'We used to tease her that Gram had talked Mom out of calling her Chastity, so she could have had it a whole lot worse!'

He couldn't help laughing, and she grinned back at him before hopping up and sitting at the other end of the table. They weren't touching. *Quite.*

She'd forgotten to put those barriers back down, hadn't she? Even though they'd veered off the subject of the window and onto something more personal. He should say something to kill this moment, move away…

But he didn't. Just a few more seconds to find out what really lay beneath Faith's high walls. The chance might not come again, and he'd be safe once she retreated behind them once more. She always did.

'It sounds as if you're close,' he said.

Faith's smile disappeared. 'Not really. Not any more. It all changed after…'

He shifted so his body faced hers more fully. 'After what?'

'You don't want to know. It's too…' She shook her head and closed her eyes. 'Your family…they're so different to mine.'

He guessed she was talking about somebody having mis-behaved. 'You'd be surprised what the rich and powerful get up to just because they can,' he said, a dry tone to his voice. 'The second Duke was a bigamist, the third Duke had more illegitimate children than he could count and the fourth Duke lost Hadsborough in a drunken game of dice and won it back again the next night. And those are just the highlights. There are plenty more stories to tell about the Huntingtons.'

Faith shook her head, but she was smiling. 'Not the same, and you know it. All those things make your family sound dashing and exciting. My family just makes people shake their heads and look sad.'

A stab of something hit Marcus square in the chest. Suddenly Faith wasn't the only one on the edge of reveal-ing something big.

'Oh, mine make people shake their heads and look sad, too,' he said.

'No, they don't…' Faith began, laughing gently, assuming he was teasing. But when she met his eyes the laughter died. 'They do?' she said, blinking in disbelief.

They did. And he found that for the first time in over eigh-teen months he wanted to tell someone about it. Someone who wasn't connected. Someone who *didn't care,* who wouldn't invest. He suddenly realised that Faith's walls made her the perfect candidate.

'I worked for my father until just before he died,' he said, his voice deceptively flat and unemotional. 'He'd started up an investment company thirty years before, and things were going really well… At least I thought they were.' He shook his head. 'I should have seen it coming. He was always so sure of himself—too sure—as if he thought he was indestructible. It made for great business when the markets were good. He liked to take risks, you see, and they often paid off.'

She nodded, waited for him to continue.

'But in the last few years, with the way the financial climate had been—' he made a face '—being *daring* didn't cut it any more. In fact he lost a lot of people a lot of money. But my father was gripped by the unswerving belief that he could turn it around. He kept risking, kept gambling, kept losing... The company went bust. People lost their jobs.' He looked her straight in the eye. 'I knew what he was like, even though I didn't know the extent of his recklessness. I should have done more. I should have stopped him.'

'It wasn't your fault, Marcus, what your father did. He made his own choices.'

Marcus swallowed. That was what he'd been afraid of.

Not on the business front. People had called Harvey Huntington a swindler, but that hadn't been true. He'd just had an unshakeable belief in himself, hadn't thought he could fail so badly. And when he had... Well, the unshakeable man had been shaken to the core. He'd never quite recovered.

'About a year later they found his car wrapped round a lamp post,' he added baldly.

Faith gasped and her hand covered her mouth. 'I'm so sorry,' she said. 'I didn't know.'

'The inquest ruled it an accident,' he said, nodding to himself. 'He'd been drinking, and he never did like to wear his seat belt. But there were rumours...'

Faith's eyes grew wide. 'You mean that he'd *meant* to do it?'

Marcus just looked at her. 'That's about the gist of it.'

'You don't believe that, do you?' she said, horrified.

'I try not to.'

Faith reached over and laid her hand on his arm. He looked down at it. They hadn't touched since their first meeting, and that one simple, spontaneous gesture completely arrested him. He looked back at her face—really looked at her—and saw warmth and compassion and gentle strength. Instead of climbing back behind her walls, he could feel she was reaching out to him, and it made him ache for her in an entirely new way.

No. He couldn't want this. Shouldn't.

But he could feel himself slipping, forgetting why.

'You can't take the blame for this, Marcus. It was nothing to do with you.' She shook her head as she talked. 'You can't carry this round with you, believe me. For your own sanity you have to find a way to separate yourself, to disconnect.'

That pulled him up short. She was good at that, wasn't she? He needed to remember that.

'Is that what you did?'

She stopped shaking her head. 'I beg your pardon?'

'Disconnect?' he said. 'I might be too wrapped up in my family, but you seem cast adrift from yours. Is that how you cope? Running away? Living in a different country? I can't do that, Faith. I have to stay and fight—for Bertie, for my children and their children.'

He knew he sounded angry, but he couldn't seem to stop himself. He was angry with her for showing him parts of herself she'd never let him have, at his father for leaving him in such a mess, even at Hadsborough for the way it hung around his neck like a millstone. Telling her the truth had opened a floodgate. And he needed desperately to break this sense of intimacy weaving its way around them both and binding them together. He needed to push her away, to make that soft compassion completely disappear from her eyes.

She pulled her hand back and glared at him, and he knew his accusations had struck home. He should have been pleased.

'You don't know anything about me, so don't you dare judge.'

'I'm not judging you,' he said. 'You're right. I don't know anything about you. Because every time anyone asks you block them out.' It irritated him that she'd been able to run from her family, to taste freedom, when he'd been trapped by his. 'So shock me. Tell me. Tell me what awful thing happened to make you avoid your home and family like the plague.'

Faith looked up at him, her eyes huge, and swallowed. For a few hot seconds she'd been furious, but then something else had crept up on her and taken her completely by surprise— the urge to do just what he suggested.

Could she tell him? Would it really be as easy as that? She never wanted to talk about this. Not to anyone. And especially not to the rest of her family.

But he wasn't family. And she was thousands of miles away in a soundproof cellar. Somehow it seemed safer to let the words out here than anywhere else.

Also, Marcus had shared something incredibly painful and personal with her, and she couldn't ignore the sense of imbalance that left her with. She needed to get them back on an equal footing again so she could put her defences in place.

'You...' she said, shaking her head. 'You've always known who you are, where you belong in the world. I don't know if I can explain it...' She swallowed. It had been so long since she'd talked about this with anyone that she didn't know if the words were still there. 'I don't know where to start,' she whispered.

He held her gaze. There was still fire in his eyes, but it was softening, brightening. 'Try the beginning,' he said in a low voice.

Faith nodded and moistened her lips. 'My mom... She's a bit of a...'

How did she put this? Calling your own mother a flake out loud, no matter how many times you did it in your head, did not seem right.

She shrugged. 'She likes to move around, has sudden passions for hobbies or places—even people—that are all-consuming.' Faith looked down at her denim-clad thighs. 'While they last. And they never do last.'

Marcus gave her his half-smile, the one that curved the right side of his mouth so deliciously. 'A bit like Bertie, then?'

She gave an exasperated puff. 'No way! Bertie is sweet and charming. Mom... Well, Mom is just...infuriating.'

He laughed a dry little huff of a laugh. 'And you don't think I find my grandfather the slightest bit exasperating?'

Faith pinned her bottom lip in the centre with her top teeth. Okay, maybe he had a point there. But she doubted he'd find her mother sweet and charming. Nutty as a squirrel, maybe.

'The same pattern applied to her marriage. She and my dad were on again, off again, for so long. And then one day he'd had enough of trying to make her see sense and he left. Or that's what I thought at the time.'

Marcus nodded. 'My mother left my father under very similar circumstances. She loved him, even though he was a bit of a cad, but she couldn't deal with all that and this place as well. Eventually she had enough.'

A well of sympathy opened up inside Faith. She knew just what that was like, to see a parent leave, promising it was nothing to do with you, that it was the grown-ups who were to blame.

'How old were you?' she whispered.

'Nine,' he replied baldly.

She nodded. Almost the same age she had been when Greg McKinnon had left the family home for the final time. She reckoned she and Marcus had more in common than she'd first thought.

'You stayed here?' she asked.

'I was at boarding school most of the time. And holidays were shared between both parents. I felt slightly divorced from the whole thing, to be honest, as if it wasn't really happening—until I came home for my summer holiday when I was thirteen and there was a new, young, blonde Lady

Westerham installed in my father's suite, wanting me to call her Mummy, and the reality of the whole situation suddenly became very clear.'

'Ouch,' she said.

Marcus smiled grimly. 'You have a gift for coming up with exactly the right word for the occasion, do you know that?'

Faith smiled softly back. 'Gram says I may not say a lot, but what I do say packs a punch.'

'Smart lady,' he said, his mouth stretching into a proper smile this time.

Faith's heart began to hammer.

She sighed. 'That wasn't all, though. But it seems so lame compared to what you've just told me.' She got up, fetched her wallet from her purse and pulled out a crinkled photograph of three women. She pointed to the polished blonde on the right. 'That's Hope,' she said, and then she tapped a blunt fingernail against the girl on the left, her fair hair caught in ponytail. 'And that's Grace.'

And there in the middle was Faith. Shorter, darker, not as pretty.

'I can see the family resemblance,' he said quietly.

Faith decided not to swallow her next comment, not to let it echo round her head as she usually did. Instead she said it out loud. 'Between the two of *them*.' She pulled in some dusty air and tucked the wallet into her jeans pocket.

The tiniest lift of Marcus's eyebrows was his only response.

'The reason my dad left was because he found out he wasn't really my dad at all. Mom had an affair years earlier, during one of their frequent bust-ups. She never told him, and when he found out it was the final straw.'

Marcus didn't say anything, but the fierce compassion in his eyes was enough to make her throat clog. When she'd first met Marcus she'd thought he was uptight and superior, but it wasn't that at all. He wasn't mean; he just was fiercely protective of those he cared about. And, dammit, if that didn't make him more appealing. She'd always been a sucker for loyalty.

The penny dropped, and she suddenly understood why those glowering looks of his got to her so. She'd always yearned for someone to look out for her that way, instead of feeling she was on her own, always having to look out for herself. One of her fathers had vanished before she'd even been born, and the other had left before she'd become a teenager. She couldn't imagine Marcus vanishing on anybody. Oh, how she could have used a man like him in her life when she was younger.

She looked at her feet, dangling off the edge of the table. 'They didn't tell me until I was eighteen, but I'd always suspected something was wrong.'

'He carried on being a father to you after he left the family home?'

She nodded. 'He's a good man, but very practical and structured—not really a good match for my mom. All three of us girls used to go and stay with him at weekends, but I could tell even then. There was something about the way he looked at me—'

She broke off, unable to continue for a moment.

'There was always this…pain in his eyes.' A giant breath deflated her ribcage. 'He didn't look at the other girls that way,' she added as she looked up at him and tried to smile. 'It was a relief to find out in some ways.'

Moisture fell hot and fast from her lashes. This was stupid. She never cried. And how selfish to cry for herself, when she really should be crying for him and all he'd had to face.

She sniffed and dragged the back of her hand across one cheek and then the other. 'I finally understood why I'd always felt the odd one out, but it didn't stop me feeling that way. If anything I felt even more of a fraud.' She shook her head and looked up at him. 'I'm glad you've still got your grandfather after all that's happened to you, to give you that sense of balance and belonging. It's a horrible thing to not know who you are and where you fit in.'

He reached for her hand. She saw his brain working behind his eyes, and his gaze sharpened and became more penetrating as his fingers covered hers. 'You said the first time we met that your father was English?'

She nodded. 'He ran a bookshop in Beckett's Run for a few years. I don't even remember what he looks like, apart from the fact he has dark hair like mine and that he always smiled at me when we visited the store. He gave me a book once. Fairytales, with a picture of Rapunzel on the cover. Inside it was full of castles, princesses and noble knights.' She paused and gave a self-conscious shrug. 'Kind of like this one.'

Marcus's eyes warmed. 'Castle, yes. The princesses and noble knights are long gone.'

Faith lowered her lids for a moment. She wasn't so sure about the noble knights. She reckoned there was one sitting right next to her, his strong hand over hers as he patiently listened to her whine on about her family. Most men she knew would run a mile at the sight of female tears.

'It was my favourite book,' she whispered softly, 'even before I knew who he was.'

'He must be very proud of you,' Marcus said, and another unexpected stab of pain got her in the gut.

'He doesn't know me.'

Marcus looked shocked. 'He's never tried to find you? Or you him?'

She shook her head. 'I'm not sure he even knows about me. And it was almost thirty years ago… He's probably got a wife and other kids now. He doesn't need me blasting in from the past and upturning everything.'

And she didn't need to invade a family she had no place in. She'd tried that once—tried so hard—and it had all fallen apart around her. She wasn't going to make that mistake again.

'He's your father. Of course he'll want to see you. How could he not?'

The look in his eyes—as if he totally believed what he was saying, that it wouldn't be just one more round of rejection—made something tiny and wavering flicker to life inside her.

And he saw it. Right deep inside her, he saw it.

Marcus was looking down at her, his jaw set, but there was a new and disarming softness in those clear blue eyes. Faith's pulse began to thunder inside her veins. Everything was still. Even the ever-vocal geese outside were quiet.

Slowly Marcus lifted his hand to her face, brushed the tips of his fingers along her cheekbone. Her eyes slid closed and she breathed in a delicious little shiver as her head tipped back.

She knew what was coming. Had known it was coming ever since that first meeting more than a week ago, when she'd slid her hand into his on that misty morning. She just hadn't realised how much she'd been waiting for it, or how badly she'd wanted it.

His lips touched hers, so gently, so softly, it made her want to cry all over again. She'd expected fierceness, but if anything this tenderness was more devastating. She met him, moved her lips against his, but she didn't want to rush, didn't want to hurry. This was too sweet, too perfect. She wanted to suspend this moment in time and make it last for ever.

His breath was warm against her mouth, and she couldn't resist touching her tongue softly to his bottom lip, tasting him, drawing in that warmth. He shuddered in response, and something swelled within her even as she sensed him resist the urge to use his superior strength to pull her to him and lose himself in her.

Faith had never wanted to be thought of as fragile. She was tough. She could cope. She could batten down the hatches and make it through. But the way he held her, touched her, as if she was made of delicate glass, unravelled something inside her—something she hadn't even been aware had been wound up tight.

He paused for a moment, pulled his lips gently from hers with exquisite softness. Just as he was about to kiss her again, just as sensitive skin was about to meet sensitive skin, there was an almighty crash on the other side of the room.

He jumped up, and Faith was left there sitting on the table, eyes closed, mouth more than ready. At first she thought one of the haphazard piles of stuff had finally given in to gravity, but when she opened her eyes and followed Marcus's trail through the dust she realised what was going on.

It was the door. Someone was trying to ram it open from the other side. They were saved.

Faith slid off the table, hugged her arms around herself and watched. Marcus yelled instructions from their side, and more crashes against the sturdy old wooden door followed. She could see it moving, millimetre by millimetre.

Using the table to gain extra height, she retrieved Marcus's phone from the window frame. The text had sent itself more than fifteen minutes ago.

Marcus stood back from the door as one final shove from the other side unjammed the slab of oak and a burly man stumbled into the room under the force of his own momentum. Marcus moved forward to check he was all right.

Faith didn't move.

She couldn't. A whole squadron of butterflies were doing aerial acrobatics in her stomach. She couldn't do anything but watch Marcus, wait for his gaze to connect with hers again, to see if the look in his eyes confirmed that what had just happened between them had really happened, that it hadn't all just been a dream.

Marcus thanked the man, shook his hand then picked the doorstop up with a flourish and wedged it under the open door. Only when that was done did he lift his head and look at her. The butterflies started dive-bombing.

It was real. It had been real.

Oh, jeepers. What was she going to do now?

Suddenly her feet were free and she found herself jogging towards the door. She grinned at the burly man, thanking him profusely, knowing she was overdoing it and sounding like a clown in a sideshow. She moved to pass him, to cross the threshold and escape.

'Faith...' A hand shot out and caught her wrist, but so lightly that she could pull away if she wanted to.

She wanted to.

Marcus's words were left hanging in the air. She licked her lips and looked away, trying not to think about the feel of his mouth there, the soft promises he'd silently delivered. Promises that shouldn't exist. Promises he couldn't keep. She looked away.

'I'll see you at dinner,' she muttered, sliding her wrist from his grasp. Then she placed his phone into his empty hand and ran up the spiral stone staircase to the ground floor.

CHAPTER SEVEN

DINNER was quiet. Faith had spent a lot of it looking in his direction without actually looking *at* him. She didn't avoid his gaze entirely, but when she did meet his eyes her expression was blank, empty. Disconnected.

Marcus felt a tug of guilt deep down in his gut, even though in the moments before their lips had touched she'd tipped her head back and all but invited him to kiss her. He hadn't meant to make her feel like this.

When instead of joining him and his grandfather in the drawing room after dinner she excused herself and headed upstairs, Marcus followed. His grandfather's eyes glittered as he left the room. Sly old fox.

Marcus caught up with her on the wide stone staircase. 'Faith!' he called softly.

She stopped, but didn't turn.

He closed the gap.

She started to move again, but he reached for her, hooking the ends of his curled fingers into hers, and that was all it took to stop her. She stared into the distance, even though the thick wall was only ten feet in front of her.

He gently moved the tips of his fingers, feeling the smaller, sensitive pads of hers beneath his own. Her head snapped round and she looked at him.

He saw it all, then—the tug of war happening behind her eyes. Something in her expression melted, met him.

'We need to talk,' he said.

She didn't nod, didn't say anything, but he saw the agreement in her eyes. However, now he had her where he wanted her he wasn't sure what to say. *Sorry?* He realised he didn't want to—because he wasn't. Those few stolen moments in the cellar had tasted like freedom.

He took a leap, giving her more honesty than he'd planned to. 'I've wanted to do that since almost the first moment I met you,' he said.

Faith let out a heavy breath, her eyes still locked on his. Once again he felt that sense of accord, harmony—and a hint of wry acknowledgement.

She shook her head and looked at their linked fingers before returning her gaze to his face. 'You? Me? I don't know what this is…' She pressed her free hand to her breastbone. 'But it can't go anywhere, even if we want it to.'

God, he wanted it to. The force of that realisation hit him like a thunderclap. It didn't help that he knew she was right. Neither of them wanted this, were ready for this.

He let go of her hand. Her eyes shimmered with regret, and a little sadness. He breathed out hard.

'It's only a couple of weeks,' she said, 'and then I'll be gone. Can we try to keep it professional until then—or at the very least platonic?'

He heard the hidden plea, knew she was balancing on a knife-edge, just as he was, torn between doing what was right and what felt right. Suddenly he had the overwhelming urge to protect her, save her. It washed over him in a warm wave, starting at his toes and ending at his ears, and then settled into a small hard rock inside his chest.

He nodded. 'Goodnight, Faith,' he said, his voice low.

Her eyes filled with silent gratitude. 'Goodnight, Marcus.'

It was only as he watched her walk up the stairs that he realised he was protecting her from himself.

Faith did her best to keep busy the next day. She got to the studio early, determined to remove the last of the glass from the old lead. Each fragment she removed was placed on the carefully drawn template she'd made. It was slow work, but absorbing, and it kept her mind off things she didn't want to think about. However, as the hand on the clock moved closer to four her heart-rate refused to settle into its normal rhythm.

Would he come?

At four-fifteen she had her answer. There was a rap on the door, but this time, instead of opening it a split-second later, he waited for her reply. Marcus was good with boundaries, she realised. He wouldn't overstep their agreement, and she knew she wouldn't have to remind him of it even once in the coming fortnight. So why didn't that make her feel any happier?

'Come in,' she called, feeling her own boundaries crumble a little further, like the scattering of grit and pebbles just before a rock-fall. Mentally, she shored them up as best she could.

'Hello,' he said.

His expression was shuttered, wary. It was almost the way he'd looked at her on that first morning, except… She had the oddest feeling that although the walls were back it wasn't that he was pushing her away, but holding himself back.

She cleared her throat. 'Hi.'

Platonic, she'd said. And Marcus had wanted to be informed of any interesting developments regarding the window. She could do this. She could do platonic and professional. She'd never had any problems with it before.

'Come and see.' She indicated the half pulled apart window on the table in front of her.

He nodded and, just as he'd done for the whole of the previous week, asked thoughtful, intelligent questions. She answered him clearly, adding in interesting facts, which had also become her habit. Anyone watching them would have thought nothing had changed, that what had happened in the cellar had stayed in the cellar.

Faith knew better.

The whole time they talked there was an undercurrent that hadn't been there before, pulsing away beneath the surface.

And they didn't deny it—to themselves or each other— but by tacit agreement decided to leave it be. It was frustrating, but it was honest. She didn't think she could have lied to him anyway. Somehow he could see inside her. It wasn't that she'd let her barriers fall—they were still tightly in place— but that to him, and only him, they were like the glass on the table in front of her.

'I've asked Shirley to rustle up some help with the cellar,' he said. 'She's sending a couple of the part-time cleaning staff down. There should be waiting for us by the time we get there.'

She nodded, knowing this was a good idea—a fabulous idea—even as her heart sank. It was a good idea to give Basil some back-up.

'Hope they like dust,' she said as she grabbed her coat, 'and badgers…'

Marcus's father had always accused him of being a contrary child with an iron will, and now that resolve served him well. Even so, the cellar-cleaning crew became his safety net over the next few days, stopping him giving in to the urge to 'lose' the doorstop one evening and do something stupid.

It didn't help him forget, though. He couldn't erase the memory of that kiss, that sweet, soft, *unfinished* kiss.

From the way Faith's gaze would snag with his, the way she'd colour and look away, he guessed she was suffering the same way. But she'd asked for friendship alone. They had an agreement and he was honouring it.

They were both back safely behind their respective walls of polite friendliness. That should have been enough, but it wasn't helping. Walls that were three feet thick were a great idea, but if those walls were transparent…

It made the whole thing worse. Now he could see Technicolor Faith all the time, but he knew he couldn't—shouldn't—reach out and touch her. Even so, he could feel his resolve slipping a little more every day. It had started with his wanting to keep her safe, to protect her, and now he was starting to want to give her other things. Things he hadn't realised he still had left to give. Maybe he didn't. And they were things Faith McKinnon didn't even want.

He just had to keep it all together for another ten days. That was all.

Late Friday morning he was passing the studio and decided to stick his head in. He found her not hunched over the table, as usual, but sitting back on her stool, hands on hips, staring at the last remaining pieces of dirty glass that she had been cleaning.

'Problem?' he said as he came and stood behind her, trying to see what was so perplexing.

She shook her head. 'Not a problem…just some interesting irregularities.'

'Not anything to do with a message?' He shaved the words *I hope* off the end of that sentence.

'No.'

He pulled up another stool and sat down next to her. 'Talk me through it.' This was safe enough territory.

She pushed her stool back, stood up and walked over to a second table, where she plucked a large photo of the window from a pile of papers and brought it back to show him. Marcus did his best to concentrate on what was in front of his eyes instead of the faint smell of rose gardens that always seemed to cling to her. What was it? Perfume? Shampoo? Whatever it was, he was finding it very distracting, even though he'd never really had a fondness for the blasted flowers.

She pointed to the top of the photograph. 'See the lead there? It's very fine and it was beautifully crafted. The work of a master glazier. No doubt about it.'

His gaze followed her slender finger down to the bottom of the picture.

'But here…nowhere near the skill. It's as if it's been repaired by a local craftsman just trying to do his best.'

Marcus's eyebrows drew together. 'Maybe the workman wasn't up to the job.'

She nodded. 'Probably. But it's not the fact that the window was repaired, but where and how that's interesting. A breakage results in a certain pattern—either a crack in just one piece of glass, or a wider area of damage radiating out from the point of impact. See this bit down here…?' She pointed to a long, wide section at the bottom of the pane. 'It's just the glass inside that border that's been replaced. All of it. You can see it quite clearly now it's been cleaned.'

She got up and looked at the disassembled window laid out on the end of the table. 'The new glass is of much poorer quality.'

Faith carefully lifted two small pieces of dark green glass and held them up to the light. One was a beautiful clear emerald, the other was slightly muddier in colour, and the newer glass had a large ripple down the centre. She returned the fragments to the template. 'It's as if someone replaced that whole section—a long, thin rectangular section. Not the sort of shape that would come from usual damage.'

'And that's significant?'

She frowned and gave him a serious look, one that made him think he wasn't going to like what she was about to say.

'I can't quite get it out of my head that someone has removed something from the window.'

He pulled in air through his teeth. 'Something like a message?'

For a second she said nothing, but then she pushed out a breath, stood up and ran a hand through her hair. She smiled at him, a weary little twist of her lips. 'Ignore me. I think I'm starting to let the magic and the mystery of this place seep into me.'

He stared at the window. Now she'd mentioned it he could see the long, thin rectangle, could imagine a phrase or word being in the place where there was now plain green glass.

'I don't think we should tell my grandfather about this. Not yet.'

If ever.

She nodded her agreement. 'There's nothing to tell, anyway. Even if there had been something else in the window, we have no way of knowing what it was.'

That was that. He should feel relieved.

He tilted his head, trying to make it look very much as if he concurred, but he couldn't quite get rid of the niggling worry that Faith had stumbled onto something.

Marcus was having an in-depth discussion with Oliver, his events manager, about preparations for the Christmas Ball when Faith came skidding into the long gallery. Her face was aglow and her eyes were shining. He knew she had something to tell him about the window. Even so, he couldn't help but smile.

She grinned back.

Oliver coughed. 'About the florist, My Lord?'

Marcus kept looking at Faith. He waved a hand in the other man's direction. 'I'm sure you're more than capable of dealing with her,' he said. He only half noticed the man's raised eyebrows as he looked between Faith and himself.

'Don't say I didn't warn you,' Oliver's low voice muttered

beside him, but Marcus was focused on the laughter behind Faith's eyes.

'What?' he said, walking towards her.

Her smile flashed wide, reminding him of how the night sky brightened after a firework exploded.

'I found it!'

For a moment his stomach dropped.

'The proof I need,' she added, her expression dimming slightly in reaction to his *non*-reaction.

Proof?

It was as if she'd heard the question that had fired off inside his head. She stepped forward, her hand held up in a calming gesture. 'Samuel Crowbridge proof,' she explained.

He paused for a moment. While he was truly relieved her news had nothing to do with his grandfather's wild goose chase, he realised he was a little disappointed, too.

'How?' he said.

She glanced over her shoulder, looked at the door that led to the main hall—the route out of the castle and back to the studio. 'Have you got a minute?'

Marcus turned round to take his leave from Oliver and discovered the man had disappeared. Oh, well.

Faith looked about her as she headed for the door. 'It's looking awesome in here,' she said.

'I'm glad you like it,' he replied.

And looking lovely it was. Christmas at Hadsborough had always been special when he was younger, but in recent years it had become a chore. Looking at it now, through Faith's eyes, he realised she was right. There was a fourteen-foot Christmas tree in the hall. Crimson candles in all shapes and sizes were dotted around—some in wrought-iron stands, some in hurricane lamps—and greenery was everywhere: holly and ivy and fir branches, draped over mantelpieces, over the door frames, wound round the banister of the staircase and dripping from the minstrels' gallery over the banqueting hall.

There was a noise in the hallway and a few moments later a walking display of red flowers entered the room. Underneath the foliage was a very human pair of legs: sturdy calves finished off with even sturdier shoes. Marcus recognised those shoes. And *now* he caught on to what Oliver had been trying to warn him about.

Janet Dixon. Florist and one-woman tornado.

Her severe salt-and-pepper hairdo appeared from behind the display and she looked around the room approvingly, as if she deemed it good enough for her arrangement.

Faith walked over and touched the papery petal of one of the fire-red poinsettia. 'My grandmother loves these,' she said thoughtfully.

'Just right for the festive season, they are,' Janet replied. 'Bringing wishes for mirth and celebration.'

Faith smiled. 'I'll tell Gram. She'll like that.'

'Oliver is around somewhere if you need assistance,' Marcus said, then cupped Faith's elbow in his hand and steered her from the room. 'Quick!' he whispered in her ear. 'She does all the flowers for the castle, and she'll tell you about every petal in great detail if you stand still long enough.'

Faith chuckled softly and began to jog towards the exit. Marcus kept pace, grinning.

When they reached the oval lawn in front of the castle they slowed to a walk. The day was crisp and sunny and he breathed in the country air. It smelled like December. Like Christmas. And there was the perfect amount of snow for the ball that night—enough to cover the grassy areas and make the castle look magical, but the paths were clear and the roads gritted.

Quite suddenly he stopped and turned to Faith. 'Come tonight,' he said. 'It's going to be a wonderful evening. You'll be sorry if you miss it.'

I'll be sorry if you miss it.

Her nose wrinkled and she grimaced. 'I don't have anything to wear.'

He had an answer for that. One she'd supplied. 'We relaxed the dress code for those that want to, remember? On very good advice.'

She made a soft scoffing noise. 'There's relaxing and then there's *relaxing*. I'm not sure you lowered it enough for jeans and a T-shirt with a few sequins, and that's the best I can do.'

He started walking again. 'Well, if that's the only problem I'm sure we can sort something out.' There were wardrobes full of ballgowns in the castle. Surely one would fit Faith? He glanced her way. 'That *is* the only problem, isn't it?'

Faith said nothing, just kept walking towards the studio, eyes straight ahead. She was glad Marcus couldn't see her face, if only for a few moments. She needed time to let the emotion show, let those stupid feelings free, before clamping everything down again.

She'd been so elated when she'd run into the castle to tell him of her discovery, but now all that was squelched beneath the slow and persistent ache in her chest. She couldn't go to a ball. Who did she think she was? Cinderella? Real life didn't work out that way. That was why they called them fairy *stories*. And she was doing her best to remember that, she really was.

You don't belong here, she told herself. *You will never belong here. Don't set yourself up for more pain by buying into the dream.*

She opened the studio door when she reached it and walked inside, back to her work table. Something solid here, at least. This wasn't clinging on to fantasies and false hope. She had proof.

She picked up the piece of glass that made up the kneeling woman's lower leg and bare foot, walked over to the large picture window and held it up. She knew the moment Marcus joined her because the air beside her warmed up.

Holding the fragment carefully between thumb and finger at the edges, she pointed to the edge with a finger from the other hand. 'I found this while I was cleaning the glass—getting rid of the dirt and grime and removing the old grout.'

Marcus leaned closer, inspecting the glass, and Faith braced her free hand on the window, hoping it would stop her quivering. So much for everything staying platonic. Somehow the *look but don't touch* agreement she'd manoeuvred him into had intensified everything, done the opposite of what she'd hoped.

'There's writing,' he said, 'scratched into the glass.'

She nodded. 'It's not unusual to find names and dates on fragments of window—little messages from the craftsmen who made or repaired it. Sometimes they are high up in cathedral windows, where nobody would ever see them, just the maker's secret message that no one knows to look for.'

He looked at her. 'So you *did* find a message in the window?'

'Yes, I did. Just not the one we were looking for.'

We? Not *we*. *You*. It wasn't her quest. She needed to remember that.

She recited what she knew was engraved on the piece of pale glass showing half a foot and some elegant toes. '"S.C. These three will abide. 1919."'

'"These three will abide"?'

She smiled softly to herself. 'It's about One Corinthians, Thirteen, I think. A favourite at weddings.' She looked around the room. 'I wish I had a Bible to check it out, though. Don't happen to have one to hand, do you?'

He shook his head. 'But I know a place nearby where we can lay hands on one.'

Faith stopped to look at the window in the chapel while Marcus rummaged in the tiny cluttered vestry for a Bible. Even with her knees and lower legs missing, and the bottom section of the window boarded up, the woman captured in stained glass was exquisite.

The expression on her upturned face was pure rapture. All around her flowers bloomed—daisies in the grass, roses beside her in the bushes, climbing ivy above her head, reaching for the stars in the night sky. Faith could see why Crowbridge hadn't been able to give up on the idea of making his vision come to life, no matter what the medium.

Marcus returned from the vestry with a worn black leather Bible and began to hunt through it. While he was occupied leafing through the tissue-thin pages, Faith allowed herself to do what she normally resisted—let her eyes rove over him. How was it fair for a man to be so beautiful?

Finally he placed a long finger in the centre of a page and smiled before looking up at her.

This time when their eyes met she didn't get that earth-shifting-on-its-axis sensation. No, this was much more subtle, and probably much more dangerous. She felt a slow slipping, like the motion of a sled at the top of a snow-covered hill as gravity got hold and it started to move. Once it gathered momentum there'd be no stopping it.

He read out a verse, and the old-fashioned language of the King James Version sat well on his tongue. "'For now we see through a glass, darkly; but then face to face: now I know in part; but then shall I know even as also I am known.'"

Faith's heart skipped a beat in the pause before he moved on to the next verse.

Know even as also I am known…

She felt as if those words had been waiting all those centuries for here and now—for her and the man reading them to her. Because that was how she felt with him: she knew him, even though they'd only met just over a fortnight ago. How was that possible?

Everyone else, even her family—especially her family—looked at her through tinted glass, only getting glimpses, never seeing or understanding the whole. Somehow this man managed to do what no one else could. But she liked her tinted glass, liked her separateness. At least she had up until now.

'It's the next one,' she said. 'Read the next one.'

He looked down again. "'And now abideth faith, hope, charity, these three; but the greatest of these is charity.'"

She blew out a breath. *These three will abide.* 'That reference makes it even more sure. He was finishing his trio of pictures. The other two weren't complete without this one.'

A sharp pang deep inside her chest cavity caused her to fall silent. That was how she and Hope and Grace had been once upon a time—the terrible trio, Gram had used to call them, with a glimmer in her eyes that was reserved only for grandparents. But they hadn't been that way for a long time, and Faith suddenly missed them terribly, even though she hadn't let herself feel that way in years.

If only she could believe that, just like Crowbridge's pictures, her sisters weren't complete without her. But the truth was that they and Mom and Dad were fully related to each other, were a complete family unit on their own; she only had one foot in and one foot out. A cuckoo. One who didn't fit in, who shouldn't even try.

'That's good, then,' Marcus said beside her.

He was closer now, within touching distance. He could reach for her if he wanted to. And she sensed he did. She closed her eyes and walked away, saw the open door of the vestry and headed towards it. She needed distance, space. Because letting Marcus take care of her, look out for her, even for just a few moments, was almost as dumb as going to the ball that evening. She couldn't let herself get sucked into this vision of a fairy tale—this place, this man. The ball always ended badly for Cinderella, so she'd much rather be Rapunzel, safe in her turret...

No, she meant *tower.* Safe in her tower.

She entered and discovered where most of the debris from

the tidy chapel had ended up. It was like the cellar all over again.

Bad idea. She didn't need reminders of the cellar right now. Or, to be more precise, of what had happened in the cellar.

She turned to go, but Marcus was already blocking the door, watching her. She glanced around frantically, looking for something to distract her, to start a conversation. There was a pile of old papers on the desk. She picked them up. On top was a note from the clean-up crew leader.

Found these in a trunk up in the tower. Thought someone might want to look through them.

'I don't believe it,' she muttered. 'Clear up one dusty dumping ground and then someone finds another one to be dealt with.' She handed him the papers. 'Sorry, Your Lordship, but this bunch is all yours.'

He took it from her after giving her a small salute. That made her smile. While he leafed through the papers, many of them torn or mildewed, Faith wandered out to look at the window once again. He followed, still flicking through the stack.

'Look…' He pulled a faded and yellowing piece out of the pile. 'Someone else has done a sketch of the window.'

She walked over and took the piece from his hands, mildly interested. Even folded into quarters Faith recognised the pattern of lines. She'd been working with them all week. But when she unfolded it her hand flew to cover her mouth.

'What?' he said. 'What is it?'

She shook her head, an expression of total disbelief on her face. Her mouth moved once or twice but no sound came out.

'Faith?'

She held up a hand and took a deep breath. 'Marcus, this is the *cartoon!*'

He frowned, and she knew he was thinking of comic books and kids' TV shows.

'The original drawing that the glaziers worked from!' she explained as she turned it round in her hands and checked the corners and edges. 'Yes! Look, there's his signature— Samuel Crowbridge!'

Marcus squinted at the drawing, but he hardly had time to focus on it before she danced away with it, spinning round and then running to the window to hold it up and compare.

'That's two pieces of evidence in one day!' she yelled over her shoulder. It was more than she could ever have hoped for.

But then she stopped smiling, stopped talking, and her eyes grew wide again. She ducked down and spread the cartoon on the floor, smoothing it out gently. She was staring at the drawing, but her brain was refusing to compute. It kept telling her eyes the information they were sending it was wrong. *Return to sender.*

Marcus walked over and stood behind her to take a look.

And so he should. Right at the bottom, roughly where the rectangle they'd been discussing earlier was, were some words. She looked up at him.

'This isn't in the window now. Somebody changed it.' She lowered her voice to barely a whisper. 'Somebody *took it out.*'

Marcus wasn't moving. His eyes were blinking and his mouth was slightly open. '"Proverbs Four, Verse Eighteen,"' he finally read, his voice hoarse. 'Why would someone want to take that out?'

Faith swallowed. 'Because to someone it meant something.' But that would make it… That would make it…

'Bertie was right after all,' she said, looking up at him. 'Once upon a time there was a message in this window.'

CHAPTER EIGHT

'PROVERBS, Chapter Four, Verse eighteen…' Faith couldn't help muttering it to herself over and over as she got dressed. A message in the window? Maybe. But a very cryptic one.

She left an earring hanging in her ear without its back so she could go and pull the piece of paper she'd scribbled the verse on out of her purse.

'"But the path of the just is as a shining light, that shineth more and more unto the perfect day",' she read out loud.

Beautiful poetry, nice sentiment, but was this the kind of message a husband would send his wife? It seemed Bertie's message in the window asked more questions than it answered.

She put the piece of paper on the nightstand and went back to getting ready. In a moment of weakness, of sheer jubilation, after finding two bits of proof that were going to put her name on the academic map, she'd relented and agreed to go to the Christmas Ball. Bertie had rubbed his hands together when he'd heard the news, and had insisted escorting her personally to a bedroom with a wardrobe stuffed with evening gowns. Another sign that hoarding went hand in hand with the Huntington genes, she guessed.

She'd chosen a red velvet dress from the early sixties, with a scooped neck and tight bodice that skimmed her hips and then flared into a full fishtail at the bottom. It was gorgeous.

Maybe a little snug, but gorgeous. Bertie had also insisted she borrow a necklace that he'd retrieved from a walnut jewellery box on the dressing table. She touched the simple V of glittering stones with her fingertips. My, she hoped they were paste.

Before she lost the matching earrings, she returned to the dresser and pushed the missing back on. The only thing to do before taking her first good look at herself in the mirror was to put on the pair of long red gloves that had been stored with the dress. She put them on slowly, avoiding the moment she had to meet her own eyes in the full-length glass.

When she had the courage to look it was as bad as she'd feared.

Not only did she look stunning, and the dress fitted like a second skin, but she had that kind of glow in her eyes a woman only got when she was halfway to falling in love.

Disaster.

She'd hoped that when she saw herself in the mirror everything would look wrong—that she'd look as if she was playing dress-up. It would be so much easier to remember that she didn't belong, that she shouldn't want to. Instead she looked like a princess. It was disgusting.

You can't want him, she told herself. He's not for you. If you didn't fit in in plain old Beckett's Run, how on earth do you think you're going to fit in here?

But she'd promised Bertie she would attend the ball, even dance with him, so she couldn't back out.

She took one last glance at herself in the mirror. *Stop sparkling,* she told her eyes. *You have no business to be doing that.* And then she took in a deep breath, held it for a few seconds and headed for the door.

The ball was already well underway when Faith made her way down the main staircase. She deliberately left it until late, hoping minimum exposure to all the glitz and glamour might help her stay strong.

She couldn't have been more wrong.

She should have come down earlier. Because she needed this. Needed the slap in the face it gave her when she walked down the stairs.

Even though she'd only been here a week or two, somehow she'd got comfortable with Hadsborough—with its little yellow drawing room and her quirky turret bedroom. Here, from her spot on the first landing, before the marble steps disappeared into a throng of people, she was once again confronted with the reality of this place.

It wasn't an ordinary home. It was a castle. And it had never looked more like one than it did tonight. Candles were everywhere, their flickering light taking the evening back into a bygone age. Glasses clinked, champagne fizzed, while guests in tuxedos and ballgowns milled and danced. The Beckett's Run definition of a 'relaxed' dress code was obviously very different from the Hadsborough one. Every single guest was dressed up to the nines and loving it.

Faith might as well have come down the staircase and stepped on the surface of Mars. It would have been just as familiar. She was used to home cooking and takeout, town festivals and barn dances. Parties where people drank to forget their daily life, not because they were partaking in some kind of fantasy.

And in the middle of it all was Marcus, looking elegant in bow tie and crisp white shirt, his dark suit screaming Savile Row tailoring. Her knees literally started to wobble. He looked so handsome, with his dark hair flopping slightly over his forehead, a small frown creasing his brow as he listened intently to an older woman in a tiara.

A tiara. This was the kind of shebang where people wore tiaras. Real ones.

Her fingers traced the necklace and she wished fervently there was a safe she could put it in somewhere. The last time Faith had worn a tiara she'd been seven years old, and it had been made of silver-coated plastic, with garish pink gems stuck on the front.

She shouldn't have agreed to come. She'd known this was a bad idea.

But there was Bertie at the bottom of the stairs, smiling up at her and holding out his arm. She swallowed her nerves and started to walk down the stairs.

Fake it, she reminded herself. *You know you look the part, even if it's just window dressing. It's like yawning or laughing. You start off forcing it and after a while it comes naturally.*

She glanced over in Marcus's direction as she reached the bottom step. He was still deep in conversation with Tiara Woman and, on the pretence of needing a drink, she took Bertie's arm and neatly steered him the other direction. The only way she was going to survive this evening was if she kept out of Marcus's way.

There was a flash of red at the corner of Marcus's eye. He didn't know why he turned towards it. When his eyes had focused on it properly, however, he fully understood why his jaw had dropped and his throat had tightened.

Wow.

Faith was on the other side of the room, in a red velvet dress that clung to every inch of her slender frame. He'd known her slim lines and understated curves appealed to him in jeans and a sweater, but tonight…

And then she turned round, revealing a low-cut back to the demure-fronted dress that made him realise he might be an earl but he was also part caveman.

She was talking to someone, smiling broadly and using hand gestures. He knew when she realised he was looking at her because she suddenly went still. A second later she twisted round to meet his gaze. Above her crimson lips was a pair of large, questioning eyes. The problem was his brain was so fried by the sight of her in that dress that he had no idea what the question was, let alone the answer.

He'd always thought her beautiful, right from that first day in the chapel, when he'd seen her studying the window, her face aglow with its colour. But here, tonight, in that dress, looking as if she was made for it, he couldn't help wondering if he should stop fighting that feeling that she was made for him.

He didn't know what to do about that.

Especially as he'd promised her he'd keep his distance.

Especially as he'd promised *himself* he wouldn't forget his own sensible plans for the next woman in his life.

But part of him ached to make the jump anyway, to give whatever was simmering between them a chance. However, the part that had been burned by Amanda's departure was backing off fast, shaking its head. Hadn't he'd thought Amanda the perfect fit too? On paper, much more so than Faith. He had to give Amanda her dues—she'd stuck with him a full six months after his father's death before she'd finally jumped ship.

That had stung. In his own charge-the-world-head-on way he'd still been grieving. He'd needed her understanding, not his spare keys in his palm and a kiss on the cheek. He'd thought she was the one person in the world he could rely on. And he'd been wrong. It didn't help to know that Faith McKinnon was a hundred times more skittish.

Even so, he excused himself from the conversation he'd been having and walked towards her, not taking his eyes from her face. He saw her heave in a breath, saw her eyes grow wide, knew the exact moment she'd decided to run but found her feet glued to the floor. It gave him a flash of male pride to know she reacted to him that way, that he wasn't the only one in its grip.

He could make her change her mind if he wanted to.

He knew that. And, oh, how he wanted to. But he'd given his word.

Nothing to say they couldn't have a platonic dance, though. Especially at a big Christmas party like this. It was practically expected.

He reached her and opened his arms. She placed one gloved hand in his and the other slid to his shoulder, leaving his left hand to rest on her shoulderblade, touching delicious bare skin. Wordlessly they started to dance, moving through the chatting guests until they joined more couples on the dance floor.

Marcus hardly noticed who else was there, waltzing with them. He wasn't really aware of doing anything—not moving his arms or legs, not dodging the other couples, just looking down at Faith, with some silent conversation going on between them.

He wished that duty and decency hadn't been drummed into him since he was in nappies. Wished he could say *what the hell* and sweep her into his arms, drag her under the large bunch of mistletoe hanging from the chandelier over the dance floor and kiss her senseless in front of all these people. Suddenly he was slightly irritated with her for making him promise, because he couldn't quite bring himself to steamroll over her feelings and take what he wanted as easily as he'd like to. That damn protective instinct of his kept him at bay.

That was why, when the music ended, he let her nod her thanks and slip from his arms, find another partner. Why he turned his back and did the same, refusing to watch her go.

But as he moved his feet to the rhythm of the music a thought started to pulse inside his head. Just for one night he wanted to ditch his blasted code of honour. He wished he could be wild and reckless and not care a bean about what the morning would bring. He'd hardly chosen a thing for himself in the last two years, always doing the right thing, always doing his duty, what was good for the family.

Tonight, for once, he wanted to choose something for himself. And he really wanted to choose Faith.

Faith had deliberately sought out the villagers of Hadsborough to talk to. She understood them, knew what they were about. And they were keen to chat about the restoration of the chapel and the stained glass window, keeping her busy, keeping her mind off where Marcus was and who he was with.

But after a couple of hours of being 'on', of having to smile and chat to one new person after another, Faith began to tire. In the back of her head she was still mulling over the puzzling Bible reference in the window, trying to work out if it meant something.

And when she wasn't trying to figure that out, and make small talk with the next person who asked her about the window, there was Marcus. Every time she caught sight of him she experienced a sudden stab of breathlessness.

'May I have another dance, my dear?'

She turned round to find Bertie beside her, smiling. He was in fine spirits this evening, and more energetic than she'd ever seen him.

'Of course, Your Grace,' she said, and offered him her hand.

Bertie shook his head as he took it and led her onto the dance floor. 'Time was when I'd have put on a good show for a pretty thing like you,' he said. 'I was quite the Fred Astaire in my day, I'll have you know.' He sighed. 'No more dips and turns for this old back any more, though. You'll have to put up with my shuffling instead.'

Faith laughed as Bertie took her in a classic ballroom hold. 'And very elegant shuffling it is, too.'

He smiled back at her. 'You'll have to get Marcus to give you another spin round the dance floor.'

She kept her expression neutral. 'You wouldn't be trying to matchmake, would you, Bertie?'

He shrugged. 'The boy needs to have more fun.'

Faith didn't say anything, just let him lead her round the dance floor. Slowly. She didn't disagree with Bertie, but whatever was going on between her and his grandson definitely wasn't fun. It felt more like torture.

The music changed, and Bertie bowed to her and took his leave. Faith tried to curtsey back, but she wobbled badly in her borrowed shoes. A warm hand at her elbow steadied her. She turned to find herself staring up into a pair of smoky blue eyes.

'Hi,' she said softly.

His lips curved upwards. 'Hi.'

And just like that her last defence fell. She'd thought it was made of cast iron, but sadly it snapped like spun sugar. The band were playing a slow number and she ended up with her head on his shoulder, one arm looped around his neck.

Try not to notice, she told herself. Try not to notice how well your head fits in the space near his neck, or how your bodies slot together like jigsaw pieces. Or how your chests rise and fall together, even when you're not trying to match rhythm.

To distract herself she started thinking about the verse in the cartoon—the one that could be the key to Bertie's past. Why hide it if it wasn't? Why would someone have gone to all that trouble if the verse had nothing to do with the story Bertie had heard about his mother? And did the numbers have significance? Or was it in the words of the verse themselves?

'Proverbs Four-Eighteen?' he whispered in her ear.

She lifted her head and looked him in the eye. 'How did you know?'

He shook his head, a rueful expression on his face.

'What do you think the verse means? Have you had any thoughts?'

He pressed his lips together, then said, 'Plenty of thoughts. Not sure any of them lead anywhere.'

Faith breathed out a little. This was easier, safer. They needed to keep talking about the window.

Marcus frowned as he pulled up a memory. 'My great uncle told me once that his brother was very fond of treasure hunts. He used to lay one out every Christmas in the grounds for the village children.'

Faith's eyes grew wide. 'So maybe the reference isn't a message in itself but a clue to something else? Another verse? Another destination?'

'We should look for key words,' he said.

'Path,' she said, nodding to herself.

'And shining light,' they both said, at exactly the same time, then both looked away and back again in complete synchronisation.

'Stop doing that,' she said. 'It's freaking me out.'

A mischievous glint appeared in Marcus's eye. 'It's not just me.' Then his expression became thoughtful. 'There are paths all over the estate, but we don't even know if it refers to something literal or figurative. As for shining lights...'

She closed her eyes, attempted to visualise the parts of the grounds she had visited. Shining light...

Her lids flipped open. 'How about that grandfather clock ·in the cellar? That has a sun on it.'

'Maybe...' He didn't look convinced. 'But if this is a clue leading to something else there should be something there to find—some more writing or another verse. Like a treasure trail. We had a good look at that clock and I didn't see anything like that.'

They'd still been swaying to the music as they'd been talking, but suddenly Marcus went completely still.

'Of course...' he said on an out-breath. 'I've been so stupid not have seen it!'

And then he went quiet again.

Faith punched him on the chest softly. 'Marcus!'

He blinked and looked down at her. She gave him a look

that said she might have to hurt him if he didn't spill the beans.

He laughed loudly enough to make some of the other dancing couples close to them look their way, then stepped back, grabbed her hand and pulled her in the direction of the door.

'I know where there are both paths and a shining light,' he said, picking up speed.

Once they were out of the ballroom he guided her towards the front door.

'Marcus! I have heels on.'

He gave her a blank look.

'And it's been snowing outside! I want to solve the mystery as much as you do, but I'd rather not get frostbitten toes doing it.'

He nodded and changed direction, heading for the small staircase that led to the kitchens. They ran right through and to the back door.

'Here,' he said, and threw a padded coat to her. Once she had it on over her dress he nudged a pair of Wellington boots her way. 'They're Shirley's,' he said, 'and she always keeps a spare pair of socks inside.'

While she kicked off her heels and sank her feet into the boots, which were at least a size too big, he pulled a coat off the row of pegs and shoved his feet into his own boots.

Then the back door was open and icy air was chilling their cheeks. Marcus grabbed her hand and pulled her out into the moonlit night.

There was something thrilling about running out of the castle with Marcus on this snowy night, her skirts caught up in her free hand, not knowing where she was going. The paths round the estate were mostly cleared, and they kept to them as much as possible. Faith kept lagging behind, caught up in staring at the formal gardens and the rolling fields beyond, all sparkling in the moonlight as if someone had dusted them with glitter, but the insistent tug of Marcus's hand in hers kept her travelling.

'Where are we going?' she asked, frowning slightly. For some reason she'd thought they might end up at the chapel, but they were jogging in the opposite direction.

He turned to grin wolfishly at her. 'We're almost there.'

She looked around. High yew hedges ran alongside the path they were running on. She didn't think she'd ventured into this part of the estate before—too busy stuck in her studio bent over bits of glass to notice what had been right under her nose.

They kept running until they came upon a gap in the hedge, closed off by an iron gate. Marcus stopped and lifted the latch, making sure he still had her by the hand.

'There are plenty of paths here,' he said softly, 'but only one is the right one. Only one winds upwards towards a shining light.'

As he led her through the gate suddenly it all made sense.

'You have a maze,' she mumbled, slightly awestruck.

'They were the craze in Victorian times. The fourth Duke had it planted, but my great-grandfather added some improvements.'

She looked up to where the hedges ended, about two feet above her head. A couple of inches of snow glistened on top, pale blue in the moonlight, making the whole maze look like a rather elaborately carved Christmas cake.

'We're going to try to navigate a maze in the dark, in the snow?' she asked, realising she sounded disbelieving.

Marcus just laughed. He pulled a flashlight from his pocket and handed it to her. 'Do you want to race me to the centre or do you want to do it together?'

She narrowed her eyes at him. 'And you're giving *me* the only light source?'

He nodded.

'I have a feeling you know your way through this maze

even in the pitch-dark, which would be cheating, so I'm sticking with you.'

She was rewarded with a broad grin at that comment. 'Smart lady,' he murmured, and then tugged her off to the right and started running again—just as her heart decided to lurch along in an uneven rhythm, making it even harder for her to keep up.

After a while Faith gave up trying to memorise their path. She just concentrated on keeping her skirt off the ground and matching Marcus's pace. When she stumbled slightly he turned, looking concerned.

'Am I going too fast for you?'

She nodded, panting slightly. 'These boots are a bit flappy, and I really don't want to ruin this lovely dress. This skirt wasn't made for running.'

He looked her up and down, a thoughtful look on his face, taking in the fishtail skirt, how it kept her thighs so close together. Feeling his gaze on her body made said thighs tingle. She told herself if was just the cold.

'Only one solution to that,' he said, and stepped towards her.

She gasped as he lifted her into his arms. Instinctively she looped her arms round his neck and held on tight. 'What are you doing?' she asked, her voice breathy. 'You can't possibly carry me the rest of the way like this!'

'Would you prefer a fireman's lift?' he replied, a ripple of humour in his voice.

She shook her head violently, thinking how the blood would rush to her head if he hoisted her over his shoulder. She was finding it difficult enough to think as it was.

'Are you flirting with me, Lord Westerham?' she asked shakily. 'Because I thought we had an agreement about that sort of thing.'

'Of course not,' he said, with a slightly devilish glint in his eye. And as he started to walk he added. 'Pity, though. That would have been a great view.'

She slapped him on the chest with a gloved hand. 'Earls are not supposed to talk like that.'

He just smiled a secret smile to himself, staring straight ahead, navigating the maze. 'I beg to differ. I've known quite a few, and I know from experience that a title is not a ticket to a clean mouth. Far from it. You should hear Ashford when he gets going...'

She slapped him again. 'You're teasing me.'

He slowed and looked down at her. 'Maybe I am. But don't let the title fool you. I might be an earl, but underneath I'm still a man.'

The glitter in his eyes as he looked down at her bore witness to that. Faith found herself strangely breathless. Wrenching her gaze onto the path ahead was difficult, but she managed it.

He picked up speed, staying silent, but his last words thrummed between them still. Yes, he was a man. A beautiful, noble man. And right at this moment, captured in his arms as she was, Faith McKinnon was feeling very much a woman. Even worse, that woman was doing just as he asked, and was forgetting all about his title and why she shouldn't just drop her gift-wrapped heart at his feet like a tiny Christmas present.

She hung on, closing her eyes.

Sooner than expected he came to a halt and slowly lowered her to the ground. Cold air rushed in between them, where their bodies had been pressed against each other. Faith shivered.

'See what I mean?' he whispered, his breath warm in her frozen ear.

She blinked and looked around. This wasn't what she'd expected. In front of them was a squat tower of stone, sloping inwards slightly as it rose maybe fifteen feet into the air.

'Come on,' Marcus said, and reached for her hand.

This time she took it without thinking. It seemed to belong there.

'We're near the end of a path that leads to a shining light.'

He led her round the stone mound until they came upon a narrow winding stairway that circled the tower. It didn't take long to climb up the twenty or so stairs, and soon they were standing on a viewing platform, surrounded by waist-high stone walls. She could not only see the whole of the snow-capped maze, but also the hills beyond, and glittering in the distance the larger of the two lakes.

The moon was in evidence, but no other light was anywhere to be seen. 'Where—?'

He placed a hand on each of her shoulders and gently turned her to face the other direction. There, in the middle of the tower, was a sundial mounted on a stone pedestal.

She walked towards it and his hands slid off her shoulders. However, they didn't drop away quickly, but trailed down her back until she was out of reach. Even through the puffy layers of Shirley's winter coat she could feel warmth, the sure pressure of his hands.

'How do you know this is what the verse is referring to? The connection seems a bit tenuous.' As wonderfully romantic as this idea was, she couldn't help think it might just be a coincidence.

'It would be but for two reasons,' he said, coming to the other side of the sundial and standing opposite her. 'First, the same man who commissioned the window also built this tower in the maze. Second...' He tapped the brass face of the sundial with a finger, before lifting up the flashlight and shining it down on it.

There, at the base of the clockface, was an inscription.

'Song Twenty-Two?' she said. 'I don't get it.'

'I think it's another Bible reference. That's why when I thought of paths and shining lights and the need for an-

other piece of the puzzle this place popped into my mind.'
He walked round the sundial to stand next to her. 'Song, I
think, is short for Song of Solomon, or Song of Songs, and
if you look carefully there, between the twos, it's a colon.'

'Song of Songs, Chapter Two, Verse Two?' she asked, her
voice barely a whisper.

He nodded.

She turned to face him, did her best to read his face in the
semi-darkness. 'You think there's something in this?'

He stared back at her and breathed out hard. 'Maybe. If it
was any of these things on their own I'd probably dismiss it,
but put them all together...'

'What about Bertie? You were really worried this would
upset him. It still might.'

His eyelids lowered briefly and he looked away. 'I know.
But if what my family has told him all these years is wrong,
he has a right to know.' Marcus looked back at her. 'I've been
trying to protect him from a lie, but I don't think it's right to
protect him from the truth.'

She saw it—the twist of guilt in his face as the dual needs
both to keep his grandfather safe and to do the right thing
warred inside him.

'The truth comes out sooner or later,' she said. 'I wish...'

She closed her eyes. She had been about to say that she
wished her parents had told her who her real father was earlier, but she suddenly realised how cruel that would have
been. There had been no easy way to handle it, had there?
Telling an eight-year-old something like that would have been
devastating. Although not telling her had wreaked its own
kind of havoc. Suddenly she understood why her mother
had swept it all under the carpet and pretended it had nothing to do with her, why she still seemed so blasé about the
whole thing.

Seeing the tortured look in Marcus's eyes a moment ago
made her ache deep inside. She wished just one of the adults

involved in the fiasco of her birth had felt that burning urge to protect *her* that way, instead of abandoning her—either physically or emotionally.

She opened her eyes and looked up at Marcus, knowing he would do the right thing no matter the cost to himself. He was that kind of man. Something deep down in Faith's soul broke free and reached for him, and where her mind went her hands followed.

It didn't have to be for ever, did it? She knew she didn't belong with him long-term. But that didn't mean she couldn't have him just for now. Why was she stopping herself?

Take it, Faith. Take something for yourself for once, instead of running away from everything.

It was only just over a week until the Carol Service, and after that she'd be gone. At least she'd have a cool story to tell—or hide from—her grandkids one day. *I once had a fling with an earl...*

She reached up and touched his cheek. Her eyes were suddenly moist and threatening to produce a black, streaky waterfall down her face. She stepped forward, put a trembling hand on his chest. He stiffened, and she knew he was doing as he'd promised, holding himself back because he'd given his word.

The only problem was she didn't want him to hold back any more.

'Faith McKinnon, are you flirting with me?' His voice was raw, despite the levity of his words. 'I thought we had an agreement.'

Faith's heart pounded so hard she thought it might knock her over. She knew she was about to cross a boundary that she herself had put in place, that the resulting fall-out could be blamed on no one else. But just for once she wanted to feel as if she wasn't alone, an outsider.

'No, I'm not flirting with you, Marcus,' she said, her voice husky as she reached up and hooked her hand round his neck to pull him closer. 'I'm kissing you.'

CHAPTER NINE

THIS was no soft, exploratory, getting-to-know-you kiss, Marcus realised. They were way past that. It was as if he already knew her this way. He could anticipate just when and where she was going to move her hands, knew just when the next breathy sigh was coming. They couldn't have been more in synch with each other if they'd been lovers for years. And if he hadn't been wearing Wellington boots she'd have blown his big old woolly socks off!

He dipped his hands inside her half-open coat, finding her tightly corseted waist inside the bodice of her dress, feeling the velvet rasp against the pads of his fingers as he pulled close. In response she buried her hands inside his hair and pressed herself against him. Faith McKinnon hadn't uttered a word, but that hadn't stopped her being as direct as usual about what she wanted from him.

That thought both set his toes on fire and stopped him cold at the same time. It took all he had to gently pull away, to disentangle himself from her. She moaned in protest as he dragged his lips from hers, and that was almost his undoing. Almost. He pulled back and held her face between his hands.

'Faith…'

Her lids were still closed and she let out a frustrated sigh. 'Don't be noble, Marcus. Just kiss me again.'

He obliged—a short, hot kiss that he was only just able to

control. 'We can't stay out here,' he murmured. 'You'll die of hypothermia.'

She opened her eyes and looked straight at him. Straight *through* him, it felt like. Her pupils were huge and he felt their tug like a giant magnet.

Her voice was low and oh-so-sexy as she said, 'Then take me back inside.'

He didn't have to ask what she meant. He almost growled in frustration. This wasn't a different-bed-every-night woman; something deep inside told him that. It also told him that she wasn't one to give all she had easily, that she didn't let that many people close. The caveman part of him rose up and cheered at the thought he wouldn't be the last in a long, long line of lovers. The Earl, however—damn him—had other ideas.

He stepped back, but kept one arm around her and led her down the short curling staircase that circled the mound.

She shivered against him. Whether from the promise of further heat or the cold night air he didn't know.

'Please tell me it's not going to take as long to get out as it did to get in. Forget hypothermia! I think I might just expire from frustration.'

'It's not going to take as long,' he said, and guided her further round the mound. After a short break the steps continued curling, but this time underground, leading them under the stone tower and under the maze.

'Oh, wow!' she said as they descended into a small grotto under the centre of the maze. The stone walls were lined with shells of different shapes and sizes, and a small fountain dribbled into a pool at one edge of the chamber.

She grabbed his arm and pulled herself tightly into his side as they passed through the grotto, down another short flight of curving stairs, and then along a winding shell-lined path, created to mimic a limestone cave with stalactites and stalagmites. At the end was an iron gate and another flight of stairs that took them out onto a different side of the maze from where they'd entered.

Faith punched him on the arm. 'You mean we could have just got in that way all along!'

Despite his sudden serious mood he felt his lips curl up at the edges. 'It wouldn't have been half as much fun.'

She looked as if she was going to argue, but then her expression softened. She pressed her lips softly against his. 'No,' she mumbled against his mouth between kisses. 'Maybe it wouldn't have.'

He looked at the path in front of them, and then down at Faith's beautiful red dress, already wet round the hem. He knew she'd be horrified if she thought she'd ruined it, even though Bertie wouldn't give a fig.

Also, there was only one way he could come up with to stop himself doing something they might both regret in the morning. So while she was distracted, looking out over the gently sloping lawn that ran between the maze and the lower lake, he bent down, grabbed her round the thighs and threw her over his shoulder.

'Marcus!' she squealed. 'Put…me…down!'

'This is for your own good,' he muttered through clenched teeth, and started walking.

She pounded on his back for a few steps. 'You're an insufferable tyrant, do you know that?' she said from somewhere behind him, but her arms circled his chest to steady herself.

'I've been told it runs in the family,' he said, a grin forming on his lips. Maybe he was a little twisted, but he was starting to enjoy himself. And he needed to keep this light, needed to keep it breezy. 'And, Faith…?'

'What?'

She sounded more than a little disgruntled. Too bad.

'I was right about the view.'

* * *

Faith had never been so glad to see a kitchen door in her life. Despite her repeated pleadings Marcus had carried her all the way back to the castle hoisted over his shoulder. When she'd complained that the guests must be leaving the ball by now, and someone might see them, he'd just taken a back route, using a path than ran past the cellar windows.

However, maybe the blood rushing to her head had done her some good. Bizarrely, she was thinking straighter now it was back where it should be, rather than making other body parts thrum with longing.

That didn't mean she regretted what she'd asked him, just that she understood why he'd held back. This would be a big deal, not some quick tumble in the haystack. Was she really ready for all that would mean, both good and bad?

On the one hand it would be a wonderful, wonderful affair. On the other… She could end up falling all the way in love with him, and then she'd really be in trouble. She didn't know which would be worse—having him and losing him, or never knowing what it would be like, always wishing she'd taken the chance when she had it.

As they entered the kitchen he skilfully managed to deposit her the right way up without making her feel like a sack of potatoes.

'Marcus…' she whispered.

He looked impossibly sexy, with his hair all messed up and his eyes all dark and serious.

He threaded his fingers through hers. 'Come.'

Her blood started heading in all the wrong directions again at the hint of promise in the word. They went up the staircase to the ground floor proper, and then through a network of corridors and rooms until they ended up in the most beautiful library. Marcus turned a single lamp on, and its glow bathed that corner of the room in warm yellow light.

On every available stretch of wall that wasn't occupied by either a door or a fireplace there were huge ornately carved bookshelves, most groaning with the weight of leather-bound books. But instead of the wood having a dark varnish, the whole room was painted a soft buttery cream. There were three peacock-coloured damask-covered sofas—one L-shaped to fit in front of the only corner bookcase. Marcus motioned for her to sit down.

He pulled a book from the shelf and came to join her on the corner sofa. He opened the book, leafed through to find a place and handed it to her.

Song of Songs.

She shot him a look and then focused on the page.

'What does it say?' he asked.

Faith skimmed down the whole of the first chapter, getting a feel for the context, before turning the page over and finding the second and reading from verse one. "'I am the rose of Sharon, and the lily of the valleys.'" She looked up. 'Rose of Sharon! Just like in the window. This *has* to be connected.' She looked down again and carried on to the second verse: "'As the lily among thorns, so is my love among the daughters.'" She met his gaze again. 'Well, that's an obvious declaration of love, I guess.'

He nodded, but he didn't look down at the book in her hands, just at her. She swallowed. All her life she'd felt like a thorn—something that got in other people's way, snagged them when they wanted to be free—but when he looked at her like that she felt as fragile and as elegant as a lily. With a rush of understanding, she suddenly understood just how remarkable those words were. What an amazing thing it was to be longed for like that, to be adored rather than merely tolerated.

She continued reading. It was beautiful. Not a sermon, or a fire and brimstone prophecy, but a poem—a declaration between two lovers, full of evocative words and sensual imagery. The man who'd used a verse from this to send a message to his wife had definitely not thought he'd made a mistake in marrying her. Far from it.

She glanced over the text again. '"Do not stir up or awaken love until it pleases…" What do you think that means?'

He leaned forward and looked at her intently. 'Maybe that there's a right time and a wrong time for everything—even love?'

She gave a huff. 'I think my mother's living proof of that. She's always falling in love with something, or someone, or some place. It always ends in disaster… It's not that she hasn't got a big heart—quite the reverse. She always gives away too much, and always too soon.' She paused and looked at the text again. '*Until it pleases*… Maybe that's the answer—her timing sucks.'

He threaded his fingers together, balancing his elbows on his knees, and looked into her eyes. 'I don't think she's alone in that. Love seems to have more casualties than it does success stories.'

She knew what he was saying, could almost see into a future where they were both limping away from each other, in much worse shape than they were now.

She exhaled loudly. 'And what about us, Marcus? Is it the right time or the wrong time for us? How do we tell?'

'I don't know…' He sat up again and ran a hand through his hair. 'But I know it's something I couldn't walk away from after just one night.'

She nodded. Her heart felt like a stone, sinking inside her chest.

There was the answer to her earlier question. And she'd wanted so much to pretend she was one of those girls who could just fall into bed with a hot man and then fall out again the next morning without a backwards glance. Why did it have to be all or nothing with her? And why did she always end up on the *nothing* side of the equation?

He reached for her, tugged her hand and brought her to sit next to him. He pressed the most delicate of kisses to her temple and then left his lips there, as if he couldn't quite bring himself to move away.

All or nothing.

What had grown already was too much to brush off as a flirtation, or rebrand and cheapen as a fling. They were hovering at a threshold, and she was too scared to cross it.

One step. Not even a leap. That was all it was.

But that one step would change everything.

The light seeping through the crack in the drawn curtains was cold and grey. Faith stirred against him. Marcus wasn't sure if he'd been dozing or not. It only seemed seconds ago that his mind had been whirring between the window, the mysterious verses and the woman nestled against him.

His arm was stretched along the back of the blue sofa cushions and Faith, still in her red ballgown and Shirley's borrowed coat, was burrowed into his side, her cheek on one side of her chest and her palm splayed possessively above his heart. He bowed his head and pressed a silent kiss to her silky hair. She moved again, just enough to signal she was on her way to consciousness.

Marcus closed his eyes and let the back of his skull rest against the sofa cushions. Even though he was cold and stiff, and his right leg was numb, he wished this night could have just dragged on and on. He hadn't quite finished relishing the feel of her curled against him, her rhythmic breathing warming his shirt. There was no way of knowing if he'd ever get the chance to have her soft and sleeping against him again, so he was wringing every second he could from the moment.

She wouldn't want to burrow so close against him if she knew what a coward he was.

Noble? *Don't think so.*

Running scared? *Oh, yes.*

He'd done a lot of thinking in the grey hours of the night. Saying no to Faith last night had been a gut reaction. He'd even managed to kid himself he'd been doing it for *her* benefit.

He was such a liar.

There was one reason and one reason alone that had held him back: fear. Nothing very noble about that.

The same strange perception that let him eavesdrop on her thoughts, anticipate her kisses, had told him something else. Something that had sent him running like a frightened deer. He knew without a shadow of a doubt that if he'd spent the night with Faith this morning he'd have been so besotted he'd have lain his heart at her feet—like some sappy knight of old who risked everything just for a wave of his lady's handkerchief.

So, as amazing as a night with Faith would be, he wasn't sure he could afford the cost.

She made a sleepy noise and used the hand on his chest to lever herself up and look him in the face.

'I feel like crap,' she said, and he couldn't help but laugh.

He brushed a wonky tendril that had escaped her pinned-up hairdo behind her ear. She didn't sugarcoat her words for anyone, did she?

She yawned, then fixed him with a steady gaze. 'What now?'

He knew her question had many layers. He decided to deal with the one he had an answer to. 'I spent a lot of time thinking last night and—aside from working out whether this new verse is a clue or just a coincidence, I thought it might be a good idea to find out more about my great-grandmother—Evangeline Huntington: the woman who started it all.'

She pushed herself away from him, so she could sit up straight, and pulled the puffy coat tighter around her. 'I didn't think your family talked about her. And they've done a hell of a job erasing any trace of her from Hadsborough.'

He nodded. 'But my family aren't the only ones who lived here, saw things. An army of servants have worked at the castle over the years, and if there's one thing that servants like to do it's gossip. Someone has to have heard something.'

She covered her mouth with her hand as another yawn escaped. 'You think the man who told you about the cellar might know something?'

'He's a good place to start.'

She looked down at her dress. It was creased horribly, and the Wellington boots were only half on, hanging off her feet. 'I'm not going anywhere like this.'

He stood up, caught her hands in his and pulled her up to meet him. She sighed as her feet dropped back into the boots with a sucking noise, and when she met his gaze he knew those other layers of questions were swirling round her head.

'Marcus? About us…?'

He shook his head. 'I don't know,' he said softly, and then he bent his head and tasted her lips one more time. He knew he shouldn't, but he just couldn't stop himself.

A week was all they had. If they'd had months ahead of them, if Faith had been going to settle down in one place for any length of time, then it might have been different. But he wasn't ready to jump right in. He had to be sure this time.

You are sure, a little voice said inside his head. *You know.*

Perhaps. But he didn't trust that little voice. He'd listened to it before—about Amanda, who had said she'd stick by him no matter what. And when his father had promised him everything was fine, that the company was just experiencing a minor blip. He'd listened to that smooth, soothing voice before and it had cost him everything. So, no, he wasn't in a rush, and he didn't think he should be.

'Then until we know,' she said, her pupils expanding, 'I suggest we maintain the status quo.'

He knew it was stupid to pretend they wouldn't get sucked in deeper, but he wasn't ready to let go just yet. One more week. That wasn't too much to ask, was it? Whatever was going on between them was balancing precariously, and it would fall one way or the other. And it would fall soon.

'A shower, a few hours' sleep and a good breakfast is in order before we do any more sleuthing,' he said, taking a step backwards.

Faith grabbed a hold of his shirt. 'Not so fast, buddy.' She used her grip to pull his face close to hers. 'I haven't finished with you just yet.'

Faith looked around her as she and Marcus walked through the terraced gardens beside the long lake.

'I don't suppose you know if there are any lilies under all that white stuff?' she asked him.

He shook his head. 'Even if I could remember it wouldn't matter. These gardens have been replanted and redesigned at least twice in the last thirty years alone. Even if that verse *is* a clue of some kind, we have to face the possibility that the lilies that were in the garden in my great-grandfather's day no longer exist.'

She sighed and stuffed her hand into her coat pocket. 'Well, let's hope this Mr Grey of yours has something enlightening to tell us.'

The walk across Hadsborough Park in the snow was gorgeous. Vast fields of white were still untouched by human feet, even though it had been days since the last snowfall and a fortnight since the first flakes.

The retired employee was visiting his son and daughter-in-law, who occupied a small stone cottage on the far edge of the estate, hewn from the same sandstone as the castle itself. Marcus used the knocker on the shiny red front door and they heard a faint voice call out from inside. He pushed the door and she followed him inside. They found Mr Grey sitting by the fire with a blanket over his knees. A middle-aged woman fussed around him, tucking it in. When she saw Marcus she stood up ramrod-straight and bobbed a quick curtsey.

'Morning, My Lord. Would you and Miss McKinnon care for a cup of tea?'

Marcus smiled. 'Thank you for allowing us to visit so early on a Sunday morning, Caroline. And, yes, a cup of tea would be lovely.'

Caroline scurried out of the room and Marcus turned to the old man in the chair.

'Good morning, Arnold.'

The old man nodded. 'Mornin', My Lord. I've been wondering when you'd turn up at my door.' He motioned for them to sit down on a large chintz sofa, which they did.

Faith and Marcus looked at each other.

'Have you, now?' Marcus said, returning his attention to the old man.

Arnold Grey smiled. 'Ever since I heard the old chapel was going to be used again I've been expecting someone to come and start asking questions.' He turned his attention to Faith. 'You're the lass who's fixing the window, aren't you?'

'Yes,' she said.

The old man nodded again, as if her answer confirmed something. 'You know the sixth Duke made that window for your great-grandmother?'

Marcus leaned forward, clasping his hands together and resting his forearms on his knees. 'That's the story,' he said, 'but until now we haven't been able to verify if it's anything *but* a story. We were hoping that you'd be able to tell us something about Evangeline Huntington.'

At that moment Caroline bustled in with the tea tray, and it took an agonising minute or two before they could resume their conversation. Mr Grey took a sip of his tea and then placed his cup back in its saucer.

'My father told me never to talk of it,' he said. 'But I reckon it's a crying shame what they did to her, and it's about time somebody told the truth.'

Faith's heart began to pound as defiance glittered in the old man's eyes.

'My older sister was her lady's maid,' he explained. 'Terrible upset, she was, when Her Grace left.'

Marcus and Faith shared a glance.

'They were more friends than employer and employee, you see,' Arnold said. 'Evie was a florist's daughter. Sweet as anything, she was, but shy and not very confident. It took a lot for the Duke to convince her to accept him, but he finally wore her down. She thought the world of him, though, and was awful upset when he died so young. But she had the baby to comfort her, and she doted on him.'

Faith reached over and covered Marcus's hand with hers. He'd gone very pale where Mr Grey had been speaking.

'You mean it's all true?' he said quietly. 'My family has been lying all these years?'

The old man didn't say anything, but the sadness in his eyes was confirmation enough.

Faith found it hard to catch her voice. 'So what really happened? Can you tell us?'

He nodded, just once, and then he smiled. 'As soon as I've had my chocolate digestive, I will.'

'That was so sad,' Faith said as they walked back across the park towards the castle.

Marcus reached for her gloved hand and enclosed it in his. He didn't like to think of her being sad, even on someone else's behalf.

She looked off into the distance, shaking her head. 'They were so cruel to treat her like that. So what if she was a florist's daughter? She was the mother of their only heir! That should have counted for something.'

He stopped, placed his hands on her shoulders and turned her to face him. Then he kissed her softly. He could feel the frown on her features, even though he'd closed his eyes, but after a moment her facial muscles relaxed and softened and she kissed him back.

That was better. He liked making Faith feel better.

When they began to walk again she looped her arm through his and he squeezed it closer to his body, keeping it there. 'They did what they thought was right,' he said with a certain amount of resignation. 'They were protecting the family.'

She looked sharply up at him. 'And what about the poor woman they harangued and belittled until she finally cracked and believed what they told her—that her husband had regretted marrying her, that she would only ever be a hindrance to her son and that he'd be better off without her? They practically ran her out of town with a shotgun.'

He sighed. 'It takes a certain kind of strength to survive a family like mine.'

Faith yanked her arm from his and walked ahead. 'I can't believe you're siding with them!' she all but yelled.

He quickened his pace to catch her up, placed a hand on her shoulder. She shrugged it off.

'I didn't mean that I agree with what they did. I just meant that I understand it.'

Head bowed, she looked at him from under her lashes. 'There are no excuses for separating a parent from their child. No excuses at all.'

He nodded, moved his hand to rub her shoulder. 'You're taking this all too personally, Faith. This isn't the same as what happened to you, and it was such a long time ago.'

She shook her head, smiling, but it was all teeth and stretched lips. 'No. You can't consign this to the distant past—not when there's a sad old man sitting by the fire in that castle, aching to know why his mother abandoned him. Because that's what all this is about, isn't it? Duke or no duke, all your grandfather wants to know is that he belongs. Why do you think he stayed away from his home all those years?'

That thought hit Marcus square between the eyes. He jammed his hands in his pockets and picked up speed. 'Is that why *you* stay away from home?'

Her mouth moved and her eyes widened. 'This isn't about me. This is about your family. Don't do what the rest of them do and blame it on the commoner—the outsider.'

He clenched his jaw. That was not what he'd meant and she knew it. He was right, though—about Faith's reluctance to return to the picture-perfect town she painted with such warm words, about her identifying too strongly with his unfortunate great-grandmother.

They walked in silence for a few minutes. Eventually she said, 'Do you want me to come with you when you tell him?'

He looked at her, then shook his head. 'No. This is family business. I think I'd better do this on my own.'

'Fine,' she said, looking anything but. Her mouth drooped and her eyes were large under her woolly hat. 'I'll be where I belong—in the studio, working on the window.'

CHAPTER TEN

MARCUS sat on the sofa, in what he now thought of as Faith's place, and watched his grandfather carefully for a reaction. Bertie had closed his eyes and rested his head against the high back of his winged chair when Marcus had finished talking. Had he done the right thing in being so open about what he and Faith had found? He'd wanted to protect his grandfather from pain, but that hadn't been possible either way.

'Grandfather?' he asked quietly. 'Are you okay?'

Bertie nodded and opened his eyes. 'I don't know if it's better to know that she loved me, that she didn't desert me willingly, or whether I'd prefer to be ignorant still and not be haunted by the idea that, had I started this sooner, I might have met her.' He opened his eyes looked across at Marcus. 'Do you know what happened to her after she left?'

'No, but I have a friend who's a genealogist. He may be able to come up with something. Would that help?'

His grandfather nodded.

Marcus looked into the fire. 'Why couldn't the family have just accepted her? Things were changing—ten years after the Great War ended the world was a different place. It couldn't have mattered so much then.'

His grandfather folded his hands in his lap. 'My uncle Reginald was a small-minded man, petty. He'd always envied my father, I was told, and once he got a chance to have

Hadsborough himself, even by proxy, I'm afraid it rather went to his head.'

Marcus got up and headed over to the window, looked outside at the still-perfect snowscape. 'No wonder you turfed him out on his ear and employed an estate manager when you were old enough.'

He heard rustling behind him, guessed his grandfather was fussing with the papers he kept close to him at all times nowadays.

'What does Faith think about all of this?' he asked.

'She went back to work on Evie's window, as she's now calling it,' Marcus said with a sigh. 'She's taking it all very personally. That's why I came to talk to you on my own.'

'You wouldn't be watching out for her so keenly if you didn't care about her.'

Marcus's insides sank further. He was trying not to care too much, but the boundaries kept getting blurry, and he couldn't always work out if he was on the right side or not any more.

He walked over to the other armchair and sat in it. 'Yes, I do care.'

Though sadness still lingered in his eyes, Marcus's response brought a warmth to Bertie's expression. 'I haven't seen you look at a girl that way since Amanda.'

Marcus expected to flinch at the mention of her name, but it washed over him. He wasn't angry with her any more, he realised. He'd let that go. In fact in the last couple of weeks he'd let a lot of things go. And he couldn't help but think that was Faith's doing. He felt as if he'd come alive since she'd been here—had started to remember who he was before life had taught him to mistrust everything and everyone.

Suddenly Amanda's parting words to him that fateful night made sense. *'I can't do it any more, Marcus,'* she'd said. *'I can't be with this angry, distant man you've become.'*

He'd thought it had just been an excuse—Amanda shifting the blame from herself to him—but now he could see the truth of her words. He'd thought she'd backed off because it wasn't the life they'd pictured together. Titles and castles had been a long way off in the future, then. But he realised now it wasn't Hadsborough and the Huntington name that had sent her running, but him. He'd stopped believing in her, in love. In anything good.

Bertie picked up the photo in a silver frame that was on the table next to his armchair and handed it to Marcus. His grandparents on their wedding day. Bertie looked as if he could burst with pride, and Granny Clara's eyes were shining.

'I knew it the moment I met her,' his grandfather said softly. 'Knew I should grab the chance to have her before she flitted out of my life and some other chap snapped her up. Proposed after one week.'

Marcus nodded. He knew. He'd heard the story a hundred times. He handed the frame back to his grandfather. 'I'm afraid I don't believe in love at first sight.'

He still wasn't sure he believed in love at all. At least he hadn't…

He shook his head. It was foolishness to think that way.

'Love is unreliable,' he said baldly. 'Look at my parents… look at yours!'

His grandfather shrugged, but his eyes were still smiling. 'Of course it's unreliable. Of course you can't pin it down and analyse it. That's what makes it so wonderful. But isn't it worth the risk when it all works out? Your grandmother and I had forty-nine glorious years together.'

Marcus looked into the fire. He knew that, too. He just couldn't quite project into the future and imagine it for himself.

'She came here for a reason, you know.'

Marcus looked up and found his grandfather staring intently at him. He didn't need to ask who he was talking about. 'She came here to fix your bloody window,' he said grimly.

'I know you've had a lot of disappointments in your life,' his grandfather said. 'I know people have let you down again and again. And I know what Harvey did… There have been a lot of shocks to recover from.'

Marcus shook his head, not wanting to hear anything else about his father.

Bertie closed his mouth and thought for a second, then he began to speak again. 'What happened to that adventurous young boy who tried to modify his kite so he could strap himself into it and launch himself off the battlements?'

Marcus blinked. He *had* done that once, hadn't he? Thank goodness the housekeeper had found him and stopped him in time.

Bertie chuckled. 'I know what you're thinking. But wouldn't it have been a marvellous adventure to actually fly?'

He couldn't help smiling. 'You're a delusional old man,' he told his grandfather.

'Maybe,' Bertie said, and then blinked slowly. 'But there's a time for grieving, for licking one's wounds and there's also a time to let yourself heal.' He reached across and patted Marcus's arm. 'The bird with the broken wing is supposed to fly again once it's mended.'

Marcus nodded even as he looked away. That was the problem, wasn't it? What if the wounds went so deep that they never mended? What if the bird tried to fly too soon and came crashing to the ground?

Faith ended the call and put her phone beside her on the table. She picked up her brush and continued working dry cement into the crevasses of the completely re-leaded window panel.

Fabulous timing, Gram.

The emotional blackmail had been hot and hard, but she'd managed to hold her ground. She knew Gram was trying to do what she thought was best for her, but her grandmother didn't understand what it was like. Gram had always been the centre of their little family unit. She'd never been consigned to the fringes as Faith had.

And the bombshell her grandmother had dropped had only made Faith want to stay away all the more.

Her dad—not the biological one, the other one—was back in town. Gram had said he and her mother had been spending a lot of time together. She'd thought that meant fireworks, but Gram had assured her they'd been getting along fine.

One side of her mouth turned down as she thought about that. As much as she wasn't sure she could deal with the Mom and Dad rollercoaster again, the possibility of reconciliation scared her more.

She could imagine it now: Christmas dinner as one big, happy family. Gram, Mom, Greg and her sisters, all laughing and talking and passing the potatoes between each other.

And her.

It had been bad enough thinking about going home anyway. Now she really would be the spare wheel.

She was disgusted with herself for wanting things back the way they had been before Dad had come back on the scene, even if 'normal' for the McKinnon women had meant fractured and dysfunctional. She was a horrible, horrible person.

She glanced up at Basil, who had now been moved into the studio to keep an eye on her. He stared back, offering no sympathy.

Slowly she put her brush down. She couldn't concentrate. She was too wired, waiting for Marcus's knock on the studio door. If it hadn't already been shut she'd have been tempted to slam it in his face when he arrived.

Because that was what he'd done to her—shut her out. Just as she'd started to believe she mattered to him. His words still rang in her head.

Family business...

And she wasn't family, was she? Never would be.

Even so, she was more angry with herself than she was

with him. Why was she surprised? She knew that already. Of course she wasn't family. She'd only been here a few weeks. How on earth had she got to a place where she was upset with him for stating the facts? Somehow she'd got distracted by things like Christmas lights and balls and moonlit mazes, even though she'd tried her hardest not to.

She decided she couldn't stand it any more. She couldn't sit here, meekly waiting for him. They weren't joined at the hip, for goodness' sake. They weren't joined in any way at all. And there'd be plenty of time to finish the window tomorrow.

What she needed was to get some space, some distance, to get her head straight. She didn't owe Marcus Huntington an explanation or a note to say where she was going. She was her own person and she could do what she liked.

She stood up, ignoring Basil's disapproving glare, and put her coat on.

Marcus had searched the entire castle and he couldn't find Faith anywhere. This was definitely a moment when having a sixteen-bedroomed monstrosity for a home was a disadvantage.

He was furious with her for disappearing like a sulky child. He'd known she hadn't liked his decision to go and see his grandfather on his own, but he'd done it for her own good. She would have hated to see Bertie sad like that. The two of them had formed a strong bond in a ridiculously short time.

At least he told himself he was furious. The longer he looked for her, the more his anger chilled into something more anxious. Still, he told himself, he was going to find her and give her a piece of his mind.

This was the third time he'd walked down the corridor that led to the turret bedroom, but this time he noticed something he hadn't picked up on before—the little door that led to the roof was slightly ajar. He stopped and looked at it. As far as he knew Faith didn't even know of its existence. Most people mistook it for a linen cupboard.

He pulled the door open and listened. Nothing. Even so, he found himself climbing the narrow curling stairs, bending his head low to prevent himself from hitting it on the stone above. When he reached the top he pushed an equally tiny door open. Cold air rushed past him. A few more steps and he could see the starlit sky.

At first he didn't see her, but then he spotted a shadow in the corner of the roof, its back to him, arms folded on the battlements, gazing over the lake. He started striding.

She heard him when he was halfway towards her. Even in the dark he saw her stiffen. He opened his mouth—ready to justify himself, ready to explain why he'd had to leave her out of his conversation with his grandfather—but when Faith whirled round and looked at him all those paper defences fluttered away.

He could see it in her eyes—the raw hurt, the disappointment. The pain that *he* had caused. It boomeranged back and hit him square in the chest.

He walked towards her, not saying anything, a bleak expression on his face, and when he reached her he lifted her off her feet, pulled her to him and kissed her as if his life depended on it. Maybe it did. Because all that mattered at this moment was wiping the pain from her eyes, making sure she never, *ever* felt that way again. He couldn't bear it.

She kissed him back, fiercely at first, her latent anger bubbling below the surface. He met her in that place and the heat intensified between them. But with each meeting of their lips they peeled another layer from each other. What had started off as armour clashing against armour slowly became skin exploring skin—and deeper.

When they had finally fought out whatever the hell had been going on between them he dropped one last sweet kiss on her lips, then pulled back and gently brushed one set of glistening lashes with his thumb.

'I didn't mean to upset you,' he said softly, letting his hand fall away.

She caught it and brought it up to her cheek, closed her eyes. 'I understand that now,' she replied, her voice thick. 'It's not that.'

Good. All that needed to be said had been said. Or kissed.

'I don't mean to cry,' she said, shaking her head as more moisture spiked her lashes. 'It's just that sometimes you have a way of making me feel so…so…' She stopped shaking her head, looked right at him. 'Like I'm something precious.'

Her eyes begged him to tell her she wasn't wrong. He placed a hand on either side of her face, stroked the soft skin of her cheeks with the pads of his thumbs. He looked deep into those warm brown eyes and gave her the confirmation she craved.

How, in all her life, had no one ever made Faith McKinnon feel special? Couldn't they see what was right in front of their eyes?

This time he kissed her slowly and tenderly. She seemed to drink it in, as if she couldn't get enough of what he gave her. Marcus knew he'd gladly empty himself of everything he had and everything he was to see her smiling and happy.

He'd done it, hadn't he? Without meaning to, and despite his best efforts not to.

It didn't matter that they hadn't slept together. It didn't matter that he could still picture the hollowness in Amanda's face as she'd walked away from him that last time. He'd leapt off these battlements, not knowing if his wings would hold or not. There was only one thing to do now.

Fly.

Faith's eyes were huge and glistening. Her mouth quivered and crumpled into a wobbly line. Tears spilled over her lashes and she dipped her head, breaking eye contact. He placed his palms either side of her neck and used his thumbs to tip her jaw upwards until she was looking at him again. For a moment he thought she was going to twist her head, or move away, but then she launched herself forward, wrapped her arms around his neck and kissed him back. Kissed him exactly the same way he'd kissed her.

That was when he knew. That was when he discovered his wings worked.

'How...?' she said in a wobbly voice. 'How is it possible? We've only known each other such a short time. Things like this don't happen...not to real people.'

She reached for his upper arm and pinched the skin hard through his sweater.

'Ow!'

She chuckled softly. 'Just checking...'

He smiled back even as he rubbed his arm. 'I thought you were supposed to pinch *yourself* if you thought you were dreaming, not someone else.'

She just kissed him again, laughing as she did so, and crying, too.

When they'd finished she drew in a deep breath, placed a palm on his chest and closed her eyes, as if she was steadying herself.

With a hammering heart, he opened his mouth. 'I don't want this to end yet,' he said. 'Stay with us for Christmas.'

He saw a flicker of something in her eyes before she answered, but he couldn't label it. Fear? Guilt? Doubt?

It didn't really matter, because she wiped all those things away when she pressed her lips against his, kissed him almost desperately, and whispered, 'Yes, I'll stay. I'd love to spend Christmas with you.'

It was dark by the time Marcus unlocked the orangery the following evening. Faith waited as he swung one of the double doors open, then motioned for her to enter in front of him.

She took a couple of steps into the dark and chilly space and he flicked a switch. Uplighters mounted on the pillars between the high windows bathed the vaulted ceiling in a warm glow, blocking out the white pinprick lights beyond the glass.

'*Wow!*' she said, tipping her head back and looking around. 'Impressive.'

'Beautiful, isn't it? There's not much point in keeping it open to the public in the winter, though.'

Low beds, mostly full of bare earth, ran around the perimeter of the vast space. Many of the seasonal plants were dormant, and even the two rows of citrus trees, in large square wooden planters, weren't doing anything interesting.

Faith walked forward and fingered a waxy leaf with her gloved hands.

They'd already looked for lilies everywhere—sculptures in the gardens, books in the library and paintings in the Long Gallery.

'Up this end,' he said, and led the way to a small semi-circular fountain against a wall at the far end. A copper pipe protruded from a marble swan's beak above the pool, and the edges were sculpted to look like wings, meeting in the middle. He shone the beam of his torch into the empty fountain, lighting up a colourful mosaic.

'Lilies!' she said.

Sure enough, against the bright blue background of the mosaic was a stylised pattern of long-stemmed flowers.

She started to hunt round the edge of the fountain. 'There's got to be something here,' she said. 'An inscription or something. There just *has* to be.'

She knelt down on the hard and dusty floor, requested the flashlight he'd brought with him by flapping a hand, and set to work. Uplighters were great mood lighting, but for treasure-hunting they needed a better light source.

After a couple of minutes searching every square millimetre of the fountain—both inside and out—they both stood up again.

'There's nothing there,' she said, brushing a wayward strand of hair out of her eyes and back behind one ear. 'I don't understand it.'

She started roaming, flashlight in hand, looking for anything that might be their clue, and stopped in front of a statue of a young woman, her long hair draped round her naked body as she stared off wistfully into the distance.

Crouching down, she shone the torch at the base of the statue. On the plinth below her feet was a worn inscription.

'I can't make out the first word, but the end bit seems to be numbers.'

Marcus squatted down beside her and she handed him the flashlight. He shone it diagonally across the indentations in the stone, slanting the beam to bring the writing into relief. 'This statue must have been out in the gardens for some years to have received this much wear and tear,' he said. 'But I always remember it being here.'

Faith squinted, trying to make out the shapes. 'It looks like roman numerals,' she said, tracing the three upright lines at the end with the fingers of her free hand.

'I don't know,' he said, shaking his head. 'The third digit isn't evenly spaced like the first two—it's further away.'

She moved her hand to investigate that spot. 'The stone's too worn to tell, but could there have been a colon between the last two digits?'

'Maybe.'

She looked back at him. 'That would make it a reference to *something* Chapter Eleven, Verse One. Can you make out any of that writing at all?'

'I think the first letter is an H,' he said, 'and there's at least another six or seven after that. This might give us enough to go on.' He transferred his gaze to the end of the orangery.

'There's quite a bit of distance between this statue and the fountain. Do you really think they're connected?'

She nodded emphatically. 'They've got to be,' she said seriously. 'They've just got to be.'

His smiled faded, even as his gaze warmed, and then he pulled her to her feet.

For the next couple of minutes they didn't do any clue-hunting of any kind. And Faith didn't care a bit.

When they were together like this she didn't doubt him. However, that didn't stop the old fears shouting high and shrill in her ears when she was on her own. Sometimes she couldn't help turning her head to listen. As much as she hated those voices, they were familiar—and they were wise. They'd saved her from heartache countless times before. But it was a miserable way to live, walled up away from everyone she cared about, never letting anyone close.

She couldn't keep running to her tower and peering at everyone from a distance. It was lonely up there, and cold, and she'd much rather be here, standing in the open door, with Marcus warm in her arms.

Eyes still closed, she kissed him softly, as if she was testing that he was still there—still real—that he hadn't vanished in a puff of smoke.

He kissed her back, pulling her closer, taking her deeper. She went willingly.

This was real. It was.

Now all she had to do was believe it.

CHAPTER ELEVEN

FAITH sat cross-legged on one of the blue sofas in the library, her feet tucked under her knees, a Bible open on her lap, feeling as if she was fizzing inside.

'Well, Hosea, Chapter Eleven, Verse One, doesn't seem right,' she said, making herself concentrate on the tiny print. 'And Habbakkuk doesn't even have that many chapters, so I'm flipping over to the New Testament to see what the only other H book says…' She parted the book nearer the book and began thumbing through the thin pages. 'Ah…Hebrews, Eleven-One…'

Marcus came and sat down beside her. 'What does it say?'

She read it in silence. All the fizzing stopped.

Then she read it again, just to make sure, before saying the words out loud. '"Now faith is the substance of things hoped for, the evidence of things not seen."' She slapped the book closed and dumped it on the sofa. 'Great.'

Marcus leaned over her, picked up the Bible and had a look for himself.

Faith waited while he read. 'There's only one Faith I can think of on this estate—apart from me, of course.'

Marcus closed the book and rested in it his lap, his finger still marking the place. 'The window…'

Yes, the window.

'It's a dead end, isn't it?' she said, finding her voice suddenly hoarse. 'Your great-grandfather never finished laying out his clues, or they were never there in the first place. We've just been stringing together bits of evidence that were never really connected. It's all been for nothing.'

She stood up. She needed to go somewhere—for a walk, preferably—but it was dark and freezing cold. The only option was to retreat to her turret.

Marcus got to his feet. 'Not for nothing, Faith… We found out the truth about Bertie's mother. You gave him that.'

'Yes, and what good has that done?'

She'd hoped Bertie would be happier, but he'd been very quiet and withdrawn since Marcus had spoken to him. She walked to the window and folded her arms, staring out at the black lake, only distinguishable from the dark lawns by the play of a half-hidden moon on its surface. The fragments of light reached for each other, trying to assemble themselves into a whole, but the wind on the water kept ripping them apart.

She looked back at Marcus, scowling at her from the fireplace, looking impossibly handsome.

She'd fallen in love with him, hadn't she? She'd done everything she'd promised herself she wouldn't and let herself believe in the fairytale.

Okay, no. She hadn't exactly let herself believe, but she'd stopped herself from *not* believing—which was just as dangerous. She'd invested in it all oh-so-much-more than she'd meant to. Just like the non-existent treasure hunt.

'That clue on the statue was probably nothing of the sort. We were just jumping to conclusions, seeing what we wanted to see.'

As she stood at the glass, staring out into the blackness, she realised she probably wasn't the first woman to look out of this window and feel this way.

'I wonder if Evie stood here,' she said softly as Marcus came to stand behind her. 'Mr Grey said she used to stare out of the castle windows crying after your great-grandfather died.'

He suddenly gripped her shoulders. 'Of *course*,' he said quietly.

She shrugged his hands off and turned to face him. 'What?'

'Something Arnold Grey said the other day that I dismissed as an odd comment suddenly makes sense. I didn't understand at the time.'

Her forehead creased. 'What was it?'

'Do you remember? He said his sister told him she didn't just stand and stare out of any particular window. She looked out of *all* of them in turn. I think Great Uncle Reginald told her about his brother's letter—about the message.'

Her heart lightened. 'You think she found it? That there really was one? Do you think she worked out what it all meant?'

He shook his head. 'I think the old—' He stopped, didn't say the word she guessed he wanted to. 'I think that dear old Great-Uncle Reggie gave her the message, but didn't elaborate. The work in the chapel was supposed to be a surprise. And why would my great-grandmother have cried so much if she'd found the comfort such a message should have brought?'

Faith's face fell. 'Oh. How cruel.' She shook her head. 'She knew the message was in a window, but they didn't tell her *which* window, and she spent years looking before she gave up and accepted the lies they fed her.'

His expression grew hard. 'Even so,' he said, his voice stony, just like on the first morning she'd met him, 'she shouldn't have given up.'

Faith turned back to the window, placed her hands on the cold glass. 'Not everyone is like you Huntingtons, you know. Some of us have blood flowing through our veins, not steel.'

'What's that supposed to mean?'

She watched his reflection in the darkened window. 'Just that you're a special breed. Not everyone is as strong as that.

Sometimes people have to know when it's time to give up and walk away.'

He was looking at her, his gaze intense. She refused to turn around.

'But think of the trail her husband was preparing for her—it was proof of some kind, a memory she could have taken forward with her. If not for herself, then she should have stuck it out for her son.'

Faith threw her hand in the air, exasperated. 'There *was* no trail! It was all in our minds. All it did was lead us right back to square one. And even if there was, Evie never knew about it!'

'Then why did someone change the window? It had to have meant something.'

She shook her head. 'They just made the same mistake we did. Thought it meant something when it didn't. They just decided not to take any chances and hide it anyway, even if they didn't understand what it meant.'

His face was hard, like the stone wall behind him. 'How can you be married to someone for five years and not believe they loved you?'

Faith glared back at him. Pretty much the same way you could believe your father adored you when he wasn't even genetically connected to you, when the overriding feeling he had when he looked at you was pain and humiliation. People could believe in the stupidest things if they wanted to badly enough.

She shook her head. 'You don't know. You don't understand what it's like to want to fit in somewhere so bad, but to know deep down that it's never going to happen. To know that one day you'll just be on your own again.'

Tears started to flow down her face and she swiped them away angrily. She sucked in a breath, trapped that quivering feeling in her lungs.

His expression softened and he moved towards her.

'Faith...I don't want to fight with you. The truth is that we may never know exactly what happened.'

He reached her, folded his arms around her and held her close. She burrowed her face into his chest and stayed there. She knew she should breathe out, release this shaky, quivery feeling inside and let her muscles relax, but she couldn't seem to work out how.

'Has your genealogist friend come up with anything?' she asked, pulling away a little and brushing the hair from her face. She needed to talk about something different before she completely fell apart.

'He left a message on my voicemail earlier,' Marcus replied. 'I'm going to call him in the morning.'

She nodded. In the morning her reason for being here would be at an end. No more window to fix, no more phantom trail to follow.

'You're right. Of course you're right. It's dumb to fight about this.' She pulled herself away from him and smiled, hid behind that outward show of happiness. 'I...I need a bath, I think.' She stepped out of his embrace. 'I'll see you at dinner.'

And then she ran, along corridors and up the winding stairs, higher and higher, until she reached her turret and shut the door behind her. She ran into the *en suite* bathroom, wrenched the taps so the bath flooded with scalding water, and stripped off all her clothes. While the water gurgled and the steam rose she covered her face with her hands and wept.

This was ridiculous. She felt... She felt... As if someone had died. As if she'd lost something precious. And all she'd done was race around for the past few weeks on a fool's errand, chasing a dream that wasn't really there.

She lay in the hot water and churned it all over in her mind. She couldn't imagine Evie as a coward, that she'd run for nothing. A mother would never leave her child like that unless she was pushed to the limit.

Poor Evie. Faith knew what that was like—to wake up

one day and realise you were a stranger in your own home, to discover the family you'd trusted had lied to you your whole life. Evie had trusted happy-ever-after and it had let her down badly. She'd believed. She'd really believed. And it hadn't been enough.

That thought had Faith springing from the tub and into her bedroom, panic rising in her chest. She closed her eyes. She loved Marcus. She knew she did. And everything inside her told her loved her, too. Yet…

She held her breath, tried to push the shaky feeling down with the air she was holding in her mouth and throat.

Marcus was her fairytale.

She wanted him so, so much. But that didn't mean the last page wouldn't close. Didn't mean the story wouldn't end the way it always did—with the words *The End*.

Faith yanked open the dresser, looking for her underwear. It sat there, plain and functional, in the ornate, perfumed walnut drawer. She looked at it for a second, then pulled all of her panties and bras out, not caring when the elastic on one item got caught somewhere and she had to wrench it free. And then she stuffed them into the front pocket of her case and zipped it up tight.

The next morning Marcus went to find Faith, only to discover she was already on her way to the chapel to put the repaired bottom section back in the window. She hadn't come down for dinner the night before, and when he'd knocked softly on her door there had been no answer. He was worried about her.

He also felt guilty. He should have realised she hadn't been in any shape to see straight about that blasted last clue.

He arrived at the chapel to find her already at work, quiet and composed. He breathed out a little and instead of disturbing her sat in one of the back pews and silently watched her. Although she didn't turn round, he sensed she knew he was there.

When all was finished she stood back, hands on hips.

He stood up and walked towards her. 'It looks wonderful,' he said.

Pity that the sky was dark and threatening rain, dulling the impact of the bright, jewel-coloured glass.

She turned and smiled, but it lacked its normal lustre. 'All done. My work here is over.'

He closed the distance between them. 'Wait until you see your window in all its glory at the Carol Service.'

She glanced over her shoulder at the window. 'It's not my window—it's not even Evie's. It's just a pretty picture made out of glass that a rich man paid for.'

Ouch. Okay. She was obviously still smarting from the whole dead end thing. He decided to tell her his news, the information that would let her know their search for Evie's treasure trail had at least turned up something good. Hopefully that would allow her to get a little perspective on the matter.

'We've located a relation of Bertie's in the East End of London.'

'Really?'

He nodded. 'My friend discovered that Evie remarried five years after she left Hadsborough, had another child. Her daughter's daughter is still alive. Bertie has a niece.' He smiled. 'You won't believe it, but she's a florist—carrying on the family tradition.'

'What does Bertie think about all of this?'

Marcus frowned. 'Surprisingly, he's a little bit cool about the idea of meeting her. But I'm going to her invite her down for the Carol Service. He'll feel differently when he sees her.'

Faith's expression darkened. 'Why don't you *listen* to your grandfather? If he doesn't want to meet her, he doesn't want to meet her.'

But now was the perfect time. He didn't want his grandfather to be engulfed by the sadness that had been creeping over him. This time he wasn't going to stand idly by while someone he loved sank further and further, stupidly trusting it would all work itself out in the end.

'I know it will help him,' he said.

She shook her head and picked up her bag.

He took a deep breath. 'A genealogist could help you find your father, too.'

Faith went still. 'Don't push, I said, Marcus. That's my business, not yours.'

A horrible feeling settled in his stomach. This was not going well. And he had no idea why. He decided to try another approach.

He reached out, caught Faith's hand. She looked down, and then back up at him. He leaned in and pressed a soft kiss on her lips—a kiss that was supposed to have been a prelude to more. But he pulled back, frowning. Her lips felt cold and she'd barely responded.

'What's wrong?' he asked.

She shook her head, her eyes blank. 'Nothing.'

'I'll butt out,' he said. 'If you don't want to find your father, that's totally up to you.'

She nodded. On the surface she looked pleased. But everything about her seemed weighed down. Grey...

'Okay. Thank you.'

That was when he realised what was wrong. This was the wrong Faith. This was black and white Faith. Where was the warm, vibrant, caring woman he'd been kissing last night? He knew she'd been upset about the window, the treasure trail... He just hadn't realised how much it had rocked her, how heavily she'd invested in it.

'It's more than that, isn't it?' he said.

He and Faith had never lied to each other before. They might have hidden behind their respective walls, but they'd always, *always* been straight with each other.

She looked away and wrapped her arms around her middle. 'I can't stay for Christmas after all, Marcus. I need to go home, to see my family.' She turned and looked him in the eye. 'I'm sorry.'

That was when he realised for the first time in weeks he had no idea what was going on in her head. And he'd seen that look on a woman's face before. Emotionally checked out. That was what it was. He didn't like that at all.

'Then I'll come with you,' he said.

A horrible idea was forming in his head—one that told him if he let her go now she'd never come back.

She hugged herself tighter, moved her weight onto her heels, as if she was going to back away from him. 'I need to do this on my own,' she said, her voice quiet. 'You more than anyone know that I have some issues to sort out back there.'

He nodded. He didn't like it, but he understood it.

'What date are you back?' he asked, testing. 'I'll come and meet you at the airport.'

This time she did step back. 'Not sure. I might have to go straight up to York.' She shrugged one shoulder. 'I'll call you.'

Now she hadn't just blocked him out, she was lying to him. He had two choices—get scared or get angry. He chose the latter.

He stepped towards her. 'Tell me what's going on,' he demanded, knowing his tone had more of a growl than he'd intended it to. Unfortunately it was the tone guaranteed to make Faith McKinnon dig her heels in harder.

That was when she let him have the truth. With both barrels.

Her chin lifted. 'I'm going to the cottage for a few days. I need time to think.'

The rage started to bubble out of control inside him. More lies. He'd been right to get worried. Faith McKinnon was putting on her running shoes.

'You're not her—you're not Evie,' he said, in a low tone full of warning. 'Don't take the coward's way out. All I'm asking is that you trust we have something we can start to build on.'

'Are you calling me a coward?'

'No.' *Yes.*

'Then what are you saying?'

He shook his head, and when he spoke his jaw was tight. He had to force the words out. 'That running away won't solve anything. It doesn't avoid the mess. It just leaves it for someone else to clear up—I think my great-grandmother demonstrated that admirably. Bertie is living proof of her mistake.'

'I'm not running away,' she said, folding her arms again, tighter this time. 'I'm going home. There's a difference.'

Well, if there was one he couldn't see it. And she was slipping away. If he didn't do something drastic in the next few moments she'd always be out of his reach.

'But I love you!'

That definitely hadn't been the tone he'd intended to use the first time he told her that, but he was good and fired up now, and he hadn't been able to help it.

She flinched at the words—actually flinched. That wasn't good.

'It's not enough, is it? I'm not sure anything I offered would be good enough for you. What would be enough to make you stay, Faith?' He really was shouting now. 'And what happens if you never find it? What legacy will you leave behind for your children? If you ever let a man close enough to have any... What is all this running going to teach them about life?'

She walked backwards, shaking her head. 'Don't you pin that on me. You don't know anything about what my life has been like.'

'Faith!' He grabbed for her, but she kept backing away. 'I'm just trying to protect you from making a mistake you're going to regret.'

'The only thing I need protection from right at this moment,' she said coldly, 'is you. And if I am making a mistake then it's mine to make.'

He'd tried to keep the caveman part of himself from taking over, to give the Earl a chance to sort this out in a reasonable manner, but now the Earl had failed the caveman pushed himself to the front and took charge. Marcus stepped forward, crushed Faith to him and kissed her stiff resolve away. He kissed her until she was breathless and panting and malleable in his hands. He would *make* her see sense.

She stepped back, wrapped her arms around her middle again and looked at him, eyes wide, chest rising and falling. 'That doesn't change anything,' she said, quietly and far too reasonably. And then she walked away.

Just like Evie. But she could do it if she wanted to. She *could* stay. His great-grandmother had just lacked the gumption.

But Marcus believed in Faith, believed she was strong enough. Why wouldn't she?

He marched right up to the window and considered putting his fist through all those pretty bits of glass to see them splinter and dance.

He'd been so stupid. After all his warnings to himself he'd been seduced by that feeling of destiny, of being soul mates— yes, even blasted love at first sight! And he'd fallen right back down into that deep pit he'd only just managed to haul himself out of. He'd let himself believe that Faith McKinnon was the woman he'd been waiting for—the woman who would stand by his side, face thick or thin with him.

But she wasn't. She really wasn't.

It made him so angry to see her giving up on herself, giving up on *them,* when he knew she was capable of more.

He followed her and stepped in front of her, making her look at him. 'Then I think it's a good idea that you go,' he said, his voice low and his teeth clenched. 'Because I need a woman who can think beyond her own selfish need for self-protection and who can *give* herself. I want a partner, not a reluctant conscript. And until that changes, you're right—you don't belong here with me.'

Faith's mouth moved and a small croaking sound came out, then she spun around and ran from the chapel, her coat flapping in her self-made breeze.

Faith dragged her last case all the way from the castle to the visitor car park and stuffed it into the trunk of her car. With every lopsided step she could feel him watching her from any one of a hundred mullioned windows, but when she turned round he was never there. When the trunk was closed and her purse was sitting on the passenger seat she pulled the keys from her pocket. They dangled in her hand.

She had one last thing to do before she left Hadsborough. One last goodbye to say.

She took the long route back to the little chapel, avoiding going close to the castle. As she half jogged she kept glancing at the greying sky. There was a tiny patch of blue off in the distance, but she didn't hold out much hope. It looked as if she'd be driving to Whitstable in the rain.

The chapel looked beautiful—finally ready for the Carol Service. Tall wrought-iron stands held thick cream candles, and holly and ivy dripped from the ends of the compact pews, tied in red ribbons. She ignored all of that and headed for the little side window—the one that had started it all.

She hadn't been able to take a proper look earlier. Not while Marcus had been pushing her and criticising her.

A flash of sadness shot through her. She wanted so badly to believe it could all come true, that she could find her happy ending here with him. But this was real life, and real life dealt in disappointment and compromise.

He'd said he loved her.

But he'd also said she wasn't worthy of him, and he was right. She was running. The only reason she'd decided to go home for Christmas was because it was less scary than trying to stay here and work it out with Marcus.

She let out a hollow laugh. Finally she'd run so far and so

long the only place she had to go back to was home. There was a sense of ironic justice in that, she guessed. But run she would. Because she didn't think she could stay here with that familiar creeping feeling that something was out of place still dogging her. Especially when that 'something' usually turned out to be her.

She shook her head. *Save the pity party for later, Faith. When you've got a glass of wine and a hot bath to console you.* She was here to look at the window, not to pick over the ruins of a dream she never should have let take root.

So she looked at the window. It really was beautiful. As she stared at the dull picture suddenly a beam of sunlight hit the outside of the glass. Faith gasped. At once the colours became bright and saturated, almost living.

The window was nothing without light. She stood there, motionless, until the wind pushed the clouds on further and everything fell dark again.

'Thank you,' she whispered to whoever was listening. At least she had that to take away with her.

CHAPTER TWELVE

FAITH sat on the end of the double bed in the ten-feet-by-ten-feet bedroom of the tiny cottage on Whitstable's seafront, staring out of the window at an angry sea. Ironically, the whole cottage had been decorated in 'New England' style, with white and blue painted wood and deep red and navy chequered pillows and curtains everywhere.

Still staring at the waves as they crashed over the beach, ripping the pebbles backwards and then hurling them onto the shore again, she reached for her cellphone and punched in the only speed dial number, then waited for the person at the other end to pick up.

'Hi, Gram.'

She heard a gasp of surprise and delight on the other end of the line. 'Hey, honey. Good to hear your voice again.'

She fidgeted and smoothed the comforter underneath her rear end. 'I'm coming home, Gram. It was only the window job that was holding me up and…well, I've finished that now.'

'Oh, Faith! That's wonderful!'

She knew she'd feel like an outsider back in Beckett's Run, but at least she knew how to handle it there; she'd been dealing with it most of her adult life.

She took a breath and revved up to ask the question she'd been dreading to ask since their last chat. 'Will Greg…Dad… definitely be coming to Christmas dinner?'

'Yes, sweetie. He's really looking forward to seeing you.'

'Oh…good,' she replied, aware she sounded less than enthused.

Gram took a breath, and Faith knew some of her grandmother's home truths were on their way. They were as famous as her chocolate cookies with powdered sugar, but being on the receiving end of them was nowhere near as pleasant.

'I know you've found it tough with him,' Gram said, and the warmth in her tone made Faith want to cry. 'It almost killed him when he found out he wasn't your biological father. I know he didn't handle it very well at first.'

You think? she was tempted to say. When an eight-year-old can tell you don't want to look at her, you're not handling it very well.

'But it was only because he loved you so much,' Gram continued. 'He did the best he could. And when he got to grips with it he really tried, but he said you were always so distant, locked away inside yourself. Many years later he told me he wondered if you'd found out, and that you didn't want him to be your dad any more.'

Tears slid down Faith's cheeks. She'd have given anything to have felt the same confidence and comfortableness with him that Hope and Grace seemed to have. She hadn't realised he'd felt it, too, though—the distance. And if what Gram had said was right, maybe the gulf between them all these years hadn't been just his doing.

Her grandmother must have sensed she was having trouble choking a word or two out, because she abruptly changed the subject. 'How's Bertie?'

Faith found herself smiling through her tears. She reached for a tissue from the box on the nightstand and dried her eyes. 'He's an old charmer—but I guess you knew that about him already.'

Gram let out a chuckle that verged on the girlish. 'Yes, I did once. It's nice to know he hasn't changed.'

Faith screwed the tissue up and aimed it at the bin near the dressing table. She missed. 'I got the impression he was in love with you once.' She got up, retrieved the wad of tissue from the floor and dropped it in its rightful home. 'If he'd asked you to marry him would you have said yes?'

'Oh, he did ask,' Gram said, sounding for all the world as if he'd merely asked her to go down to the store for a quart of milk. 'I turned him down.'

Faith's mouth hung open. She'd always assumed that Bertie hadn't asked because Gram wouldn't have been 'suitable'.

'Why?' she said, so quietly it was almost a whisper. 'Because you knew it wouldn't work? That you wouldn't fit into his life?'

Gram sighed. 'Because he was a wandering soul, honey. He was always restless, and I knew that was never going to change. I wanted roots and a family and a home—that's why it wouldn't have worked. Not because of who we were or where we came from.'

'But that *would* have been a problem if you'd wanted to, right?'

'Maybe. I don't know.' Another sigh. 'I worry about the same thing for you.'

Faith swallowed. Gram was the most sensible person she knew, and if Gram could see problems with a romance between a girl from small-town Connecticut and a man who would be a duke one day she was probably right.

'It's okay,' she said. 'I'm not thinking about marrying the grandson.'

Not any more.

Gram chuckled. 'I'd be delighted if I thought some nice young man was going to propose, but I meant that you remind me of Bertie in other ways—you've got those same restless feet.'

Faith frowned. That was nonsense, as Bertie would say.

All she'd ever wanted was to find somewhere she could unpack for good and finally belong.

'Well, just be glad those restless feet are bringing me home for the holidays,' she said, with more levity than she felt.

'I am, honey. I am.' There was that tone again, warm like maple syrup. Faith reached for another tissue from the box, just in case.

'Listen,' Gram said, 'this call must be costing you a fortune. Let's save the rest of the catching up for when we're face to face.'

'Sure.' Faith breathed in deep. 'Love you, Gram.'

'Love you, too, honey.'

And then she was gone. Faith discovered her reach for the tissues had been somewhat prophetic.

The front door to the little white cottage was painted a summery sky-blue. It seemed artificially bright in this pretty but deserted off-season seaside town only a few days before Christmas. Marcus bunched his fist and rapped on the matt paint. He and Faith McKinnon had unfinished business, and he wasn't letting her run away until they faced it.

A few moments later he heard footsteps in the hallway, and then the door cracked open. By the look on Faith's face she was considering slamming it closed again. He opened out his hand and applied gentle pressure to the wood.

'We need to talk before you go,' he said.

Indecision swirled in her eyes.

He didn't push the door. 'And I've got something for you—a Christmas present,' he added, lifting up the large paper bag that was weighing down his left arm.

She nodded and let the door swing open, but she retreated down the hallway and into a small living room before he got too close. He followed, leaving his left arm behind him so not to bang the bag on the walls of the narrow passageway.

She stood by the window of the tiny living room and folded

her arms. He stayed by the door and gently lowered the bag to the floor. He cleared his throat. 'There were things we both said that we shouldn't have, and things we probably didn't say that we should.'

She nodded again. It didn't mean she'd dropped those mile-high barriers an inch, though.

'I was angry,' he said, 'because I think we have something unique, and I don't want us to throw it away without giving it a chance.'

Her arms squeezed tighter around her midriff. 'I am giving it a chance.'

He took a shallow breath. No, she wasn't. She wasn't going to let her drawbridge down an inch, was she? Well, he might as well carry on saying what he'd come here to say.

'I want you to know that I heard what you said—about you and about Bertie. No more pushing.'

A faint smile flickered at the corners of her lips. 'You can't help it, Marcus. But the way you look out for those you care about is what I lo—' She broke off and looked away. 'What I admire most about you. Don't change on my account.'

'I have changed. But *because* of you, not for you.'

And then, because she didn't respond, and because there was no point in having a one-sided conversation with a brick wall, he picked up the paper bag and offered it to her. 'Merry Christmas.'

She frowned slightly, but she accepted it from him. The present inside wasn't gift-wrapped, so she spotted what it was as soon as she looked down. Her mouth fell open.

'You're giving me Basil?'

Yep. It had been staring at him when he'd gone back to Faith's empty studio. He'd decided it needed a good home.

She put the bag down and carefully lifted the creature out, now with a big red bow tied round his neck, and placed him on the sofa. Basil stared warily at his new surroundings with his orange glass eyes. Marcus decided that if he'd been able to talk he'd have probably asked to go back inside his filing cabinet.

Faith shrugged, her hands flapping as she searched for something to say.

'Nothing says *I love you* like a stuffed badger,' she finally managed, and he saw her regret at her choice of words even before she uttered the last syllable.

'Quite.'

She raised a hand to her eyes and rubbed them. 'Don't make me cry, Marcus. I've done enough of that already.'

'Then don't cry,' he said softly, stepping towards her and holding out his hand. 'Say goodbye.'

Goodbye. It sounded so final. And she knew it, too. She didn't say anything about *au revoir,* or it being just for now. At least she'd stopped lying to him.

She looked at his open palm with a similar expression to the badger's, but she eventually relented and slid her smaller, paler hand into his.

There it was again. That feeling. The sense that something deep in the core of him resonated with her. She blinked but didn't look away. Neither of them moved.

Marcus realised he didn't want to let go, didn't want to spend the rest of his life wondering if he'd ever find this again with someone else. But after a few breathless moments he released her fingers. He wasn't going to chase her if she ran.

He prepared himself for what he'd really come to say—properly this time.

'I love you,' he said, and waited for a response.

He thought it would feel as if his skin was being flayed off, to hear those words come out of his mouth and receive no echo, but instead a weight lifted from him. It was liberating.

Her eyes filled with tears and her lip wobbled. And then she did say it back. Not with her mouth, but with her eyes, still refusing to pull down those walls.

He lifted his chin. 'I said you didn't know how to give yourself. I was wrong.'

He saw it in her face, the moment she relived the other things he'd shouted after her.

You don't belong...

He stepped forward and saw the panic in her eyes. The pure fear. It confirmed his worst suspicions.

'That wasn't true either,' he added, picking up on her silent communication. 'I think you belong at Hadsborough with me, but...' He paused, prepared himself to deliver the truth he could no longer protect her from. 'But until you *let* yourself belong somewhere you never will. And no amount of chasing after you will change that,' he said. 'So if you want to go...go. I'm not going to stop you.'

He clenched his jaw. Even though he understood it, it still made him angry. She was wasting so much.

'I want to,' she said, her voice wavering. 'I really do.'

There was such pain in her eyes that he truly believed her, and seeing it there made him want to pull her to him and wrap his arms around her. Instead he clenched his fists and held them rigid by his sides. It was either that or start yelling again, which probably would make her bolt all the faster. He'd promised himself he'd end it properly this time—leave with some dignity, not behave like some raving Neanderthal.

Even if she tried she'd fail. Because until she was truly ready she'd always end up running out on him. And that would just set the cycle of rejection spinning again. Faith McKinnon was the only one who could stop it, and he had to accept that she didn't know how. Not yet.

He couldn't resist one last parting shot, though.

'I've one last thing to say. You were right—Evie didn't know the truth when she ran from Hadsborough. But *you* know. Deep down, you know. And you're still running.'

And then he was walking back down the hall and out of the cottage. As he passed the window he glanced in and saw

Faith standing there, the moth-eaten badger clutched to her chest, plinth and all, with tears streaming down her face.

Basil was now sitting on top of the bookcase in the tiny cottage's living room. Faith spent most of that evening staring at him and sipping red wine. The television remained unplugged and her paperback book remained unopened. The badger stared back at her, no help at all.

She turned the events of the past few weeks over and over in her mind—much in the way the endless surf captured and rolled the pebbles on the shore outside her window. She thought about another window, about the stupid romantic trail that never was, and about Evangeline Groggins—her maiden name—florist's daughter and runaway mother.

Had Evie been a coward?

Was *she?*

Had she identified too strongly with Bertie's mother, as Marcus had suggested? It had been so easy to understand why she had left, how she must have had her fill of trying to fit in, always feeling out of place, always feeling like an unwanted reminder. Who wouldn't crumble under that sort of pressure?

Marcus, she thought, as she took another long sip of her wine. Marcus wouldn't crumble. He wouldn't give up. He just wasn't made that way.

But she was. She was a coward. Too scared to stay and fight for the man she loved. Even when he'd given her a second chance she'd just stood there, frozen to the spot, too much of a jellyfish to think, let alone speak.

But Evie hadn't got off lightly. She'd paid a high price for her freedom. Bertie had, too. Marcus had been right about that as well, damn him. And she suspected he'd hit the nail on the head when he'd told her running away didn't solve anything—that you just left others to foot the bill for you. Had she done that to her family? Had she hurt them in ways she hadn't even realised?

She thought of Gram, of her sweet lilac letters and how she ached for her girls to come home...

Yes. The Earl had been right about that, too.

And about what Gram had said about her being a wandering soul? Well, she could see now that she had taken as much as she could from her family, and then had just...checked out. For so long she'd tried to play peacemaker, felt the responsibility for keeping them all together, but once she'd found out the truth she'd shut down, and she'd never really woken up again.

She put her wine glass down. 'Oh, Basil,' she said, standing up and moving over to place a hand on his rough, patchy fur. 'I've been such a fool.'

How could anyone get close if she was keeping them at arm's length? And how could they include her if she walled herself up in her own little tower like Rapunzel and refused to come down?

She'd made herself an outsider, hadn't she?

She grabbed the wine bottle and sloshed some more Merlot into her glass, because the thoughts that followed really had her shaking.

There was only so much time a woman and a badger could spend cooped up together in a tiny little fake New England cottage without one of them going stark staring mad. Faith suspected the badger might be doing the better job of staying sane and so, despite the driving wind that lifted her hair by its roots and made it dance, she ventured out into the cold winter morning.

It was a Sunday, but plenty of cute little coffee shops and art galleries and nice little boutiques were open. She didn't stop at any of them, but when she passed a little florist's shop she paused at the window. It wasn't even a trendy one, with big bouquets in bulbs of cellophane keeping the flowers hydrated. It was the sort of shop you'd go to get your elderly aunt a pot plant, but a little white ceramic planter in the window drew her attention.

She stared at it for a second, then stepped inside the shop and looked around. 'Excuse me,' she said to the woman behind the counter. 'What is that plant in the window? The little shrub with the yellow flowers.'

The woman looked skyward for a second. *'Hypericum calycinum,'* she said, with the air of a woman who knew what she was talking about. 'One of the plants also known as the Rose of Sharon. Pretty, isn't it? Make a nice Christmas present,' she added hopefully.

'I'll take it,' Faith said, surprising herself. There was no way she could take it home on the plane—especially as she already had an unwieldy badger-shaped bit of hand luggage to deal with.

The woman fetched the plant. 'A hundred years ago someone who planted this in their garden would have known what it meant,' she said as she put it in a thin blue-and-white-striped carrier bag.

Faith got the idea the shop had been quiet for days and its owner was in desperate need of someone to chat to. 'What *does* it mean?' she asked almost absently as she rummaged for some cash.

'Love never fails,' the woman said, sighing. 'It's sad no one understands the language of flowers any more... Some of these *avant-garde* things that florist up the high street does! She has no idea of all the horrible things she's wishing her customers.'

Faith stood open-mouthed, staring at the plastic bag. She felt as if she'd been slapped upside the head with her grandmother's iron skillet.

A florist.

Evie Groggins had been a *florist's* daughter!

* * *

Once again a stranger was sitting nervously in the corner of the sofa in the yellow drawing room. The middle-aged woman was squeezing her handbag ever so tightly, Marcus thought. She looked as if she might jump like a frightened rabbit if either he or his grandfather even breathed hard.

'It's very kind of you to come, Donna,' Bertie said, smiling as he stirred his cup of tea.

Donna nodded, but her eyes were wide. 'I can't get over it,' she mumbled. 'The likes of you and me being related... I always knew Granny was a bit of a lady, but...' She shook her head again. 'I can't get over it,' she repeated faintly.

'And you're a florist?' Marcus asked, trying to draw her out, to make her feel more comfortable.

'That's right. Third generation. I run the shop that Granny and Grandpa started before the war—' She looked nervously at Bertie, then back at Marcus. 'Sorry... I didn't mean to mention him.' She squeezed the handbag harder.

'That's quite all right, my dear,' his grandfather said. 'I'm just glad to know a little bit about what happened to her.'

Donna looked up and smiled. 'She was a nice lady. Gentle...quiet... She had a lovely way about her—like you do, if you don't mind me saying, sir.'

'Was she happy?' his grandfather said, doing a good job of hiding his pain behind his smile.

'I think so.' Donna looked across at Marcus. 'At least she didn't seem *un*happy.' She stopped abruptly, as if a thought had just popped into her head. 'Except at Christmas,' she said, smiling faintly. 'Which is odd, isn't it? Because that's normally a happy time.'

'How so?'

She pulled a face. 'It's nothing, really. Something silly... It's just that every Christmas morning, when everyone was laughing and shouting and opening presents, she'd put on her hat and coat and go for a walk—no matter what the weather. She'd be gone for a few hours and then she'd come back again, smile, say she was ready now and then she'd cook the Christmas dinner. Did it every year like clockwork.'

Bertie's tea cup rattled on its saucer and Marcus raced forward to take it out of his hand.

'Oh, dear!' Donna said, standing up so quickly she almost knocked her own cup over. 'I haven't said something out of turn, have I?'

Bertie shook his head. 'No, my dear. Quite the opposite, in fact.'

Marcus picked up Donna's tea, handed it to her and motioned for her to sit down again. 'Christmas Day was my grandfather's birthday, you see…'

'Anyway,' Bertie said, and placed his hands on the arms of his chair to push himself to standing, 'no matter, my dear. Now…let's go and take a look at this window that started all the fuss…'

All three of them were standing in front of the window, admiring it, when there was a crash at the other end of the chapel. Marcus turned to see something come flying through the door.

It took him a second to realise that something was Faith.

She waved a couple of crumpled sheets of paper at them as she kept running towards them. They looked like something that had been printed out from the internet and then chewed up and spat out by a dog.

'The window! It's been there all along!' she said breathlessly. 'The message has been there all along—right under our noses!' She was standing in front of them now, and she paused to rest her hands on her knees, hunched over, and dragged in some much-needed oxygen. 'Flowers…' she said weakly. 'The language of flowers…'

Donna turned to look at the stained glass again. 'Oh, yes! I can see what you mean! There's ivy and daisies, lemon blossom and lavender…even roses…'

Faith stood up so fast Marcus guessed she was seeing stars. 'You mean you know about this stuff?'

Bertie, who was looking far from displeased at Faith's sudden and unscheduled interruption, smiled at her. 'Faith, I'd like to introduce you to my niece—well, my half-niece— Donna.'

Faith's eyes grew wide. She reached forward and shook the other woman's hand. 'Lovely to meet you.' She waved the sheets of paper again. 'There was only so much I could find on the web, and I wasn't sure what some of them were...'

Donna was touching some of the flowers lower down on the window, frowning.

'Do you know what they all mean?' Faith asked. 'Would the words fit together to form a sentence or a phrase?'

The other woman smiled softly at her. 'Much simpler than that. Some of these flowers represent the same things.' She looked at Bertie. 'Did you say your father made this for Granny?'

His grandfather nodded.

Donna's smiled warmed further. 'She would have liked this if she'd seen it.'

'What does it all mean?' Bertie asked.

Donna turned back to the window. 'Well, the roses symbolise love, with each colour and type meaning something slightly different. The daisies and lemon blossom mean fidelity and loyal love, and the others...they all have meanings to do with ardent devotion and marriage. Oh, how odd...' Donna tipped her head on one side. 'That woman in the middle of them...she looks like photos of Granny when she was younger.'

That made the other three stop and stare at the window again.

Faith couldn't stop looking at Marcus all the way through high tea, while Donna and Bertie chatted away like old friends in the background. It wasn't that he looked any different, just that she felt different—just like the window. Now she was looking at him in the right way she could suddenly see all the things she'd been blind to.

She desperately wanted to find some time to be alone with him, to tell him Rapunzel had finally hired a bulldozer and done some much-needed demolition work. But after tea it was time for the Carol Service, and everybody wanted to talk to Bertie and Marcus about the chapel, about how perfect it looked and how excited they were it was going to be used again.

Faith stood beside Marcus, singing softly in the candle-light. All around her songs of hope and faith and love swirled in the air, and she started to understand just how intricately those three things were connected—just how they fed and supported each other—and she saw how poor she'd been in each until she'd met Marcus.

Heart pounding, she looked at his hand down by his side. It seemed to be waiting for something. Missing something. Slowly, keeping her breath in her throat, she slid her fingers into his. They fitted perfectly.

He started a little, but he caught her hand and held it firmly before she could react and pull away again. It felt so good it was all she could do to stop the tears sliding down her face. Finally that thing inside her that had always fluttered around like a trapped bird, making her restless, came to rest.

He didn't let go after the service. He kept her hand in his even though she knew she could have pulled away if she'd wanted to. People came up to congratulate him on resurrecting the old tradition, to tell him what a great time they'd had at the ball, and he smiled and chatted, all the time still holding her hand. She suspected he didn't want to let go in case she disappeared again.

Eventually the last person went out through the door and they were alone in the candlelit space.

She turned towards him and wound her other hand into his free one, tugged downwards to pull him towards her. He obliged, but stopped just short of kissing her, his lips hovering millimetres above hers. She closed her eyes and bridged the gap, softly exploring. In some ways it was like kissing him for the first time.

Even though she'd felt his skin beneath her fingers before, felt the touch of his lips on hers, part of her had been guilty of seeing him like a figure in her storybook—or in the windows she repaired. A noble knight or a prince. Beautiful, but not real. Not something she could have or hold. Or keep.

Marcus groaned and drew her close to him, kissed her both deeply and tenderly. This time she saw everything she'd missed before—the evidence of things she'd been too scared to hope for.

She pulled away and smiled at him. 'I'm sorry,' she said.

He just smiled back, making her knees feel like half-melted chocolate.

'You were right. I was running away. I was being a coward.'

He shook his head. 'I pushed too hard. I made you run.'

She wished she could let him take the blame, but she couldn't. 'No,' she said, looking into his eyes with frankness, making sure every last barrier had been smashed to the floor. 'You might have been right about the other stuff, but I said it was my choice, my mistake, and I was right about that.'

Marcus let out a soft little laugh. 'Okay. No arguing about that one.' He dipped his head and kissed her again. 'What matters is that you're back.'

'And I'm staying,' she added. 'If that's okay with you?'

Marcus growled, then kissed her soundly. She could have sworn she'd heard him mutter 'impossible woman' at some point.

'Oh…but I still need to go home for the holidays,' she said.

'I have things I need to say—to my sisters and to my mother…
to my dad. Especially to my grandmother!'

He nodded. 'Of course you do,' he said. 'And I know it's
not going to be an easy visit. That's why I'm coming with
you—no arguments.' He reached for her hand. 'You don't
have to do this on your own, Faith. Let *me* be the outsider
for once.'

'I love you!' The words burst out of her before she could
even think about stopping herself, but then she realised she
didn't want to. 'Don't ever stop believing in me—even when
I'm stupid enough to stop believing in myself.'

Marcus smiled that wolf-like smile of his before setting
her down and stepping back. He gave her a look that sent a
million volts charging through her, before dipping one hand
in his pocket and pulling it out again. Faith couldn't see what
he was holding. It was too dark in the candlelit chapel, and
his fingers almost covered the small object.

It was only when he brought it up right in front of her face
that she realised it was a box, and only when he eased it open
and she saw a flash of candlelight reflected in its contents
that she guessed its contents.

'That's…that's a…ring,' she stammered.

'I know,' Marcus said. 'Straight to the point, as always.
That's my Faith.'

He took the ring from the box and held it out to her. It was
stunning. An antique, she guessed. Art Deco, with a large
square cut diamond.

'It's beautiful,' she said.

He blinked slowly. 'It was my grandmother's. I thought
about giving you Evie's ring, but it has too much of a sad
past. I wanted something connected with a lifetime of happy
memories.'

She looked at the ring in its cushion. 'Marcus, I can't take
this! It's a family heirloom! Some day somebody in your family might need to give it to the woman they want to marry.'

He stared at her, his eyebrows raised and an off-centre smile twisting one side of his mouth.

Oh.

Oh!

He just had.

The next day Faith woke in her turret room again. The light was so bright that she wondered if they'd another significant snowfall, but then she looked at the clock and realised it was halfway through the morning. She leapt out of bed and started getting dressed in so much of a flurry that she put her panties on the wrong way round. Twice.

Her flight was in less than two hours. They were never going to get to the airport in time!

Not bothering with socks and shoes, she bolted out of her room and ran down the large stone staircase, looking for someone. Anyone.

She found Bertie, sitting as usual in his armchair in the yellow drawing room.

'Plane!' she said breathlessly. 'Airport...'

'Do sit down, my dear,' he said, hardly looking up from his paper. 'Don't worry. Marcus has got it all under control.'

Faith did nothing of the sort. 'But—'

'And congratulations. I'm very much looking forward to having you as part of the family.'

That stopped her in her tracks. She looked down at the diamond on her left hand. In her panic she'd almost forgotten. She made herself take a deep breath before leaning over and kissing her soon-to-be grandfather-in-law on the cheek, smiling.

'Thank you,' she said, glancing out of the window. 'But about the plane...'

Bertie waved her away. 'Just go and finish getting dressed. Marcus will be back soon. And tell that boy I want a few great-grandchildren before I pop my clogs.'

She made herself take a deep breath before leaning over and kissing Bertie again.

'You're a meddling old man,' she said, smiling at him, 'and if I didn't know any better I'd think you and Gram had cooked this whole thing up together.'

That stopped her in her tracks. They *hadn't,* had they…?

But before she could interrogate him further Bertie flicked his newspaper, making it stand up straight.

'Didn't you say something about catching a plane?' he said, smiling like a cat. 'You might want to go and finish getting dressed.'

The plane! Gram was going to kill her if she didn't make it home for Christmas.

She ran back up to her turret bedroom and got herself packed as fast as she could. When she had just put her toothbrush back in her overnight bag the door opened.

'Ready?' Marcus said, but he didn't let her pick up her bag or leave the room. Instead he crossed the room and kissed her thoroughly.

Faith didn't resist at first, but then she started softly nudging his arm.

'What?' he said, as he bent to kiss one eyelid and then the other.

'We haven't got time for this!' she said. 'We've got to go. As it is I might miss the flight, and any chances of getting a standby at Christmas are practically non-existent!'

Marcus said as he reluctantly set her free, 'You mean *we* might miss the flight. I booked a ticket last night. I meant what I said about coming with you. Besides, I need to talk to your father about something while I'm there.'

And then he led an open-mouthed Faith out through the castle and onto the large oval lawn. Faith gasped when she saw what was sitting there.

'A helicopter?' she said, hardly able to take her eyes off the sleek machine.

'Quickest way to get to the airport,' he said, smiling.

When she got closer, she could see their luggage inside, and sitting on top of it all was Basil the badger, still with his red bow tied snugly around his neck. He looked ready for an adventure. Could stuffed badgers actually smile?

Faith reached over to stroke his head as she climbed inside and clipped herself into her seat. Then the blades began to whirr and the machine lifted itself straight up into the air, sending tiny ripples in every direction on the moat. She reached for Marcus's hand as the helicopter climbed higher in the air, banking slightly as it circled over the top of the lake and both islands, preparing to head off in the direction of the airport.

Faith looked down through the large window and her heart stalled. The castle looked even more beautiful from up here, with the turrets and chimneys reaching for them, the bright grass peeping from beneath the patchy snow. She felt a twinge of sadness at leaving it behind, even for a week or two.

Marcus leaned over and kissed her cheek, whispered in her ear. 'It won't be long before we're back,' he said.

She smiled at him, glad he was able to read her mind still.

'Good,' she said. 'Because I'm going to be looking forward to coming home. With you.'

She stopped smiling while she concentrated on the stinging at the backs of her eyes. She was *not* going to miss this wonderful view by spoiling it with tears. And she didn't mean the castle and lake below—she meant the wonderful man sitting next to her.

She leaned in and kissed him, not caring what the pilot thought.

He was hers, wasn't he? She just hadn't understood that, hadn't ever thought of it that way round. It wasn't just about her belonging to someone for it all to work, it had to be reciprocal.

'You're mine, Marcus Huntington,' she shouted at him over the noise of the blades. 'You belong to me now.'

He shook his head, took her hand, kissed it and looked deep into her eyes. 'No,' he mouthed, smiling. 'We belong to each other.'

* * * * *

Sleigh Ride
with the Rancher

Donna
ALWARD

A busy wife and mother of three (two daughters and the family dog), **Donna Alward** believes hers is the best job in the world: a combination of stay-at-home mum and romance novelist. An avid reader since childhood, Donna always made up her own stories. She completed her Arts Degree in English Literature in 1994, but it wasn't until 2001 that she penned her first full-length novel and found herself hooked on writing romance. In 2006 she sold her first manuscript and now writes warm, emotional stories for Mills & Boon®'s Cherish™ line.

In her new home office in Nova Scotia, Donna loves being back on the east coast of Canada after nearly twelve years in Alberta, where her career began, writing about cowboys and the west. Donna's debut romance, *Hired by the Cowboy*, was awarded the Booksellers Best Award in 2008 for Best Traditional Romance.

With the Atlantic Ocean only minutes from her doorstep, Donna has found a fresh take on life and promises even more great romances in the near future!

Donna loves to hear from readers. You can contact her through her website at www.donnaalward.com, her page at www.myspace.com/dalward, or through her publisher.

CHAPTER ONE

THE cold air penetrated clear through Hope McKinnon's jacket as she stepped out of the rented car and looked up at the home base of the Bighorn Therapeutic Riding Facility. It was December in Alberta yet it felt like the arctic! It was a shock to her system after she'd reluctantly left the hot brilliance of the Sydney sun only hours before.

She huddled into her woolen coat and popped the trunk for her bag. The wheels of her suitcase squeaked and dragged on the snow covering the path to the wrap-around porch of the big log home. Coming up the long lane, she'd thought it had a fairy-tale quality, like a romantic ski chalet nestled in the mountains. Twinkling fairy lights were intertwined through evergreen boughs on the railing, glowing softly in the waning light of late afternoon.

But that had been in the warm car, with the heater going full blast. Now she shivered. The house was rapidly losing its winter magic as she gave the case a tug over a ridge of packed-down snow. She heaved it up the stairs one at a time, growing more and more irritated until she plunked it down beside her leg and rang the doorbell.

Three times.

She huddled into her jacket as she waited.

By this time her legs were cold and her feet were beginning to go numb in the soft leather boots she wore. She looked around and saw a truck parked next to the barn. She was supposed to meet a man named Blake Nelson, the guy who ran the ranch. She'd been guilt-tripped by her grandmother into coming and taking pictures of his operation, and she wasn't all that pleased about it. She could think of a million other places she'd rather be in December than in the icy cold of Alberta.

But she was here, and she was freezing, so she left her suitcase by the door and made her way across the yard toward the barn. A light glowed from a window within, a warm beacon against the grayness of the afternoon shadows. It would be warm inside, wouldn't it? She quickened her step as she neared the door.

The next thing she knew she was slightly airborne as her boot hit a piece of ice camouflaged by a skiff of snow. The weightless sensation lasted only a second and was immediately followed by a bone-jarring, breath-stealing thump as she landed squarely on her rump.

"Ow!" she cried out as her tailbone struck frozen ground. She fought for a few moments as her emptied lungs struggled for air, and then gasped it in painfully, closing her eyes.

When she opened them she was looking at a pair of worn leather cowboy boots that disappeared into two very long, denim-clad legs. Humiliation burned up her neck and into her cheeks as she forgot the pain in her bottom. What a way to make a first impression!

"You must be Hope," said a warm, deep voice with just the barest hint of a drawl. "Let me give you a hand up."

The rich voice sent shivers down her spine and she struggled to keep her breath even. She looked up then, and couldn't help the gasp that escaped her lips. This Blake guy—assuming it was him—was stunning. Incredibly tall, and the form he cut was that of the quintessential cowboy, complete with sheepskin jacket and a dark brown cowboy hat to match. His breath made white puffs in the wintry air.

Her photographer's eye was already framing him as if she were behind the lens, capturing him like a great Western icon.

"Did you hit your head or something?" He still held out his hand and she realized she'd been staring at him like he was the eighth wonder of the world.

"Sorry," she said, holding up her hand and grasping his wrist. He gave a quick tug and she was on her feet again. She hid her flaming face by twisting and brushing the snow off her pants and the tails of her jacket. She didn't stand much hope of dignity now. She might as well make the best of it.

"You have to watch out for the odd bit of ice in the yard," he cautioned. "Those boots don't look like they have much tread. I hope you brought something heavier."

She tried to ignore the humiliation that seemed to burn her cheeks at his chastising tone, making her feel foolish and about five years old. She lifted her eyes and tilted her head to look up, studying his profile as he turned to inspect her heeled boots.

The looking up was a rarity. At five-foot-ten, and with a modest two-inch heel, she stood an even six feet. And she still had to look up at Blake Nelson. He had to be at least six-four, six-five. Most of the time she felt like an ungainly giant, but next to his strong build she felt positively feminine. Or she would, except she could still feel the bump on her butt, reminding her of her grand entrance. Perfect.

He turned his head slightly so he faced her squarely, and the part of his face which had been shadowed by his hat was now clearly visible. Her heart seemed to drop to her toes, and a small cry escaped her lips before she could stop it.

For the space of several heartbeats she was back in the hospital again, trying terribly hard to look at her best friend Julie in the face as the bandages came off. To smile when she felt like weeping; to tell Julie it wasn't that bad when in truth the raw shock and ugliness of her friend's injuries had made her sick to her stomach. The same queasiness threatened now and she gulped in air, needing to steady herself. This cowboy wasn't so perfect, after all. A long scar ran from his right temple clear to his jaw—pink, ugly, and puckered.

"Are you sure you're okay? You've gone quite pale."

The words were polite but Hope was aware enough to realize how very cold they were. He knew exactly what had happened. She'd taken one look at the mess that was his right cheek and she'd been repulsed. What he didn't understand was why and she was too fragile right now to explain it. The last thing she wanted to do was break down in front of a stranger.

There wasn't a day went by that Hope didn't see Julie's smiling face in her mind and feel the hole that her death had left behind. Julie had been the most beautiful girl Hope had ever known—beautiful inside and out. It had been six months since her funeral, but Hope couldn't get the image of Julie's ravaged body out of her head. It had all been so unfair, especially since Julie had been the one person Hope had let herself get close to in all these years. Julie had understood about Hope's family, about her dysfunction and frustration and the futility of hoping that someday it would all work out.

And then Julie, like everyone else in Hope's life, had abandoned her. Not by choice. Hope knew that. But when she was alone in the apartment they'd shared, when there was no one to text during a slow workday, or catch a drink with on an outdoor patio, it felt like the same thing.

Hope fought for control and shut the feelings down before they overwhelmed her completely. She had to keep focus.

"I'm Hope," she announced, trying desperately to sound normal. It shouldn't matter that he'd been injured and left disfigured. Except that it really did. It smashed into the concrete wall she'd put around her feelings with all the subtlety of a wrecking ball, reminding her of everything she'd rather forget.

"Blake," he replied, but the coolness remained in his tone. "And I'm guessing you're pretty cold right about now. Let's get you up to the house."

As they walked back to the house she was constantly aware of his hand by her elbow, waiting to catch her if she slipped again. It was courteous, considering their shaky start, but unsettling, too. He opened the door—unlocked, making her feel foolish once again—and held it for her to enter before grabbing her suitcase as if it weighed nothing at all and bringing it inside.

She almost wept in relief at the blast of heat that greeted her, and forgot about all her reservations at staying in a private home. She could think about that later. Right now she would focus on warming up and that was all that mattered.

He started up the stairs with her case. "I've got your room ready. I put you on the west side of the house. I thought you'd like that. It's got a view of the mountains, and the early-morning sun won't bother you. Not that it rises that early this time of year."

He was being terribly polite, and Hope was beginning to feel doubly guilty about her obvious reaction to his face, half wanting to explain and half wanting just to forget all about it and start over.

"Thanks," she said, injecting as much warmth as she could into the word. "I'm pretty jet-lagged. I'm lucky I know which end is up."

He stopped in front of a door and opened it, but his closed expression told her he hadn't exactly thawed toward her yet. "You can always nap for a while if you want," he offered. "I've got chores to finish up in the barn."

He was getting away from her as fast as he could, she realized, her heart sinking. So much for starting over.

She considered taking a nap, but she knew it would probably be better if she stayed up awhile longer and tried to go to bed later, so she didn't end up being as nocturnal as a koala.

"I think I'll wait a while, try to adjust."

She stepped into the bedroom and momentarily reconsidered. The rustic cabin-style decor in what she'd seen of the house was repeated in this room, with knotty pine paneling climbing the steeply pitched walls. Along the center of the outside wall, lined up with the peak of the pitch, was a heavy wooden bed that looked like it had been hewn from logs. It was covered in a gorgeous raspberry-and-cream quilt with several fluffy pillows on the top.

While definitely not her personal decorating taste, Hope found the room surprisingly cozy and welcoming. She could hardly wait to sink into the softness of the mattress, snuggle beneath that quilt with her head cushioned on the pillows. A stone gas fireplace was tucked in one corner. Hope almost swooned with pleasure. All it would take was a flick of a switch and she'd have toasty flames to heat up the room.

Blake put down her suitcase as she went to the window and looked out. For miles the white foothills rolled, leading to the gray hulking shapes of the Rockies—so large that they appeared closer than she suspected they actually were. In all her travels around the world as a photographer she'd never been here, and she suspected that on a clear, crisp day the white-capped peaks were stunning.

She turned and chafed her hands together. "Thanks. Mr. Nelson…"

"Just Blake," he corrected, straightening. "I'm not so much into formality around here."

"Blake," she continued, unsure how she felt about him calling her Hope instead of Ms. McKinnon for the duration of her visit. The last thing she needed was anyone getting overly personal. She preferred to keep her distance, after all. "Doesn't this feel weird to you? A stranger in your home?"

He looked taken aback by her question. "You city people," he said. "It's not like that around here. Consider it Western hospitality."

The words should have been friendly, but to Hope they still held the stiff veneer of politeness. Great. So he was as awkward about her being here as she was. She should have stood her ground and told Gram no. But she'd never been able to say no to Gram…

Hope considered telling him she hadn't always been a city girl. She'd spent lots of time climbing trees and swimming and picking wildflowers. Getting grass stains and skinned knees from falling off her bike, and in a town where you could knock on anyone's door for a quick glass of water or a Band-Aid to heal a scrape. The memories caused a pang inside. They hadn't been ideal yesterdays but they weren't all bad, especially all the times spent in Beckett's Run with Gram. That town was about as far from a big city as you could get.

She looked up at him, smiled politely, and kept her mouth shut.

He shrugged. "After what Mary said on the phone, there's no trouble with you staying here. Really."

Hope's brow furrowed. What did Blake mean? The only reason she was here was to take pictures, right? She replayed her conversation with Gram in her head. *Pictures and...*

Something uncomfortable wound its way through Hope's chest. *Pictures and down time,* Gram had said. Time spent not working. In a house with a single man...

Gram wouldn't be matchmaking, would she?

Hope banished the thought. Gram didn't even *know* Blake. The very idea was ridiculous. Boy, Hope really did need some sleep, didn't she?

She looked into Blake's face and thought she saw his eyes soften with what looked like compassion. Compassion for her? Ridiculous. "I don't know what she told you. Why don't you enlighten me?"

At her sharp tone the soft look in his eyes disappeared and she wondered if she'd imagined it. He tilted his head the slightest bit, his keen gaze feeling a bit like an assessment as he paused.

He shook his head. "You look dead on your feet. We can talk about things later, after you've had a chance to rest and have something to eat. I've got to get back out to the barn, but I'll put on some coffee in the kitchen before I go."

He looked down at her legs and back up again, his expression knowing. His examination made her feel about two inches tall.

"If I were you I'd change out of your wet pants. The snow is starting to melt. You're going to be quite uncomfortable in about thirty seconds."

She looked down and saw a puddle by her boots. She

hadn't taken them off when she came inside. Hadn't done anything but march dutifully up the stairs. She looked back up, but her head seemed to lag half a second behind her eyes. Uh-oh. Having the equivalent of an out-of-body experience was no time for a conversation about the whys and wherefores of the next few weeks. It would keep.

"Coffee would be great, thank you."

He went to leave but turned back, his right cheek facing her so she couldn't look at him without seeing the scar in all its angry, beastly detail. The funny tingling sensation she recognized as anxiety crawled down the backs of her legs again but she forced herself to hold his gaze.

"I'll be back inside at dinner. Anna put a roast in the crockpot this morning, so we can eat when I come back."

Anna? Hope felt a rush of relief. Perhaps they weren't going to be alone, then. Maybe Gram had been wrong. Maybe Blake had a wife, or a girlfriend.

That would be very welcome news, because while Hope certainly lived in the twenty-first century, there was a small part of her that felt odd knowing it was just going to be the two of them under the same roof.

Wouldn't her friends have a chuckle about *that?* Who knew she would be so *traditional,* after all? Of course she might just be feeling that way because, despite the scar and the cool attitude, she did find Blake rather attractive in a raw, rugged sort of way...

"Is Anna your wife? Girlfriend?"

He grinned then, and the sight of it changed his face completely, making her catch her breath.

"That'd give her a laugh," he chuckled. "Anna's my part-time housekeeper. You'll meet her tomorrow."

He stepped back and touched the brim of his hat, a gallant gesture that took her by surprise.

"Make yourself at home. I'll be back in a few hours.

And, Hope?" The momentary smile was wiped away as he frowned, and his face was all planes and angles again. "Get some rest before you fall over again."

His boots clomped down the stairs and she heard the front door slam.

She sat to take off her boots and her pants chafed against her legs.

Dammit, he was right. About the pants, the falling over—all of it.

And it was probably a very good thing that she was too tired to care. It was going to be a very long ten days.

CHAPTER TWO

BLAKE opened the gate and brought the horses from the corral. Each one plodded to its own stall, where it was warm and where fresh flakes of hay and water waited. A storm was brewing. Blake could feel it in the air—a blend of moisture and expectation that he recognized after living his whole life in the shadow of the Rockies. The gray cloud cover that had made the day so bleak and the air raw was bringing snow. This close to the mountains it was bound to get ugly.

It was a good thing Hope had arrived when she had.

He closed up the stall doors and frowned. His grandmother had called after it had all been set up, and then Hope's grandmother had followed up, calling him personally. He'd said yes to Hope staying here for one reason only: because Mary had promised that Hope would take pictures for him, providing professional shots to be used on the facility's website and in promo materials for organizations all over western Canada. He appreciated the favor because money was tight and he tried to put every cent he could back into the facility. Bighorn needed a better professional presence, and he wasn't going to get it with a few snapshots and a website he'd put together from a template. He knew where his strengths were. IT support wasn't it.

But then Mary had insinuated that Hope was in desperate need of a holiday, too, that she was really struggling and a place like his was just what she needed.

He'd tried to ignore that last part because he had no desire to get personally involved. It was uncomfortable enough having her stay in the house with him, but what else could he do? Say no and ship her off to a hotel miles away? His mother would have something to say about that and the Western hospitality he'd been sure to point out to Hope just minutes ago. He'd resigned himself to having a house guest, and made sure that Anna had prepared the guestroom for her in welcome.

But he hadn't expected a tall, elegant blonde with sleek hair and the slightest lilt of an acquired Australian accent to show up. She was the kind of girl who, in his high school days, had intimidated the hell out of him. The kind of girl who wore the best clothes and hung with the cool people and looked down her nose at guys like Blake. Guys who were less than perfect. He'd had her pegged the moment he saw the expensive high-heeled boots and the stylish scarf looped around her neck in some crazy, fashionable knot.

She'd hooked her hand into his and he'd felt the contact straight to his belt buckle as he helped her to her feet. Before he'd even been able to put the reaction into perspective she'd looked into his face.

He'd seen that look before. Revulsion. Disgust. Over the years he'd grown more patient with people. He knew the scar was ugly. Shocking, even. And the reactions were just that—reactions. People naturally expected a perfect face, and his was anything but. He never faulted anyone for a moment's reaction. So why did Hope's make him scowl so?

Maybe because she'd been worse than the others. Not surprise or a small wince before glancing away. She'd ac-

tually paled and swayed on her feet. His pride had taken
a hit and he'd heard the echoes of his school nickname in
his head… *Hey, Beast.* The *Beauty and the Beast* movie
had been out a few years earlier than his accident and all
the girls remembered the words from the songs, taunting
him with them through the hallways when the teachers
weren't paying attention.

There was nothing he could do about his disfigurement.
Nor had they understood the fact that the pain of it was
nothing compared to the agony of losing his twin, Brad.

Enough time had passed now that the memories had
become a part of who he was, so intrinsically a part of him
that he usually forgot all about it. But not today. Today
he was off his stride and *she'd* shown up with her superior airs, making it sound like he wouldn't want her here
when it was clear that *she* was the one who would rather
be somewhere else. It was only his sense of hospitality
and the promise he'd made his grandmother that had kept
him from answering with the words that had hovered on
his tongue.

His mother had raised him to be a gentleman, after all.
And so by the time he'd got Hope's suitcase to her room
he'd calmed his temper and attempted pleasantness.

He shut the last stall door and slid the bolt home with
a loud *thunk.* Before he left he ventured into the storage area of the barn and ran his fingers over the wood
of the sleigh he'd bought from a rancher near Nanton.
It was old, but solid. The green paint had been chipped
when it was delivered. Now it was stripped and sanded,
the runners reinforced, and the whole thing waited to be
repainted. He'd been planning this for a while, keeping
his eye out for a used sleigh he could refinish—one big
enough to seat a driver upfront and a group of kids in the
back. A group of kids who needed help making the kind

of Christmas memories that Blake had known growing up. The kind that came with hot cocoa and cookies and visits from Santa Claus.

It shouldn't bother him that a look of surprise and aversion had touched Hope's face. He had more important things to think about. But it irritated him just the same. His hands moved over the gentle curves of the wood as he considered, picturing her flawless skin, her waterfall of soft hair, her sweetly curved body... She was tall and long-limbed and, despite being jet-lagged, moved with an innate grace he admired.

Maybe he'd been working with physical disabilities too long if he could make that complete an assessment of her based on a five-minute acquaintance.

As usual, working with the animals helped him sort out his thoughts. While the ranch catered for children with visible disabilities, he was well aware that not all problems could be seen by the naked eye. He dedicated his life to helping people look beyond the scars and disabilities of others. Not a day went by that he didn't think of Brad and how they'd planned a life that was no longer a possibility. It was the driving force behind Bighorn Therapeutic Riding, after all.

Maybe, just maybe, he owed that same courtesy to Hope. If he didn't, he'd be as closed-minded as all the people who had turned away from him over the years. So, he mused, as he turned out the barn lights and closed the door, he'd put his first impressions of Hope aside and give her the benefit of the doubt.

It was silent inside the house, and for a minute Blake wondered if Hope had taken a nap. She'd been dead on her feet, her eyes slightly unfocused as she'd stared at him in her room. The scent of roasting meat, garlic and bay leaves permeated the hall from the kitchen and his stomach growled. Should he wake her for dinner or save her a plate?

And then he found Hope sitting at the breakfast counter, laptop open, her delicately arched brows wrinkled in the middle as she focused on something on the screen, prissy little glasses perched on her nose. The stylish kind of spectacles that looked more like an accessory than anything else.

"So, not asleep, after all?"

She started at the sound of his voice. "Oh, goodness!"

"You didn't hear me come in?"

"I tend to block things out when I'm editing," she explained, tucking a silky sheet of her hair behind her ear. "Sorry."

"Editing?"

"Of course. I find the imperfections in the pictures and then work to make them better. Come look," she said, turning the laptop a few degrees so he could see the screen better.

He was off step again, expecting one thing and finding another. He'd been about to apologize for his earlier coolness and here she was looking refreshed and businesslike, as if things hadn't been awkward at all.

He went to the counter and peered over her shoulder.

The picture was of a female model, posed in a white overcoat and stilettos, her hair artfully blowing around her face.

"Looks good," he said. Truthfully, it looked a bit sterile and lifeless. There was too much white and the model looked like she might be blown away with the first stiff breeze to ruffle her umbrella. With her hair blowing like that, and a coat on, he would've expected an outdoor shot rather than…what? It looked like she was standing inside a cube. Why would she need an umbrella in a cube?

"Let me show you the original." She brought up another picture and put them both side by side. "See?"

Her smile was wide and expectant as he looked at the screen again. Honestly, he couldn't see much difference.

"You're clearly a pro," he commented, stepping back.

Her brows knit closer together. "Don't you see? Look right here." She pointed to the model's jaw. "This line is totally different now. And that spot?"

He had to lean right in to see where she indicated.

"It's gone in this one. And I lightened everything just a bit as the exposure wasn't quite right. It's totally different. Now it's nearly perfect."

"And perfection is important?"

She looked at him like he'd suddenly sprouted an extra head. "Of course," she chattered. "I mean, I'm always looking for the perfect shot. That's what I do. I haven't found it yet, but I will someday." Her lips took on a determined set. "Until then I keep trying, and I tweak and fix what I have. It's so different than in the old days, before digital."

Perfection. His mood soured. If she was looking for perfection, boy, was she in the wrong place.

"Yeah, well, I've always been a point-and-shoot kind of guy."

He went to the counter next to the sink and took the cover off the Crock-pot. Steam and scent assaulted him and he breathed deeply. No one did elk roast like Anna.

"Dinner's in ten—I'm going to make some gravy," he said, taking out a large platter.

He put the roast in the center and scooped out potatoes, carrots and golden chunks of turnip, arranging them around the roast. Then he tented them all with foil while he poured the broth into a saucepan and set it to heat, mixing flour and water to thicken it. He marveled at the change in her. Not only had she traded her wet clothes for dry, but the dazed look in her eyes was gone and she seemed full of chatter. Like she was two entirely different people. Which one was the real Hope?

The chatter was annoying on one hand but somehow pleasant on the other. The house often felt too quiet with just him here in the winter months. He supposed that one of these days he should get off his butt and think about having a family of his own.

And yet every time he considered it something held him back. Something he didn't want to examine too closely. Things were better the way they were now.

"Mr. Nelson?"

He paused, his hand on the flour bin. "It's Blake, remember?"

"I just… I want to apologize for earlier. I think we got off on the wrong foot. I was terribly tired, you see…"

Her voice trailed off, but her blue eyes looked both hopeful and perhaps a touch bashful, which surprised and pleased him. They were both aware that she hadn't slept, so he saw the apology for what it was—trying to smooth the awkward moment over. He could be graceful and accept it, or reject it. Considering they had to spend the next week and a half together, rejecting it probably wasn't such a smart idea.

"What brought you around?" He chose to move the conversation along and start over. "When I left you, you looked ready to drop."

He turned his head and looked her square in the face, waiting for her answer. To his surprise she smiled.

"Your coffee. It's very good."

"Kicking Horse. Comes from a place a few hours that way." He thumbed ambiguously toward the west.

"Oh. Well, it's delicious. And I snooped in the pantry

and happened to find a jar of the most delicious cinnamon cookies. Caffeine and sugar have given me my second wind."

"Good to know."

He turned back to his broth, now bubbling on the burner. "Can I help?"

"You can set the table if you like," he replied, focusing on running a whisk through the gravy, trying not to think about how soft and sweet her voice sounded. "Plates are to the far right of the sink. Glasses one door in."

As she busied herself setting the table, he whisked thickener into the boiling broth. "So, what are you editing, anyway?"

"Just a shoot I did a week or so ago, for a fashion magazine. I'd rather wait to sleep tonight and try to reset my clock—know what I mean? Working keeps me alert."

"You brought work on your vacation?"

She shrugged. "It's hardly a vacation, is it? I'm here to take some pictures for you to use for promotion, right?"

"And take some downtime. Mary said you needed it."

Hope's hands paused on the knives and forks. "What exactly *did* my grandmother say anyway? That's the second time you've mentioned that I 'need' to be here."

Satisfied with the gravy, he poured it into a glass measuring cup which doubled as a low-class gravy boat. Ah, so he'd struck a nerve, if the edge to her voice was anything to go by.

"All she said was that a place like this could do you a world of good. She didn't elaborate."

"'A place like this'?" she repeated, her words slow and deliberate. "This is a rehabilitation ranch for children with injuries and disabilities, isn't it?"

"Yes, it is. And clearly you're not a child. Nor do you have any disabilities that I can see."

He met her gaze then, and something sparked between them. She was about as close to flawless as any woman he'd ever seen. Without her hip-length coat now, and changed into casual jeans and a soft sweater, he could appreciate the long length of her legs and the perky tilt of her breasts beneath the emerald-green material. Her eyes looked the slightest bit tired, but her lips were the perfect balance between being full without being overly generous, and her eyes were the color of bluebells when they bloomed in the pasture in summer. Her silky hair framed a flawless face. Yep—she was beautiful, and his reaction was purely physical.

But he wasn't sure what could be responsible for the reciprocating spark on her end. He certainly wasn't anything to look at. He'd accepted that long ago. In a way he considered his disfigurement part of his penance for being the one left behind after the accident.

The marks were a part of who he was. Take it or leave it. All it took was a look in the mirror to remind him why the ranch and the program were so important. It was all because of Brad and a desperate need to have something good come of their family tragedy. And as Blake had been the one who'd made it out alive, the one who'd been left behind, it was up to him to make it happen.

Her lips thinned as she straightened, her posture was flawless, too. Regal, even. He felt a flicker of admiration.

"I think there's some mistake," she said, her voice clear. "I don't know why on earth my grandmother would have said such a thing, but rest assured, Mr. Nelson. I am perfectly fine and I'm only here because I would walk over broken glass for her."

So he was Mr. Nelson again, and she had made it perfectly clear that she certainly wasn't doing *him* any favors.

"She sounded like she would do anything for you, too."

Blake chafed at her abrasive tone but kept his patience. Tired or not, Hope's pronouncement sounded an awful lot like denial. And he'd put money on it having something to do with her extreme reaction to his face.

"I'll take pictures for you, as she promised on my behalf. But I'm hardly in need of any sort of rehab. In any way. As you can see, I'm perfectly fit."

Oh, she was fit, all right. The way he was noticing the soft curve of her waist and the swell of her breasts beneath the soft sweater was proof enough of that.

"She didn't say it was physical. She led me to believe that it was more..." He was used to talking about these things in a practical manner, so why was it suddenly so difficult with her? So trite and clichéd? "More emotional," he finished. "A different kind of hurt."

Something flickered through her eyes. Fear, vulnerability, pain. Just as quickly it disappeared, but he'd seen it. Her grandmother was right, wasn't she? Hope was doing a fair job of hiding it, but something was causing her pain.

"She's wrong. She hasn't even seen me in over two years," Hope replied coolly, folding her hands. "Sorry. Nothing to fix here."

He shrugged, knowing better than to push right now. "It's okay. I'm just happy to have the pictures for our promo materials. And you never know. Sometimes a few days of R & R can do miraculous things. It doesn't have to be any more complicated than that. I'm just a rancher, Hope. I don't have any interest in prying into your personal life."

Indeed not. He'd been dreading her arrival for days. He might be good at his job but he was hopeless at playing host. Social situations were so not his thing, and as a rule he avoided them as much as possible.

His words did nothing to ameliorate the situation. If

anything they seemed to make it worse. She straightened her shoulders.

"Since that's the case, perhaps it would be best if tomorrow I find another place to stay nearby."

There was an imperious arrogance to her voice that grated on a particular nerve of Blake's. There was being private, and then there was just being uppity, as his father would say. And Hope McKinnon was being uppity. He wondered what it was that put her on the defensive so completely. Clearly she wasn't any happier about being here than he was.

"Suit yourself," he replied smoothly, refusing to take the bait. He had enough to worry about without babysitting a woman who didn't want to be here. At this point as long as he got his pictures he was a happy boy.

He took the platter to the table and put it down in the center. He was very good at being patient. Maybe he was annoyed, but she could issue all sorts of decrees and pronouncements and she wasn't going to fizz him a bit. He'd had tons of practice at hiding his true feelings. Years of it.

Besides, he had more important things to worry about. Like Christmas. And making sure the program kids had some extra good memories to carry them through the holidays. And a sleigh to paint. All of which would keep him out of her way.

Hope sat down at the table and opened a paper napkin, spreading it over her lap like a visiting princess.

As Blake grabbed the carving knife, he set his jaw.

Nothing was going to get in his way. Especially her.

Hope stretched beneath the covers, luxuriating in the soft blankets. The light coming through the window was strange…dim, but somehow bright at the same time. She rubbed the grit from her eyes and checked her watch.

Seven-thirty in the morning. She'd slept for ten hours. Considering the time difference, that was very close to a miracle. She had worked after dinner until she could barely keep her eyes open. That had been the plan. Work. Fall asleep. No time to think.

No time to feel.

She could be very productive this way.

The floor was cold beneath her feet as she tiptoed to the window. Ah, the reason for the odd light was fresh snow. Mounds of it piled up around the barn and fenceposts. Great dollops of it balanced on the branches of the spruce trees in the yard. It looked like a winter fairyland and it kept falling—big, fluffy flakes of it. She felt as if she were looking out on an interactive Christmas card. The kind that landed in her in-box this time of year, with snowmen and Christmas trees to click on.

For a moment it reminded her of home—of Gram's place in Beckett's Run. She imagined Gram would be baking Christmas cookies and getting out the decorations by now. Something that felt like homesickness swept through her as she stared at the snow, so familiar and yet so foreign.

In New England they'd always hoped for a white Christmas. She and her sisters had put on hats and mittens and boots and made snowmen and had snowball fights. Grace had accused Hope of being too bossy about where to put Frosty's nose and Faith could no longer play peacemaker.

Hope smiled to herself. Poor Faith. Hope and Grace hadn't made things easy on their middle sister. Things were slightly better with their relationship now, in so far as Faith wasn't *not* speaking to Hope. Grace was still put out with Hope for not agreeing to go on an assignment with her. In Hope's defense, the opportunity to do a shoot for *Style-Setter* magazine was too good to pass up, but Grace hadn't understood.

Now Faith was in a similar predicament to Hope— Gram had asked a favor of her, too, and she was doing some special stained glass project for an English earl.

Sometimes it seemed like the three of them were on different planets.

A movement to the right caught her attention. It was Blake, bundled in a heavy coat with a black knitted cap on his head and huge gloves on his hands, shoveling the walkway that ran from house to barnyard. Snow flew off his shovel in great puffs as Hope took the time to study him more carefully.

He'd annoyed her with his assessment last night, making her react when she'd truly wanted to be pleasant after getting off on the wrong foot. And in his words he was no therapist. Just a rancher.

Looking at his scar, though, she knew he wasn't any ordinary rancher. This was personal for him, wasn't it? Someone didn't run a place like this without a history. She'd bet it was all wrapped up in how he'd got that scar.

And just like that she knew it would be best if she did move lodgings. What good would come of any sort of curiosity? She didn't want to get caught up in anyone else's drama. She'd had enough of her own to last a lifetime. She had a good life now and she'd fought hard for it, worked hard. Gram was wrong. She didn't need fixing at all. What she needed was to keep busy.

She wished she could snap her fingers and it would be Christmas already. She'd spend it with Gram and then head back to Sydney, where she belonged. She'd rather just forgo all this nonsense altogether.

Hope showered and dried her hair, then got dressed, did her makeup carefully and straightened her unruly curls with a flatiron until they lay soft and smooth to her shoulders. When she finally went downstairs Blake was inside, curling his hands around a coffee cup while steam rose in wisps in the air.

"Good morning."

He turned and smiled as if the tension of last night had never existed. It appeared they were both making an effort.

"Morning."

"Is there more of that?"

He moved his head, gesturing to the coffeemaker. "Help yourself. How'd you sleep?"

She reached for a cup. "Better than I expected. Maybe it's the mountain air. Or going without sleep for nearly forty-eight hours. I slept right through."

"It was still dark after sunrise, thanks to the storm. We really got dumped on overnight. I figured we would."

She poured the coffee and took the first sip—*ah*. The restorative, caffeine-injected brew suddenly seemed to make everything a little more right in the world.

"How much came down?"

"Maybe a foot and a half, and it's still falling."

Her bubble of happiness popped and the coffee didn't taste quite so good. "A foot and a half? Like, eighteen inches?"

"Yeah. Afraid the roads are closed from here to the highway unless you've got a four-by-four. And of course there's always the problem of trying to realize where the road ends and the fields begin. Try it and you're in a ditch and calling a neighbor to haul you out. No one's going anywhere today."

And there it was. Her brilliant plan to be friendly but

insist on going to nearby Banff to find a hotel room blown out of the water. "For how long?" she asked.

"Oh, rest of today for sure. If it lets up things'll be clear by tomorrow sometime. Added to what we already had, there's no doubt it'll be a white Christmas this year."

He grinned with satisfaction—only the second time she'd seen him smile. It seemed the gruff rancher had a soft spot for the holidays. Good for him.

Well, there was nothing to be done about it now. She could manage one more night. She could make some calls today and book a room. She let out a breath.

"You should have some breakfast. I ate early, but Anna's here. She'll fix you up. Anna?"

"You called?"

A raspy voice came from the hall and a woman appeared just after it. She was small—barely over five feet—with eyes black as night and golden-brown skin. "Hope, meet Anna Bearspaw."

The woman smiled, making the skin around her eyes wrinkle, and now Hope understood why her question about whether Anna was his wife or girlfriend had made him laugh. The woman was easily fifty, her graying black hair pulled back in a sleek low ponytail.

"Hope." She grinned. "Blake says you liked my elk last night."

"Elk?" she struggled to keep the pleasant smile pasted on her face. She'd assumed the flavorful meat was beef. Didn't Alberta boast about its beef?

"The roast," Blake offered. "No one does it up like Anna."

Hope had to swallow the saliva that pooled in her mouth at the thought of eating what had to be hunted game. She rarely ate red meat, but had made an exception rather than rock the hospitality boat. She was used to meat coming in neatly wrapped packages at the market. Her stomach turned as she imagined the process of getting a wild animal to the table.

"It was…uh…delicious," she offered weakly.

"My boy John's the hunter. We kept some for ourselves and gave the rest to Blake in trade."

"Trade?"

"It's nothing," Blake said, putting his cup in the sink.

"Oh, it's *nothing,*" Anna parroted. She looked at Hope. "Blake has given me a job, and now that it's just me and John at home he looks after us, whatever we need. He's a good man."

It made no sense to Hope why she'd be curious to know more about Anna, but she found herself asking, "Looks after you?"

The woman beamed. "He's a good neighbor."

"We all look after each other out here, that's all," Blake replied.

That was just the sort of thing Hope tried to avoid. She didn't like having to rely on other people. She'd rather rely on her own two hands and abilities. She liked being independent. She liked her job and her circle of friends in Sydney. She had life just the way she wanted it, didn't she? And it was a good life. Relying on help meant people thought they had the right to pry into personal matters. She much preferred privacy.

It hadn't always been that way, though. Not when she'd been a child. Once upon a time the three sisters had stuck together. After their parents had finally split for good they'd had to—they'd only had each other. And Gram.

It had been Gram who had told her to stop trying so hard to hold them all together. And Gram who had witnessed her complete breakdown at eighteen, when stress had meant she'd blown her exams and lost her scholarship. It had been Gram who had picked her up and helped her get back on her feet again. No one but the two of them knew how much it had cost Gram. And Hope had paid back every cent. She'd made sure of that.

She was still working on paying back the personal cost to her grandmother—which was why she'd agreed to this stupid scheme in the first place.

She pushed the painful memories aside and tried to smile for Anna. "If the roads are closed, how did you get here this morning?" She was almost afraid to know the answer. Wondered if she'd look outside and see a dogsled. This all seemed so surreal it didn't feel out of the realm of possibility.

"My snowmobile."

"Of course," she said faintly, quite sure now that she'd ended up in a parallel universe.

"We won't have any clients today. But the snow's supposed to stop, and I've got to scout out a Christmas tree. You can come if you want—see more of the ranch. You could probably use the fresh air after being cooped up in a plane for the better part of two days."

Hope looked over at Blake. He was leaning, completely relaxed, against the kitchen counter. With Anna on one side and Blake's long legs blocking the escape to the hall Hope felt utterly trapped.

"I thought I was supposed to be taking pictures," she replied, scrambling for an excuse. There was no way she was going to straddle a snowmobile and wrap her arms around Blake.

"Bring your camera. I'll take you up to the top of the ridge. The view from there is phenomenal. Mountains as far as you can see. They'll be pretty now with the new snow."

"I don't do landscapes," she explained desperately.

The two of them? Alone in the wilderness? Briefly it struck her how many shoots she'd been on with complete strangers. This was no big deal.

Only it was. Because this didn't feel exactly business-like. And it was impossible it could be anything else. They didn't even like each other, did they?

"A picture's a picture, right?"

He was undeterred, and she was feeling more irritated the longer the conversation went on. Anna proceeded to unload the dishwasher as if they weren't even there. A picture was only a picture if you were an amateur. She kept away from nature photographs because she preferred to have control. Her photos were carefully set up, lighting adjusted, models just so. If there were variables *she* wanted to control them.

But she wasn't about to explain that to Blake any more than she'd try to tell him how to do his job. He'd probably find it supernaturally boring. Not many people understood her quest for perfection. Truthfully, she wasn't sure she'd ever find it, but she still kept trying. It was a constant challenge and one she thrived on. Some days that challenge was what got her up in the morning. The possibility of perfection, out there waiting for her to make it happen. Something no one could ever take away from her.

"I don't think I have the right clothing." She tried for a final excuse, knowing this would surely get her out of it. She'd research some hotels instead and book a room, so she could be gone once the roads were cleared. And she'd explain her reasons so he understood. Gram was just trying to look after her, but she was doing just fine looking after herself. She didn't need to impose on his "Western hospitality" for the whole ten days.

"I think we've got gear that'll fit you," he said. "Any more excuses?" He lifted an eyebrow in challenge. "You're not afraid of a snowmobile, are you?"

She really couldn't come up with anything else. She thought about having to climb on the back of the snowmobile, wrapping her arms around his middle. She swallowed. She'd die before explaining about the whole physical proximity thing. It wasn't that she was shy. It was more...

She looked into his face. His eyes were focused on her in a way that made her heart flutter unexpectedly. This was the problem. In the small bit of time since her arrival there'd been an awareness she hadn't either expected or wanted. The angry scar on his face added a sense of danger, and she tried to ignore it as best she could—and the dark feelings it evoked. But his size alone practically screamed masculinity and she wasn't completely immune to that. It was the way he looked at her, the husky but firm tone of his voice that set her nerve endings on edge.

Blake Nelson, for all his broodiness and imperfections, was exciting. It was the last thing she'd expected and it totally threw her off guard.

And now he'd issued a challenge.

She could do this. Besides, after two days of stale recirculated air on the plane she could use the crisp bite of the wind in her face, right?

"I'm game. I guess," she added. He didn't need to know he'd tapped into her competitive streak.

"I'm going to finish up a few things in the barn, so I'll be back in about an hour, okay? Anna knows where the winter gear is. She'll help you."

"Sure I will," the woman answered from behind Hope.

Hope smiled weakly. Well, if nothing else the ride with

Blake would give her the chance to talk to him about switching accommodation.

That was one argument she wouldn't lose.

CHAPTER THREE

BLAKE handed over the helmet and watched as Hope put it on. He hid a smile, wondering if she was worried about messing her perfect hair. "Put down the visor when we start out. It'll keep the wind and snow off your face," he suggested, straddling the padded seat of the snowmobile.

Anna had bundled Hope up in borrowed winter boots, ski pants and jacket, and a thick pair of gloves. She looked different. Approachable. He was enjoying seeing her out of her comfort zone. After last night, with her reading glasses on like armor and her laptop flashed up, he got the sense that her work was her shield.

"Hop on," he called, starting the machine, letting it idle for a few minutes. She slid on behind him, her legs cushioning his. He swallowed and for the first time wondered about the wisdom of the idea of disappearing into the foothills with her.

Then she slid her arms around his ribs.

Even through the thick material of their jackets the contact rippled through him. He scowled and set his teeth, rejecting the surprising whip of arousal. What was the point of being attracted to her? A woman like Hope would never be interested in a man like him. They never were. He and Hope came from different places. He kept his life simple, without frills and fancies. And she was a city girl through and through. A modern woman, independent and successful—not that there was a thing wrong with that.

But nothing good would come of the two worlds colliding.

He hit the throttle. "Hold on!" he called, and gave it a shot of gas, taking them up and over a snowbank before heading over the snowy field to the crest beyond.

The zipper of her jacket seemed to dig into his back but he ignored it as they cruised over the undulating hills. The snow had stopped, only the odd errant flake drifting lazily down now to settle gently atop the pristine white blanket covering the meadow. In the summertime he wandered these hills on horseback to calm his mind. But in winter he used one of the snowmobiles that Anna kept at her place for her and John.

He reached the crest of the ridge and slowed, coming to a stop by an outcropping of rock that sat oddly out of place in the middle of the land. He cut the engine, dismounting. It was his favorite place on the ranch when all was said and done.

It was where he and Brad had come as boys. Identical twins, they'd done everything together. They'd made campfires and built a hooch in the shade of the rock, unrolling sleeping bags and spending the night with nature. They'd talked about hockey, talked about playing in the NHL someday, talked about the farm and, as they got a little older, girls.

Now Blake usually came alone. Sometimes to remember. Sometimes to look down at the awesome view—the way the land dipped and then extended straight out to the mountains—and to realize that he was just one small part of the big world out there. It helped him put things in perspective after a bad day.

He'd been surprised at himself for issuing the invitation

to Hope. Perhaps it was that little glimpse of vulnerability that had prompted him to do it. And the knowledge that he felt the need for the wind on his face and it wouldn't be very hospitable to take off and leave her stranded at the house alone.

Maybe he wasn't entirely pleased with the houseguest arrangement, but he liked to think his parents had taught him decent manners.

"This is nice," Hope said, climbing off the snowmobile and peeling the helmet off her head. Her hair was matted down beneath a thin toque and she pulled the hat straight. Pieces of blond hair stuck out like straw around her ears.

"Nice?" he repeated, somehow deflated by her bland reaction to the spectacular panorama before them. He breathed deeply, watched as his breath formed a frosty cloud that disappeared. "It's kind of a miracle, don't you think? That places like this exist?"

"I suppose," she answered, taking a few steps through the snow toward him. "It certainly is a big view."

He turned his head to study her. "The best adjectives you can come up with are 'nice' and 'big'?"

She smiled then. "So my attempts to downplay it are a major fail?" She shrugged, then took a deep breath and let it out. "Okay, you win. I admit it. It's stunning up here."

"That's better." He nodded and went to the biggest rock, used his arm to dust the snow off its surface. "Care to sit, Your Highness?"

He offered her his hand but she ignored his gesture, climbed up nimbly and perched on the rock, drawing up her knees and looking out over the landscape. "What is this place, anyway?"

"The outer edge of the ranch property. We used to own more, but I sold a chunk of it off years ago."

"Why?"

He was a little startled at her question, especially as she'd shown very little interest in the ranch side of things since her arrival. "I didn't need as much grazing land once I sold off the cattle. I just needed enough for the horses and feed."

"You had cattle?"

"My family did, yes."

"Why did you sell them off?" She was quiet for a moment but he knew she wanted to ask something more. Finally she looked over at him. "Was the ranch in trouble?"

He shook his head. "No. But when my dad decided to go into early retirement after a heart attack scare the ranch was left in my hands. It was up to me to make the decisions. This is what I chose." He shrugged. "The therapy part and the funding I receive covers the operational expenses. The horses I board give me something to live on."

And it hadn't been easy either. Despite being in charge, he had wanted his parents' support. His father had thought he was crazy when he'd broached the idea of selling off the majority of the ranch to fund a rehabilitation program. Once the assets of land and cattle were gone they were gone for good. But when he'd explained about how difficult it had been, growing up with not only the scarring but the lingering effects of the accident, about how he needed to do something worthwhile, they'd come around. Now his parents helped out during the spring and summer. In some ways this program was a living memorial to Brad.

"Where are your parents now?"

"Phoenix. They're snowbirds. They have a condo down there and avoid the cold Canadian winters. They'll be back for Christmas though, flying in Christmas Eve. Mom always says it doesn't feel like Christmas without snow."

Hope didn't answer, and Blake studied her profile. She was tanned from living in Sydney, her blond hair streaked from the sun. She turned her head and looked at him and he realized the combination made her eyes stand out. Right now, in the cold crisp air, they were the precise color of a mountain bluebird.

"What about you? What are you doing for Christmas?"

She shrugged, but he thought he saw a shadow pass over the brightness of her eyes. "I'll fly out of here to Boston, and then on to Beckett's Run to spend the holidays with my grandmother. And I suppose any other members of my family who might show up."

"You're all spread out, then?"

She rubbed her hands together as if they were cold. "So what made you switch from cattle producer to equine therapy?"

She was changing the subject. Clearly her family was a sore spot with her. Was that the problem that her grandmother had mentioned? He reminded himself that it was none of his concern, but found he was curious anyway. Were they estranged?

But she'd turned the tables and asked a question and he knew she expected an answer. He pointed at his scar. "This."

She looked away.

"I know it's bad," he said. "I see it every day."

"It's not that bad," she said quietly, but she looped her arms around her knees, shutting him out. "I've seen worse."

Those three words seemed to explain a lot and nothing all at once. "But it does make you uncomfortable?"

She looked at him. "I suppose that makes me a bad person?"

She was so defensive. He let out a breath. "Depends. Depends on why, right? Someone like you—you're used to dealing with beautiful models all day long. You're probably not used to—"

He broke off. He refused to refer to himself as ugly. He'd spent too long digging himself out of his hole of grief to allow negative thinking.

"Now who's judging and making assumptions?"

It bugged him that she was right.

She looked him square in the face—not to the side, not over his shoulder—dead in his eyes.

"If it makes me uncomfortable it's not for the reasons you think. I just… It just reminds me of someone, that's all."

"And remembering hurts?"

She looked back out over the fields, but he saw a muscle tick in her jaw. "Yeah. I guess it does. So I try not to. It's easier that way."

He could relate to that more than she'd ever know. Instead of answering he let the quiet of the winter day work its magic. He sat on the rock beside her—far enough away that they weren't touching—and listened. To the wind shushing through the stand of spruce trees nearby. To the faint sound of the sparse flakes of snow touching the ground. No traffic. No nothing. Just space.

"How did it happen?" she finally asked.

He'd explained it many times, but each time his throat clogged up a little. The memory never dimmed. It was never less horrific, even after all this time.

"We were coming home from a hockey tournament in British Columbia. We had an accident."

"You played hockey?"

He tried to smile. "Still do—a little pond hockey. You'll see. Some of the neighborhood teenagers come over and have a go at it. I'll have to clean the rink off tomorrow. It's covered in snow now."

"You're a real kid person, aren't you?"

"I suppose I am." He aimed a level look at her. "Kids are great. Full of energy and curiousity."

"Loud, destructive, unpredictable…"

She was smiling a little now. She looked awfully pretty when she smiled like that.

He cleared his throat, uncomfortable at her observation. He liked to keep his personal life personal. It was easier to talk about the ranch and his program than it was to talk about himself.

"Perhaps. But they're also generally accepting." At least the younger kids. Older ones could be cruel—his high school experience could attest to that—but the teens around here had known Blake long enough that his face was no big deal.

"The way most adults aren't?" Her smile slipped. "I suppose it has something to do with loss of innocence. It makes us grown-ups a bit jaded after a while."

Damn, but she had a knack of saying a lot without revealing much of anything. He kind of admired that. "I take it you're not much of a kid person?"

"I don't think I've actually thought about it much."

"You've been too busy searching for the perfect picture?" Burying herself in work, if he could venture a guess. He got the feeling that Hope McKinnon was a pro at losing herself in her job. They had that in common, then.

Her lips twitched. "Something like that. It's not something I'd want to do on my own, if ever. I'm only thirty. I haven't really thought much about the whole marriage and kids thing."

There was something about the way her gaze slid from his that made him think she was lying. "Building your career, I suppose?"

She brightened. "Of course. I love what I do, and with

all the long hours and the travel it's not really conducive to husbands or kids. Anyway, I still have time, right?"

Her smile was bright—possibly too bright.

"I don't know." He shrugged. "How much time do any of us really have?"

"You're a great one for philosophical questions, Blake."

"I have a tendency to overthink."

She put a hand over her mouth in feigned surprise, then dropped it to her lap. "A fault? Surely not? I was starting to think you didn't have any."

"How could you possibly know in less than twenty-four hours?"

"Oh, I'm a quick study. Occupational hazard. And you're an easy read."

Something inside him started to warm as he realized with some surprise that they were bantering. Was she flirting? Hard—no, impossible—to believe. "Are you teasing me?"

"I am. You're awfully serious."

"That's what I thought about you."

She shook her head. "No. I'm focused. Big difference. I know I probably seemed serious yesterday, but really I do know how to have fun. I know how to relax. Who wants to walk around stressed all the time? I like my job, my apartment, my social life. No worries and all that."

They were silent again for a few minutes, but then Blake had to ask the question that was burning in his mind. "If that's true, then why does it seem you carry the weight of the world on your shoulders?"

And there it was. That flash of vulnerability. Just for a moment, but there all the same. Hope might put on a strong, capable show but underneath there was more. A lot more.

And Blake knew that unfortunately he had a soft spot

for birds with broken wings. Seeing as he'd been one once upon a time. He should take her back to the house and keep it strictly business from here on out. But Hope McKinnon was intriguing. The face she showed the world wasn't the real Hope, was it?

Hope hopped down from the rock. "I'm cold. I'm going to walk around a bit and take a few pictures."

He let her go, holding back the observation that she'd said she didn't do landscapes. He watched as she took her camera out from beneath her jacket and moved around, studying angles and light as she snapped. The camera was what had dug into his back on the drive out, he realized. He liked watching her in action. Her face took on a determined set as she focused. But he noticed too that she frowned a lot, a crease forming between her brows. That search for perfection again?

He looked around him at the splendor of the Rockies. It never failed to catch his breath and fill his soul. What could she find to fault in such a magnificent creation?

He hopped down, too, now that the cold of the rock was seeping through his lined pants, making his butt chilly. "What's the matter?" he called, wading through the snow to where she stood, glaring at a particular peak.

"It's not right. The lighting is wrong. With this cloud, that side of the mountain is going to be too shadowed."

"Can't exactly control *that,* right?"

"Exactly. This is why I don't do landscapes and nature shots. There are too many variables. I like to be able to set it up, get the conditions right."

"Yet in all that planning you still haven't found the perfect shot?"

The look she threw in his direction was annoyed. "No. Not yet."

"I think I know the problem," he said, starting to smile. "You're missing the magic."

Her mouth dropped open. "Did you just say *magic?*" She made a sound that was both sarcastic and dismissive. "There's no such thing."

"And that's why you haven't found it. You're a nonbeliever. You can't organize perfection. You can't plan it. It just happens. And when it does, it's magic." Confidence filled his voice.

"You're talking nonsense," she said, shutting her camera off and tucking it back inside her jacket.

She zipped up the coat right to her neck. If she'd been vulnerable before that was all gone now. Instead she was defensive. He supposed she had a right. He did seem to enjoy challenging her, and they barely knew each other.

"I'll bet you that by the end of your time here you'll have your perfect photo, and it won't have a thing to do with planning or staging the scene."

She laughed—a sharp sound in the stillness. "That's an unfair bet. I'd win."

"What if I win? What do I get?"

She stalked back to the snowmobile. "It won't matter anyway. I'll take your pictures, Blake. I'll do promo shots for the ranch and the program. But I think I'd rather stay somewhere else. This is your private home. I don't belong here. I'm going to make some calls and book into a hotel in Banff."

Blake stared at her. He'd really struck a nerve if she couldn't even stand being in the same house as him for a few days. And, while the whole arrangement had been odd from the beginning, he was somehow a little offended that she was so desperate to leave.

Not that she was actually going anywhere. This close to Christmas there wouldn't be a room to spare in the resort

town. She was stuck here even if she didn't know it yet.
And he wasn't about to be the one to tell her. He doubted
Ms. McKinnon liked to be told anything. She could fig-
ure it out on her own.

"Can we go back now? I'm getting cold."

"Sure," he answered.

They got back on the snowmobile and he started the
engine, revved the throttle and turned them around, heading back to the warmth and comfort of the ranch house.

As they glided over the rolling hills Blake thought
about all she'd said, and what she hadn't. If he were a bet-
ting man he'd guess that she was a workaholic and she was
lonely. Hope was in some serious need of holiday cheer.
Problem was, he was the last person able to give it to her.

Hope hit the "end" button on her cell phone and scowled
at the display. That was the fifth hotel she'd tried and
there were no vacancies anywhere. She didn't even consider calling the Banff Springs—she wasn't hurting for
money, but the hundreds of dollars a night price tag was
definitely out of her budget for a ten-day stay.

She should have known. Major resort town, so close to
the holidays… She was going to be stuck here at Bighorn.

The thought made her stomach turn nervously. Not
just because she'd been borderline rude to Blake up at the
ridge and now had to make nice. But because on one level
she'd actually enjoyed talking to him. She'd let down her
guard for a few minutes and had nearly told him about
Julie, nearly mentioned her family. For a moment, as she'd
stared at the awe-inspiring peaks and snowy valleys, she'd
been tempted to confess that the weight on her shoulders,
her search for perfection, came from years of trying to
make everything right, to create a perfect family that had
never existed and never would.

They'd all let her down. Even Julie. Hope had thought to create her own special family, based on love rather than genetics. But the result had been the same. At the end of the day she stood alone. It was time to accept that she just wasn't good at family.

That she'd wanted to unload all of that on a virtual stranger hadn't just surprised her—it had been scary. The last thing she wanted to do was open the Pandora's Box that was her childhood. It was easier to keep it locked away and focus on the here and now. The present was all anyone had control over anyway.

She flopped back on the bed and sighed. She hadn't been lonely, as such. And she wasn't bitter, just guarded. Careful. She didn't share secrets or confidences. She wasn't even close to her sisters anymore. She and Grace always argued and it wasn't much wonder that Faith had chosen a calmer path than trying to run interference between them.

It *had* been lonely, she supposed. At times.

Right now she had to even things out with Blake in order to make the best of the next several days—especially as she had no place to go.

Problem was there had been a moment today when he'd looked in her eyes and she'd had the most irrational impulse to tell him *everything*.

She'd have to watch that.

She put her phone on to charge and decided to wander downstairs. She could always check the pictures from today and see if any were salvageable. And she really needed to talk to Blake about more practical matters— like what sorts of shots he wanted for his promo materials and how they were going to make that happen. She needed to think of this as a job. It would make the time go faster—and easier.

She'd booted up her laptop and inserted her memory card when she heard the back door open and close, followed by a heavy stomping of boots.

Blake came in, his cheeks ruddy from the cold, his eyes glowing even brighter than before. His hair was disheveled from wearing the heavy hat, giving him a boyish, roguish appearance. If it weren't for the jagged gash on the side of his face he'd be gorgeous, she realized. The men she knew paid stylists a fortune to achieve that tumbled, rugged look, and spent hours at the gym to gain a physique that Blake had mastered from simple physical labor on the ranch.

She'd been staring at him far too long. She dropped her gaze back to the computer screen and used the mouse to bring up the day's photos. "You look cold," she remarked blandly.

"The temperature's dropped. Animals are in for the night, though. Snug as a bug."

"That's good," she said, skimming the photos. A few weren't half bad, she realized, though her instincts had been correct—the lighting wasn't right. She might be able to play around with them, but none stood out as anything special or noteworthy.

"Anna's gone?" he asked, rubbing his hands together and going to the sink. He ran water and washed his hands, reaching for a towel hanging on the inside of a cupboard door.

"I think I heard her leave just before it started getting dark. When I came downstairs I checked, and there's what looks to be a lasagna in the oven for dinner."

"Gosh, that sounds good." He hung the towel back up. "I'll throw together a salad and some garlic bread to go with it."

"You're quite the cook."

"Lots of guys cook, you know."

She did know, but she had a hard time picturing Blake in the kitchen. He was so…large and manly. She smiled to herself. Maybe she'd been working in fashion too long. "So why keep a housekeeper if you're so capable?"

He lifted a shoulder. "Anna needs the work. I know how to run a washing machine and the vacuum and kitchen appliances. But it's nice sometimes, especially after a long day, to not have to worry about it. I cook for myself on the weekends. I make a French toast to die for."

She imagined Blake pushing a vacuum over the living room rug, pictured his long fingers wrapped around a spatula, flipping eggy bread. She found the image strangely attractive.

"What's so funny?" he asked.

She looked up and grinned. "I was just picturing you in an apron."

Something odd and strangely exciting seemed to curl through her stomach as she looked up at him. He was so reserved. Not just reserved…guarded. He'd mentioned an accident today but stopped short of giving any real insight. She found herself growing more and more curious about him.

"Blake, about this afternoon…"

At her serious tone he put a loaf of French bread down on the countertop beside her. The breakfast nook and stools were a great place for her to work but she suddenly felt like he was very close and her pulse quickened in response.

"What about it?"

"I think I owe you an apology. Some of your questions made me uncomfortable and I think I came across as rude."

He studied her carefully until she wondered if she was

starting to blush beneath the scrutiny. There was something simmering between them, something she couldn't quite put her finger on, but it felt suspiciously like he could read her mind. She wasn't sure she liked someone poking around in her thoughts.

"No hotel rooms available, eh?"

Heat flashed to her cheeks. She was definitely blushing now. He'd seen clear through her apology, hadn't he? She was totally busted. A bit irritated, too, though—because her remorse was genuine.

"Even if there were," she said quietly, "I was snippy with you and you didn't deserve it."

"Why were you?"

"You always ask the hard questions, don't you?" She put down the cover of her laptop and looked up at him.

"Not hard. Just real."

"From where I'm sitting they're the same thing."

His gaze softened. "I'm used to challenging people, I guess. Pushing to break through what's holding them back."

"I'm not here to be fixed or rehabilitated," she reminded him firmly. He'd been rather cryptic himself, out on the ridge. But she wouldn't bring that up right now. She was trying to smooth things over, not begin another argument. "I just keep to myself, you know? When I said today that your scar reminded me of someone, you asked if it hurt. It does."

"Who was he?"

She paused, surprised that he'd assumed it was a man she was speaking of—though she supposed she shouldn't be. She was thirty years old. Blake probably assumed she'd had relationships before. And she had, though never anything serious.

"Not a he. A she. My best friend. Her name was Julie."

She took a breath, surprised that she'd actually come right out and said it. She never talked about Julie. Her throat tightened but she forced the heavy feeling away, shutting it out.

She swallowed away the pain and forced herself to continue. "We shared everything. Work, interests, TV shows…an apartment."

"What happened?"

"There was a fire at a nightclub." Hope's throat felt like it was going to close over, and she fought to swallow, to keep going without thinking about it all too much. She could say it, offer a basic explanation so they could move on, right? "She was burned very badly. It was the worst thing ever to see her like that. First with all the bandages and then, briefly, without."

"What happened to her?"

Hope blinked, but her eyes were stone-dry. "She died. It was too much for her body to take and she went into organ failure."

She didn't have to say more for them both to understand how it had been a long and painful illness.

"I'm sorry."

She felt grief hover around the edges and began to panic. She had to change the focus. Put it somewhere else. She looked up and saw Blake's scar before her eyes. Painful truth slammed into her heart. "I saw you yesterday…" She heard her voice shake and tried to steady it. "I saw you and it was like seeing her…"

She couldn't finish.

Blake's hand closed over hers, warm and strong. The contact rippled through her, past the wall she usually built around herself, past the wall she sensed he kept around himself, too. Oh, it felt good to be connected to someone again. Terrifying but reassuring all at once.

All too soon he pulled away. It was just as well, she thought, tucking her fingers into her lap. She didn't trust it. Didn't trust the caring, tender gesture. Didn't trust herself to be objective.

"When?"

The simple question took her by surprise. "When what?"

"When did she die?"

Her gaze was drawn to his. There was no judgment in the blue depths, just patience. "About six months ago," she found herself answering.

"You haven't grieved yet."

He was getting too close to the truth. It wasn't any of his business if she had or hadn't. What was the point in indulging in a fit of grief? Crying and self-pity wouldn't bring Julie back and it wouldn't fix anything—another lesson learned the hard way at too young an age.

If only tears had the power to make things right life would have been so different. For all of them. She and her sisters wouldn't have been dragged from pillar to post. There wouldn't have been the arguments that Hope had always heard, even through walls. There wouldn't have been the crying for Daddy in bed at night with the covers over her head. She would have been able to hold them together. They would have been one big happy family instead of the mess they became.

"Of course I have," she lied, more shaken than she cared to admit.

"Grief can be crippling in itself," he explained. "At some point you have to deal with it."

She was starting to get angry now. How dared he talk to her like he had her all figured out? He knew nothing about her.

She took a slow, deep breath and held her temper. Losing it wouldn't do either of them any good. Instead she tried a smile that felt stretched and artificial. "Look, I just didn't want you to think it's…well, that it's you. Or that I'm…" She found she couldn't go on, couldn't say the word that had flashed into her brain. *Superficial.* The words trailed away.

"That you're prejudiced?"

Her gaze clashed with his. "Why would I think less of someone because of a scar?"

"I don't know. It makes me wonder if you look for perfection in people like you do in your pictures."

"People aren't perfect. Everyone knows that."

His lips curved up a little bit. "I agree. And apology accepted. Let's eat."

She felt utterly off balance as Blake let the topic drop and shifted gears into dinner mode. She put the photos away and went to help him with the garlic bread and salad. The sound of the evening news on the television provided a welcome chatter in the silence. But as she set the table his words echoed uncomfortably in her mind. *Did* she expect people to be perfect? Or was it knowing they weren't that made her keep everyone at arm's length?

CHAPTER FOUR

THE snowplows had been and the roads were open the next day. The ranch yard was a hub of activity by midmorning. There were extra cars in the driveway. Blake had had the chores done before Hope was even out of bed, and she'd eaten breakfast alone in the kitchen—Anna had the day off to do Christmas shopping in Calgary.

Hope looped her camera strap around her neck before putting on her puffy red jacket. It looked cold, so she put mittens on her hands—the kind with flaps that flipped up to leave her fingers exposed—and a knitted hat with a small funky peak on top of her head. Maybe she needed to be warm, but that didn't mean she had to be styleless. It had been a while since she'd put up with a northern winter but she did know how.

And after last night, and the confidences she'd shared with Blake, she felt the need to hit a reset button. It would be better to keep things businesslike from here on in, right? Professional. She was here to take pictures, and that was exactly what she was going to do.

The barn was warmer than she'd expected, considering the frosty bite to the air outside. Voices came from the riding ring and she made her way in that direction, taking in the scent of horse and hay as she walked down the corridor. It was a pleasant scent, and reminded her of early adolescence when, typical for her age, she'd gone through a horse stage and wanted her own. The answer had always been no, though eventually she'd worn her parents down and they'd agreed to riding lessons.

She'd had exactly three wonderful lessons when Mom had left Dad—again—and they'd moved.

She sighed. And people wondered why she didn't let herself count on anyone—or anything—too much. Her parents' marriage hadn't been an easy one. Whoever said opposites attract was dead wrong. It was a recipe for disaster. Her mom and dad hadn't balanced each other out. They'd driven each other crazy—Lydia with her flighty ways and Greg always trying to clip her wings. Hope had felt left in the gap—a child herself, but with the responsibility of raising her sisters. She hadn't done a very good job.

She stopped and took a few pictures of the long corridor of stalls. The floor was neat as a pin, and the inside of the tack room was exactly the same—saddles lined up precisely, bridles hung on thick pegs, a stack of heavy blankets a splash of color in a room that was decidedly brown. She liked it, actually, the leather and wood were rich and redolent with character and a certain Western charm.

She experimented with a few different angles and adjustments for several minutes, losing herself in the task. Finally, when she was satisfied, she made her way to the entrance to the riding ring.

The first thing to catch her eye was Blake. He stood in the middle of the ring, boots planted a few feet apart and his hands on his hips. He wore a red long-sleeved shirt with a puffed black vest over the top and a cowboy hat on his head. Her gaze traveled up his long legs to the worn pockets of his jeans and her lips went dry.

On impulse she lifted her camera, turned it to capture

him from top to bottom. She zoomed in so that his tall figure filled the viewfinder. There was no posing, no setting the scene, but right now he didn't need it. Besides, this wasn't an official photo for the site or anything. She'd work with him on that, so he'd have some sort of head shot he could use for promotion. This, she admitted to herself, was purely self-indulgent. A whim. She'd probably end up hitting the "delete" key in the end anyway.

Two horses with riders slowly circled the ring, and Hope watched as the first rider—a girl of perhaps ten—looked at Blake and smiled widely. He called out some encouragement, and then something else to the next rider—a boy who looked to be a similar age. As Hope watched the girl stopped her horse and stayed to the side, while the boy trotted up to Blake, turned and trotted back to his first position. Then it was the girl's turn.

It wasn't until Hope took a moment to take a full look around the perimeter of the ring that she saw two women, probably the moms, standing to one side, smiling and chatting.

There was too much activity right now to get the pictures she wanted. She'd rather the ring was empty. In her mind she analyzed the different views and vantage points, the available natural light and what fixtures were installed within the building. Wouldn't it be neat to be able to get a bird's-eye view of the ring? But she had no idea how she'd get up to the rafters to take it. She'd done some daring things to get a shot before, but suspending herself from a ceiling was one she hadn't tried yet.

The lesson ended and the boy and girl dismounted and began leading their horses to the exit. Hope slid aside, pressing herself to the wall to give them lots of room as they passed. She tilted her head as she watched them go by. They didn't look disabled in any way. They looked like a normal boy and girl.

Blake was right on their heels and he gave her a brief nod, but that was all. She hung back and watched as he efficiently cross-tied the animals in the corridor. The kids, barely five feet tall, began the process of removing the tack. Blake stepped forward and helped take the weight of the saddle from each of them. But the rest he let them do alone.

He came over to her then, keeping an eye on the children the whole time. "Hey," he said. "Wondered if you were ever going to get up."

"My days and nights are still a little messed up," she commented. "You were out here already when I dragged my sorry butt out of bed. It was a pretty cozy nest I had going on."

His gaze fell on her and she tried to ignore the warm buzz of awareness that ran through her.

"They do all that themselves?" she asked.

He grinned easily and she realized he was quite different out here in his element. More relaxed, less of a chip on his shoulder. He moved his attention from her and nodded in the direction of the children. "They do now. Not at first, though. Both Jennie and Riley are autistic. It took quite some time for us to get them to this point."

"I wondered. They look like normal kids."

He frowned. "They *are* normal kids."

Oh, she'd hit a nerve, she realized. Quite unintentionally, but she probably should have chosen her words better. "What I meant to say is they don't have a visible disability."

"I know what you meant. It's a bit of a battle, though. Drawing the line between normal and abnormal is what can make it so hard for these kids, you know? It really shouldn't matter what challenges they have. They have feelings like anyone else."

There was a sharpness to his tone that made her look up. The line of his jaw was firm and, if her guess was right, defensive. "Of course they do. I never meant to imply otherwise."

"I find it hard to take off my crusader's hat at times."

She wondered if that was because at one time he had been one of those kids. Had he been teased, picked on? Had there been more to his injury than facial deformity? She wasn't any stranger to that either. She'd been a head taller than every other kid in her class from an early age. The names "Beanpole" and "Spider Legs" had hung on for years. Her prom date had been two inches shorter than her, and she'd worn plain flats when all her friends had on heels. Her own father had called her Stringbean.

It was a far cry from a disability, but the teasing had hurt just the same, making her sensitive to the situation of both Blake and his clients. Even now she had to remind herself to stand up straight, rather than slump in an attempt to conceal her height.

"Don't apologize for being passionate about what you do. You're clearly good at it," she said gently.

She bit back her questions about why he'd become that crusader. Even if she did want to know more about him, now was not the time or place. Any answer she got would be short and unsatisfactory.

He leaned against the wall and folded his arms, watching as the little girl returned from the tack room with a bucket of brushes and began grooming her mount.

"Why don't you tell me a little about them?"

The question seemed to satisfy him, and the harsh expression melted away as he watched the duo closely.

"Well," he said, affection warming his voice, "take

Jennie, there. I put her on Minstrel and Riley on Pokey from the beginning, because the gelding and mare are gentle and work well together. That's important when there's more than one rider involved. We couldn't actually put them together at first. It took a lot of work. But they have similar issues and are a similar age. By pairing them up it's not just the two horses that work well with the riders, but the riders work together, too."

"They clearly like you," she added. Blake was quite easy to like, after all—at least in this setting. Easier than she was comfortable with. "The way Jennie smiled at you out there…"

"She's something, isn't she?" He grinned as he watched the youngsters work. "At the beginning she nearly froze in the saddle and didn't say a word. I had to walk Minstrel around the ring while her mom stayed alongside. Finally she started taking the reins herself, but her mom was always right there. Now Heather watches from the sidelines. Seeing Jennie that comfortable and confident—well, that's what this program is all about."

His easy speech took Hope by surprise. In the two days she'd been here he hadn't ever said so much, and so freely. "Is it always just you? It must be a lot of work running this by yourself."

"Oh, no. Jennie and Riley are at a point now where I don't need extra staff or therapists for their sessions. We have to look at the individual child's needs. Safety is the first priority."

Hope looked up at Blake again, examined the dark scar running down his face. Julie had needed someone like Blake. Julie—who'd cried pitifully and without tears when she'd realized her career was over. When she'd understood that she'd never be beautiful again. Hope's throat swelled and she found it hard to swallow. Julie had realized that she'd never get married, have children, be a grandmother. Seeing a person's face when they understood they were going to die was a terrible, terrible thing.

She turned her attention to Riley for a moment as she pulled herself together. He wasn't smiling, and his tongue was between his teeth as he ran a brush over Pokey's hide. "Riley looks tense."

"Riley's very precise. He likes things a certain way, and it's easy for him to get overwhelmed. Riding's only part of it. Right now they're grooming. Once they put the horses back in their stalls they'll make sure they have fresh water and a little treat."

"Really?"

He nodded. "Jennie and Riley both have autism but they're very highly functioning. It works putting them together because they both get overwhelmed and stressed very easily, and frustrated when they can't communicate. Riding is soothing—the gait is very rhythmic and calming—and working with the horses is tactile. And by having to care for them they are practicing making connections, you know? That's so important."

"Mister Blake!" Riley came running up. "Mom brought carrots for Pokey."

Blake smiled at the boy and nodded. "When he's brushed, you can give him one."

Riley looked over at Jennie. "Maybe Jennie would like one for Mist…Mist…"

"For Minstrel? Why don't you ask her?"

They watched curiously as Riley hesitantly approached Jennie.

Jennie nodded at Riley, her ponytail flopping, and Blake smiled. "I'll be…" he murmured. "They don't talk to each other much. Mostly to the horses. It's a big thing that Riley went to her just now. Look."

Riley's mom gave him two carrots, and he promptly took one to Jennie. "Not 'til they're all brushed," Riley instructed.

Jennie nodded solemnly and tucked the treat into her jacket. Blake laughed as Minstrel nudged at Jennie's pocket. "Not yet," she chided the horse. "Soon."

"You're not taking any pictures," he noted, keeping an eye on the kids but confident things were well in hand.

Truth be told Hope had forgotten about her camera. Her interest had been captured by the workings of the place and talking to Blake. "I got a few of the barn while you were in the ring."

He wrinkled his brow. "None of the session? There's no problem with having our kids in the photos."

She looked past him when she answered. "If you're going to use the pictures for promotion you'd have to get all the parents to sign a release. This way is just easier."

Jennie came over. "I'm done. Can I put Minstrel in his stall now?"

Blake laughed. "That carrot burning a hole in your pocket?"

Jennie looked puzzled as she took his joke literally and didn't understand, so he turned to Hope. "Hope, this is Jennie. Jennie, this is Hope. Hope takes pictures, Jennie. She's going to take pictures of the ranch for me."

Hope said a quiet "Hi," but Jennie's smile faded and she seemed to withdraw.

"It's okay," he said to Hope as Jennie turned and trotted back to Minstrel. "She finds meeting new people daunting. That she even came over while you were standing here is progress. She hardly talked when she started."

"How do you know all this stuff?" Hope asked, looking up at him curiously.

"I had to be certified through the Canadian Therapeutic

Riding Association. That's the national board that governs everything. Anyway, we're still pretty small here, and this time of year isn't as busy—especially the few weeks leading up to Christmas. Spring and summer, when the weather turns nicer, it really books up. We do outdoor trail rides then, and other activities rather than just using the ring—including summer camps. I have some volunteers who come in to help, and some of our kids have medical teams that we work closely with—like physios or occupational therapists. This afternoon you'll meet Cate Zerega. Completely different situation than Jennie and Riley."

"How so?"

He kept one eye on the kids' progress as he answered. "She's got cerebral palsy and she's in a wheelchair. It's a lot to deal with when you're six."

Riley was having trouble getting Pokey unclipped so Blake stepped forward. "I'll be back in a bit," he said, leaving Hope standing there alone.

She watched as he smiled at Riley and soothed the boy's nerves. Together they unclipped the horse, and Riley put him in his stall without further incident. It was then that the carrots came out, and Blake laughed as he showed them how to hold out their hands flat. Jennie giggled as her horse's fuzzy nose touched her hand. Blake spoke for a few minutes with the mothers.

Hope had been thinking a lot about what Blake had said last night about her expecting people to be perfect. She wasn't quite sure what to make of it. She liked things a certain way. Didn't everyone? But it had made her think about growing up, and how many times she'd wished her parents had been different—wished they'd stop fighting, stop getting on and off the merry-go-round of their marriage.

That was what had kept her awake late into the night last night. She'd remembered how for a while things would be good, but then the arguing would start again, and then Dad would have had enough, and Mom would decide to take the girls on a new adventure. It hadn't always felt very adventurous. Hope and her sisters had had little stability through those years. Gram had been it.

Hope had tried her best for her sisters. She'd tried to hold it all together by getting perfect grades and trying to fill the gaps that their mother had left in her wake. She'd always felt like a failure, though. Every time Grace got in trouble or Faith got tears in her eyes from having her feelings hurt. Hope, being the oldest, had always felt she understood more about what was happening than the other two. Faith, the tenderhearted one, and Grace, the defensive one. It had been Hope who'd had to step in to dry tears or fix what was broken. Hope who had made sure everyone had a packed lunch and their homework completed.

And now the sisters hardly spoke. How was it she had messed it all up despite trying so hard, and Blake seemed to manage to put pieces back together so naturally?

A more grounded man she'd never met. He seemed comfortable in any situation, didn't he? He had his place in the world and was secure in it. It was evident in his business, his house, the way he grabbed a dish towel and washed dishes or shoveled a walk. This was his corner of the world. And, while Hope loved her life in Sydney, she'd never quite called it home. Home was Beckett's Run, and even then it had never had the permanence that she craved.

She turned away from the cozy scene with the kids and bit her lip. She'd been here two whole days and already it was bringing back things she didn't like to think about. What was the use of dredging up past mistakes? She couldn't change the past. And the truth was she couldn't make everyone fit into the ordered existence she wanted—

she *needed*. They'd all left her anyway. Every single one. She'd given up trying so she could save her own sanity.

It was time she got out of her own head and back to work. She went back into the ring and walked around the edge, snapping different angles. If she could get a good picture of the barn—despite the snow—and a long shot of the stable area, she could probably put together a good spread featuring the main facilities. It wasn't exactly art, but that wasn't what Blake was looking for, was it?

He found her standing in the middle of the dirt floor, much in the same way she'd found him standing only an hour before. "Hey."

She turned and watched him stride across the loam, his long legs eating up the distance. He moved purposefully, with a loose-hipped grace that was sexy as all get out. His cowboy hat shadowed his face, but she could see his lips were set. Her fingers tightened around the camera and without thinking twice she began snapping—rapid shots, one after the other.

"What are you doing in here?"

"Trying some things out. Do you think I could get up there somehow? It'd be cool to get a bird's-eye view of the ring from above."

His eyes opened wide and there was a long pause. Then, "I could get a block and tackle," he mused, rubbing his hand along his chin.

"Really?" She stared up at the beams and then heard his low chuckle. He was making fun of her. "Ha, ha."

"You took off before you could meet the moms."

"I didn't realize you wanted me to."

He frowned. "I wanted you to talk to them about including Riley and Jennie in your pictures. They'll be back next week for the Christmas party. You could get shots then, I suppose. But we won't have a regular session with them again while you're here. You missed the opportunity."

"I didn't know you were serious about that." She looked up at him and felt a little spiral of guilt as she offered the teensy white lie. "I thought it would just be easier if I took pictures of the rig empty."

"Shouldn't your pictures include what we *do,* not just where we do it?"

She bit her lip, unwilling to confess that she'd had to escape the corridor because she'd gotten emotional. "But those pictures are harder to get right. Do you really think Jennie and Riley would take to being positioned and posed, and all that goes into a photo like the ones we're looking for?"

"Why would they have to pose? Can't you just snap as we're working? You're a pro, Hope. You'll come up with something that'll work."

Her lips dropped open as he unwittingly brushed aside all the hard work that went into her job, treating it as if it were nothing. "Something that will work? You're right about one thing, Blake. I *am* a pro. And if I'm going to put my name on something it's not going to be merely adequate. It has to be the best."

He stepped closer and she felt the proximity of his body practically vibrating against her. She had to tip her chin up to meet his gaze, and for one delicious moment his eyes dropped to her lips before moving back up to her eyes again.

"I'm not interested in perfection." His voice was an intense rumble in the quiet of the riding ring.

"And I never settle for anything less," she retorted.

"I bet you don't," he replied.

His voice was so *knowing* that she wanted to smack the snide smile off his perfectly shaped lips.

"How about compassion, Hope? Do you have any of that?"

If he'd reached out and slapped her it wouldn't have stung more. "Ouch," she said quietly. "You do know how to aim, don't you?"

He glowered at her. "Me with my scar. Jennie and Riley with their issues. Cate with her deformity. All of us—we come as a package deal. That's what Bighorn Therapeutic Riding is about. That's what you're hired to take pictures of. Not an empty barn."

Could he insult her any further? Goodness, she hadn't meant him—or the children. She'd meant perfection in *herself.*

She ignored the tiny voice that said he might be a little bit right and let her anger build up a head of steam. "Hired? I wasn't *hired.* I'm doing this for free, remember? You couldn't possibly afford what I charge an hour."

The indignant light in his eye dimmed and she felt like an utter heel for bringing money into it. He was doing a good thing here, and she knew his operating budget was probably a precise work of art from year to year. It had been a low blow. Maybe even lower than his dig about compassion.

It was only remembering his low opinion of her that kept her from apologizing—again.

"You're right, of course," he replied, his voice dangerously low.

"Take it or leave it."

Her words hung in the air for several seconds.

Blake stepped back, his eyes icy and his expression hard and closed-off. "Take your perfect pictures," he stated, then he smirked. "Oh, wait. You're *still* searching for the perfect shot. Good luck with that."

He spun on his boot heel and strode out of the ring, leaving her standing there alone.

She looked down at her toes, trying to put her jumbled emotions in order, surprisingly stung by his harsh words. There was anger at being told how to do her job. Guilt for lashing out. And, most surprising of all, attraction. With their bodies close together and his gaze flashing at her there'd been a shiver of excitement that had zinged up her spine.

But all that aside the kicker was that he was right. She'd never accomplished perfection, no matter how hard she tried. She did settle for less—all the time. And, truth be told, seeking perfection was becoming rather exhausting.

Worse than that was that she knew how he'd taken her words. No one was perfect here, and that was the whole point. Everyone was scarred, flawed in some way. There was no cure. No permanent fix. There was just acceptance—and she'd essentially thrown that back in his face just now. He'd actually looked hurt underneath the angry set of his features. Because she hadn't just put down this place, she'd put *him* down too—even if it had been misconstrued. And she felt utterly rotten about it.

She had to fix it. Soon she'd be heading to Beckett's Run and Christmas with Gram. Somehow between now and then she'd find a way to give both herself and Blake what they wanted.

And then she'd get back to her previously scheduled life.

CHAPTER FIVE

IT WASN'T often that Blake was in danger of losing his cool, but little Miss Perfect Pants had just about driven him there. He was used to people's misconceptions and, frankly, misunderstandings when it came to his work. He considered it part of his job to work to dispel them.

What he wasn't used to was this feeling of impotence that seemed to envelop him whenever Hope looked at his face. He hated that she could make him feel like a self-conscious boy all over again. The boy who'd been pitied at first, because of his tragedy, and then scorned for his appearance. Scorned and laughed at by his schoolmates, with adults frowning and shaking their heads in what he now recognized as condolence and sympathy. As if he'd died right along with his brother somehow. In some ways he'd preferred the teasing to people always feeling so damned sorry for him. At those times he had always felt like he was somehow too pitiful to be *worth* teasing.

And then there had been the girls who'd cringed when they looked at his face. He hadn't even gone to his own prom. He hadn't had a girlfriend and he hadn't wanted a pity date for the rite of passage either.

He'd grown older and wiser and had developed the confidence to know what he wanted to do with his life. Not everyone turned away in disgust. He'd even started dating along the way—and one relationship in particular he'd thought had potential. Until a few months in when the offhand comments about his scar got more regular. And then she'd suggested plastic surgery.

He'd never forgotten that moment. He'd thought that girl was different. But she'd come right out and said it. *You can't possibly want to go through life with that atrocity on your face.*

Any dating he'd done since then had been short-lived. A man couldn't live like a monk, but he never quite trusted that anyone would see past his face to the man beneath. And he could never accept anything less.

Hope McKinnon made him feel all those uncomfortable, powerless feelings again and he hated it. And he hated himself for letting her get to him and making him say things he already regretted.

So he'd walked away before he could do any more damage and left her in the ring to take her precious pictures.

Now, an hour later, he pushed all his thoughts aside to focus on Cate Zerega. Cate was one of those children who reached in and stole your heart without you seeing it coming. Dark curls touched her shoulders and enormous brown eyes dominated her face, but her body appeared twisted and her muscle control and coordination were impaired. Cerebral palsy had made it impossible for her to walk without forearm crutches, but it hadn't taken away her bright smile, even though now and again her speech would slur when she was excited, Blake had accepted long ago that Cate was someone special.

When Cate had her appointments one of Blake's volunteers attended, too. Shirley was a physiotherapist from Canmore who had been donating her time for nearly two years. Together with Cate's mom, Robbi, they formed a strong team.

Today he'd saddled Queenie, one of the ponies he kept for the smaller children. Queenie was eighteen, and had never been overly ambitious. She was a dull gray, and not the prettiest equine specimen on the ranch, but she was gentle as a lamb and ten times as patient.

Cate's eyes lit up as Blake led Queenie to the ring.

"Hi, Mister Blake." Cate's eyes were round as dollars and Blake's earlier irritation slipped away.

"Hey, cupcake. You ready to ride?"

She nodded. "I've been waiting all week."

Her words were clear, with only the slightest hitch.

She gave her crutches to her mother and Blake lifted her in his arms. He took in a breath and was enveloped in a sweet cloud of little girl smell…strawberry shampoo, fabric softener and what he guessed was a fruity sort of snack eaten during their drive out from Calgary.

As gently as possible he settled her in the saddle. "There you go, munchkin. Queenie's all ready for you." He reached up and made sure the black helmet was secure on her head, then gave it two knocks with his knuckles.

"Who's there?" she asked.

"Ya," he said solemnly.

"Ya-who?" she asked, equally sober.

"Yahoo? Are you a cowboy, too?"

She giggled and he saw Robbi roll her eyes as she grinned. "Do you two never get tired of that joke?" she asked.

"Nope," Cate answered for them both.

Blake looked at Shirley and Robbi. "She's ready to go. Shall I lead first?"

They started the session in the ring, Blake leading Queenie around the perimeter while Shirley and Robbie walked along on either side. They stopped occasionally to adjust, and invariably Cate gave Queenie a pat on her mane before they started again. Blake smiled. Cate had improved since starting here months earlier, due to the simple act of riding. It got her blood pumping, helped with her core strength, posture and muscle tone.

"I think she's ready," Shirley said quietly, and Blake halted the team.

"Your turn," he said to Cate. "My arm's tired. Do you think you could take the reins now?"

She nodded. "I can."

"That's good news. Now, your mom will be right beside you. Just take her in a nice slow walk around the ring, okay?"

He put the reins in her hand, ensuring they were even and secure before stepping back. "I'm going to watch from over here."

He backed off and watched as Cate seemed to sit up even straighter from the simple act of being in charge. He smiled to himself. It was amazing what a little confidence and pride could do. She loved being in control of Queenie, even if it was just plodding around the ring endlessly at a walk.

"I'm doing it, Mister Blake!" she called out.

"You sure are!" he shouted back. "Good job, sweetie!"

Something caught the corner of his eye. He looked over and saw Hope, her camera raised, clicking away.

She lowered the camera and caught his eye. Something passed between them; something wordless and honest and accepting. It was an apology from Hope, a willingness to bend demonstrated by her returning to the ring to take some shots of Cate.

Blake dipped his head in a subtle nod—a tacit thank-you and his own apology—and the tension and bitterness that had snapped between them earlier melted away.

Instead something else hummed in the air between

them—something warm and exciting. He now understood why he'd felt as he had earlier—powerless. He wasn't in high school anymore but it was the same jumped-up feeling he'd gotten when he'd liked a girl…when he'd been attracted to someone…and when he'd considered that someone out of his league. Back then the girls had always looked away when he'd met their eyes.

The difference now was that despite her angry words Hope wasn't looking away. She was looking directly at him. No flinching. And as the seconds spun out he started thinking about her long blond hair, and the blue of her eyes that was clear as a glacier stream, and her long thoroughbred legs. He loved that she was so tall. So… He swallowed. *Accessible.* At six foot five, he usually towered over women—and a number of men, too.

"Good girl, Queenie!"

He snapped out of the moment at Cate's cheerful words as horse, rider and entourage passed by. He heard the clicking of Hope's camera as the group passed close to where she was standing.

Blake shoved his hands in his pockets. He was a smart man. He knew well enough what was going on. Curiosity. Awareness. Back and forth arguing that set off sparks in both of them.

And strategic retreat—him to the barn and her behind the lens of her camera.

But it was there all the same. The big question was, would he be smart and do nothing?

Or stupid and see what would happen?

He kept his gaze on horse and rider. He wasn't—and never had been—a stupid man.

Hope blinked furiously against the stinging in her eyes and focused on what she saw within the frame of her camera. She took picture after picture of the little girl sitting atop the aging pony. That was what Blake had asked of her and that was what she was going to do.

Even if it hurt. Even if parts of her heart that she'd thought closed off years before were coming slowly, painfully to life at the sight of the gruff rancher smiling at a poppet of a girl on a horse.

She hadn't known he could be this way.

But she'd keep the camera focused on the little girl and pony, even though she was tempted to turn around and take pictures of Blake. The way he rested his weight on one hip. The soulful expression in his eyes as he gave her that tiny no-fuss nod. The way his eyes lit up and his smile broke over his face like a prairie dawn when he spoke to the child on the pony.

She was far too aware of Blake, so she resolutely kept her eye on the team of people in the center of the ring and not on Blake on the sidelines.

When the session ended Blake moved forward and took the reins. He led the horse and rider to the edge of the ring and the concrete floor. Hope stayed to the side, still snapping, as one woman retrieved the forearm crutches and Blake reached up and lifted the girl from the saddle. He put her down carefully and helped her with the crutches.

Hope swallowed tightly. The girl wore small brown boots, and with the black riding helmet looked like the perfect tiny equestrian. The way she was looking up at Blake was pure hero-worship. And why not? He was a big, strong man who treated her with gentleness and kindness. He was good with kids. No, more than good. He was a natural, and it made her long for something she had stopped hoping for years ago. For someone—for *him*—to turn that gentleness on her. To make her feel as special, as treasured, as the little girl on the pony.

The center of someone's world.

"There you go. Time to put Queenie away."

"Mom says there's no more lessons until after Christmas."

Blake tipped back his hat and squatted down in front of her. "That's right. Everyone gets a bit of a vacation over the holidays."

"But I don't want a vacation," Cate said, her lower lip pouting just a bit.

Hope hid a smile, but didn't turn away from the scene.

Blake smiled at Cate. "Well, you're in luck. Because next week instead of riding we're doing something else."

"We are?"

He nodded. "Yep. Next week we're having a Christmas party."

"With cookies?"

"Of course."

"And hot chocolate?"

"Naturally."

Cate used her crutches to step closer, and Hope couldn't hold back the smile now, even as the sight of her sent a pang through Hope's heart. The girl was playing Blake like a violin. Whatever she asked for Blake would probably agree just because she'd asked it.

"And Queenie?"

His smile fell. "Nope, not Queenie." He waited a beat and then added, "But better. We're going on a sleigh ride."

"A sleigh ride?" The excitement was back. "With bells on the horses?"

He slapped a hand to his forehead. "I plumb forgot about bells."

"You can't have a sleigh ride without bells."

Hope heard how excitement put a slight lag on the girl's

speech. How could anyone remain immune to such an enchanting creature?

Hope stepped forward, her heart pounding with uncertainty. "If there are bells to be had, Blake'll find them." She smiled tentatively.

The dark eyes were turned up at her now. "He will?"

It was such an honest, heartfelt question that Hope didn't stand a chance either. Hard as she might try to keep her distance while she was here, there was something about this little girl that reminded her of herself at that age. She blinked as she realized it was her name—Hope. Cate had it in spades. And Hope missed having that trusting innocence.

"Has Blake ever let you down before?"

Cate shook her head.

"Well, there you go, then."

The girl turned back to Blake with more questions and Hope straightened. She turned to the pair of women looking on and smiling.

"Hi," she said, holding out her hand. "I'm Hope McKinnon. I'm doing some photography for promotional materials. I wondered if it would be okay to use today's shots? I'll have an official release drawn up, but for now your okay would be great."

"I'm Shirley, and of course you can. I'm a physiotherapist from Canmore, and I volunteer to work with a lot of Blake's more physically challenged clients."

"Then *you* must be the mom of this angel," Hope said, shaking the other woman's hand. "She's got Blake wrapped around her little finger, hasn't she?"

"Oh, and the other way around, too. I'm Robbi, and I'm happy to let you use any photos you like of today, Ms. McKinnon. Anything to help the facility. This place means a lot to Cate and our family. It's just wonderful."

They chatted a few minutes more. Out of the corner of her eye Hope saw Blake remove Queenie's tack while Cate, using her crutches, followed him like a faithful pup, keeping a safe distance as instructed, chattering the entire time. Hero-worship indeed. What was amazing was that Blake didn't seem the least bit fizzed by her incessant talk. He looked like he enjoyed it.

At the end he grabbed an apple, took out a jackknife and cut it into quarters, and then knelt beside Cate on the concrete floor. "You want to give Queenie a treat now?"

Cate let go of one of her crutches and balanced on the other, then held out the apple on the palm of her hand. Queenie lapped it up and crunched lazily while Cate laughed.

Robbi sighed. "Every time I see them together I wonder why that man isn't married with a bunch of his own kids."

Something seemed to expand in Hope's chest. She'd never even thought to ask if Blake had a girlfriend or if he was interested in anyone. Did Robbi have designs on him? She wondered how many of the moms talked about Blake like he was the next best thing to sliced bread. The idea made her feel unusually plain and un-special—especially as she was already aware that she stood a whole head taller than this very attractive mom.

Robbi laughed. "If I weren't already happily married…"

Well. That answered *that* question. Robbi looked at Shirley.

"You coming to the sleigh ride?"

Shirley shook her head. "Afraid not. We're heading to Cranbrook for Christmas the day before."

"Have a good holiday, then." Robbi called to her daughter, "Are you ready, honey?"

"Awwww," Cate complained, "do we have to?"

Robbi looked at Hope. "And this is why we love it here.

School is a bit of a challenge this year, but when she's here she seems so incredibly typical. Does that make sense?"

Hope smiled. "It does. Thanks for your permission."

"You bet. See you at the sleigh ride?"

Hope had been thinking she would give it a miss, but now she was curious. And she was thinking. She didn't normally do candid shots, but what if she did some at the party? If none of them turned out well, she wouldn't have to use them. But there'd never be a better chance to get a variety of clients all together. Staging shots was difficult, but one group shot might be doable. If nothing else she could give it to Blake as a present. She got the feeling he'd like something like that.

"Yes, I'll be there," she replied.

"Be where?" Blake's voice said behind her shoulder.

She turned and pinned on a bright smile. "At the sleigh ride, of course. I wouldn't miss it."

His eyebrow was raised. She suspected it was half in surprise and half unspoken challenge. "You're sure? It's going to be hectic."

It was her turn to raise an eyebrow. "You're forgetting I deal with temperamental models all day. If I can handle the divas, I think I can handle this."

He grinned. "Suit yourself. And in that case…"

"What?"

"Oh, nothing. Yet. I'm still working on some ideas."

He moved off to say goodbye to the group.

What ideas? And why did she have a very bad feeling they were going to involve something she didn't want to do?

For the rest of the week Hope and Blake managed to form a truce. Quite often Anna ran interference between them in the house during the day, contributing to the status quo, and Hope spent a lot of time in and around the barn taking pictures.

As she watched during Saturday's session it continually amazed her how hands-on Blake was with the kids, and how he genuinely enjoyed working with them—even when things didn't go particularly well. She'd started thinking along the same lines as Cate's mom—why on earth hadn't he married and started his own family? Clearly he liked kids. He was stable, secure…and despite the scar on his face not bad to look at either. For the right woman he'd be quite the catch—so what was the holdup?

Of course *she* wasn't that woman. Marriage, kids, the whole settling down thing? The very idea scared her to death. She'd already attempted to raise one family and hadn't done such a great job of it. It wasn't something she wanted to screw up twice.

She focused on the job. Soon she'd really have to sit down and start organizing the photos—picking and choosing the best ones and doing some editing. But for now, in the evenings, she found herself more often than not alone in the house while Blake spent his time in the barn. He was painting the sleigh and getting things ready for the party, he explained. There was always a glint in his eye when he mentioned it, and she was afraid to ask what had put it there. Truth be told, she was enjoying her evenings of solitude. A cup of tea and a book or a DVD while curled up next to a blazing fire was not a bad way to spend an evening. Whenever she felt like she was being indulgent she thought of Gram. Gram would be happy to know she was taking some downtime, if that was her worry.

Sometimes, before she went to bed, Blake would come and sit for an hour and watch a program with her. During those times they'd let the television do the talking. It was amazing to Hope how they were both comfortable to do so.

* * *

Anna had taken the day off to finish up her Christmas shopping.

Hope wandered downstairs at half-past nine, dressed in pyjama pants and a sweatshirt. The sun was bright and the light through the windows was diamond-sharp as it glinted off the snow. She squinted her way to the coffee-pot, and was pouring her first fragrant cup when Blake came through from the laundry room.

"Hey, sleepyhead," he said, reaching for a mug.

"You're too cheerful for this early in the morning," she remarked, affecting a scowl.

He chuckled. "Chores done, *and* I threw a load of laundry in."

"Disgusting," she commented, but his good mood was contagious. She took a sip of coffee and closed her eyes. The man did know how to brew a decent cup of joe.

"I haven't eaten yet, and my morning appointment has cancelled today. Doctor's appointment. You hungry?"

"I guess."

"Great." He reached beneath the cupboard and plunked an appliance on the countertop.

"What on earth is that?"

"A griddle. I'm making French toast. I told you it's my specialty."

Her mouth began to water. "Real French toast? Like dipped in egg batter and drowned in maple syrup?"

"Of course. And bacon to go with it."

Sweet mother—bacon, too? She'd be as big as a house after ten days of eating this way—first Anna's fine cooking and now Blake's. "I love bacon."

"Then you're in charge of that." He grabbed a pound from the fridge and got her a frying pan. "Cook it all. I'll use what's left for BLTs later."

They worked around the kitchen easily, Hope turning

the bacon and putting the crisp pieces to drain on paper towel while Blake mixed up milk and eggs. Out of the corner of her eye she saw him add vanilla and cinnamon. The first slice of French bread soon sizzled on the griddle, and as it cooked Blake got real maple syrup out of the fridge, along with butter and orange juice. When the slices were done he put them in the oven to stay warm and repeated the process.

When all the bread was gone and the bacon was cooked, they sat down at the kitchen table to eat. The earth was frozen and white outside the windows, but inside Hope was warm and relaxed. There really was something about this place. The dominance of natural wood in the design and the rustic decor was growing on her, and her new favorite thing was the stone hearth and the flue for the fireplace.

It was about as far removed from her modern apartment in Sydney as you could get, but there was something here that her apartment would never have. She looked around and realized it was permanence—rock and logs and land. This place was built to last. The people here *stayed* here. The reality of that was foreign to Hope, but the dream wasn't. It was what she'd searched for her whole childhood and never found.

She'd given up believing in it, but Blake lived it every day. She wondered if he appreciated it.

And yet…his parents weren't here. They'd gone off to warmer climes and sunnier days. There was no wife, no babies bouncing on his knee. Maybe Hope was only seeing what she wanted to see. She certainly had a habit of doing that. How many times over the years had she painted castles in the air only to have them tumble back to earth again?

How many times had she put her trust in people only to have them let her down?

He turned on the radio and a local station played country music interspersed with Christmas carols. Hope poured syrup on her toast and took the first delicious bite. When was the last time she'd had French toast? Probably the last time she'd had breakfast at the pancake house in Beckett's Run. She'd always put maple syrup on the first piece, and then load the second with icing sugar and whipped cream and fruit for "dessert."

Good memories. She took a hasty sip of juice to hide an unexpected burst of emotion. So many of her memories were tied up in anger and disappointment that it was a revelation to have such a simple, positive one pop up out of the blue.

"What are you smiling at?" Blake asked, helping himself to bacon off the plate.

She cut another piece of toast, savouring the rich vanilla and cinnamon flavor. "I was just remembering going to the pancake house in the town where Gram lives. She'd take us there when we were kids and we'd eat until we were nearly sick. This brought back memories, that's all."

"You spent a lot of time with your grandmother?"

She nodded as she finished chewing and swallowed. "We moved around a lot as kids, but we spent holidays and summers at Gram's. That's the real home I remember."

"What about your mom and dad?"

She shrugged, determined not to let things get dark and depressing. It was what it was, and nothing would change it now. "They were on again, off again a lot. My mom's a free spirit type, and my dad's more...*traditional*," she finished. "For lack of a better word. He always wanted her to settle down and face reality. She wanted him to lighten up. There was a lot of friction. They went their own ways a lot."

"But...?"

Explaining her family dynamic had always been a challenge. "But they usually tried again. It was pretty confus-
ing. Hard on my younger sisters, mostly, I think. Faith
was shy and didn't say much, and Grace tended to act
out for attention."

"And you?"

She put down her fork and picked up her coffee, half
hiding behind the cup and curls of steam. "Oh, me," she
said easily. Perhaps too easily to be believable. "I tried to
help where I could."

Which was the grandest understatement of the century. She'd tried to provide the stability that the three
girls had been missing. And, as much as she'd understood
her mom's need to spread her wings, she'd wished in the
deepest corners of her heart that her dad would come and
sweep them all home and tell Lydia that this was enough
nonsense.

She'd wanted them to be a regular family. Desperately.

"You've gone quiet," he observed softly.

She cleared her throat and busied herself cutting into
her breakfast. "Never mind," she said briskly. "Look,
Blake. I've seen the kids that you work with all week.
I could boo-hoo about my past all I want, but the truth
is, I've never had to deal with what those kids and parents are dealing with. I just need to get over myself, and
that's that."

His wide hand closed over hers and the fork stilled.
"That is easier said than done, and I know it."

She stared at his fingers, at the way they completely
dwarfed her hand, how strong they felt wrapped around
her skin, and before she could think about what a bad idea
it was she turned her wrist so that her hand rolled and their
fingers clasped together.

Not just a gesture of comfort now, but a real, honest-to-goodness physical link between them, and Hope felt it clear to her toes.

His thumb rubbed against her wrist, warm and reassuring, and she made no effort to pull away. Just another few moments. It felt so good to feel like a part of something, even if it was as simple as holding hands at a breakfast table. She'd been alone a long time. By choice, but alone just the same.

"*You* got over yourself," she reminded him. "You didn't let your accident stop you."

His fingers tightened on hers. "Didn't I? There were a lot of years between the injury and starting this place. I felt plenty sorry for myself. Plenty guilty."

"Guilty?" Hope looked up into his face. "What on earth did you have to feel guilty about?"

His eyes were the saddest she'd seen them as he said, "My brother was in the car, too. He didn't make it."

CHAPTER SIX

"Didn't make it?"

Hope felt like she needed to pull her hand away, but she couldn't. It would be a deliberate withdrawal and a step back—not at all what she should do at this moment.

Blake had had a brother? She swallowed. As much as she'd argued with her sisters, having them had always been a blessing. Because of them she'd never felt alone. Despite the strain of the responsibility she'd felt, and it hadn't been easy, they'd been there, given her a purpose. Even if they'd acted out in their own ways, the reason for it had tied them together.

She couldn't imagine what it would have been like to lose one of them.

"I'm so sorry," she whispered. "That must have been terrible for you."

"Brad was my twin," he said roughly. "We did everything together. The bond between twins is…"

"I've heard it's different. That the connection is deeper."

"I knew what he was thinking, sometimes what he was feeling. We played hockey together and sometimes we were so in tune with each other it was like music." He pulled his hand away then, and gave a sad smile. "I think of him when I watch the Sedin brothers play now. We could have been like that."

Hope didn't know who the Sedin brothers were but she didn't need to know to understand that Blake still felt the loss keenly.

"I can't imagine not having my sisters," Hope replied. "You're close?"

She looked down at her plate, annoyed with herself for bringing the conversation back to herself when she really wanted to learn more about him.

"Not particularly. But…I know they're there."

She suddenly felt guilty about not keeping in touch more. Not making more of an effort now that they were all grown up and leading their own lives. Faith and Grace weren't her responsibility any longer, but instead of trying to redefine their relationship, they'd drifted apart. Anytime either of them had asked her for anything she'd turned her back. Maybe it was time that changed.

"I spent a lot of time wishing for Brad back," Blake said. "It felt like a piece of me was missing. And I really struggled with why he was taken and I was left behind. At the same time I was a teenager, going through all the things that teens go through. We'd talked about going to the NHL together. All the dreams and plans were ours, and without him I had nothing."

"So what did you do?" She looked up at him, feeling strangely bereft at the grief still shadowing his voice. Had Blake hit rock bottom like she had?

"Got by day to day. Lived in a shell. Shut people out."

Hope's throat swelled as she remembered the day she'd finally given up on holding her family together. She'd broken down, and Gram had been there to pick up the pieces, but things had been different from that point on. Ever since she'd kept people at arm's length. She wasn't blind. She knew that if she didn't let anyone too close she didn't have to worry about disappointments or goodbyes.

Blake had come out of his shell and built this place. She hadn't, and she hid behind a camera.

"How did you come out of it?"

Blake had, and he'd done something extraordinary.

"My dad." Blake seemed to relax, and resumed cutting into what was left of his pile of French toast. "He and Mom took the accident hard. It was awful around here. But he showed up in the barn one day and handed me a pair of skates. I hadn't played hockey in three years—the accident ended my season and I never went back. He told me he'd lost one son and he'd be damned if he'd lose another and told me to put on the skates."

"And you did?"

He grinned. The way his mouth pulled made him look rakish. "You haven't met my dad. You don't argue with him. We went to the pond over at Anna and John's, laced up our skates and took shots at a net for three hours."

He mopped up some syrup with a chunk of bread.

"After that I spent some time deciding what I wanted to do. I read an article about the therapeutic benefits of riding and it clicked. The one thing I'd done through it all was work with the horses. They were my saving grace. The more I looked into it, the more I knew. And when Dad retired I made it a reality."

Hope pushed away her nearly empty plate. "You're very good at what you do, Blake. And very good with kids. I'm kind of surprised you don't have any of your own."

His gaze touched hers. "Been wondering about me, have you?"

"Don't flatter yourself," she replied, feeling heat rise in her cheeks. "I'm not the only one to speculate. Half the women that walk through your stable doors wonder the same thing."

His eyes looked confused for a moment, but then they

cleared and he brushed off her observation. "Women don't tend to be interested in a man like me."

"What's that supposed to mean?"

His blue gaze pinned her again. "You know. They take one look at my face and..." He put his knife and fork on top of his plate. "It's a lot to get past."

Was he serious? Hope didn't know what to say. Sure, she'd reacted to his scar, but she hardly noticed it now. It was hidden by his other fine qualities. His kindness, the way he smiled at the children, the light in his eyes and the strong, sure way he carried himself. Once she'd seen him in his element she'd glimpsed the real Blake. He was the kind of man who could be quite dangerous to a woman like her.

She could reassure him, but that would reveal way too much, so she came up with the only paltry platitude possible. "Someday the right woman will come along and sweep you off your feet." She smiled. "You'll see."

She pushed back her chair and picked up her plate. But Blake caught her wrist as she went to move past him.

His fingers were strong and sure as they circled her wrist. "This place is the most important thing to me right now. And I haven't said it yet, but thank you for what you're doing. You were right. I couldn't afford you by the hour."

She stared into his honest face. "I'm sorry I ever said that. You touched a nerve that day with the perfect thing."

He let go of her wrist. "I know I did."

"Not the way you think," she answered. "It's not *you* I expect to be perfect, Blake, or the children, or anyone else except me. It's *me* who keeps falling short of the mark."

That little bombshell dropped, she escaped to the sink to rinse off her plate.

She heard the scrape of his chair as he pushed back

from the table, knew he was behind her. She kept her back to him, the water running uselessly in the sink now that her plate was rinsed.

"There are things in life that happen and that we can't see coming. That's just reality," he said, his voice quiet but full of conviction. "Expecting yourself to be perfect is setting yourself up to fail."

"How can you say that?" she asked, turning back around and facing him. "How can you, when you are so good at what you do? Do you even have any flaws, Blake? And I don't mean physical ones."

"Plenty," he whispered. "I'm far from perfect, Hope. I just try to stay on the positive side. To find joy in things."

"But sometimes the heartache doesn't allow you to trust in the joy," she replied. "Because you know it could be ripped away at any moment."

There was a long silence. Finally he lifted his hand and placed his palm along her cheek. "I look at you and I know that there are many ways to grieve without having experienced death. What are you grieving for, Hope?"

"When my friend Julie died..." She scrambled to put together the words, but he shook his head. His hand was warm, comforting on her skin and she bit down on her lip so it wouldn't tremble.

"No, it's more than that. There's something else. Something you lost and never got back."

She blinked and sidestepped away from his hand, away from his eyes. "Don't," she warned. "I told you when I first got here not to go all shrink on me, remember?"

"I just want to help."

"Then leave me alone. Let me be, Blake, please. It's been a good week. I took some pictures and got fresh air and I've relaxed. Just let that be enough, okay? In a few days we have the sleigh ride, and then I fly out to Boston."

"For a family Christmas?"

"Yes. Let's just chill for the next few days, okay? No more digging into our personal lives. I won't if you won't."

She wanted to know more about him, but fair was fair. She couldn't expect him to open up while she remained a closed door, could she?

There was a long pause, and then Blake's shoulders dropped. "Okay."

"Okay. Now, since you cooked I'll tidy up. And this afternoon I'm going to start going through the pictures I have. Layout's not my specialty, but I'll put together a portfolio of shots you can take to a good designer."

"I've got a few jobs to do, as well. I'll be back by midafternoon. Maybe you can show me then."

"That'd be good."

He looked like he wanted to say something more, but then he shook his head. "All right. See you later."

"Later."

When she saw him again she was sitting at the table listening to the hum of the dishwasher, her laptop open before her. Her gaze caught a glimpse of a thick red hat above his black ski jacket. He wore heavy pants, too, and she gathered that whatever he was going to do it was going to be out in the bitter December weather. He'd be cold when he got back in. Maybe she'd make some cocoa to warm him up.

She shivered and turned back to her photos. Scratch the cocoa. After this morning she'd realized she was spending far too much time concerned about Blake's welfare. She could still feel the gentle touch of his hand along the side of her face. *Aw, hell.* She was starting to care for him more than she was comfortable with. When he'd talked about his brother her heart had cracked just a bit, and she'd had the crazy urge to take him in her arms and comfort him.

Which made her just about as starstruck as the moms who gazed at him like he was perfection in a cowboy hat.

He'd seen it on their snowmobile ride, and now Blake trudged the last hundred feet into the barnyard, towing the toboggan behind him. The perfect Christmas tree— eight feet of spruce, perfectly tapered, just the right size for the vaulted ceiling in the family room—was sprawled over it. A good shaking to get the snow off, a couple of taps with the hatchet on the trunk and it would be ready for the tree stand.

He expected Hope would balk at the idea of putting up a tree, but he wanted it up for the Christmas party, and his parents would be arriving Christmas Eve. He gave the rope a hard tug and pulled the toboggan over a small snowbank. If she didn't want to help decorate, that was fine. He'd done it by himself lots of times. Usually with a hockey game on in the background.

He'd seen the look of longing in Hope's eyes this morn- ing, though. Felt the squeeze of her fingers in his. She wasn't as immune as she wanted him to believe. And ev- eryone deserved to have a good dose of Christmas spirit. It didn't have to go any further than that. Shouldn't. No matter how attractive he'd found her.

No matter how much she'd surprised him by saying what she had this morning.

Her reaction to his face had been the worst, but now she was acting as though it didn't matter anymore.

Well, *fool me once,* as the saying went. They were just words, after all.

But it didn't change the fact that he sensed she was sad and wanted to cheer her up. He knew what it was like to be in that abyss. So he'd dig out the decorations and make the best of it.

He stood the tree on the porch and went inside, clomping his boots to get the snow off before disappearing into the basement to the storage area for the stand. When he came back up, Hope was looking down the staircase curiously.

"What are you up to?"

He held up the stand. "Christmas tree. Wanna help?"

Just as he'd expected, she took a step back. "You were out getting a tree?"

"Of course. After the sleigh ride we'll have cookies and hot chocolate in here. The kids will expect a tree."

He didn't mention the second part of the plan—the part where he'd be dressing up like Santa Claus and needing an elf. He wanted to hit her with it at the right moment, and give her as little chance as possible to try and get out of it.

"Oh."

She stepped aside, but he handed her the stand and bent to unlace his boots. He looked up as he shrugged out of his jacket and hung it on a peg.

She looked awkward and uncertain, and he smiled on the inside. "Come on," he prodded, nudging her through the door and toward the family room. "Help me move some furniture to make room."

Together they rearranged the furniture that sat next to the fireplace by moving the sofa down a bit and shifting a heavy side table to the other corner, pushing it against a matching table so that it made one wide rectangular surface. Blake eyeballed the vacant space and put down the tree stand in the precise spot he wanted it.

"You loosen the screws and I'll bring in the tree," he suggested, and without waiting for her response went out on the porch in his stockinged feet and picked up the spruce.

Together they fit the tree into the stand, and he held it level while Hope knelt on the floor and tightened the wing nuts. When it was secure she stood up, and he stepped back, admiring. It was the perfect fit. The perfect amount of fullness except for one spot that was a little sparse. He turned that side toward the wall—problem solved.

"Oh, my gosh, that smells so good!" Hope exclaimed, brushing off her hands.

"Wait until we get lights on it," he said, finally feeling some Christmas spirit. There was nothing like the scent of a real tree to put you in the holiday mood.

"I haven't had a real tree since…"

"Since?" She'd hesitated, leaving the sentence incomplete. Good memories or bad ones? he wondered.

"Since our family Christmases with my grandmother."

He looked over at her and caught her smiling wistfully.

"We always had a real tree, too. And Gram did her holiday baking and the kitchen always smelled good."

"You don't have a real tree now?"

She shook her head. "I live in an apartment and I travel a lot. A small artificial one is enough."

"Not this year, eh?" he asked, thinking that the idea of spending the holidays alone in an apartment with a plastic tree sounded very lonely indeed. "I'll go bring up the boxes of decorations." He nodded at the television. "There's a Christmas Classics channel in the music section. Why don't you turn it on?"

"Really?"

She sounded skeptical, and that just wouldn't do.

"You can't decorate without Christmas carols," he decreed.

By the time he found the boxes and got them upstairs Christmas songs were playing and Hope had disappeared.

"Hope?"

"In the kitchen."

Her voice came from around the corner, and he put the first box in the living room before going to find her.

She was standing in front of the stove, stirring something in a pot that smelled fantastically spicy.

"Mulled cider," she announced. "I found the seasonings when I was looking in the cupboard the other day. This is as good a time as any, right?"

"It's perfect. I'll start on the lights while you finish up. The lights take the longest."

He was halfway through putting multi-colored twinkle lights on the tree when she came into the room carrying two mugs, steam curling off the top. He took a break and stood up, stretching out his back as she held out the mug.

"It looks good," she offered.

"I like lots of lights," he replied, thinking back to when he and Brad had been boys and their job had been to stand back and squint. The lights had all blurred together, and any blank spots in their vision had meant there were holes that needed to be filled. One year the tree had been so big that their dad had used over fifteen hundred lights on it. "It's kind of a family tradition."

He took a sip of his cider and raised his eyebrows. "Mmmm," he remarked, angling a sideways glance at Hope.

Her lips were twitching just a little.

"I found some spiced rum in the cupboard, too. Thought it might warm you up after your cold hike."

He swallowed the warm cider, felt the kick of the rum in his belly. It wasn't just the rum. It was her, wasn't it? She could have a fun side if she let it out to play more. She put a wall around herself most of the time, but behind that wall he had a suspicion there was hidden a warm, giving woman. A woman he could like. A lot.

Right now she looked barely past twenty, with her straight hair in a perky ponytail and hardly any makeup. He could think of more pleasant ways than mulled cider to warm up, and all of them included her, in his arms.

Which would be a very, very bad idea. They were hardly even friends. It was a big leap from their new-found civility to being lovers. And there was no point in starting something he didn't intend to finish.

"It's good," was all he said, and he took another drink for fortification. It didn't help that she looked so cute in her snug jeans, when her long fingers curled around the mug as she blew on the hot surface of the cider with full pink lips.

He got to work putting on the rest of the lights while she dug through the boxes for ornaments and the tacky red and green tinsel garland he put on the tree each year. By the time he'd finished she'd pulled out a box and was sitting on the sofa, surrounded by nearly a dozen porcelain shops and buildings—his mother's Christmas village.

"This is adorable," she said, lifting up an ornament that depicted a red square building with a steeply pitched roof and the word *Schoolhouse* on a sign above the door.

"My mom's. Every year we got her a different building until she could build a whole town. Look." He reached inside a large plastic ice cream container and took out a tiny LED light. "Put this inside and it lights up."

"Pretty. Where do you normally put it?"

"On the long table in the hall."

Hope held the porcelain carefully in her hands and looked up at him, dismay turning her lips downward. "But you can't enjoy it there. You only see it as you pass through." She looked around and then her eyes lit up. "Look. What about the two tables we pushed together?"

"It's big enough."

"We need a white cloth. Just a minute."

She disappeared upstairs and returned with a snowy white towel. He watched as she draped it over the tables and put the schoolhouse down. She stood back and put a finger to her lips, then went back to the box again and again. She went into the kitchen and came back with something in her hand he couldn't discern, but she tucked it under the towel and before his eyes a hill of snow seemed to appear. Tiny figurines of children followed, punctuated by green bottlebrush-like trees and a snowman in a black top hat. Before he knew it she'd arranged the whole village—church, school, bookshop, houses—along the table, with snowy white hills forming a backdrop.

"How did you do that?"

She beamed. "Do you like it?"

"I do. What's more, I think my mom will, too. It's a shame you're not going to meet her."

Not meet her…not be here for Christmas Eve and then Christmas morning…it surprised him to realize he wanted her there. He liked having Anna around, but there was something right about Hope being in the house, wandering through the barns. She added something to the place—a sense of sophistication and class that he found he appreciated. And ever since that first day with Cate he'd been able to tell that even when she held back, there was something about the children that she responded to. She was fitting in rather well, considering the hoity-toity photographer who'd arrived only days ago.

Perhaps fitting in too well. Considering lately he couldn't stop thinking about her.

* * *

Hope saw the look in Blake's eyes and nerves bubbled in her tummy. She'd seen that look before: a softening of the features, a warming of the eyes, the slight parting of lips. There were times she tried to elicit this precise expression for the camera. Other times she'd seen it in the moments before she'd been kissed.

And Blake was looking at *her* that way, making her knees turn to jelly and her pulse pound.

Kissing him would not be the smartest move. All it would do was complicate things. This was supposed to be an easy ten days, then off to Gram's for Christmas and back to her life in Sydney, just as she'd created it. Granted, she'd been thinking about him a lot. Granted, she'd had to move past her own "rules" and face some old demons in order to give him what he wanted for the facility. That had put her out of her comfort zone.

Funny how out of her comfort zone it seemed kind of… well, cozy and right.

But in the end everything would go back to normal— which was Hope looking after Hope and not fretting about everyone else. Not getting involved.

She suspected that kissing Blake was definitely something a girl wouldn't walk away from without fretting on some level, so she nodded toward the boxes, breaking the spell of the moment while the music station shifted to a horrendous version of "O Holy Night."

"We should probably put on the rest of the decorations. Are they in this box?"

The warm intensity of his eyes cooled and he stepped back. "Oh, right." He opened the box and pulled out the bag that had ropes of red and green garland poking out of the top. "This is next."

It was tacky and cheap and slightly gaudy to Hope's artist's eye. Still, it was his tree, his house. And having grown up with Gram she did hold the slightest remnant of knowledge that traditions were not to be messed with—especially on the holidays. She took the first mass of tinsel in her hands and began looping it around the tree in a precise scallop pattern while Blake held the end.

"You're very exact."

She frowned and adjusted a swoop of garland. "I like things balanced. If they're imbalanced they have to be intentionally so, you know?"

"Not exactly. But you're having fun with it, so go for it."

He was teasing her now, and she didn't know whether to be pleased or annoyed.

Together they added ornaments to the tree—cutesy homemade types that were hand-painted or stitched: old-fashioned gingerbread men and knitted skates and bells, red and green boots with paperclips as blades, and gold-shot yarn bells with tiny brass jingle bells dangling from the centre, catching the light of the bulbs.

It was a long way from her red-and-white tree and the delicate glass balls that she had at home.

It was, she realized, a family tree. A tree with years of memories and love. And Blake was here alone. His brother was gone and he was stuck decorating the tree with a stranger.

Well, not exactly a stranger—not anymore. But definitely not family.

She wondered if the tree was up at Gram's. Wondered what Beckett's Run looked like, dressed for the holidays. Wondered if Gram had baked Hope's favorite holiday cookies—the chocolatey ones in powdered sugar.

Good heavens. She was homesick.

"Are you all right?" Blake's voice brought her back to earth and she realized she was standing holding an ornament, the string looped over her finger.

"Oh. Of course. Just thinking."

"About what?"

She drew in a breath that was shakier than she liked. "It's silly, really. I was just remembering Christmas in Beckett's Run. No matter what was going on in our lives, we always went home for Christmas."

"Good memories, then?"

She nodded. "Mostly."

She hung the ornament and saw Blake was holding a small oval one in his hands. His face changed, a mixture of love and pain twisting his features. When he'd hung it gently on the tree she could see it was a photo frame, and when she stepped she closer realized it was black with a big red "C" on it—the logo of the Calgary Flames. Inside the frame was a picture of two boys in oversize jerseys, hockey sticks on the ice, grinning widely for the camera.

Blake and his brother, Brad. Eleven, maybe twelve years old. Blake without the jagged scar down the side of his face, before puberty hit full force. His twin, Brad, looking so much like Blake it was uncanny, but with something different around the eyes and mouth.

She touched her finger to Blake's figure. "That's you, right?"

"Not everyone could tell us apart."

"It's the eyes and the shape of your mouth. And you're big as a barn door now, Blake…stands to reason maybe you were a little taller than Brad."

"I was the better checker," he said softly, "but Brad had faster hands."

"I'm sorry."

"You have nothing to be sorry about." He stared at the photo a while longer. "It is what it is. I miss him every day. But nothing will bring him back. I stopped making those sorts of wishes long ago. Now I just remember."

"And put this ornament on the tree?"

Blake's mouth twisted, and once more Hope noticed how the stiffness of his scar pulled his lips slightly. She wondered how horrible it must have been for him as a teen, dealing with that sort of disfiguration. Dealing with people's reactions. It wasn't much wonder he'd been curt with her when she'd arrived. The first thing she'd done was stare at him like he was some sort of freak.

But he wasn't. He was the strongest man she'd ever met.

"There's just one thing left to do," he said, clearing his throat. "Put the angel on the top."

He reached into the box and took out a rectangular carton. He opened the flap and carefully took out the most beautiful Christmas angel Hope had ever seen. A flawless porcelain face was framed by a coronet of hair the color of cornsilk; a white circlet atop her head was a halo. The dress was white silk shot with gold thread, and softly feathered wings flowed from the center of her back, the tips nearly reaching the hem of the dress. It was a work of art—a family heirloom.

"Do you want to do the honors?" he asked.

"Oh, I couldn't." She put up her hands. "That's gorgeous, Blake."

"It's been in the family a long time."

"It's your tree," she said. "You should be the one to put it on."

Blake disappeared to the kitchen and came back with a step stool. He put it on the floor and held out the angel. "It's your tree, too," he said.

"Blake…"

"Please?"

Her hands trembled as she took the delicate figure from his hands and stepped up on the stool. He stood beside her, and she was acutely aware of his shoulder next to her rib cage as she leaned forward and carefully placed the angel over the top bough of the tree. The cone inside the skirt slid over the pointed top and settled firmly into place as Hope let out the breath she'd been holding and turned around.

The step stool put her higher than Blake, so that his face was just below hers. He was standing close…so close she could feel the warmth of his body, smell the faint spiciness of his aftershave.

"Perfect," he whispered.

He wasn't looking at the tree. He was looking at her. Gazing into her eyes with his own deep blue ones.

She felt herself going, losing what was left of her common sense in the depths of them. Before she could think better of it she lifted her hand and laid it along his cheek—the one with the scar. She ran her finger down the length of it slowly, carefully, her heart breaking at the difference in texture of the scar tissue, its smoothness oddly perfect when its very presence was a symbol of such pain and loss.

His hands spanned her ribs and lifted her from the stool, put her feet firmly on the floor.

And once she was steady he took her hand from his face, squeezed her fingers and kissed her.

CHAPTER SEVEN

"Perfect," Blake had heard himself say. But he couldn't drag his gaze away from her.

The way she was looking at him made it impossible. He'd never talked about Brad like that before—not to anyone but his parents. It made people uncomfortable. But not Hope. She'd spoken in such a matter-of-fact way that it had been a relief to express how he missed his brother.

And then she did the last thing he expected. She rested her hand on his scar, tracing the length of it with warm, soft fingertips. Exploring. Caressing.

He spanned her waist and lifted her down, never taking his gaze off hers. She wasn't backing away this time. The music played softly and the lights glowed around them. And right now all he wanted to do was feel close to someone. To her. He knew in his heart that this could never truly go anywhere, but what she'd given him broke down all his resolve. With nothing more than a touch she'd accepted him, scar and all.

He covered her hand with his, pulled it away and squeezed her fingers—the fingers that had given him back something he'd lost long ago: faith. Faith that someone would see past the scar and see who he really was. Inside, where it mattered.

He dipped his head and kissed her lips. Warm,

cinnamon-spicy lips that opened beneath his and for one breathless moment made him believe that anything was possible.

All Hope's senses were on full alert as Blake touched his lips to hers. The glow of the Christmas lights beside them. The scent of the tree and mulling spice in the air. The sound of Christmas songs on the television. It was the kind of holiday moment she saw in the movies and read about in books; the kind that never happened to a girl like her but kept her up late on Christmas Eve under a blanket, with a DVD, a box of tissues beside her glass of wine and a packet of store-bought shortbreads that were never quite as good as Gram's.

But here she was, closing her eyes as Blake's warm lips beguiled her, tasting of cider and something far more potent than the tot of rum she'd put in his mug. His arm slipped around her, drawing her closer, and she put her hand on his shoulder, feeling the exciting firmness of his muscles beneath her fingers. He drew back slightly, their breaths mingling in the charged silence as the song switched. She bit down on her lip and chanced a look up at him, desperately wanting more and terribly afraid he might just realize it.

Looking up was a mistake and a blessing. The first petals of curiosity had been plucked and had been replaced by the more exotic bloom of desire and need. Blake's embrace tightened and Hope wrapped her arms around his neck as their mouths met again, hotter, more demanding. Her breasts were crushed against his shirtfront and his wide palm pressed against the curve of her back, molding their bodies together as their breathing quickened.

She hadn't expected this explosion, this powerful craving for him. It would only take a word and they'd be in bed together. Hope knew it, and the thought made her blood race. It would be fantastic. Blake was the kind of man who would be gentle and physical all at once. Careful, yet thorough. Sexy, yet loving.

And that last was what made Hope hesitate, back away from the heat of his touch and the glory of his mouth.

This wouldn't be a casual one-nighter. A brief encounter with no strings. Blake wasn't that kind of man.

And she wasn't that kind of woman either. She wouldn't be able to simply get up and walk away.

The alternative was getting in way too deep...or backing off.

She gathered all her fortitude and took another step backward, nearly tripping over the step stool, righting herself while her cheeks flamed and her heart seemed to pound a mile a minute.

"Hope..."

"Don't," she whispered, her voice hoarse. "We can't do this, okay?"

"You're afraid?"

Damn straight she was. Afraid of everything she was feeling lately. Afraid of getting caught up in holiday nostalgia. And most of all afraid of getting caught up in *him*. It would be so easy.

"I'm here for a few more days and then I'm gone. I don't do temporary flings, Blake. I'm not built that way."

"What *do* you do? Because it's perfectly clear that you don't do serious or commitment either. What's holding you back, Hope?"

Panic threaded through her limbs. "I'm just here to take pictures, okay?"

"Liar," he said softly, taking a step forward. "Those pictures are just a reason our grandmothers gave us both. Surely you'd figured that out by now?"

The very idea frightened her to death. "Are you saying you're…?" She choked on the next words. "On board with this? That you planned…?"

Oh, Lord. She was really starting to freak out now. Blake was looking at her in his strong and steady way, and she felt like a baby bird flapping its wings and still falling steadily toward the ground, waiting for the inevitable thud.

"Of course I didn't plan it. When you arrived I knew you were the last person I'd be interested in."

Ouch. That smarted. Even if it was what she wanted to hear, it stung just the same.

"Ditto," she replied.

"And now we have this." He swept out his hand. "It would appear we weren't quite as right as we would have liked to believe."

"It…it was just a kiss," she stammered.

"Yes, it was." He came closer and put his hands on her upper arms. "So why all the panic?"

"Because… Because…" But she couldn't form the words for a coherent explanation.

Because she didn't do emotional intimacy. And here she was, talking about it with him. Here she was, at his place, wiping away tears as she watched a young boy hug a horse or listened to the laughter of a girl who had very little to laugh about. This whole place was opening her up to a world of pain she'd shut the door on years ago. It was getting harder and harder to pack those feelings back into the box where they belonged. And what terrified her most was that she was afraid there would come a time that she couldn't, and then she'd break.

"I know."

His deep voice slid over her soul. He really did know, didn't he? It was in his eyes when he looked at the photo of his brother. It was in his smile when he lifted Cate from her pony or sent Anna home with the little bit extra left over from dinner. He didn't seem the least bit afraid of caring. But he knew she was. Because he'd been there.

She hadn't truly cried in years, but right now tears threatened as everything—past, present, future—seemed to overwhelm her. It was like she was standing at a cross-roads and it was too painful to go back, too frightening to move forward, but impossible to stay where she was.

She'd never felt more alone.

"What do you want from me, Blake?"

There was a long pause. "Nothing."

"It doesn't feel like nothing. *That* didn't feel like noth-ing." She lifted her chin, challenging. "Do you want to sleep with me?" she pushed. "Or was it just a kiss? Out of the blue, perhaps? Maybe you just got caught up in the moment? Or were you looking for something more from a poor confused girl who needs fixing?"

He ran a hand over his hair. "Dammit, Hope, I don't know!"

The words rang out, followed by a crystal clear silence between them.

"No, you don't," she said quietly. "And it's unfair to take things further when neither of us knows what we want."

"Why did you touch me, then?"

He turned the tables and butterflies started wing-ing their way through her stomach again. She could still feel the texture of the skin on his cheek, marveled at the strength of him and the vulnerability, too.

She ignored the question. "Blake, we both know this is a mistake. Let's just chalk it up to some spiced rum and holiday spirit and leave it at that. There's no sense com-plicating it with things that will never be, and we both know it."

"So reasonable," he replied, his eyes blazing.

"I don't want to get hurt," she answered.

"You think you could?" He took a step closer.

"I might," she admitted.

He didn't know how many feelings had truly come to the surface during this trip. Didn't know how many barriers he'd broken down simply by being himself. He could *never* know that.

Shaken, she looked up at him. "I need some time. A little while to…"

He nodded. "Fine. I'll clean up here."

"You're sure?"

His eyes seemed to see everything, to see right through to the heart of her as he nodded. "I'm sure. You go on."

She turned and fled the room, heading for her bedroom. When she got there she closed the door carefully and sat on the bed. She bit down her lip. Longings she hadn't allowed herself for years had surfaced, all resurrected by the power of his kiss. She'd felt beautiful, cherished, strong and capable of anything. But now it was over she was faced with the truth. She was an emotional wreck. She didn't know how to love, didn't know how to trust anyone. She'd failed so many times to hold her family together. She'd wanted so many things for them all and instead they'd ended up at opposite ends of the globe. Her mother, father, Faith, Grace…all spread out.

She remembered Gram's weary words the day she'd finally given up.

"You can't take the happiness of so many on your own shoulders," Gram had said wisely. "It's okay, Hope. You can let it go."

She'd let go of the responsibility, but she'd let go of her family, too.

And she missed them. Despite their differences and distance, she missed them.

She dried her tears and blew her nose. She had to stop thinking about Blake and put things in perspective. A few days from now and she'd be in Beckett's Run.

She decided to forget about long distance and roaming charges and dialed Faith's number. She needed a sister, and in her fragile state she wanted Faith, who had always been the gentlest of the three of them. Faith, who would be easier to talk to than Grace right now.

"Hello?" came a sleepy voice after the fourth ring.

"Crikey, I forgot about the time difference." Hope calculated in her head and realized that it was nearly midnight in England.

"Hope?" Incredulity colored her sister's voice.

"I really am sorry, Faith. Go back to sleep."

"I wasn't asleep." There was a sigh from the other end. "Is everything okay?"

"How did you know it was me?" Hope lay down on the bed, sinking into the pillows.

"I don't know many people who say 'crikey' in an American accent."

"Right…"

"Are you okay, Hope?" Faith's normally gentle voice held a note of worry. "You *never* call. And you sound…" She paused. "Is Gram okay?"

That was part of the problem, wasn't it? She never called. And now that Hope had her sister on the phone, she didn't know what to say.

"Gram's okay and so am I."

"Well, that's a relief."

Hope sighed and leaned back on the pillows. "I was just wondering… Does it strike you funny that Gram has asked all three of us to do favors for old friends? I mean, me with the photos, you and the stained glass—and Gram said Grace is going back to Beckett's Run…"

"I don't follow."

"Well…" Hope brushed her hand over her eyes. "I mean right smack in the middle of all three are…"

"Men?"

There was an acerbic tone to Faith's voice that made Hope sit up. *"Yes,"* she said emphatically. "You know Grace is going to see J.C. when she's back? And this Marcus guy, for example…what's his deal?"

"You mean *Lord* Westerham?" Faith huffed out a sigh. "He's a thorn in my side, that's all."

"I hear that," Hope replied, sitting cross-legged in the middle of the bed. "Blake is driving me crazy."

"Crazy good?"

Now, *that* was a loaded question. "Truthfully?"

"I could use a diversion. What happened?"

"We kissed. That's all."

She could nearly hear Faith's smile through the phone. "You kissed? That's all?"

"That's what I said."

"You didn't sleep with him?"

"Faith!"

Faith's soft laugh echoed in Hope's ear. "All this fuss over a kiss? Imagine what Grace would say."

The unstoppable Grace always took life by the tail and never angsted over a simple kiss, did she?

And in that moment Hope realized something strange and important. She envied her youngest sister. She admired her. Grace had never been burdened by the responsibility of keeping the family together. It showed in the way she lived her life—on her terms and with no apologies. Grace, of all of them, was the most courageous.

Hope had never been that brave. And it showed.

"Hope? You still there?"

"I'm here."

Faith's voice was serious again. "Are you okay, really? You never call like this."

"I just got to thinking about when we were kids and stuff. We had some good times, right? Especially at Gram's. I was pretty put off by being told I had to go home for Christmas, but I'm sort of looking forward to it now. How about you?"

There was a pause, and then Faith sighed again. "Hope, there's something you should know before you fly home."

Alarm bells started ringing in Hope's head. "What is it?"

"It's Mom. It seems she…and Dad are both in Beckett's Run for the holidays."

Hope didn't miss the pause before the word *dad*. It had always been really hard for Faith once she'd found out that she had a different father from her two sisters. It had been the nail in the coffin of her parents' marriage, really. The moment that their father—Greg—had finally had enough.

"That must be tense," she managed to say.

"Apparently not as tense as you'd think."

Faith's voice held an implication that was startling. Hope sat back and let that tidbit of news sink in. Their parents were actually getting along?

"I'm glad you called," Faith continued. "This way you've got a heads up."

The line was silent for a moment or two. Did Hope want to open the Pandora's Box that was their relationship with their parents? She closed her eyes and pressed her hand to her forehead. Not tonight. It was too complicated. They'd be on the phone for hours.

"Does Grace know?"

"I don't know."

Another telling pause. Hope wondered what Faith thought of it all. And Grace… The three girls were so different. But they all bore the scars of their inconsistent childhood in their own way.

"Faith, listen. I just wanted to call and say…" Say what, exactly? It was going to sound stupid and emotional, and that wasn't Hope's style.

"Say what, Hope?"

"That I'm sorry. I gave up on the family and I shouldn't have. I wish we'd stayed closer, you know? We're sisters." She thought of Blake and Brad. They wouldn't have another chance. But Hope did.

"You tried too hard, that's all." Faith's voice was warm and reassuring. "You tried to step into Mom's shoes and we resented you for it."

"Not you. You were never as hard to handle as Grace."

"I just handled it differently. I quit playing peacemaker and walked away. I'm as much to blame as you, Hope."

Hope's lower lip trembled as the simple words of truth touched her heart. "I think it's going to be good to see you this Christmas."

Faith laughed. "Me, too. Goodness, I don't know who this Blake guy is, but he must be something to bring all this about."

A hot flush seemed to crawl up Hope's body. Something? Oh, he was something all right. Not that she would go into details.

"He just makes me think, that's all."

"Right. So what's the problem? Why not see what happens? When was the last time you were involved with someone?"

The answer to that was long and complicated. She gave her sister the short version. "I'm flying out in a few days. I hardly know him. The only alternatives are to drop everything in Sydney to be with him, or try a long-distance thing from Australia to Canada. Based on what? Ten days? Either option would be crazy." No matter how great a kisser he was.

"You're right. That doesn't sound very practical. And you're not the risk-taker in the family."

Hope let out a breath. "See? You *get* it. What about you and the Earl?"

"Oh, no," Faith replied. "You called *me*. We're talking about you. Not me."

"For now."

"You should go. This has to be costing you a small fortune."

Hope recognized a diversion when she heard it, but things were going too well for her to persist and risk the fragile connection they'd made. "It is, but I'm glad I called. I'll see you in a few days, yeah?"

"You got it."

"Bye, Faith." She hit the end button and put the phone on the night table.

It had been right to call. Right to reconnect. And it had felt good to put into words how she'd been feeling about Blake. No matter how attracted she was becoming, no matter how much she was drawn into caring for him, anything more was a ridiculous idea doomed to disaster. Look at her parents. They'd dated briefly and jumped right into marriage and they'd *all* paid for that mistake. The very idea that both of them were in Beckett's Run now, making nice, made Hope roll her eyes. Why would this time be any different than before? She hoped Faith wasn't getting her hopes up for some big reconciliation. Hope was sure that this time would be exactly the same as all the others.

It was insane to think of anything coming of her time here with Blake. Anything serious was inconceivable in this short amount of time. And anything else was just pointless, wasn't it?

And there was still his Christmas party to get through.

She was just going to have to toughen up and Scrooge her way through—to keep them both from being hurt in the end.

Blake turned his head at the sound of heels on the concrete of the barn floor. His first appointment wasn't due for another half hour, and he knew that particular sound anyway. Hope's heeled boots—the silly ones she'd worn the first day and that he'd hoped she'd wear again each day since. Totally impractical, yes. Also totally sexy.

He stepped out of the stall, stood the shovel on its end and rested his arms against the handle.

"You're up early."

"Just wanted to let you know I'll be gone for the day. I don't have a present for Gram or my sisters, and the last thing I want to be doing is shopping at the airport."

"Nothing says love like an airport gift shop."

She smiled. She had on that red puffy jacket again—the one that made her cheeks look extra rosy.

"Exactly. Even worse would be the shops in Beckett's Run on Christmas Eve, after everything's been picked over."

Never mind that he understood exactly what she was doing. Putting distance between them. Things had been strained ever since that kiss, despite their attempts to keep it casual and pleasant. There was an *atmosphere* now.

But he wasn't going to do anything to stop her. She'd brought him up short the other night, asking him what he wanted from her. He didn't have an answer. He wanted her. He wanted to feel close to her. But beyond that she was absolutely right. She was leaving in a few days. A rough-

and-ready tumble in the hay might be on his mind, but it wouldn't help matters any—not in the long run.

And it was probably better if she was out of his hair for the day. Being so close to her, smelling her shampoo in the moist heat of the bathroom after her shower, the hint of lipstick on the edge of a coffee cup...

Everything about her was driving him crazy. In all the very best and worst ways.

"Drive carefully and enjoy yourself," he advised, keeping a bland expression on his face.

She looked at him strangely but smiled, shifting her purse over her shoulder. "I will."

Her boots clicked over the concrete once more and he resumed shoveling.

But damned if he could get her out of his mind, or decide what he was going to do about it.

Hope headed toward the downtown core of Calgary, hoping to get there early and finish before lunch. There was one place in particular she needed to stop on the way home and it was quite a bit out of the way. She had found the perfect present for Blake. One that he'd never see coming. She couldn't keep herself from imagining the look on his face when she presented him with bells for his sleigh. It had taken some searching but she'd found them.

And if it looked like he was going to make too much of it, she'd say they were for Cate. It had been the little girl, after all, who had looked up at him with huge, innocent eyes and insisted that the sleigh have a set of bells.

She parked and wrapped her scarf around her neck, enjoying the walk through the bustling streets. It felt familiar, the crush of people going to work, cell phones pressed to ears and random conversations happening all around her. It was vital. It was teeming with life.

Then she thought about standing on the crest of the ridge with Blake, looking out over the mountains. That was vital, too. And awesome. A place where a person could be quiet with their own thoughts.

She stopped at an intersection and waited for the light to change. Frowning, she stared at the flashing orange hand. Had all the noise of her life kept her from thinking too much?

The light changed and she hotfooted it across the street surrounded by men and women, all headed to their destinations. Where was she headed? She hardly knew anymore. But she rather suspected that her old way of living wasn't going to fit quite the same way again. And where did that leave her?

Stephen Avenue Walk was awash in holiday spirit. Banners hung from old-fashioned-looking light posts, and above her head Christmas lights were strung across the walk. No vehicles were permitted on the street so pedestrians mingled freely. In front of one store she marveled at an intricately carved ice sculpture of a Christmas tree and presents. Each storefront was draped in ribbons and bows and sparkled with red and green and gold. She could only imagine what it would look like at night, all lit up, and could almost see herself wandering along with a gingerbread latte in hand.

And someone to share it with.

She took her camera out of her handbag and snapped a few pictures. It wasn't good that she was imagining strolling through the walk with Blake, holding hands and admiring the decorations, doing some last-minute shopping. She tucked her camera away and zipped up her bag. She was here to shop for her family, and that was what she was going to do.

Venturing on, she entered an upscale shopping center.

At a bookstore she found a hardcover book featuring a beautiful stained-glass collection. She bought a stunning cashmere scarf and glove set in the department store for Gram, wincing at the price tag but wanting to treat her grandmother to something fancy and upscale.

She browsed through the store, admiring the fine clothes and gazing at perfume bottles with longing. But today wasn't for her. She resisted the urge to treat herself even as she passed the lingerie section. She had a weakness for pretty underwear and nearly gave in when she spotted an emerald-green silk bra and panty set on sale. But she turned away, knowing she didn't need it. Knowing that there weren't any occasions to warrant it in her future.

And yet she hesitated, just for a heartbeat, remembering the look in Blake's eyes as he'd kissed her. There could be, couldn't there? If she allowed it. If she let him in.

Getting away for the day had been smart. Even this morning, in the barn, there'd been a light in his eyes that was hard to resist.

In the end she gave it one last longing glance and moved on.

She still had to find something for Grace—the hardest present of all. What could she get for a woman who didn't settle down? Who lived her life from a suitcase? Perhaps Faith and Hope lived oceans apart, but they'd made lives for themselves in one place. Grace traveled endlessly.

At a gallery she spent more than she'd planned on a small painting for Grace—a grove of trees leading to a river. It reminded Hope of summer days in Beckett's Run. The colors were soft and blended, giving it a lazy, nostalgic feeling. Looking at it, she felt her throat tighten. Her sisters hadn't given up on her, had they? She'd given up on them. Or, more accurately, she'd given up on herself.

It was too late now to get those years back. Grace in particular was angry with her, and rightfully so.

Before she could change her mind, she handed over her credit card and bought the piece. Grace traveled, but she did still have an apartment. A home base. Maybe the girls couldn't go back to those days, but if they were all going to be together for Christmas perhaps they could remember some good times.

With her sisters and grandmother taken care of, that just left Blake. As Hope wandered farther into the historic district she saw a store boasting Westernwear. Unable to resist, she went inside.

It smelled of leather and cotton, and Hope couldn't hold back the small smile that touched her lips. This was Blake's world, wasn't it? Boots and leather, jeans and belt buckles. She didn't know why she was here, really—her plan had been to pick up the sleigh bells and that was it. But there wasn't anything wrong with getting him a small something to say thank you, was there? After all she'd been staying in his house and eating his food for more than a week already.

And she was giving him plenty in return—professional photos, a part of her argued.

She ignored the thought. She could buy someone a present if she wanted. She ran her fingers over the soft fabric of a red long-sleeved shirt. Blake looked good in red. It set off his complexion and made the blue of his eyes stand out somehow. Kind of like it had just before he'd kissed her in front of the Christmas tree.

She swallowed. It was just a shirt, right?

And she really should get something for Anna, she justified. After all, Blake was her host but Anna cared for the house and did most of the cooking. That was all these things were—host and hostess gifts. Nothing deeper than that. She found a silver hair clip set with turquoise that was gorgeous, and added it to her purchases.

Ten minutes later she walked out, hands full of shopping bags and well satisfied with the morning's work. A quick stop at another department store secured wrapping paper and bows. She was all set now, wasn't she? To her surprise she found she was actually excited for the holiday—something that hadn't happened in years.

Her stomach growled, so she stopped for a sandwich and a coffee and opted to eat outside. It was cool, but not cold; she took her simple lunch to Olympic Plaza and sat, enjoying the sight of skaters swirling around what was a wading pool in summer, and admiring the arches built for medal presentations during a previous winter Olympics. She sipped her coffee and sighed. She liked it here. It was a big city, with big oil and gas money, but there was still a feeling about it—a down-to-earthness that she appreciated. She'd bet this place was beautiful in the summertime.

And the mountains were only an hour away.

And so was Blake.

Disturbed at the direction of her thoughts, she threw her wrapper and cup in a garbage can and made her way back to the parking lot. She still had to drive to the southwest corner of the city to pick up the bells, and then make her way back to Bighorn before dinner.

As she brought up the address on her GPS she frowned. She'd taken a day away from the ranch to get away from Blake, to stop thinking about him. And instead he'd been in her thoughts all morning. More than in her thoughts.

He'd been everywhere. And it was more than just appreciating the sight of him in well-fitting jeans and boots. It was inside. She cared for him. When he was with her it was like someone lit a candle inside her, warm and bright. She was falling for him, and that was *so* not the plan.

It was only the indisputable knowledge that nothing could come of it that kept her from moving forward, from exploring what might be between them. As she'd told Faith, the idea of a long-distance relationship was ludicrous, as was the notion that she'd leave everything behind in Sydney without a hint of a guarantee.

She only had a few more days. If she and Blake gave in to temptation it would only make leaving more difficult, wouldn't it?

Hope headed south on Macleod Trail and let out a huge breath. She just had to get through this party thing, which shouldn't be too difficult, right? There would be plenty of people around running interference. She'd probably hardly even see Blake during all the ruckus.

And damned if that didn't make her feel even more lonely.

CHAPTER EIGHT

HOPE tried to stay out of Blake's way the next day. She sorted some laundry and wrapped her presents, and waited until she saw him walking across the yard to the barn before heading for the kitchen to scrounge some breakfast.

She put her bowl and coffee mug in the dishwasher before booting up her laptop. Today she was going to go through the pictures she had and make a short list, then start editing. Blake needed a good dozen images to use in his brochure and on his website.

She frowned as she moved two unusable pictures of Cate into her discard folder. Blake had more than one PR problem. Hope could give him the best photos in the world, but his current website design wasn't doing him any favors. She wondered what his plans were. He could do with a redesign. Something that captured the feel of the place and the program rather than a standard template straight from a hosting package. She knew of several people who had the know-how to set it up, and then it would merely be a matter of updating; something Hope, even with her basic skills, could show him.

Except she wasn't going to be here, was she? And she'd guess that Blake would find it hard to take money from his budget to hire a web designer. Which left him with his basic site.

It was past noon when Hope lifted her head and rubbed her eyes. She gazed absently out the living room window and saw Blake walking back and forth with a gigantic snow scoop. Curious, she went to the window. She could see now. He was clearing a large patch of ice. With the snow removed Hope could see that the rink was bordered by planks, forming a perimeter. He put the scoop aside and brushed off two huge logs beside the rink. Seats? She smiled to herself. Benches?

His hat was pulled low over his head, his breath making frosty clouds in the air as he picked up shovel and scoop together and headed back to the barn. She swallowed. She couldn't deny—at least to herself—that she found his strength and physicality incredibly attractive. She'd never considered herself a fan of the big, rugged outdoorsy type, but Blake's roughness was what made him different, made him stand out. Paired with what she knew now was a gentle heart... Well, it made a devastating combination.

She managed to keep a grip on her hormones when he came in for lunch. Anna had fixed her a sandwich. She ate sitting at her laptop and then went to change her laundry over to the dryer while Blake ate his standing at the counter.

"Sorry to rush," he said between mouthfuls. "The guys will be here anytime."

"The guys?"

"Weekly game. We usually have it on a Sunday, but now that high school's out for the holidays we planned it today. Anna's son, John, comes over and captains the other team, and a bunch of local teenagers keep us on our toes. You can come and watch if you want." He waggled his eyebrows. "Be a puck bunny."

He seemed to be oblivious to everything that had happened before. The long looks, the dim lights, the way they'd kissed next to the Christmas tree. It was like nothing had ever happened between them, and on one hand she was relieved and on the other annoyed. The least he could do was show a bit of the awkwardness that *she* was feeling when they were in the same room together. But there was nothing. He was completely at ease.

She blinked and stared at her monitor without really seeing. Maybe *she* was the one making too big a deal out of everything. Maybe she was the only one who stared at the ceiling at night, unable to go to sleep, knowing he was just down the hall. She'd asked him what he wanted from her and he'd said nothing. Maybe he was right and she was making a mountain out of a molehill.

She ignored the puck bunny reference deliberately. "I really should keep working. I only have a few more days to get this sorted for you." She looked at him out of the corner of her eye. Part of his figure was obscured by the frame of her reading glasses.

He shrugged. "Suit yourself."

He went out the door minutes later and Hope let out a breath. Shortly after she heard the low drone of a snowmobile go past the house, and then a few trucks pulled into the yard. Her concentration shot, she watched curiously as nets were set up at either end of the rink and a line of boys—men, rather, looking at their size—sat on the logs, lacing up skates and putting on helmets.

One by one they stepped onto the ice, sticks riding close to the surface. A puck appeared and there was some passing back and forth, and shooting at the empty nets. Two players shuffled onto the ice in full goalie gear—pads, mask, glove and blocker. They smacked their sticks on the ice in a testosterone-fueled show of hubris as they began making practice saves.

And then the disorganized scrimmaging became a game.

It was easy to tell Blake from the others. He stood a good three inches taller than anyone else on the ice, and he moved the puck with a grace and finesse that the other players lacked. For the first few minutes he didn't get a chance at the net: a pass was intercepted, and a poke check turned over the puck. But then she saw it…the opening. And Blake did, too. With fast feet he zoomed up the ice, let the puck sit on his stick, before flicking his wrist and sending it flying—straight over the glove of the goalie and into the mesh at the back of the net.

Hope let out the breath she'd been holding and laughed. She hadn't watched hockey in years, but spending time in Massachusetts meant that she'd watched her share of Bruins games. She knew enough about the sport to appreciate the players below.

A few congratulatory slaps from his teammates and they were off again. Hope looked over at her computer and then at her camera, sitting in its bag at the end of the table. She couldn't resist.

Within five minutes she'd dressed in heavy coat, hat and boots and made her way toward the ice, camera dangling around her neck. She waded through the snow to the edge of the fence—Blake wouldn't see her here unless he was looking, but she had a clear view and could zoom in to capture everything she needed.

She took pictures for over an hour. Pictures of the men swooping and swirling on the ice. Pictures of sticks raised in victory after a goal. Of Blake, his long legs extended as he raced for the puck, his arms lifted as he released the puck, and—the best one of all—Blake laughing. His eyes sparkled blue fire and his mouth was open as he laughed, his cheeks ruddy with color beneath the black helmet.

She could hear the glorious sound of it across the

snowy field and it warmed her from the inside out. She found herself smiling in response. Blake's laugh made her happy, she realized. And she also realized that while she'd shed tears this past week she'd also laughed more, smiled more—more than she had in a really long time.

She felt alive here.

And she was going to miss it when she left.

That was the biggest surprise of all. Never in her life had she lived in a place this isolated. She couldn't even see another house from here. It was a long drive just to the nearest convenience store, and almost an hour to the closest city when she was used to everything being within a few blocks. But it had little to do with the place. It was bigger than that. It was Blake, and the simple acceptance he offered toward everyone who passed through the gates.

She didn't have to pretend to be anyone she wasn't when she was here, and it had made the pressure inside her seep away. She couldn't remember ever feeling this relaxed, without the weight of expectation and responsibility on her head. Being here, with Blake, had made her want things she hadn't wanted in a very long time.

The game wound up and she continued taking pictures. There was one she knew she was going to like—six huge male bodies, their backs to her, sitting on a log taking off their skates. Their voices mingled in the crisp air. And then she was sure one of them caught sight of her. She paused, her heart seizing, as he elbowed Blake and nodded in her direction.

She didn't need to zoom in to know that Blake's gaze had found her. His teeth flashed as he smiled, and he picked up the bag that held his gear.

Then he started walking toward her.

His stride was long and purposeful and as he drew closer Hope could make out the impish smile on his face and…oh, yes. A glint in his eye. He dropped his bag and catcalls echoed out behind them. Intuition told her she was in trouble, and she hurried to zip her camera back into the vinyl case sitting on the snow beside her.

"Taking pictures, are we?"

His voice was deep and rich, and it sent tingles down her spine it was so delicious.

She lifted her chin even as she continued walking backward. "Isn't that my job?"

Blake scooped up some snow, molded it in his hands, and kept walking.

"Did you get everyone to sign a release?" he teased, his steps menacing as he drew closer.

"D-don't," she stammered, stumbling backward and feeling the oddest temptation to burst out laughing.

A snowball fight? Just when she thought she had him figured out he came up with another surprise. His sense of humor was definitely suited for children…

"I mean it, Blake!" She would *not* engage in a silly snowball fight.

The first snowball hit her in the arm.

She bent down to grab her own snow and quickly pressed it into a ball—she had to defend herself, after all!

"Blake…"

He had more snow in his hand. She drew back and let her snowball fly, needing the distraction so she could get away. The ball just grazed the top of his head and he laughed, letting go with another and hitting her square in the chest. A clump of thick snow clung to her zipper. She stared at it for a millisecond before throwing another, missing him completely. As she bent for more snow he ran through the white fluff and captured her, circling her with his arms before she could throw the next one.

She struggled against his embrace, losing the battle

against laughter. "Let me go, you big goon!" she gasped, throwing out her elbows. But it was no use. He was laughing, too, and not even close to letting her go.

"You show 'er, Blake!" came a call from behind them.

Hope's mind raced, searching for a strategy to get free.

She looped one foot around the back of his boot, stopped struggling long enough to place her hands on his chest—and shoved.

Blake toppled over like a felled tree, just as she'd planned. But he grabbed her jacket and pulled her over with him—not what she'd planned at all.

They hit the ground in a mass of tangled legs and arms, with Hope most definitely sprawled on top of him in a most undignified manner, her face inches from his as the other hockey players let out whoops and cries.

Time seemed to hold still for several seconds as she looked down into his eyes. "Blake..." she warned, but it only added fuel to the fire.

"I'm sorry, Hope," he murmured. "I can't help it." And then he lifted his right hand, cupped the back of her hat, and pulled her head down until he was kissing her.

His lips and nose were cold, but his mouth was warm as he held her head in place. She knew she shouldn't—not after the other day, not after she'd decided there'd be no more flirting or intimate moments. But she couldn't resist his kiss and she let herself go, let herself enjoy the feel and taste of him. She reveled in the sound of his breath in the winter stillness, loved how the kiss teased and played.

He shifted his weight and suddenly she found herself beneath him, pressed into snow that was sharp and cold and yet somehow insulating.

"I've wanted to do that since the other day," he murmured. "Told myself I wouldn't. You make it hard on a man, Hope McKinnon."

He wasn't kissing her now. He was just looking at her, and she was looking at him. She couldn't seem to stop gazing into his eyes. And just when she wondered if he was going to let her up, he lowered his head again and made her go all soft and swoony by using his lips in a very effective manner. She didn't stop him. It felt too perfect, too wonderful. The flame inside her that he seemed to kindle so easily flickered to life. When he looked at her this way, kissed her this way, she felt alive. Beautiful. Cherished. Like anything was possible.

She was dimly aware of the sound of vehicle doors slamming, engines starting and trucks disappearing, and still they went on kissing. Soft kisses, light kisses, deep and passionate kisses. His body was heavy and warm as it pressed against her and she shifted the tiniest bit. Blake groaned into her mouth and a surge of feminine power raced through her veins.

She and Blake could take this inside. It would take very little convincing to move this to a warmer location with fewer clothes.

And it would be spectacular. She knew that instinctively.

Everywhere he was touching her now—even through clothing—felt like it was on fire. Blake would be gentle and thorough and intense. The blaze of desire flared inside her. All it would take was the right word.

The right word and he could be hers.

But was that really what she wanted? For the next hour, *yes.* Absolutely. His lips touched her neck and she struggled to breathe. But what about after that?

It always came back to the same thing. She stilled beneath him and he lifted his head. He was so beautiful, she realized, scar or not. It was more than that. It was how the man inside shone through his eyes and the set of his jaw.

She blinked against the moisture that gathered in the corners of her eyes. She cared too much. It wasn't love—it couldn't be and she knew that. But there was a connection between the two of them—perhaps there had been from the moment he'd offered her his hand when she'd fallen on the ice. He'd broken through the wall she normally kept around her heart like it had never even been there.

And she hadn't seen him coming.

His gaze deepened and he kissed each eyelid with such tenderness she thought she might fall apart right there in his arms.

"What is it?" he murmured the words in the silence. "Tell me, Hope."

How could she explain it without making herself even more vulnerable? "I can't do this," she whispered.

His eyes smiled down at her. "We can move it inside. I'm pretty sure Anna's gone home by now."

"That's not what I meant," she began.

The gaze that had been gently teasing before now sharpened hungrily. "I want to be with you," he answered. "Really be with you. Even if it's just this one time. I've never met anyone like you."

Oh, glory. If only he knew how much she wanted to say yes. He wasn't making it any easier. But then nothing was easy with Blake.

In the end, her need for self-preservation won out.

"It would be a mistake. We'd both regret it, Blake." She bit down on her lip, because even as she said it she was thinking about kissing him again.

Her legs and bottom were getting numb from the cold snow, she realized. She should get up and walk away. But she couldn't make herself push him away. Not yet.

"Why?" he asked. He shifted one leg so it rubbed up

against hers. "We've got means, motive and definitely opportunity."

Why did he have to be so charming?

He brushed his lips over the crest of her cheek, his breath warm as it slid over her skin.

"We're both grown-ups," he continued, sprinkling kisses over her face, little flecks of heat in contrast to the chill. "Both consenting adults. With a house to ourselves." He added the last with special significance.

All good reasons on the "for" side.

But it really only took one good "against" to throw a kink into the works.

"I can't be casual about this," she answered, wishing for the first time ever that she could be more free and easy about things rather than take everything to heart. "I'm leaving, remember?"

"You don't exactly let me forget it."

"Blake, I don't bounce back easily." She put her hands on either side of his face and forced his head around so that she could look him square in the face. She knew she guarded herself closely, and as a result she could often seem like she didn't care, but the truth was she often cared too much. "If we do this it'll make leaving even worse, don't you see?"

"Because you have feelings?"

"Because I can't do this *without* feelings."

She gulped, wondering what he'd think if he knew how much it had cost her to be that honest. Wondered what he'd think if he understood exactly how inexperienced she was and that she didn't take sex lightly. There'd been one time at the end of high school, which had been a horrible, horrible mistake, and twice more—both in her twenties, both relationships that hadn't panned out. Instead they'd fizzled out before they'd ever had the chance to get serious.

His gaze cooled. "That's clear enough, then."

She suddenly realized that he'd misunderstood. She'd meant that she wasn't a woman who could be casual about sleeping with someone. It had always been more than physical gratification to her. She'd meant—God help her—that her feelings were already involved. But he'd taken it literally—presuming that she had no such feelings for him. He was so wrong. He had no idea how completely he held her in the palm of his hand. How close she was to breaking. How much he made her feel about everything.

She wished she could explain, but she couldn't possibly open up about her real feelings. She didn't know how to have a holiday romance and still leave with herself intact at the end.

He pushed himself off of her and, just like the first time they'd met, offered his hand to help her up. She took it, feeling a mixture of relief and regret, and definitely unsatisfied in the most primal, physical sense.

"Blake, please understand." She tipped up her face and on impulse peeled off her glove and put her hand to his cold cheek. "It is going to hurt enough when I have to leave on Sunday. This would only make it hurt more."

"Why should it hurt?"

And there he was—still pushing her emotionally. He wanted her to say the words and it was unfair. It made her feel naked, with no defenses.

"Don't make me say it, okay?" There was a lump in her throat. "Isn't it enough that I've said this much?"

The air between them hummed with the words she hadn't said but they both knew.

"You can't keep kissing me like this. We need to keep it businesslike from now on." She didn't dare tell him that it was a very real possibility that he would wear her down.

A girl could only hold out for so long—especially when a giant part of her wanted to give in.

"Businesslike?"

She nodded. "If you care about me at all, please do as I ask," she said, hoping to appeal to his sense of honor.

His brow wrinkled and he reluctantly gave in. "All right," he replied. "No more kissing in the snowbanks."

"Or anywhere else," she cautioned.

"Or anywhere else," he confirmed.

"Thanks," she said, and skirted around him to retrieve her camera case.

He picked up his bag and followed her to the house, and Hope was relieved. At least that was what she told herself. But she was also disappointed.

She really did have to get out of here—back to Sydney and real life. It was far less complicated and way less painful—just the way she liked it.

Too bad she'd got the funny feeling that it wouldn't be the same.

CHAPTER NINE

THE morning of the Christmas party Hope kept her lap-top packed away and helped Anna with the preparations.

There was to be hot cocoa for the kids and hot spiced cider for the adults, as well as cookies and treats. While Anna went to work making iced shortbread, Hope donned a red-and-green apron and began making an old family favorite—Gram's Chocolate Truffle Cookies.

She'd called for the recipe yesterday, and been shocked to hear that Grace was out doing something Christmassy with J. C. Carson. She'd wondered if J.C. would make it through the evening uninjured. She'd said nothing to Gram, though, who'd sounded satisfied at the whole thing. And neither of them had mentioned Hope's parents.

She melted chocolate and then went to work on the dough, beating the butter and sugar while Anna hummed along with "Frosty The Snowman" on the radio as she spread icing on shortbread bells and stars.

Hope was up to her wrists in dough when Blake strolled in, cheeks ruddy from the cold and a smile on his face. "I think the sleigh is ready to go," he said. "And what have we here?" His gaze traveled from Hope's feet to her face. "In an apron? Surprising fashion statement, Hope."

"Oh, I'm full of surprises," Hope responded, rolling a spoonful of dough into a ball and placing it on a cookie sheet. "My grandmother's Chocolate Truffle Cookies. To die for. Wait and see."

"Full of surprises, hmmm?" he speculated, snatching a cookie from Anna's freshly frosted tray. He bit into it and a smidgen of green icing remained on his lip.

Hope stared at it and swallowed. It would be tempting to remove it personally, but she'd sworn off that sort of thing and Anna was right there, after all.

"You've got a…" She pointed at her own lip and then watched, fascinated, as his tongue slipped out to swipe the sweet bit of frosting away.

"Thanks."

She shrugged, rolling another cookie, filling the sheet. "Actually, I have an early present for you. Let me slip these into the oven and set the timer."

"A present?"

She nodded, butterflies swirling around in her stomach. Why on earth was she nervous? But she was. She avoided his gaze as she washed her hands and dried them on a towel. "I'll be right back," she said to Anna, who merely nodded as she worked on piping a red outline on a star.

She only had ten minutes—enough time to give him the present, not enough for them to be alone together for too long.

She hoped.

Blake followed her down the hall and into her room—the first time he'd been inside it since that afternoon she'd arrived and he'd carried her bag upstairs. The bed was neatly made and her suitcase was nowhere to be seen. Her laptop sat closed on a side table, the mouse pad and mouse precisely lined up at a right angle beside it.

Her perfectionist streak manifesting itself again?

Clearly Hope was nervous. She could barely look at

him, and her shoulders were tense. He smiled a little as he saw a smudge of cocoa on her apron. That had been a total surprise. Hope always seemed so put together, so... He wasn't sure how to explain it. Untouchable, perhaps. Out of his league with her tall, elegant looks. Either way, baking cookies in an apron made her look different. Put them on the same level somehow.

Maybe she was starting to unbend just a little bit. He hoped so. If anyone needed to unwind and let go of tension it was Hope. He only wished he knew what had her so tied up in knots. It wasn't just her friend Julie. He understood that now. She needed to grieve, and not just for her friend. But what? Why was she so demanding of herself?

She disappeared into the closet. She'd bought him a Christmas present and that surprised him—especially after the episode in the snow. She'd told him she didn't have feelings for him. She was a damned liar, but he knew she didn't *want* to have feelings for him and that essentially amounted to the same thing. Hands off. No matter what he was feeling in return.

Trouble was, he didn't want her to go. He wanted her to stay, to see if what was between them was real. For the first time since he'd broken up with his ex he trusted a woman to see beyond the surface. It had all changed the day she'd touched his scar with a tenderness and reverence that had humbled him.

He wasn't sure if he was in love with her or not, but he wanted the opportunity to find out. And he couldn't do that if she left for good tomorrow.

"I hope these are what you were looking for," she said, coming out of the closet carrying a gift bag very carefully as if what was inside was incredibly fragile.

He took the bag from her hands and heard a funny jingle. He opened the bag and peered inside. His heart gave a little catch. He reached in and pulled out a leather strap. The clear sound of bells filled the room.

"Cate said she wanted bells on the sleigh, so…"

He looked in her eyes. In the bright sunlight of her bedroom they were stunningly blue, full of hope and uncertainty. It hit him then. The professional manner, the precision and perfection—it wasn't confidence. It was covering up a massive case of insecurity. Was she worried he wouldn't like them? That they wouldn't suit? There were so many more layers to Hope than he'd first thought. It touched him that she was so obviously trying to please him. That she'd bothered to find something so appropriate, so personal.

He slid the leather over his palm and smiled. "They're perfect, Hope. Where ever did you find them?"

"In an antique store just outside Calgary," she replied. "You're sure they'll work?"

"Oh, they'll work. They'll be perfect." He looked up and smiled. "Thank you, Hope. It was very thoughtful of you to go to the trouble."

She blushed. Color infused the crests of her cheeks much to Blake's delight. The more she let go of the veneer she protected herself with, the more he liked her. Right now, with a bit of flour across the breast of her apron, her hair in a ponytail and a glow to her cheek, she looked adorable.

Was he actually considering a relationship, then? It would be a mistake to think that way. No matter how much he was starting to care for her, he knew she would never be happy here. Their lives were so different, and his first priority was the program.

She was right. He probably shouldn't have kissed her. Too bad he couldn't quite muster up an appropriate amount of regret.

"You're welcome. I thought…I thought the kids would like them."

"They will. They'll make tonight perfect." She was looking at him so hopefully he knew he had to keep the mood light before he got himself in trouble yet again. "I have something for you, too."

Her eyes widened. "You do?"

He nodded. "Not a present as such… Well, hold on. I'll get it and explain."

He made a quick trip to his room and grabbed the shopping bag from his closet. There was no guarantee she would go for it, but he hoped she would. Hope needed to let her hair down and show some silliness. They needed to have fun, and he had to stop thinking about her in ways that would get him nowhere. Their kisses before had been surprising and spontaneous, but there was something more now. A gravity between them. He couldn't quite put his finger on when or how it had changed but there was something—something important and a little sad and slightly desperate in these last twenty-four hours before her departure.

Back in her room, he handed her the bag. "I'm dressing up as Santa tonight and handing out some small presents to the kids. I was kind of hoping you would help."

She opened the bag and stared at the contents. "This is…" She put the bag down on the bed and drew out a hat, green-and-red striped, with a bell on the end. "This is an elf hat."

"Santa needs an elf," he said lightly, but he wasn't encouraged when he saw her frown.

She pulled out the tunic and tights and his favorite bit—the shoes, curled up at the toes and with bells attached to the tips.

"You can't be serious."

"Hey, at least you don't have to stuff your costume with pillows and wear a scratchy beard," he remarked, forcing a chuckle.

"You do realize I was hired to take pictures?"

"I know that. I thought over the last few days that had changed into something more." He remembered hearing her laugh as he tackled her in the snow, the taste of her lips all the sweeter because she'd been a willing and equal participant. He took her hand. "I thought we were something more," he said quietly.

"You know that's impossible."

And yet there was a hint of longing in her voice that he didn't miss. "So we're not friends?"

She pulled her hand away. "I didn't think that was what you meant. I hadn't really thought about it," she said, but her gaze slid from his. She *had* thought about it. They both had—too much.

"Have you never done something silly? Something just for fun, Hope? Have you seen the look on a kid's face when he or she sits on Santa's lap? It's Christmas. I want to give them something awesome—there's not enough fun in their lives. And I want to give you something, too."

"What's that?" She put the costume back on the bed and faced him, her guard fully up and functional again.

"A memory," he said. "A good Christmas memory. Because I think you need one—desperately."

The guard slipped just a little as her eyes widened and he saw his chance.

"Trust me." He lifted his hand and touched her cheek with his finger. "Can you trust me for tonight, Hope?"

"I leave tomorrow, Blake."

"I know that. Believe me, I know." He wished he had more time. Time to get to know her better. Time to…

Aw, hell. Maybe it was better this way. He was already

getting too involved. Much more and she'd really be able to hurt him. He knew for a fact that she wouldn't be back. She'd go back to her life in Sydney and that would be that, wouldn't it? Girls like her didn't stay. They didn't settle.

But it didn't stop the wanting. Or the need to do this for her. For all of them.

"Trust me," he repeated. "Wear the costume. Be my elf. Drink hot cocoa and eat cookies and let yourself be a kid again, Hope. Just this once."

She looked down at the costume and back up at him again. "You are *so* going to owe me for this."

And he was going to enjoy paying the price. "You'll do it?"

"I'll do it. For the kids, mind you."

"For the kids," he repeated. "You'd better get back to your cookies."

"The cookies! They've probably burned!" She rushed from the room, leaving the elf costume scattered on the bedspread and the scent of her perfume and dark chocolate behind.

He shook the bag of bells and smiled as the sound rang out. If this was the end of their time together he was at least going to give her a good memory to take away. He'd deal with his own feelings later.

Anna had saved the cookies from burning, and Hope had baked the rest without incident. They sat prettily on a plate now, dusted with icing sugar like snowy mountaintops. Hope had sneaked one earlier and they tasted as delicious as when Gram made them, making her long for the comforts of the one place she truly considered home.

Blake had remained scarce for most of the afternoon, getting the chores done ahead of his guests' arrival.

At three-thirty the kids and parents started arriving,

and the house became a hubbub of activity as Anna set out a Crock-Pot of hot cider, carafes of hot chocolate, plates of cookies and bowls of potato chips and pretzels.

Hope hadn't yet changed into her costume, and questioned whether or not she would. She would look ridiculous. Like an overgrown female Peter Pan with bells.

But when it came down to it she'd probably play along. She couldn't escape the memory of the look on Blake's face as he'd implored her to help him. Lordy, he was so handsome—and *kind*. She'd stopped noticing his scar days ago. What had once been ugly was now simply a part of the bigger whole, and that whole was something really special.

The carols playing on the stereo could barely be heard over the chatter and happy laughter of the kids. Cate arrived, using her crutches to get around, and Hope felt a surge of pleasure knowing that the little girl would have her sleigh ride complete with bells.

Hope looked around the busy room with a lump in her throat. This was how things should be, she realized. Loud and crazy and happy, with the sound of children's voices echoing through the house and the lingering scent of fresh-baked cookies in the air. It all felt so right that it caused an ache deep inside her. This was what she'd wanted for her sisters. For herself. And despite Gram's best efforts, and Hope's, it had never quite come to pass. But here—here it happened so effortlessly.

It was a bit of a miracle, really, and she wondered if Blake truly appreciated the magnitude of what he was doing with Bighorn. It was more than therapy. It was *home*. This was his family, she realized. Not by blood, but by love. He was the cord that bound them all together.

She blinked away a sheen of moisture on her eyes. If she wasn't careful she was going to leave a bit of herself behind when she left, and she wasn't sure she had too many pieces to spare.

"Ready for the first sleigh ride?" Blake's voice sounded close to her ear, the warmth of his breath sending tingles over her neck and down her spine.

"There's more than one?"

"I'll need to do two for sure, to fit everyone in."

"Won't I take up a valuable seat?" She turned her head slightly, angling her chin to look into his face.

His eyes were twinkling—he really enjoyed all this Christmas stuff, didn't he? He was going to make a wonderful Santa Claus. He'd make a wonderful father too—if he ever settled down and started a family. She wondered again why he hadn't.

"You can sit up with me," he said. "And get the carols started."

"Carols?"

He shook his head dolefully. "Hope, are you telling me you've never been on a sleigh ride?"

"Never."

"Then you'd best get your coat and boots and bundle up warm. It's high time you experienced one."

And then he was gone, to organize the first round of kids.

She met them outside, bundled as warm as she could be in heavy mittens and a hat, and one of Blake's goose-down jackets that was too big but the warmest thing she'd ever worn. The sleigh waited, hitched to two huge horses that stood so patiently Hope was sure they qualified as gentle giants. One shook his head, making the bells ring out merrily.

Cate clapped her hands at the sound. "Mister Blake, you *do* have bells!"

Blake tucked blankets around the knees of the passengers and rubbed the top of Cate's pom-pommed hat. "Didn't Hope promise you we would?"

Cate spun around to look at Hope. "You were right! He *does* have bells!"

The research, the drive, the money, the awkward moment with Blake this morning—all was worth it when she saw the smile on Cate's face.

"Of course!" she replied with a laugh. "What's a sleigh ride without bells?"

Hope climbed up front with Blake and nudged him with her elbow. "You've made Christmas for her, you know. Probably for all of them."

"They make mine, too," he replied quietly. He turned sideways and called back, "Everyone ready?"

"Yeah!" went up the chorus.

He gave the reins a gentle slap and the team started off. The runners squeaked on the snow, and Hope could smell the freshness of the air mingled with the pleasant smell of horses. Once they passed through the open gate to one of the pastures Blake urged the team into a trot, picking up the speed and causing some squeals in the back. Before long the first chorus of "Jingle Bells" started without any prompting from Hope, accompanied by the percussion of the bells on the harness. After "Jingle Bells" came "Silent Night," the young voices so sweet that Hope felt a stinging behind her eyes.

"You okay?"

She nodded. "You were right. This is special, Blake."

"Didn't you have fun Christmases at home?"

She shrugged. "Not so much. I tried, and Gram definitely tried, but most of the time either my parents were split and my dad was missing, or they were together and things were so tense that it just felt wrong, you know? After they split for good it was worse. We usually spent

Christmas with Gram, but our mother wasn't always around."

"I'm sorry, Hope."

She shrugged again, not wanting to delve too deeply into those feelings. "It is what it is, you know? I tried for a long time to step into that role, but it was a bit much to expect from a young girl. After a while I gave up."

"You were too young to be the mother."

She shrugged. "My sisters resented me for it, I think. I was only trying to help, but to them I was being bossy. I forgot how to have fun—thought that if I somehow kept things together maybe things would work out. That it would help Mom so she'd want to be around more. And if she were around more she'd be happier with Dad..." She paused, wondering how much to confess. "It was too much pressure to put on myself. The snowball fight the other day...? I haven't done anything spontaneous like that in years."

"Everything's precisely planned?"

"I don't get disappointed that way. I've had a lot of disappointments, Blake. I've learned not to have high expectations."

The song changed to the more upbeat "Rudolph the Red-Nosed Reindeer." The bells rang out merrily and the cold made their skin pink and vibrant.

"I hope you're not disappointed now," Blake replied, handling the reins easily in one gloved hand as they maneuvered through another gate into a grove of trees.

He put his free arm along the back of the seat, not quite an embrace, but she felt the intimacy of it anyway. It made her long to lean against his shoulder and let all her troubles go.

The tall spruces on either side made the setting even

better, adding the spicy scent of their needles to the winter potpourri.

"Today's a good day," she said simply, afraid to say any more lest emotion get the better of her.

Truthfully, today felt like a fairy tale. In her quest for perfection over the years she'd forgotten what it was like to enjoy simple pleasures. She'd pushed so much of her old life aside—things like hearing children's laughter and baking cookies and not worrying about how she looked and enjoying the moment.

Her quest for the perfect picture wasn't important right now. Perhaps it wasn't important at all anymore. She was living a sterile, scheduled existence, hiding behind a camera instead of participating in her own life.

She needed to fix that. She wasn't quite sure how, but she hoped that the trip to Beckett's Run would help. It was a start, anyway.

The horses picked up their pace as the back of the house came into view again, their necks bobbing as they led the way home.

"You coming on the next run?" Blake asked. "Or are you too cold?"

His shoulder buffered hers, and it would be so easy to slide over another inch or two and lean against him, swaying to the rhythm of the horses' gait. She was tempted, but she knew it wouldn't solve anything. Leaving was going to be difficult enough.

She shook her head. "I think I'll help Anna in the kitchen."

"Don't forget, when I get back it's Santa time."

Her heart thudded. "I haven't forgotten."

They pulled to a stop and Blake hopped down, then offered his hand to Hope to help her out of the seat. She put her mittened hand in his and jumped, landing so close to him the zippers of their jackets touched. For a prolonged second they paused, looking in each other's eyes.

Hope finally looked away. "Santa'd better get a move on," she murmured, and skirted around him toward the house.

As she went inside she heard his cheerful voice instructing the next round of kids where to sit, more laughter. She felt a strange sense of belonging and yet not belonging. Because this wasn't hers. She was only borrowing it for today. And it was getting harder and harder to remember that.

Blake had thought he was prepared for Hope as an elf, but he'd been very, very wrong.

Once the horses had been unhitched and put in their stalls he'd come in the back door to get ready for his stint as Santa. He was sneaking down the hall when he caught sight of her, all dressed in green. He should have known that, with her height, her legs would go on forever. The green tights clung to her legs, emphasizing the lean length of them, and the tunic with its scalloped edges skirted the tops of her thighs. Even with the ridiculous hat and shoes she was one heck of a sexy elf.

He changed into his Santa suit, stuffing the coat with a fat bed pillow and hooking the white beard over his ears before putting on his cap. Black boots rounded out the costume, and Anna had stitched him up a red sack made from fleece. Inside were presents for each child—a toy and a treat. He hadn't been extravagant, but that was hardly the point. Each item had been carefully chosen and wrapped.

"Ho, ho, ho!" he boomed, stepping into the living room with the sack over his shoulder.

Eyes widened, and one small voice whispered reverently, "It's Santa!"

Blake wasn't sure how convincing he was going to be—he was probably a good deal taller than most Santas, he only hoped the beard concealed his scar, and keeping up the deep, booming voice was going to be a challenge. But he took a seat in a chair by the tree and did his best.

"Santa's got a good little helper this year! Do you all know Hope? Doesn't she make a pretty elf?"

He nearly laughed at the mortified expression on Hope's face as all eyes turned to her.

"Well," she replied, clearing her throat, "if Santa came *all* this way for our party, it's only right he should have a helping hand, don't you think?"

"Yeah!"

Excitement bubbled up and out, and everyone looked to Blake again. Hope sent him a wink that said she knew what he was up to—and she was going along with it.

"Hope, maybe you can give Santa a hand by taking the presents out of that sack." He looked down at the children. "Did you all want presents? My elves have worked very hard this year. I hope you've all been good."

"I've been good, Thanta!" one girl called out with an adorable lisp.

There were more shouts and laughs and Blake chuckled at one little boy who was so excited he was almost vibrating.

Dutifully Hope came forward and reached into the bag, pulling out the first present. She handed it to him and he let his eyes twinkle up at her. Little did she know, but this was only the first of the surprises in store for her today.

"Says here this present is for Chad," Blake boomed. "Come on up, Chad, and get your present."

Chad, who had suffered a spinal cord injury when he was three, shuffled up to Blake with a wide smile. "For me?"

"For you," Blake said, handing over the present.

And so it went on until, just as he'd planned, there was one box left in the bottom of the sack.

"Ho, ho, ho," he said deeply as he picked it up. "It feels like there is something else in here."

Hope had a wrinkle between her eyebrows. "But everyone has a present," she said.

He reached into the bag and took out the small box. "Says here this one is for Hope. Ho, ho, ho!" He looked up at her expectantly. "Hope, come sit on Santa's knee while he gives you your present." He patted his thigh.

"I think I'll stand—thanks anyway, Santa."

"Sit on his knee!" called Cate.

"Yeah," shouted a few others, "sit on Santa's lap, Hope!"

With a dark look aimed just at him, Hope came closer and perched on his knee. "I'll get you for this," she murmured, just loud enough that he could hear.

"I'm counting on it," he whispered back, but then continued on in his booming, jolly voice, "Now, Santa has a long trip after this, so I think he needs a little something to keep him warm."

"Hot chocolate!" shouted someone.

His grin widened. "Need to watch the waistline," he said, patting his round stomach. "After all, I'll be getting lots of milk and cookies very soon. What about a kiss from Hope here?" He touched a finger to his cheek. "Come on, Hope. Give Santa a kiss."

Her eyes were like daggers, but she smiled sweetly and dutifully pecked his cheek. "Santa's beard is scratchy," she announced.

He handed over the present. "Don't open it here," he whispered, then boosted her off his lap and picked up the empty bag. "Well, Santa must be getting back. Reindeer-training, you know. Merry Christmas, everyone!"

He added in a few extra *ho, ho, ho*s as he waded

through wads of wrapping paper to the door and slipped outside. Then he made his way to the back of the house and stripped down to his T-shirt and long johns. So no curious eyes would catch sight of the bright red suit he left the suit on the back step to collect later and hurried out of the cold, darting inside and sneaking to his room, where he changed into his jeans and shirt. He pulled on his jacket, went out the back door and around to the front, and made a show of coming back in again.

"What'd I miss?"

"Oh, Mister Blake, Santa was here!" Cate's excitement quivered in her voice. "And he got me a new doll!"

"Santa? When I was stuck out in the barn putting the horses up for the night?"

"You missed it! Hope sat on his knee and kissed him an' everything!"

His gaze strayed to Hope. She was still in her elf getup, still strikingly beautiful. As their eyes met he suddenly wished for the party to be over, so he could put the next part of his plan in motion.

This was their last night together. No more television in the evenings. No more watching her work on her laptop with those silly glasses on her face. No more kisses in the snow or by the flickering light of the tree. He didn't want the day to be over, but he did want the evening to get started. He'd promised her a good memory, after all. He wanted it, too. If this was all he was going to have from her he wanted it to be a night to remember.

"Well, I'm sorry I missed *that*," he replied to Cate, dragging his eyes away from Hope.

"Okay, everyone, before you go I want a group picture," Hope called out, picking up her camera once more. "In front of the tree. Blake, you get on your knees. And, moms and dads, if you could help out..."

Blake followed orders, wondering how Hope was dealing with the chaos of trying to set the shot. She was always so worried about lighting and balance and things being in the right place. But before he knew it she was directing them to smile and say "Merry Christmas" and it was over.

Things started to wind down after that; parents got kids ready to go home, Anna and Hope began clearing away platters and bowls and cups.

Blake retrieved his Santa suit and put it away, and as Hope changed out of her elf costume he packed a Thermos of fresh cocoa and a basket of goodies. It was fully dark outside, crisp and cool, and if his hunch was right nature was going to put on a show later tonight. A show he didn't want Hope to miss.

CHAPTER TEN

HOPE packed away the elf costume and changed back into her jeans and a fuzzy sweater with pockets. She tucked Blake's present inside one, running her fingers over the foil wrapping and soft ribbon. Her lips still tingled from kissing his cheek, and the fake beard had been soft, not scratchy as she'd said.

The whole day had been disturbingly perfect—a word she didn't use often. But there wasn't another word to describe the way she was feeling. Happy. Complete. Wonderful.

Perfect.

The only thing marring the perfection was knowing it was going to be over and tomorrow she'd be saying goodbye.

Anna was putting on her coat when Hope wandered back to the kitchen.

"I'll see you in the morning, yeah?" Anna asked. "To see you off?"

"I don't leave until eleven," Hope assured her, a heavy feeling settling in her stomach.

She really was leaving here tomorrow. On the one hand she was actually looking forward to seeing Gram and her sisters…and, if she were being honest, even her mom and dad, if what Faith said about them getting along was true.

But on the other hand, she was going to be sad to leave. Only a little over a week ago she'd been determined to find a hotel and stay somewhere else. Now it was hard to imagine spending Christmas anywhere else.

As Anna's car pulled out of the drive Blake came back in. It felt odd somehow, intimate, and with a layer of tension that was unexpected just by being alone together. He had his outdoor gear on again, and she wondered if he had late-night chores that needed doing.

"Bundle up," he suggested, standing in the doorway. "Night's not over yet."

A strange sort of twirling started through her tummy as his gaze seemed to bore straight through to the heart of her. "It's not?"

"Not by a long shot. I have something to show you. I hope. Meet me outside in five minutes?"

She nodded. It was their last night. She couldn't imagine not going along with whatever he had planned.

When Hope stepped outside first she heard the bells. Once down the steps and past the snowbank she saw that Blake had hitched the horses to the sleigh again. It was dark, but the sliver of moon cast an ethereal glow on the snow and the stars twinkled in the inky sky. A moonlight sleigh ride. She'd guessed there was something of the romantic in him, but this went beyond her imagining.

The practical side of her cautioned her to be careful. But the other side…the side that craved warmth and romance and intimacy…the side that she'd packaged carefully away years ago so as to protect it…urged her to get inside the sleigh and take advantage of every last bit of holiday romance she could. It was fleeting, after all. And too good to miss.

Blake sat on the bench in the driver's seat, reins in his left hand while he held out his right. "Come with me?"

She gripped his hand and stepped up and onto the seat. He'd placed a blanket on the wood this time, a cushion against the hard surface. A basket sat in between their feet.

Blake smiled. "Ready?"

Ready for what? She knew he meant the ride, but right now the word seemed to ask so much more. She nodded, half exhilarated, half terrified, as he drove them out of the barnyard and on a different route—back to the pasture where they'd first taken the snowmobile. The bells called out in rhythm with the hoofbeats, the sound keeping them company in the quiet night.

Neither said anything until they reached the ridge several minutes later. The foothills rolled in shadow, a palette of grays and blacks that curled up next to the mountains. Blake hooked the reins and reached down for the basket.

"We didn't have a proper dinner, but if you can stand a few more cookies I can." He opened a container with an assortment of sweets, and then took out two mugs and a Thermos. "And hot chocolate with a little extra something."

He poured her a cup and handed it over, steam curling into the air with the rich scent of creamy chocolate. She took the cup in both hands, leaving her mitts on. At the first sip she grinned—he'd laced it with Irish Cream.

"Delicious," she said, peeling off a mitten and reaching for a cookie. "And proper dinner is overrated anyway."

The heat of the chocolate and the buttery richness of the cookies soon had her feeling warm and lazy, and she leaned back against Blake's shoulder, looking up at the sky.

"The sky is so big here," she whispered, staring at the carpet of stars. "Do you know that in Australia I don't see the Big Dipper?" She angled her head so she was looking at his profile. "It's like we don't even see the same sky, Blake."

The thought made her feel disconnected and lonely. It would have been nice to go home and at least think that maybe they were looking at the same thing, even though they were miles apart. But it was a foolish, romantic notion. The time difference didn't even add up. It was the kind of thing Hope the romantic would have thought of when she was fifteen. Not the realistic Hope at thirty.

They sat in silence for a long time, gazing at the stars, sipping their chocolate, until Blake pointed toward the north horizon. "Well, you won't see this in Australia," he said, his voice holding a note of excitement. "Hope—look."

She followed his finger and stared at the sky. "What am I looking at?"

"Give it another second...*there*. See it?"

The sky somehow shifted before her eyes. There was a swirling and a wash of white, like spilled milk, that suddenly caught edges of green and hints of yellow.

She sat up straight in the sleigh and stared. "Oh, wow! That's the northern lights, isn't it?"

"I hoped—with the moon not so full tonight and it being so clear and cold. You can't always see them this far south. Up north, around Fort McMurray, they're amazing. Bigger, more colors."

"Oh, but this is amazing, too, Blake. Look at that."

It was like the ripples of a blanket, all curves and shifts and soft hues. She was suddenly overwhelmed by it all— the sleigh, the picnic, the stars. It was like Blake was bewitched, able to take all the elements of a perfect winter night and hold them in the palm of his hand, releasing each one like a wish at his command. Even the Aurora Borealis. How did she stand a chance against such a man?

"I wish you didn't have to go tomorrow," he said, his voice low in his chest. "I wish you could stay for Christmas. Meet my parents. Have eggnog in your coffee Christmas morning and eat bacon and waffles and unwrap presents in your pajamas."

"It sounds lovely," she said wistfully, reluctantly drawing her gaze away from nature's display. "But I promised Gram. And I need to see my family. I didn't realize how much until I came here."

"So your grandmother's plan *did* work?" he commented, sipping his chocolate, which she now figured had to be cold because they'd stargazed so long.

"Gram's always known me better than everyone else. When I told you today that I gave up trying…I'd been burning the candle at both ends and I blew my exams. I lost a big scholarship and at eighteen—well, it felt like my life was over. Gram was there for that. She was the one who stepped in and made it right. It was the lowest I ever remember being until…"

"Until Julie died?"

"Yes." She breathed out the word with relief. "Julie was the first person I'd trusted in a long time. We were like sisters only without all the drama." She gave a small smile. "Losing her was…"

They watched the lights a little longer, until Blake interrupted the silence, carrying on with her last thought as if there'd never been a break in the conversation.

"Only you didn't really grieve. Which is why you reacted the way you did when you saw me."

"You know it is." She finished the last mouthful of lukewarm chocolate and tucked her mug back into the basket. "But, Blake, I stopped thinking about your scar after the first few days. It's not all there is to you. I know that. You're so much more. You're…" She stopped before she could say *everything*.

"Maybe you're more than your scars, too, Hope. Have you considered that?"

She swallowed thickly. "Of course I've considered it."

"But you're afraid?"

"Wouldn't you be?"

They sat in silence for a few more moments.

"I think I need to start doing that, Blake. Grieving for Julie, I mean. She came from a messed-up family, too. She respected that there was stuff I just didn't talk about. She didn't expect anything of me, which was a revelation. I let myself rely on her, and then she was gone."

Really gone. No second chances, forever gone.

The stars blurred and the lights disappeared as she blinked rapidly. "After the funeral I had to go home and pack up her things. I had to meet with her mother and send everything back. I had to go home to an empty apartment every night. I missed her." She swiped her hand over her face. "I do miss her. And I'm angry."

Blake put his arm around her and held her close against his side. "Angry with her for leaving?"

"Of course! That's what people *do,* Blake. They teach you to love them and count on them and then they leave. It's not worth it."

"Of course it is. It just hurts. It hurts when I think of Brad, but I can't imagine not having those years with him, not having those memories. Not everyone leaves, Hope. You've just had more than your share."

"The last week or so has been good for me," she admitted. "But it's a small bit of time. Temporary. It's not really my life. I needed it, yes. But now I have to figure out what comes next. Some of that is reconnecting with my family."

"And after that?"

"I don't know."

She really didn't. She had her job and her apartment in Sydney, but the thought of it seemed empty and lonely now. There would be no Gram. No Blake. No one who really mattered.

He took her mittened hands in his. "Come back."

"What?" Her gaze darted to his and she found his eyes dark and utterly earnest.

"Come back. I don't have all the answers, but I don't want tomorrow to be goodbye forever. There's something between us, Hope. I know you've felt it, too."

"Well, of course I felt it. But like I said, it's temporary."

"Why should it have to be?" He turned in the seat and gripped her wrists. "I've seen you with the kids, I've seen the way you light up. I know you've had a hard time of it and you're cautious. Don't you think I understand? This quest for perfection...it's what you rely on. You don't want to be disappointed. I get it. And I also know how I feel when you're around, Hope. I light up. I haven't felt this way in a really long time."

"It's just Christmas. People get all weird and sentimental at the holidays," she answered, but her voice felt tight and choked in her throat.

The worst of it was she suspected he really did get it. And she wanted to believe him. Wanted it so badly because it meant she wouldn't be alone.

"It's not just Christmas," he contradicted.

He leaned forward and pressed his forehead to hers, the thick knit of their caps touching. He kissed the tip of her nose before dipping lower and kissing her lips gently, sweetly, so perfectly that she half expected Christmas angels to start singing right above the northern lights. She allowed herself a taste of him...chocolate and the nip of whiskey cream, and butter and a man. A delicious combination that was tough to resist. The problem was that Blake was perfect. And for the first time in her life she didn't trust perfection.

"Be reasonable," she said, pulling away from the kiss, running her tongue over her lips for one last tantalizing taste. "We've only known each other ten days, Blake."

"I know, and that's why I want you to come back. So we can figure this out."

She shook her head, feeling the beginnings of panic settling in, cramping her chest, making it hard to breathe in the frigid air. "My job is in Sydney. My apartment is there. My life is there. I can't just pick up and leave when I want. I have obligations."

"Another few weeks," he suggested. "You never vacation. You must have time coming to you."

"And then what?" she asked, sliding away, putting inches between them.

He was going to make her say it, make it difficult, wasn't he?

"I leave after a few more weeks and it's even harder to say goodbye? It wouldn't work, Blake. You've built something amazing here. The program is your life and it's important. You can't just pick up and leave either. You belong here. And I'm not crazy enough to pack up and leave my life behind after ten days of...whatever it's been, with no guarantees."

"And you need guarantees?" he said coldly.

"You know I do. Come on, Blake. What happens to me if suddenly it doesn't work out? How can I give up the little security I've built? And what would I do? No home, no job..." She lowered her voice, leaving out the most important word...*alone*. "I'm not resilient enough for that."

"Then..." He lifted his chin. "People do the long-distance thing every day."

Her heart sank. This was not how she'd wanted things to go. She'd wanted to leave smiling and with fond memories, not with hurt feelings and…well, broken dreams seemed a little dramatic, but it was certainly feeling that way at this moment.

"Be realistic, Blake. Canada to Australia? Long distance aside, how often would we see each other? Do you know the cost of flights between Calgary and Sydney?"

"You're not even willing to try," he accused, sitting back against the seat of the sleigh. "You're going to leave tomorrow and write me off, the way you write off everyone who disappoints you!"

"That's not true," she defended. "I don't write people off. They write *me* off." She was getting angry now, was tired of always being made to feel like she was the one lacking. "I didn't kill Julie, and I sure as hell didn't ask my parents to split up and drag us from pillar to post so that we never really knew what home was. I'm the one who tried to keep the family together, and instead we ended up scattered all over the damn globe. That's not my fault!"

"I know," he said quietly. "And now you know it, too."

Silence settled uncomfortably as Hope sat there, feeling worn-out and, worse, played.

"I told you in the beginning that I didn't need to be fixed." Her voice was low and held a distinct warning. "I'm not one of your clients, Blake. I didn't come here to be psychoanalyzed. You said you were a rancher with an ear, but that's not true. You're a fixer."

"That's unfair—" he started, but Hope held up a hand.

"You fix people. That's what you do. You need to be needed. You see someone hurt and you make them better. You find someone troubled and you give them the answers—the kids that come here and even Anna."

"Anna?"

"She needed money and you gave her a job. She told me things about herself—about how she lost her husband when she was so young and brought up John on her own. And Blake swooped in to the rescue, right?"

"When did helping people become a flaw?" he defended.

"Why do you suppose you try to fix everyone? Does it have anything to do with not being able to save your brother?"

He couldn't have looked more shocked if she'd slapped him and she instantly felt sorry for the words. Losing his brother had been devastating; she knew that.

She sighed. "I'm sorry. That was uncalled for."

"No, you're right. I couldn't save Brad. But I can help others rather than letting the accident and my loss cripple me."

She understood the implication, even agreed with it. In his grief he'd found a way to reach out. *She'd* found a way to withdraw and protect herself.

She swallowed against the lump in her throat. "Oh, Blake. What happens when I'm all fixed? Will you be done with me then? Or what happens when you figure out that you can't fix me? Do you give up and walk away?"

"It wouldn't be like that."

But he couldn't know that, and they both knew it.

"Why haven't you ever married, Blake? It's clear you'd make a great father, so what's holding you back?"

He looked nonplussed, sitting back against the seat of the sleigh and staring at her with wide eyes. "What do you mean? I suppose I haven't found the right person."

"And will you ever? Face it, Blake. You're married to the program and those kids are your children. You get to fix them and send them on their way. Yes, you get close to them—but not too close, right? Because then you don't have to be afraid of losing them the way you lost your brother."

He looked so shocked she knew she'd gotten it right. She lowered her voice. "You made them your family so you don't have to take a risk on your own, didn't you? So how can you ask me to take a risk on you if you're not capable of doing the same?"

"Hope..." he said hoarsely. But that was all.

He had no rebutting argument. Hope felt relieved that the truth was out, but horrible that she hadn't been kinder with it. Blake deserved better.

If they'd been back at the house she would have made her apologies and left it at that. She would have walked away before they could hurt each other further. But where could she go here? She was stuck in his sleigh in the middle of nowhere. What would she do? Walk home? In the dark?

She pulled away and stared stubbornly at her boots. "I think we should go back now."

"So you can run away again?"

"Maybe I'm running *to* something this time."

He sighed and studied his hands. "I'm not saying you're wrong," he admitted. "Hope, despite everything we've said to each other, everything that's happened, you must know I care about you."

He looked up and met her gaze, so earnest and artless her heart turned over a little bit.

"I know you're hurting. Tonight when I looked at you I could tell that you wanted to belong so very badly. You do, Hope. More than you know. You *do* belong."

They'd argued and struck nerves and he still managed to see past it. The truth was he could never know how badly she wanted to stay. To see where things might go between them. And perhaps if she didn't live half a world away she would try it.

But her job was there—a good job—and it would be foolish to throw her career away for a maybe. Her mother chased those sorts of rainbows. Hope didn't. She knew how awful the thud could be at the end. She wasn't sure she could bounce back one more time.

"I can't," she said, her voice raw. "I'm sorry, Blake."

He looked at her for one long moment before picking up the reins and giving the team a slap. The sleigh lurched forward and Hope hugged her arms around herself. The wind picked up and the cold seeped through her coat and mittens.

It seemed to take forever to get back to the house. Blake halted the horses and Hope jumped out, grabbing the basket and taking it with her.

"I've got to look after the team," Blake said.

"Good night," she answered. "Thank you for the ride."

It was paltry and it rang a little false. The first part had been magical and then it had all fallen apart.

"I'll see you in the morning," he replied, and with a *hup* he had the sleigh moving again toward the barn.

Morning. As Hope turned toward the house she felt the first cold tear slip down her cheek. On one hand her leaving seemed too soon, but on the other she wanted it over with. Maybe then she could stop hurting. Because what Blake didn't understand was how badly she'd wanted to say yes. How much she'd wanted to be able to trust blindly and take a leap.

She was falling in love with him—perhaps had been from the start. And he'd offered her no guarantees because there were none.

She wouldn't have believed him even if he had, because deep down they both knew guarantees didn't exist.

CHAPTER ELEVEN

BLAKE made sure the chores were done and he was inside by midmorning. Hope was planning on leaving by eleven, and already a light snow was falling. The roads probably weren't going to be bad, but there was no guarantee of that.

Guarantee. There was that word again. She was expecting the impossible. He'd stopped believing in absolutes when Brad had died in that crash. He'd offered her more time—their time together had been too short; he was just now starting to really understand what he felt for her. It didn't really have anything to do with fixing her, did it?

And yet her words still echoed in his head, because he thought she might be right. He'd invested in his surrogate family because the idea of going through what he'd gone through—what his parents had gone through—after Brad died wasn't anything he wanted to experience again. Whether it had been intentional or not, that was what he'd done. And it had been easier to let Cindy go and say it was about her nonacceptance of his scar than it was to face the fact that he'd done exactly what Hope had done—protected his heart from being hurt again.

He was wiping dishes for Anna when Hope came downstairs, carrying her suitcase. She was dressed in her silly boots again and the wool jacket that looked like a winter coat but which they both knew was useless against real cold. Her hair was up in some sort of artistic twist and her makeup was flawless.

Oh, yes, her barriers were well in place, weren't they? And he'd been the one to make them go back up after he'd worked so hard to tear them down.

"You're all ready," Anna observed, drying her hands on Blake's dish towel.

"Ready as I'll ever be," Hope replied, trying to sound perky.

But he heard the wobble.

"I have something for you," Anna said, going to her recipe book. "Recipes for your favorites." She held out a sheaf of cards. "It's not much, but…"

Blake watched as Hope took them.

"It's perfect," she said warmly. "Whenever I get to missing this place I'll be able to make them and think of you. Thanks, Anna, for making me feel so welcome while I was here."

"You take care."

Anna barely came up to Hope's chin but Hope bent down a little and gave Anna a hug.

"You, too," she replied.

Anna stood back and flapped the dish towel at Blake. "Go on," she said. "Get out of my kitchen, you two, so I can get some work done."

He knew what she was doing. Making sure he and Hope had a smidgen of privacy to say goodbye. But voices carried in the house.

Blake followed Hope down the hall to the front door. "Wait a sec. I'll put on my boots and help you with your bag."

Hope paused by the door. "I left a CD with my pictures on it on top of your desk," she said quietly. "My email's there, too, if you have any questions or need a little more editing. I've saved them all."

So a glimmer of hope for more contact. But not nearly enough, and more of a formality than an invitation.

"Thank you." He opened the door and picked up her suitcase. "Careful. We've had a bit of snow. The walk could be slippery."

Like it had been when she'd arrived. He remembered seeing her go down, flat on her back, and the moment his breath had caught, hoping she hadn't hurt herself. That same breathlessness had happened again when she'd taken his hand and he'd helped her to her feet.

And again the first time he'd kissed her when they'd decorated the tree.

Damn. That had been the moment. The precise second that he'd begun his freefall, when he'd dropped the shield around his heart and let her in in a way he'd never let anyone in before.

She popped the trunk of her rental and he stowed the bag inside. "Be careful. The highway should be fine, but these side roads might be slippery. Is your phone charged?"

"Of course. Don't worry. I've got time. My flight doesn't leave for a few hours."

She stopped by the driver's-side door and fiddled with the keys. She was as nervous as he was, it seemed. It hadn't been this awkward since the very beginning between them.

"Hope, about last night..."

"I'm sorry," she whispered, looking up at him with tortured eyes. "I shouldn't have said what I did. I didn't mean to hurt you."

"Nor I you." He stopped just short of admitting she was right; it wouldn't change a darned thing now. She was determined to go and nothing would change her mind. Not even if he bared his heart and soul to her. "I don't want you leaving with this negativity between us. I want a good memory to hold on to when you're gone."

She swallowed, her throat bobbing as her lower lip quivered.

"Ah, hell," he said, giving up and stepping in.

He cupped his hand around her neck, feeling the soft skin beneath his fingers and the silky texture of her hair. If this was the last time he was going to see her, he'd be damned sure to kiss her goodbye.

Her mouth opened beneath his and she gave a little breathy sigh that only served to fuel both his desire and his frustration. Maybe she was right. Maybe it was impossible. At the very least it was crazy to feel this way after such a short time. He nibbled on her lower lip for just a moment before pulling away. And yet he still held her, one hand on the nape of her neck and the other resting on her rib cage, unwilling to let her go, because when he did it would be for good.

He was relatively certain now that the feelings he had went deeper than he had ever expected. Why else would it hurt so much to watch her leave? He kept the words inside, though, not wanting to make it any harder for either of them to say goodbye. Because they must say it. There was no other thing to do.

"I've got to get going," she whispered.

"I know."

He reached around her and opened her door. "Be safe."

She got in behind the wheel and started the car, letting the engine warm up. A swipe of the windshield wipers swept the snow away from the glass.

Blake kept his hand on the top of the door for one more

minute. "Merry Christmas, Hope. Enjoy your time with your family."

"Merry Christmas, Blake."

He shut her door, not wanting to, not knowing what else to do.

She started off down the lane and he watched as she reached the road and turned left, heading out toward the highway, on to Calgary, to Massachusetts, to Australia.

A world away.

It was only when she was out of sight that he remembered she hadn't opened his present.

Beckett's Run hadn't changed much. Even at night it was clear the old businesses were much the same. And, like it did every year, the town had gone all out in Christmas decorating—perhaps even more than Hope remembered. Lights twinkled like multicolored stars, porches were strung with evergreen garlands, and the statue of town founder Andrew Beckett sported a plush wreath around his neck. Even nature had been accommodating, supplying a blanket of pure white snow for the holiday.

A few weeks ago Hope would have rolled her eyes at the blatant demonstration of peace and goodwill toward men. But now the familiarity of being home made the backs of her eyes sting as she drove through town in yet another rented car, heading toward her grandmother's house. She'd found them stinging more often than she was comfortable with ever since leaving Alberta.

Despite her resolve, she'd left a bit of herself behind, after all.

She turned the corner and saw Gram's house. A delighted laugh escaped her lips. The blue Cape Cod–style house was decorated just like it had been when they'd been kids—every single shrub and tree frosted with lights, a giant wreath on the door, and a candy cane walkway leading to the porch. She pulled in the yard and cut the engine, content just to look at it for a while, feeling the fulfillment of being *home*. She should have come back before now. Should have made the time instead of avoiding the place.

She got out of the car, and had grabbed her suitcase from the back when the front door opened and Gram stood in the doorway, wearing a reindeer apron and a wide smile.

"You're here!" she called, excitement and welcome filling her voice.

"I'm here," Hope answered, grinning, and then on impulse she left her suitcase in the snow and ran up the steps to give her grandmother a hug.

"Oh, my precious girl," Gram said, hugging her back. "I wasn't sure you'd come."

"Of course I came."

"And the drive?"

"The drive was lovely. Roads were terrific."

Gram stood back and held her by the arms. "Have you eaten?"

Hope shook her head. It was the same old pattern and it felt good: love, questions, followed by food. "I only had a sandwich on the plane."

"Hours ago," Gram stated. "Bring in your bag and I'll heat up some chowder."

Hope took her bag inside and slid off her boots before carting it up to her old bedroom. The spread and wallpaper were exactly the same as they'd been the last time she'd visited—just before taking the Sydney job. In the desk drawer were old notebooks and pens, and a really old lip gloss that had dried out but had once been waxy and strawberry-flavored.

Gram had kept all her things just as she'd left them. In the hope that one day Hope would come home? An ache spread across her chest. For all her grievances and reasons she knew they were mere excuses. She had stayed away too long. Gram deserved better. If anything had come from this trip at all it was her determination that she'd get it.

Back downstairs, Hope got a good look at her grandmother. A little older, but still with her cheerful face, sparkling eyes, and soft white hair. She wore a sweater with a holly pattern on it. Gram had always loved the holidays, no matter what was going on. Maybe she was getting older, but she kept herself young.

"Sit down, honey. I've got some fresh bread to go with that."

Hope sat at the table and looked around. "Oh, it's good to be home," she said at last, as Mary put a bowl in front of her. "Where's Grace?"

"Oh, I'm guessing she's with J.C., putting the final touches on the plans for the festival tomorrow. She's been helping him out, you know."

"Grace? And J.C.? Working together?" She raised an eyebrow and gave her grandmother a telling look. "How many trips to the E.R.?"

Gram's face took on an innocent expression. "They seem to be getting along just fine."

"And Faith?"

"Faith and Marcus arrive tomorrow."

"Faith *and Marcus?*"

Hope's spoon clattered to the bowl. *What?* Last she'd spoken to Faith she'd claimed the Earl was getting on her nerves. But then, Hope remembered, there *had* been a particular tone in her voice that suggested something quite different...

"It appears Faith has decided to hold on to her earl," Gram said, picking at the crust of a slice of bread. She put it down, folded her hands on the table and looked at Hope. "And what about you, dear? How was your trip to Alberta?"

Hope studied her bowl. "It was good. Mr. Nelson..." how strange it was to call him that! "...has a great facility, and the children were wonderful. I left him with a CD full of pictures."

"And that's it?" Gram sounded disappointed.

Hope schooled her features and looked up. "Was there supposed to be more?" she asked innocently.

Gram watched her closely but didn't say anything.

"You wouldn't have been playing matchmaker, would you, Gram?" She sent her grandmother a sly look.

"Of course not!" Gram protested, but roses appeared on her cheeks. "Well, maybe. He's very good-looking, and right around your age, and I know he's from good people..."

Hope fought the urge to laugh and patted Gram's hand. "This chowder is as good as I remember. And the ten days away were good for me—so you're forgiven for issuing ultimatums."

Mary's face relaxed. "It's good to see you, Hope. I never thought I'd see all my girls under one roof again."

"It's good to be back."

But a bit of Hope was still stuck in a sleigh in an arctic breeze, watching the northern lights. She missed it already—the coziness of the log house, the barn, the sight of the mountains in the distance and Anna's cooking in the kitchen while Blake teased.

How was it she could be homesick for a place she hardly knew? She'd only been there for a few days. And she'd been gone for hours, not years.

"You all right, Hope?"

Hope shook the thoughts away. "Just tired. I think I might have a hot bath and an early night. Can we catch up more tomorrow?"

"Of course we can. You go ahead. I'm not going to be far behind you. Gotta keep up my energy for tomorrow's hoopla."

Hope kissed her grandmother good night and headed up the stairs. In the bathroom the scent of pink rose soap was in the air—a scent she always associated with Gram. She started the bath and went to her room while it was running to open her suitcase and take out pajamas. She found the flannel pants toward the bottom and was pulling them out when Blake's present fell out onto the floor.

She picked it up and examined the wrapping, touching it with her fingertips, feeling the texture of the silver foil and the soft curve of the ribbon. She went to the bathroom and turned off the bath, and then went back and sat on her bed. Slowly she untied the ribbon, putting it carefully on her dresser. She split the tape with a fingernail, wanting for some odd reason to leave the paper perfectly intact.

Inside was a square box. She removed the lid to find an exquisite dream catcher inside, lying on a nest of soft cotton.

She lifted it out, admiring the intricate weave and the gorgeous gray and black feathers drifting down. She wondered if Anna had made it. She wouldn't be surprised; the woman could do just about anything.

Folded on top of the cotton was a note. Her heart pounded as she took it out of the box and opened it.

There are different stories of the dream catcher, but this is my favorite: the hole in the center of the dream catcher is to let good dreams pass through

*and bless your sleep. The web is to catch all your
bad dreams so they disappear with the dawn.
     May all your dreams be sweet ones, Hope.
     All my love, Blake*

All my love. Hope stared at the note, stared again at the
beads and feathers, and touched each bit tenderly.

All my love. The words repeated in her head and she bit
down on her lip. Was that the feeling she couldn't seem to
pinpoint? Was it love? It must be, because why else would
she feel so miserable?

CHAPTER TWELVE

CHRISTMAS Eve morning dawned as all Christmas Eve mornings should—cold, clear, with a robin's-egg-blue sky and beams of sunlight that bounced off crystalline snow.

Hope slept in past the sunrise, waking shortly after nine. In Alberta it would be just past seven. Blake was probably up already and finished with the chores. His parents would arrive today from Phoenix for the holiday. He'd open his presents tomorrow, including the one she'd placed under the tree for him before she left.

The idea made her so lonely she curled up in the covers once more, soaking in the last bit of warmth.

But it was Christmas Eve, and there were things to be done. The festival was today, and events were going on all over town. She forced herself out of bed, straightened the covers, and looked in the mirror.

Should she straighten her hair? She looked at the curls tumbling over her shoulders, tighter than usual because it had still been damp when she went to bed. She'd been straightening it for years, but today she wanted to let it go. It looked...relaxed. And she was going to try to relax more. Accept things as they were rather than trying to be in control.

Besides, everyone in Beckett's Run would remember her with corkscrew curls. She smiled to herself as she dressed in jeans and a long-sleeved T-shirt. Why shouldn't she enjoy the holiday? There'd be street vendors with food and hot chocolate, music and events all over town.

And if she joined in maybe she wouldn't think of Blake quite so much.

That plan was soundly thwarted when she arrived downstairs. Grace was standing at the kitchen counter, pouring a cup of coffee. When Hope walked in Grace simply got another cup out of the cupboard and poured her a drink.

"Hey," Hope said quietly, wondering if Grace was still mad at her. Their last conversation hadn't exactly gone well. "Where's Gram?"

"Hey, yourself." Grace handed over the cup. "Gram's helping out with one of the events today. She said you went to bed early. I got in late…"

"I heard you. That board on the porch, remember?" Hope grinned at her sister. "It always did cause you trouble. With J.C. then, too, if I remember right."

Grace raised an eyebrow. "There was a lot to do to get ready for today. I need to be out the door soon." She paused. "It's good to see you, Hope."

"Really?" Hope sat down at the table. "After our last talk…"

But Grace waved a hand. "It doesn't matter now. It was good for me to come back. To see Gram. To…"

But she didn't finish the sentence. "Anyway, how was ranch life? Gram said you were taking pictures for some therapy-type place."

"It was good." Hope felt her cheeks heat but ignored it. "It's a therapeutic riding facility. I took pictures, had a chance to recharge."

"Is that all?"

The same question Gram had asked. Suddenly Hope

felt like she needed her sister very much. Perhaps that had been a lot of the problem—she'd never let herself confide in Grace or Faith. She hadn't wanted to burden them with her troubles. But they were all grown up now. And, while Hope didn't want to spill her guts to Gram and get her hopes up, she had the strange urge to tell Grace everything.

"No, it's not all." Shyness and a fear of being rejected made her backpedal. "But I doubt you want to hear it."

Grace sat down at the table. "Try me."

"I thought you had to skedaddle?"

"I can manage a few minutes."

Something passed between them then—a simple sort of acceptance, a closeness that had been missing for too long. "The guy that owns the place—Blake—and I...we kind of got involved."

"How involved?"

Hope felt her face flame yet again. "There's a slim chance I may have fallen a little bit in love with him."

Grace sat back in her chair and laughed. "A *slim* chance? You *may* have...? Oh, Hope. You haven't really changed, have you?"

"What do you mean?"

"You always hold back, refuse to let in people who would help you. Who would care for you. You're so busy protecting yourself from getting hurt that you forget how to live in the process."

"Don't sugarcoat it on my account," Hope said, still feeling the sting of Grace's words. "I'm sorry I said anything."

She made a move to get up, but Grace's next words made her sit right back down again.

"Does he love you, too?"

Did he? He hadn't said as much.

"I don't know. He asked if I'd come back after Christmas for a while. But it's impossible, right? I mean… I live in Australia. It's no way to run a relationship. And I'm hardly going to throw all that away after a ten-day… well, whatever. Flirtation?"

"You want to know how I see it?" Grace pushed her coffee cup across the table. "You were the oldest. You tried really hard to fill the gaps, especially when we weren't here with Gram. You tried to be perfect for everyone. But no one is perfect, Hope. And no matter what any of us did you were the responsible one. Faith never wanted to rock the boat, and me…? Well, I tried to get attention in other ways. But none of it made a bit of difference. And now you're so afraid of getting hurt that you push everyone away."

She reached over and in a move that was so not Grace, touched Hope's hand.

"I know a lot of people think I'm the most like Mom. I never stay in one place for long. I'm always after the next thing. But I think *you* are, Hope. Because you are spending so much time fighting who you really are by trying to be who you think you ought to be. No wonder you're exhausted."

In an odd, twisted way Grace made perfect sense.

"I'm scared," Hope admitted. There was a slight tremor in her voice; it was a tough thing to confess. "I'm scared to take that leap."

"After our upbringing, of course you are! All I'm saying is don't let your job stop you. If you love him, wouldn't he be worth it? You're a brilliant photographer, Hope. Why else did you think I asked you to do that assignment with me? I've been freelancing for years—nothing to say you can't do the same. Your job is just an excuse."

Hope chuckled. "Today is one day I appreciate your

bluntness," she said. "I'll think about it. In the meantime, there's Christmas to get through, right?"

She didn't have to decide anything right now.

"Which reminds me—I really need to get out of here."

"What about you and J.C.?" Hope asked.

Grace grinned at her. "Like I said, I really need to get going. See you around town, Hope."

"Don't think you're off the hook," Hope replied as Grace put her cup in the sink.

"Believe me," Grace replied acerbically. "I'm nowhere near off the hook. Anyway, bring your camera today."

She slipped out of the kitchen, leaving Hope in peaceful silence. With plenty of time to think. Was Grace right? Had she forgotten who the real Hope was? When had she disappeared? And was there a chance she could find her again?

She'd had hopes and dreams once. She'd wanted things—like love and a family. She'd been so sure, knowing that if she had them she'd never let them go like her mother had.

And it hadn't been any one particular thing that had caused her to throw those hopes away. No, it had been a constant chipping away. Every time they moved, every time there was a disappointment or an argument, or every time Hope tried to hold things together and failed. She'd been eighteen and the girls had been teenagers. Of *course* they hadn't wanted to listen to her. But years of insecurity, of little failures, had drained her of energy. Of hope. She gave a bitter laugh. Ironic that that was her name, when she thought of it.

She'd given up hope a long time ago, and her other plans with it. Someone to share her life with. The sound of a child's laughter. Blake had given that back to her, even if it was just for a brief moment. Those kids weren't just his surrogate family, they'd been hers, too, for a very short time.

She went back upstairs and fired up her laptop, sitting at the small desk where she'd once written in her journal and sometimes done her homework. Within seconds she'd brought up the pictures. Looking at Blake's laughing face during the hockey game made her both smile and feel weepy. She clicked through each image. Each one was attached to a memory. The picture wasn't always perfect but the memory was. The boys unlacing their skates. The farmyard during a snow flurry, with flakes softening the edges of the barn and the trees. Anna in her apron, holding a casserole in her hands.

Hope hadn't even looked at the ones from the party—just copied them to the disk for Blake. But she clicked through them now, each one a tug on a tender heartstring. The children in front of the tree, Blake in the middle. The two kids she'd met the first day, sitting together and sharing a plate of cookies. A small boy playing with a new set of toy cars, his grin dominating his whole face.

This *was* Blake's family. She understood it now. This was the reason he got up in the morning. The reason he sacrificed. She blinked. They really were alike, weren't they? They would do anything to make life better for the ones they loved. Except Blake hadn't closed off his heart, had he? She'd accused him of doing that, of not having a family of his own, but he'd opened his heart by choice, to those who needed him.

The final picture popped up on the screen. Blake was holding Cate in his arms with the Christmas tree behind them, its colored lights muted and providing a warm backdrop. Cate's hands rested on each side of his cheeks and above their heads was a sprig of mistletoe. Blake's eyes were closed and his lips were in an exaggerated pucker as the little girl kissed the man she clearly idolized.

In all her years of taking pictures Hope had never accomplished it—not until now. But *this* was the perfect picture. Not because of the lighting or the balance or the colors or exposure. But because it hit her square in the heart and squeezed, making it difficult to breathe.

Blake's words—the ones she'd dismissed so easily from the first—came back clearly, echoing through the empty chambers of her heart, filling them with bittersweet love.

"You can't organize perfection. You can't plan it. It just happens. And when it does, it's magic."

Magic.

To start with, she'd been in control. At the first sign of stinging behind her eyes or wetness on her lashes she'd locked it down—even when Blake had got her talking about Julie. But it was impossible now, as she stared at the courageous little poppet and the man who held her in his arms.

The man Hope had fallen in love with. She was sure of it now.

Tears rolled down her cheeks as, for the first time since she was eighteen, she let her heart out of its prison. She wept for the girl she'd been, and the one she'd become. She cried for Julie and the loss of someone who'd been more than a friend. And her heart cracked as she thought of Blake. He'd seen past it all to the truth of her—something she hadn't even been able to see in herself. And now he was there and she was here.

She heard again the words she'd said to him that last night and felt the heavy weight of regret. She hadn't been fair, and he'd been right all along.

After she'd mopped up her eyes and washed her face,

she picked up the phone in the quiet house and dialed Blake's number.

"Hello?"

It was a woman's voice—probably his mother, already in from Arizona.

"Hello, is Blake there?"

"I'm sorry, he's out. Can I leave a message?"

She paused. What could she say? *Tell him Hope called* was too little. Anything more was too much.

"No—no message, thank you," she said, her voice faltering as she put the receiver down.

She stared at the phone for a few minutes and then took a deep breath. Okay. So it wasn't going to be fixed today. She could accept that. She *had* to accept it. Right now she needed to get ready and head downtown to the festivities, enjoy the time the family had together. Faith would be here later, and after this morning's peacemaking session with Grace it would be good to hang out.

But when she got back she was going to call the airline and switch her ticket. She was going back to Alberta and she was going to face her feelings rather than run away. Everything after that she would take as it came.

The batteries in her camera had run out and a check of the camera bag had come up empty. Rather than stand in line at the drugstore, Hope walked the extra few blocks home to grab a new set.

She'd enjoyed the day. The variety of food had been staggering—including the chowder lunch she'd had at the Steaming Mug. The spiced cider had been piping hot, the decorations had been splendid, and the children's activities had put a smile on her face. And yet it had all left her feeling a little down, too, because each time she saw a couple pass by holding hands she wished Blake were there to share it with her.

He'd love this sort of thing—a real sense of togetherness and holiday spirit. Hope had spoken to the few journalists in town, covering the events, and she was proud of what J.C. and Grace had accomplished. Grace was a writer and Hope took pictures. It was better late than never—maybe they could do something together about Beckett's Run.

She shut the front door behind her and heard the porch board squeak beneath her feet. Smiling, she'd turned to go down the steps when she saw someone standing at the end of the driveway.

She looked up and everything in her body seemed to drop to her feet, then rebound to fill her whole body with joy.

He came.

Blake Nelson was here in Beckett's Run, dressed in boots and jeans and a soft sheepskin jacket and his *hat*. The brown cowboy hat made him seem impossibly tall and, yes, even a touch exotic, and she swallowed, thinking he looked absolutely gorgeous.

Anything she'd thought of saying to him deserted her. All her apologies were jumbled in her head. All her proclamations seemed small and paltry next to the reality that he'd flown all the way to New England on Christmas Eve and shown up on her doorstep.

He took a step through the snow, and another, and when he was close enough for her to hear him clearly he stopped.

"I don't want to fix you," he said.

The air stilled between them, carrying only the faint sound of music coming from downtown and the soft plop of clumps of snow dropping off cedar branches.

"I don't want to fix you, Hope. I love you just the way you are."

It was like she could suddenly hear the "Hallelujah Chorus" in her head. She slowly dropped her camera bag and went down one step, then another. He took one step forward, then a second. A smile blossomed on her face and she was rewarded when he smiled back, slightly sideways as his scar pulled at his lip. It didn't matter. She adored the roguish tilt to it.

When she reached him she stopped and tilted her face up to his. "You came."

"I had to. I shouldn't have let you go in the first place. It was all wrong from the moment you left. I knew I'd made a terrible mistake."

"So you came after me?"

He put his gloved hand on her collar, squeezing the inside of her shoulder. "It was high time someone did."

Oh, he *did* get it! She threw her arms around his neck and pulled him close. It had been so long since she'd felt she was first in someone's life.

"It wasn't trying to be perfect that made me put up walls," she whispered, holding him tight. "It was wanting to feel like I mattered. No matter what I did I never felt like anyone thought I was important enough to waste time on. Never thought anyone would ever think enough of me to stay, you know? Gram was the only anchor I had."

"Now you have me," Blake said softly, wrapping his arms around her. "No matter what happens between us, Hope, you'll have me. Because I know you matter. You matter to me. More than you can imagine." He gazed into her eyes, his wide and earnest. "I didn't say it right that night on the sleigh. I'm not sure I'll say it right now. I know you're scared. I know this is crazy. But I didn't expect to feel this way. You were right. I don't even think I knew I was doing it. I was afraid. I *am* afraid. Of loving someone so much and losing them."

"So what changed?"

"You drove away and I'd lost you anyway. Lost you and missed out on all the wonderful things we might have had. I couldn't let you go—not when I'd found what I'd been looking for all along." His throat bobbed as he swallowed. "I realized that you need to hang on to wonderful things in life with both hands when you have the chance. So they don't get away."

He gripped the sleeves of her coat in his fingers and gazed deeply into her eyes.

"With both hands."

"Oh, Blake."

He wasn't sure of her. She got that now. And why should he be? She hadn't been sure herself until this morning—until she'd been without him and seen the reminder of all she'd left behind. She stood on tiptoe, feeling utterly feminine for once, and not like the awkward beanpole who'd been too shy to take the initiative. She tilted her head and kissed him. Really kissed him—without hesitation, without reserve. He angled his head and her hand bumped his hat, knocking it to the ground, but they didn't stop. Not until the kiss had settled from a question into a certainty. He could be in no doubt of her feelings now.

"We can make it work," he said, holding her close. "I know we can somehow..."

"I was going to change my ticket this afternoon anyway," Hope said, grinning. "I was going to come back after Christmas. I wasn't sure what would come after that, but I knew that yesterday couldn't really be goodbye."

"You were?"

She nodded. "I had a rather interesting conversation with my sister this morning. She told me I was using my job as an excuse to avoid intimacy. She's right. My feelings for you scare me. But I don't like who I've become, Blake. You did fix me—or at least you started to while I was with you. You reminded me of things I once wanted but had given up on. Family. Closeness. A house full of children. And presents and get-togethers."

"You want those things?" He leaned back and looked into her face. "But you always hung back."

"It seemed easier not to hope at all rather than continually be disappointed," she replied. "But I was just pretending to be something I wasn't."

"When you were standing in the kitchen in that apron with flour on your nose I knew," he said. "You belonged there. I didn't know how to make you see it. But you looked happy. It seemed right."

"It was right. You gave me the greatest thing of all, Blake. Acceptance. *You* accept people. Yes, you try to fix them—not to make them someone different from who they are, but to show that they are already valuable and worth your time. I love you, Blake. I didn't expect to, and I certainly didn't want to, and I wasn't even sure I could. But I do—so much. You're my Christmas miracle and I wasn't even looking for one."

His eyes sparkled at her. "Hope? I want to kiss you again, but we're still in the middle of your grandmother's yard. And if this town is like most small towns then nothing is private. Do you suppose we could go inside, where it's warmer and more…um…?"

She took him by the hand and led him up the porch, over the squeaky board, and inside. He immediately swung her about until she was in his arms and he was kissing her—without the caution of that first time by the tree, and not in the lazy way they'd kissed in the snow, or even the desperate, unsure way they'd kissed only minutes ago in the yard. This one was deliberate, confident. Like coming home and Christmas morning and all the good, fine things she could imagine rolled into one.

When it broke off they were both smiling, and the weight that had been on her shoulders—the one he'd seen right from the beginning—suddenly rolled away. She laughed as she realized she had one final present to give him.

"I finally did it, Blake. I took the perfect picture."

"You did?"

She nodded. "Stay here. I'll show you."

She raced upstairs, boots and all—she'd clean up later—and grabbed her laptop. "I haven't had a chance to print it yet, but look." She brought up the picture and held it out. "It's you and Cate in front of the tree."

"And this is the perfect shot?"

She nodded again, watching his face and not the screen. "It has everything I truly want in it." She took the computer from his hands and put it down. "I saw my mom and dad today. I think they might finally be on the road to happiness. But, Blake, I've realized that I don't want it to take me so long. I want happiness *now*. I want love and a family of my own. Anyone who sees you work with the kids knows you'd be an amazing father. You're kind and loving and you make me laugh."

"Why, Miss McKinnon, it almost sounds like you're proposing."

Was she?

"That might be moving a little too fast," she admitted with a sideways smile, "but Grace was right. I can freelance anywhere. It doesn't make sense to stay in Australia when my heart's in Alberta, does it?"

"Definitely not," he agreed. "So, tell me. What are we doing for New Year's Eve?"

"Still have those sleigh bells?"

He reached out and touched her cheek. "Always," he murmured.

"In the meantime you need to meet my family. Come to the rest of the festival. It's my first freelance gig with Grace. She just doesn't know it yet."

Blake grinned and took her hand.

They stepped outside just as Gram's Christmas lights came on with the timer. In the waning afternoon the yard was transformed into a twilight fairy tale.

She squeezed his fingers. "Merry Christmas, honey."

"I like the sound of that," he replied, tugging on her hand and leading her down the candy cane path.

* * * * *

Mistletoe Kisses
with the Billionaire

Shirley
JUMP

New York Times bestselling author **Shirley Jump** didn't have the will-power to diet, nor the talent to master under-eye concealer, so she bowed out of a career in television and opted instead for a career where she could be paid to eat at her desk—writing. At first, seeking revenge on her children for their grocery store tantrums, she sold embarrassing essays about them to anthologies. However, it wasn't enough to feed her growing addiction to writing funny. So she turned to the world of romance novels, where messes are (usually) cleaned up before The End. In the worlds Shirley gets to create and control, the children listen to their parents, the husbands always remember holidays and the housework is magically done by elves. Though she's thrilled to see her books in stores around the world, Shirley mostly writes because it gives her an excuse to avoid cleaning the toilets and helps feed her shoe habit. To learn more, visit her website: www.shirleyjump.com.

CHAPTER ONE

THE envelope sat on Grace McKinnon's hotel-room desk in Santo Domingo for a good three hours before she picked it up and glanced at the return address.

Beckett's Run, Massachusetts.

Her grandmother had to be pretty determined to track her down all the way out here. But that was Gram. When she wanted something, she got it. A stubbornness Grace had inherited—a curse, her mother called it, a blessing Gram always said. Either way, right now, Grace had bigger issues to deal with, so the envelope would have to wait.

"I just turned in the Dominican Republic piece a couple hours ago," Grace said into the phone. "Where do you want me to go next?"

The cell connection faded as she paced the room, passing the desk and the letter several times before coming to a stop again. She shifted back to the window, perched against the farthest southern pane. Below the ten floors of the hotel, cars congested the roads of Santo Domingo, impatient horns blaring an angry chorus in the bright morning sun.

Grace's hip nudged the desk and dislodged the envelope again. She leaned on the corner of the desk, toward the strongest cell signal she could find, and fingered the envelope while she listened to her boss's latest rant.

"I don't want you to go anywhere next. I skimmed what you emailed and the Dominican piece was okay, full of the usual hotspots for tourists and that kind of thing, but honestly, that New Zealand one was a mess. You kept veering off on other tangents, like the tents set up by the homeless. What tourist wants to see that? That's the kind of piece someone would write for that tearjerker *Social Issues*. Not what I hired you for and not what you said you wanted to write."

"It is what I want to write."

"Yeah? Then why do you keep sending me these change-the-world things?"

She bit back a sigh. "Wouldn't it be nice to run something different once in a while?"

"Hell, no. The advertisers don't want different. Neither do the readers. So just give me what I'm paying you for."

"I will." She shifted her weight again. In the last couple of years, all those happy vacation stories had gotten on her nerves. She wanted more. The problem was, she didn't have the chops to write more. She'd sent a few pieces to *Social Issues,* thinking she'd be a shoo-in because the editor, Steve Esler, had been her mentor in college and a good friend since then. For years he'd encouraged her to come over to the magazine and write something with "depth and meaning." She'd sent him those pieces, then sat in his office and watched him shake his head.

"You're a better writer than this, Grace. You need to put your heart into your stories. Then the reader will laugh and cry right along with you. These articles...they feel like you're afraid to care."

So she'd gone back to travel writing, to the empty kind of writing about the best hotels and zipline tours she'd written before. She told herself she was happy, that she didn't want to be one of those starry-eyed fresh-from-college journalism grads who thought they could change the world with their pen.

Except a part of her had always felt that way. And still did. Even if she wasn't a good enough writer to do that.

"I don't want humanity's woes smeared all over the page," her editor was saying. "I want happy destination recaps and most of all laughing people, who are completely unaware there is a single issue in the world worth worrying about while they sip their margaritas and enjoy a relaxing massage."

Paul Rawlins let out a long sigh. Even all the way from Manhattan, she could hear her editor's discontent.

"You let me down, Grace. Again. I can't count on you anymore."

"One mistake, Paul. The pictures—"

"It's not just one. It's many. Your stories are flat lately. Uninspired. You even made Fiji boring, for Pete's sake. *Fiji*. What happened? You used to be my best freelancer."

"Nothing happened."

But something had. Something had shifted inside her when she'd been in Russia and seen that little girl on the streets, wearing nothing more than a thin summer dress in the middle of winter while she peddled newspapers that no one wanted to buy. Grace had taken a photo and, through a translator, gathered enough information to write a story, thinking maybe someone somewhere would see it and champion the cause of homeless orphans.

But the article hadn't made it past the *Social Issues*

editor's desk because it hadn't done its job—moved the reader to act. The editor there was right. Grace McKinnon's heart was surrounded by a wall, one Grace had never been able to break. She should stick to what she knew and stop trying to be something she wasn't.

She'd get back to work, and somehow it would all work itself out. If she buried herself in work she'd be fine. Just fine.

"Why don't you take a break, Grace?" Paul said. "Just a couple weeks. Take a vacation, then come back to work."

She bristled. "Take a break? But I'm at the height of my career here."

"No. You're not."

His words, flat and final, drove the last spike into Grace's hopes.

She had lost her groove somewhere along the way. For years she'd jetted from here to there, flitting around the world like a hummingbird in a flower garden. Her career as a travel writer for one of the largest destination magazines in the world had suited her just fine. No real ties to anything or anyone, and a job that depended on one person—herself.

Then she had run into an assignment that had changed her life, changed her thinking, and everything since then had paled in comparison. She'd left the travel magazine world for the deeper pieces of *Social Issues,* and when that hadn't panned out she'd returned to travel writing, but something was wrong, an off beat, a missed step.

She kept trying to find a way back to the writer she had been before, and failing. Maybe if her sister had come when she'd called, Grace could have taken that last piece to the next level. Hope's photographic eye always saw the best in everything. But, no, Hope had refused her. Grace still smarted about that turndown. The one time she'd needed Hope—

Hope had said no.

In the last few months the magazine assignments had trickled away to almost nothing. And the last few jobs—

Well, Paul was right. They hadn't been Grace's best work. They hadn't even been her close-to-best work. Still, the thought of having all that time over the holidays stretching ahead of her with no way to fill it—

"Paul, let me do the Switzerland piece that I pitched last week. There's this train there that takes people up to the mountain. Real travel hotspot. I can cover it from the point of view of the locals—the people who live up there and need to take it down to the hospital—"

"Give it a rest, Grace. Seriously. It's almost Christmas. Just take some time off, get your wind back and call me after the holidays. We'll be needing pieces on romantic holiday destinations then. And if…" He paused. "And I mean *if* you are really ready to come back, *then* we'll talk about you going to Switzerland."

In other words, take the vacation. Or else. At least he hadn't outright fired her. The job would be there as soon as the holidays were over. She'd sit on a beach somewhere and sip margaritas and tell Paul she'd recouped like crazy. What choice did she have, really? She needed this job, and if Paul thought she needed a vacation to keep it, well, she'd do that. Or pretend. "Sure. Will do."

"Good." The relief bled through his voice, across the miles and around the world. He said goodbye, and then he was gone.

Leaving Grace alone in her hotel room, without a job or a destination. She hadn't been this adrift in…years. Maybe more than a decade.

Outside, the constant busy stream of traffic beeped

and chugged its way through Santo Domingo. She crossed to the window, watching people hurrying on their way to their jobs. Landscapers hitching rides on the back of flatbeds, hotel workers riding three to a moped, taxi drivers weaving in and out of the dense traffic jam. The salty tang of ocean air mingled with the constant fumes of congestion, giving the city a curious sweet/sour smell. All around her stood stone buildings as old as time, the foundation of North America's history, the first stepping stone for Christopher Columbus himself. Santo Domingo was a beautiful, tragic city. One she had loved. Her digital camera was full of images for her scrapbook. Not a one of them featured the beautiful beaches of Punta Cana or the bustling open air markets. No, the pictures Grace took featured other sides of the city, of the countries she visited. The kind of pictures her editor didn't want, the kind that would never accompany a story about the best vacation spots in Latin America. The kind that she had once thought would launch a career built on depth, meaning.

Why couldn't she just give up that idea? Be happy she was employed and paid to travel the world? Why did she keep searching for the very things she wasn't meant to have?

She paced around the room some more, then started packing. She loaded the last of her things into her duffle bag, then hefted it off the bed and set it by the door. Then she stood in the center of the room—

Lost.

Where was she going to go from here? The beach? Alone? At Christmas?

If anything screamed *loser,* that would be it. Sitting in some romantic destination, sipping margaritas by herself, watching all those families and couples on holiday frolic in the surf. Grace liked to be alone, but not in a place where everyone was paired off like the animals on Noah's ark.

What she needed was a destination that could serve two purposes—give her the vacation she'd promised Paul she would take, and give her an opportunity to write a bonus piece, one that really showed him she still had what it took. Sure, a little quiet time might be good, too. Give her a chance to catch up on her emails. Finally figure out that social media thing, perhaps.

But where?

Grace's attention landed on the letter from Gram. She'd almost forgotten it. She retrieved it from the desk, then tore it open, expecting the usual Christmas news and a gift card to the mall.

Instead, a plane ticket slipped out and tumbled to the floor. Grace's gaze dropped to Gram's loopy writing.

Dearest Grace,

I hope this letter finds you well. I've missed seeing you and was so disappointed when you had to cancel your trip home last year. And the year before that. I've decided that this is the year I'll see all my family for the holidays. I'm not getting any younger, and seeing you is high on my list for Santa. So, please, come home to Beckett's Run. It promises to be a wonderful holiday here, what with the town's two-hundredth-year celebration and all the festivities planned for that shindig. You wouldn't believe the event that is turning into! Something worthy of the front page, that's for sure.

I've enclosed a plane ticket. So no more excuses, sweetheart. Come home.
Love always,
Gram

Grace picked up the ticket from the floor. Go home to Beckett's Run for Christmas. To anyone else, a visit to the cozy little Massachusetts town with its snowy, magical holiday setting would sound perfect. Very Norman Rockwell-ish. But to Grace...

It sounded like torture.

Beckett's Run. The very place that contained everything—and everyone—she had run from years ago. Did she really want to revisit all that?

Then she glanced at the letter again. Two-hundred-year celebration. Big events planned. The cliché of a small town getting together for the holidays. The wheels in her head began to turn, and she made her decision. She hefted her bag onto her shoulder and headed out of the hotel.

And back to Beckett's Run.

The holiday had descended upon Beckett's Run like ten feet of snow. In a matter of days, the town had gone from winter doldrums and hues of gray and white to bright red and green, with cheery music piping from the storefronts and crimson swags swinging from light to light. The bench sitting in front of Ray's Hardware and Sundries boasted a bright red bow, the statue of town founder Andrew Beckett had a wreath necklace, and even the cement frog sitting on the front of Lucy Wilson's lawn sported a bright red Santa hat.

J. C. Carson slowed his Land Rover as he passed Carol's Diner, sending a wave in the direction of the Monday Morning Carp Club—Al, Joe and Karl, who claimed the carp was for their fishing trips, but in J.C.'s opinion it was for the observing and reporting they did from the bench in front of Carol's every day. J.C. turned right at the stop sign, then circled back around to the town park. Volunteers filled the snow-dusted space, while they worked like bundled-up bees to complete the setup for the town's holiday celebration. The first Beckett's Run Winter Festival had been planned by Andrew Beckett himself, and in the two centuries since the event had grown to include visits from Santa, sleigh-ride races down Main Street and Christmas-tree-decorating competitions. That meant the two-hundred-year-milestone celebration had a lot to live up to and a lot to outdo.

J.C. had heard one TV crew was already camped out at Victoria's Bed and Breakfast. No one was surprised—Beckett's Run had recently been voted "Most Christmas Spirit" by a world-renowned magazine, and that had the media spotlight focused on the tiny town's party.

That meant J.C. had to ensure one thing—the smooth running of the holiday event. Ten years ago no one would have pegged J.C. as the one to keep the town running on an even keel. Heck, he'd been tearing up these streets and running wild. But that had been before, and he had stopped being that J.C. a long time ago.

Beckett's Run wasn't exactly overrun with crime—a fact evidenced by the five-person police department—so J.C. didn't expect any real trouble, but planned for it just in case. The kind of publicity the article would bring would also bring in tourist dollars—something struggling Beckett's Run needed. Too many shops had been shuttered, too many houses sold. In the last couple of years J.C. had done all he could to shore up the town's waning economy, but finally realized if no one else believed in the town, there was only so much one man could do.

It was part of the reason why he'd volunteered to head up the committee for this year's celebration. He'd seen

Beckett's Run die a little more each year, after economic and personal blows hammered away at the town's core. He loved this town, and if a Christmas celebration could restore the town's faith in itself, J.C. wanted to be part of that effort. And in the process attract some much-needed tourist dollars to the coastal Massachusetts town.

But there was more, much more, he hoped the Winter Festival could do. What had started as a way to help Beckett's Run—and stop Pauline Brimmer from calling him and begging him to chair the committee—had become something personal to J.C. Something that mattered more than an economic boost to the town.

The day his life had turned upside down, J.C. had taken a leave of absence from his position at Carson Investments, given his Boston apartment key to his housekeeper, then driven out to Beckett's Run and moved back into his old room at his mother's house. He was too tall and too old for the rickety twin in his baseball-filled room, but sometimes there were more important things in life than whether his feet hung over the end of the mattress. Soon he'd have to return to Boston.

Which meant he needed to make some hard decisions. And fast.

But for now there was the Winter Festival. One challenge at a time.

J.C. turned the last corner, then released an easy breath. The downtown area all looked good. The perfect image of a serene yet festive holiday.

A sense of ownership and pride filled J.C. as he looked around Beckett's Run. When he was a kid, he'd hated this place and wanted nothing more than to leave. He'd broken the rules, come close to spending some time in the police station, even. Then he'd grown up, gone to work, and put that past behind him.

He might not have pictured himself returning to this town, but he could see why people put down roots and raised their children here. Beckett's Run offered stability, a sense of home, in its predictable schedule and dependable sameness. Something J.C.'s family needed right now. Desperately.

He heard a screech, the sharp whine of tires arguing with ice. J.C. swung the S.U.V. around just in time to see a cherry-red convertible slide past a stop sign and plow into a snowbank.

J.C. was the closest to the accident, so he pulled over and got out of the S.U.V. The cold air hit him fast and hard, whipping icy breath along his skin. He zipped his jacket, fished in his pockets for his gloves, then stepped over to the driver's side of the car.

The glass slid down, but all J.C. saw was the back of a woman's head. Long blonde hair, swept into a pony-tail that swung around a thick dark blue jacket with a faux-fur-trimmed hood. "You okay, ma'am?"

"Sorry, Officer. My license is in here somewhere," she said, cursing as she rooted through the front pocket of a backpack. "Ah, finally."

She spun back, a white piece of plastic in her hand, but J.C. didn't need to look at her ID. He already knew who she was. He recognized her even with the oversize Hollywood sunglasses on her face, the bright pink lipstick on her lips, and the cherry-red convertible.

"Grace McKinnon." The words came out flat, without a single note of surprise. Though if anyone had forced him to name ten people he never expected to see in Beckett's Run again, Grace would have been in the top three.

She leaned back against the black leather seat and cupped a hand over her eyes. "J.C.?"

"The one and only."

She laughed. "Oh, my goodness. The last time I saw you…well, I can't remember the last time I saw you."

Did she truly not remember? Because he sure as hell did. Or maybe she didn't want to remember. Probably a good thing. A damned good thing. The past was behind him for a reason, and it would stay that way.

She leaned both elbows on the windowframe and shook her head. "God, I thought you were a cop. That's the last thing I need right now. I'm glad it was just you."

"Just me?"

She shrugged. "Someone who knows me."

He didn't know what to say to that. He'd once thought he knew Grace as well as he knew himself. He'd been wrong.

"And what are you doing, calling me *ma'am?*" she went on. "That makes me sound grown-up and old, and I'm neither of those."

His gaze traveled over her curves, making a quick detour down the open V of her red shirt. Damn. He begged to differ on the grown-up part. Grace had grown up and out in very nice ways.

He tried to remember why he was here. Oh, yeah. Reckless driving. Not reckless thoughts.

"You were speeding, Grace." He waved at the streets behind him. "The roads are slick, and there are a lot of people around here. I'm not a cop, but I am a concerned citizen. Do me a favor and take it easy."

She snorted. "J.C., come on, you know me. Since when do I take it easy on anything? And when did you ever want me to, at that?"

He braced a palm on the roof of her car, then leaned in until his gaze connected with those fiery hazel eyes and sent memories of the two of them together rushing through his mind. He shrugged them off. What had happened between him and Grace happened a long time ago. Hell, a lifetime ago. One where he'd been a different person, with different goals, wants and needs. "I do know you, which is why I'm asking you to take it slow."

"You sound like my father when you talk like that. What happened to the J.C. I remember?"

"He grew up." J.C. gave the roof of the car a tap, then stepped away. "Welcome back to Beckett's Run, Grace. Where life moves slower than you, remember?"

He left her sputtering and returned to his S.U.V. As he pulled away and headed down the street, Grace McKinnon gave him a very unladylike—and very Grace—glare. He was pretty sure she also shouted something he didn't want to hear.

Grace was back. And that meant Trouble had arrived in Beckett's Run.

CHAPTER TWO

GRACE pulled to a stop outside the robin's-egg-blue, Cape-Cod-style house. She hadn't been here in years, but she knew every nook and cranny of the rooms inside. Knew which board on the porch squeaked an announcement to past-curfew footsteps. Knew which way to jiggle the back doorknob when it stuck in the summer heat. Knew how many steps it took to get from her room to Faith's, and how many more to Hope's.

Of course neither of her sisters were here now, so there'd be no giggling and running down the halls. Not that they'd done much of that anyway. Serious Hope, always so worried about the younger two. Cautious Faith, the middle sister, who wouldn't have been caught dead speeding down the main thoroughfare of Beckett's Run. And then there was Grace.

That was how most folks in Beckett's Run referred to the sisters: Hope, Faith, oh, yeah, and then there was Grace. The wild one. The troublemaker.

Grace had spent nearly every summer and school break of her life in this little four-bedroom house. Her mother off on yet another vacation with yet another man, or pursuing yet another hobby she claimed would be her new career, while her three daughters spent the summer months under Gram's supervision.

Gram had gone all out on the decorations this year—as she did every year. Twin trees sat on either side of the porch, strung with white lights that swooped from balustrade to post, and all around the porch. A giant wreath filled the front door, while a candy-cane fence marched along the front walk. Blinking multicolored lights drenched every shrub, and coiled up the lamp post at the head of the driveway.

Grace got out of the car and walked around to the front. No damage from the snowbank. Thank God. The last thing she needed right now was an expensive car repair bill—on a rental, no less. J.C. had made it sound like she was committing a federal crime when all she'd done was skid a little. Okay, maybe she had been speeding. But not much. J.C. just needed to get a grip.

The last time she'd seen J.C. he'd turned away from her. Odd that they'd repeat that scenario—except without the crying and the broken heart—all these years later. He'd gotten taller, more mature, and she supposed so had she. They'd become different people, and whatever might have been between them before had surely died in the interim.

She shrugged off the thoughts of J.C. She wasn't going to be in town long, and certainly not long enough to run into him again, not that she even wanted to. He was a memory, a past she had put to rest a long time ago. Then why did she wonder what he was doing in town? How his life had turned out? If he remembered her the way she remembered him?

Before Grace could climb the stairs, Gram burst out of the house, a wiry, agile woman with a pouf of white hair and a wide smile. A reindeer-decorated apron swung around her hips as she rushed forward, arms out. "Grace! You're here!"

Grace stepped into her grandmother's embrace. A sense of warmth and home enveloped her, the same kind of steady comfort that being around her grandmother inspired. Grace may have hated Beckett's Run, with its quirky traditionalism and uninspired living, but she loved her grandmother. "Hi, Gram."

"I'm so glad you came." She drew back and smiled at Grace. Tears brimmed in her gentle blue eyes and the wrinkles on her face eased into a well-worn smile. "I've missed you so much."

"I've missed you, too." Grace shrugged her duffle higher on her shoulder and avoided the real question in Gram's eyes—why had it taken so long for Grace to return? "So…what's for dinner?"

Gram laughed and turned to lead the way into the house. "How'd I know you were going to say that?"

"The same way I know whatever you make will be fantastic." Grace pressed a hand to her belly. "And I'm famished, so I hope dinner is ready soon."

"It will be. And it'll be a great time to talk and catch up." Gram took Grace's coat and hung it in the little closet by the door, still stuffed with coats from years past—thick snowsuits, playful bright raincoats, matching gingham jackets—as if the McKinnon girls would age backward at any time. Nothing changed at Gram's— which was exactly what Grace loved about this cluttered, charming house. She dumped her duffle on the floor, then turned toward the living room.

Christmas had exploded in her grandmother's house, or at least that was what it seemed like. A thick, chubby fir tree sat in one corner, every branch lit by twinkling white bulbs or shining with an iridescent rainbow of ornaments. Gram's Santa collection marched along the fireplace mantel, up the staircase, and down the long side table in the hallway. The usual navy throw pillows had been switched for ones in festive reds and greens, and Gram's favorite pink afghan had been stowed, replaced by the reindeer one Aunt Betty had knit for her at least twenty years ago. Electric candles centered the windows, and bright red bows hung from the corners of the curtains.

Grace paused when her gaze landed on the fireplace. "You put out the stockings."

"Do you want me to take your bag up to your room?" Gram asked.

"Gram, why are the stockings out?"

"Because it's Christmas. I fixed up your old room. Clean sheets on the bed and a nice thick down comforter. You've been globetrotting so much you might have forgotten how cold these New England winter nights can get. If you need an extra blanket, look in the closet. There's—"

"Gram, you only put out the stockings for people who are going to be here on Christmas Day." Grace turned back to her grandmother. "Why did you hang up Hope's, Faith's and mine?"

Gram shrugged. Avoided Grace's gaze. "I was thinking we'd have a nice, traditional family holiday."

Nice and *traditional* meant sitting down at the table, all of them together, just like when they'd been children. Pretending they were happy, that their world was a rosy, perfect place. Grace had long ago given up on such fantasies, and had no desire to feign happiness with either of her sisters. Especially since she wasn't talking to one of them and the other was on the opposite side of the world. "Are Hope and Faith here? In town?"

"No." Gram turned away and busied herself with putting on a pot of coffee. "Not exactly."

"What's that mean?"

"I invited them for the holidays, too."

Grace bit back a sigh. Her grandmother was always doing things like this. Thinking if she just got the three McKinnon sisters together, they'd bond like glue. Turn into a happy family right before her eyes. The chances of that happening were so slim no sane oddsmaker would place a bet. And after the argument she'd had with Hope…

Well, those odds became darn near anorexic.

"I can't stay long," Grace said, already itching to be back in the convertible and heading for the closest airport. If she left soon enough she'd miss the holiday rush of travelers. And miss her sisters. That would be one way to ensure a happy, stress free holiday. "Just popping in for a couple days."

Gram's light blue gaze met hers. "Why? Do you have an assignment to get off to?"

Grace wanted to lie, she really did, but she'd never been able to lie to Gram. She loved her grandmother too much to do that, and respected the woman who had been instrumental in Grace becoming the person she was. "No. I don't. Not for a while."

An indefinite while.

"Good." Gram grinned and clapped her hands. "Because I have a favor to ask you."

J.C. strode into the Steaming Mug Coffee Shop shortly after ten on Tuesday morning and greeted the girl behind the counter. "How you doing, Macy?"

"Just fine, Mr. Carson." She grinned, revealing the same gap in her front teeth that marked her as Ron's daughter. J.C. had known Ron almost as long as he'd known his own name, and had watched Macy grow from a fussy baby to a perky, cheerful high school senior. Damn, the time passed fast. Every time J.C. saw Macy he thought of how his own life path had detoured away from a family.

"That's good to hear."

"Oh, I've been meaning to tell you," Macy said. "You were right. That Comparative Societies class was amazing. I love the professor."

"I'm glad you're enjoying it. I remember taking Professor Smith's class. He made even the most boring topics interesting."

Macy nodded. "He's wicked smart. I just love that school. I can't thank you enough for helping me out. I never could have afforded it on my own. It's just so cool that I can finally do what I dreamed of doing."

He waved off the thanks. "It was nothing, really. I just knew you deserved a good education."

"It was a lot to me," Macy said quietly.

J.C. just nodded, uncomfortable with the praise. He'd paid for Macy's education to help a friend, nothing more.

A part of him envied her the chance to go after her degree in Graphic Design. As long as he'd known Macy she'd been doodling something or other. He remembered when he'd been her age and thought he could make a career out of music. A foolish moment, J.C. reminded himself, and far in the past.

Macy brightened and grabbed a coffee mug from the tower of them beside her. "The usual?"

"Oh, yeah, sure. Thanks." He waited by the counter, drumming his fingers on the oak surface, while Macy poured a mug of the café's special dark brew. She slid the mug across the counter, and waved off—for the thousandth time—J.C.'s attempt to pay.

"My dad would have a cow if I ever let you pay," Macy said.

He stuffed the bills into a squat clear jar on the counter, emblazoned with the image of a local resident raising money for a children's charity. Macy gave him a knowing smile, then went back to work.

J.C. turned around, his gaze roaming over the small shop, looking for a free table. He picked up a copy of that day's paper from the rack by the register, sliding the thirty-five cents across the counter to Macy. If he was lucky, he'd have enough time to finish his coffee and a few headlines before he had to get to the meeting for the Beckett's Run Winter Festival. His to-do list was long, and the stress of all that—coupled with a family who seemed to need him more every day—weighed on J.C.'s shoulders.

A burst of laughter came from the couches at the back of the room. J.C. smiled. The Tuesday morning book club. A nice bunch of older ladies, who made their opinions about the literary classics well known. They'd been here every week for as long as he could remember.

That was life in Beckett's Run. The same things, with the same people, every day. When he'd been a kid, he'd hated that. A part of him missed the hustle and bustle of Boston, the friends he met for an after-dinner beer and watching the game on the big screen. He missed having his own space, his own sofa, his own bed. Staying with his mother was definitely a temporary plan. Still, there was something about this town, something so basic, the kind of thing people built foundations on and lives on. Every time he was here, it was like he was...

Home.

Maybe he should think about making a more permanent stamp on the place. Hell, half the time he was here more than in the city. He shook his head. Who was he fooling? He wasn't the settling down kind. He had a busy, demanding company and a life in Boston. A sometimes-girlfriend living in the Back Bay. And a whole lot of people depending on him keeping the company running and profitable.

The problem was, J.C. had already made his money, and didn't give a damn about making more. He wasn't lacking in work.

But in purpose, yeah.

He thought of the changes his family's life had taken in the last few months. The forty-pound reason he'd come back to Beckett's Run, and that had him living in his old room even though a part of him would rather be in the spacious king bed in Boston. The same reason that had him considering chucking it all and staying here.

"What are you? An idiot? Throw away a company like that? If you did, you'd be nothing."

There were days when his father's voice rang loud and clear in J.C.'s head, even though John Senior had been gone for four years. His father, a stern, brooding, unforgiving man, who had expected his son to take the helm of the family company and multiply it tenfold.

"You take care of your family by providing for them. Not doing something foolish like slaughtering the golden goose."

If J.C. stepped down from the financial management company that two prior generations of Carsons had built it would probably survive, certainly keep going. But it wouldn't be the same. How many clients had said they invested with Carson Investments because they had a personal relationship with J.C. or with his father? When it came to money, people wanted trust, and trust came from relationships.

The problem was that there were days when J.C. had to wonder whether he was pursuing the right things. At some point his own dreams and goals had gotten swallowed in the quest to expand, grow, become all he'd been tasked with being. But if he walked away—

Would he hurt or help those he loved?

J.C. heard a curse from behind him. He turned to find Grace McKinnon standing in the doorway of the coffee shop, her hair windblown from the winter air, her cheeks red and her gloved hands clutching a bag from a local bookstore.

"They're here," she said.

"Who?"

Grace jerked her gaze up to his. Those same fiery hazel eyes he remembered, the kind that could hold a man's gaze for an hour. He wondered what she was doing in town—and why she was still here. He hadn't seen her in years, and now he'd seen her twice in the space of a couple days.

"What did you say?" Grace said to him.

"You said, 'They're here.' Who did you mean?"

"Grandma's book club." Grace gestured toward the group at the back. "She said they probably wouldn't show because it was the holidays and everyone was busy."

"I can't remember a Tuesday they've missed. Well, except when they were reading one of their books and Mrs. Brimmer got into a scuffle with Miss Watson about a particularly offensive passage." J.C. grinned at the memory of being called over to settle the literary dustup. "For retirees, they can get pretty rowdy."

"Rowdy. My grandmother's book club." Grace snorted. "Right."

J.C. stepped to the right. "See for yourself."

A burst of laughter rose up again in the group, followed by the rise and fall of excited voices. Mrs. Brimmer slapped the arm of the chair she was sitting in to emphasize her point, and Mrs. Simmons got to her feet to argue it back. Their voices rose louder, over the music coming from the sound system, as the two sides voiced their opinions.

Grace groaned. "Why am I doing this?"

"You're running Mary's book club? How did that come about?"

"She asked me. And she didn't play fair." Grace leaned in closer. "She baked cookies."

When Grace closed the distance between them, J.C. bit back a groan. Damn, what perfume was that? And why did it affect him so? The dark vanilla notes lingered in the air, teasing, tempting. Overriding common sense. "Let me guess. Peanut butter blossoms?"

"And chocolate chip. The ones with the big hunks of chocolate, not those weakling little chips."

J.C. chuckled and his stomach rumbled. He'd known Mary McKinnon nearly as long as he'd known Grace. Mary's cooking far surpassed anyone's in town, and her desserts…people talked about them for years. "You're right. Your grandmother doesn't play fair."

"No, she doesn't." Grace shook her head. She pulled out a copy of Jane Austen's *Persuasion* from her purse. "Any chance you've read this book? And want to talk about it?"

"Couldn't do it even if I wanted to. I have to get to a meeting."

"Come on, J.C., help me out." She put out a hand, as if she was going to touch him, then pulled it back. "Those ladies like you. Look, they're waving."

Indeed, Mrs. Brimmer was sending J.C. a friendly

wave, and Mrs. Horton was shooting him a friendly smile. Both women had single daughters—and an eye for an eligible, employed male. "They just want me to marry their daughters."

Grace turned toward him. Surprise lit her face. "I thought you married what's-her-name."

"I didn't." He left it at that. No need to rehash a long personal history, one Grace hadn't been around to witness.

"Oh." She bit her lip, which he knew—too well— meant she was biting back a few words. "I should probably get to the book club and talk about…" She turned the bag over in her hands. "Whatever it is that happens in this book."

"Did you read it?"

"Heck, no. But I looked it up online and got a plot outline. Jane Austen, trying to fix up everyone in the boring little town where she lives. Happy ending. Done."

He chuckled. "Wow. Speed reader." Then he leaned in toward her. He told himself it was to keep their conversation private, but then he inhaled, and knew it was really an excuse to catch a whiff of that perfume again. "And speed driver."

"This town can't plow its roads. It's not my fault I slid."

"You've been to Beckett's Run enough times to know not to speed in the winter. And in a car like that, no less. Don't blame the town for your recklessness."

She perched a fist on her hip. "Are you calling me reckless?"

"Aren't you?"

Grace bit her lip again, then shook her head. "You haven't changed at all, J.C. Carson. Not one bit."

"Oh, I've changed, Grace, more than you know." He

shot her a grin, then turned toward the door. "Have fun with the book club. And don't let Jane Austen get to you. Just because she believed in happy endings doesn't make her wrong. They do happen. For lots of people." Then his gaze met hers, and a wave of memories surged forward. Memories that tasted of honey and lemon, sweet and bitter, memories that haunted his nights and whispered *what-ifs* every time he saw her. Memories that would do nothing but open a door he had sealed shut a long time ago. "Just not for you and me."

CHAPTER THREE

GRACE tried to concentrate. Tried to pay attention to the women around her. But her mind kept straying to J.C.

He'd aged well. Very well. Still had the same deep blue eyes and short dark hair as always, but there was an added ruggedness to his features, a depth to his face, that spoke of loss, experience. A part of her wanted to sit on the banks of the creek with him, watching the minnows dart around their feet in silver arrows while she and J.C. talked until they could talk no more. Another part warned that everything between she and J.C. was over, in the past—

Where it should stay.

He'd left after their brief conversation this morning, letting in a burst of chilly air as he exited the coffee shop. Leaving his last comment hanging, like some mystery waiting to be solved.

She already knew the answer.

Years ago, she and J.C. had been inseparable. Two peas in a pod, her grandmother had called them. He'd been the one bright spot in her miserable summers spent in Beckett's Run, the one thing she'd looked forward to every time her mother dumped her and her sisters on Gram's front porch and left so fast the dust didn't even have time to settle in the driveway.

Then J.C. had dumped her, the whole event cold, heartless, cowardly, and it ended just like that. She'd left Beckett's Run—and never looked back.

Until now.

"I think the persuasion part of the novel was all about Anne trying to persuade women to be stronger," Mrs. Brimmer said, drawing Grace back to the book club. "She was a regular feminist, that Anne."

"Are you completely daft, Pauline? Anne caves to conventionality in the end. Why, she takes three steps back for the women's movement." Miss Watson shook her head, and several gray strands escaped from the messy bun on top of her head. "Makes me glad I never got married. I wouldn't want some man making all the decisions."

"I would disagree," Mrs. Brimmer said. "Anne is one of the strongest women I've ever seen in a book."

Miss Watson huffed. And puffed. "Strong women don't settle down with spineless men."

"Captain Wentworth is far from spineless. He encourages Anne to be strong and independent. Much like my dear Harvey did with me." Then Mrs. Brimmer swung her attention toward Grace. She leaned her tall frame forward, and put one bony hand on Grace's arm. "Tell us, Grace, what do you think? You're part of the younger generation. What did you think of Anne?"

"Me? I…" She glanced down at the book in her lap, the spine as pristine as it had been on the shelf at the bookstore. The internet hadn't given her a ready-made opinion. "Well, I didn't exactly have time to form a concrete judgment about her."

"You didn't read the book?" A collective gasp went up from the group. "Any of it?"

"Well, no, I mean, my grandmother just told me about this and—"

"But, dear, Jane Austen is required reading for any woman who wants a happy ending of her own." Mrs. Horton's hand landed on Grace's other arm. "Her novels are like...well, a guide to finding true love."

Several "amens" went up from the other women. A chorus of Austen recommendations started up, with each of the book club members tossing out their pick for top romantic guide by the famed writer. "Mary told us that you haven't settled down yet," Miss Watson said. "She's set us all on a mission of sorts, too."

Mrs. Brimmer smacked Miss Watson's arm. "Shut your trap."

"Mission?" Grace put the book aside. Alarm bells clanged in her head. "What mission?"

Miss Watson glanced at Mrs. Brimmer, who shook her head. "Oh...nothing. Just an idea she had. You know us old ladies. We're always looking for something to do."

"That's why we have *book club*," Mrs. Brimmer said, stressing the last two words. "So we talk about books, and nothing else."

Miss Watson nodded. "Okay, back to Jane. And Anne."

Grace agreed. Being one half of someone's matchmaking equation wasn't on her agenda. Now or later. Her grandmother didn't really expect these women to find Grace a happy ending, in the next few days, did she? Gram knew Grace would never want to settle down here. What was she thinking?

The coffee shop door opened and a trio of people walked inside. A man in a suit and tie, trailed by a young man and woman, both scruffy in stonewashed jeans, oversize anorak jackets and sturdy boots. "Oh, Lordy, it's Carlos Fitz from the local news," Mrs. Brimmer exclaimed. "If I was twenty years younger—"

"You'd still be old enough to be his mother," Miss Watson cut in. "Do you think they're here about the celebration?"

"What celebration?" Grace asked, playing dumb. Often the best information came if one pretended one didn't know anything. She was half tempted to get out her notebook and start jotting notes, but figured that would be obvious. At Gram's house she had read the local paper's accounts of the event, and done a cursory internet search, but hadn't really found anything that leapt out as a career-saving story yet.

"Why, the Christmas one we have every year," Mrs. Brimmer answered. "Two hundred years this year."

"And you remember every last one," Miss Watson quipped.

Mrs. Brimmer went on, ignoring her friend. "Didn't you know Beckett's Run was named 'Most Christmas Spirit' by that magazine?"

Grace glanced back at the trio from the television station. That meant the media had already latched on to the Beckett's Run event. She needed to come up with her own unique angle if she was going to impress her editor. "So who's in charge of this celebration?"

"J.C. Carson." Mrs. Brimmer let out a sigh. "Why, he's been a one-man wonder, getting this town back on its feet in the last few months, thank the Lord. The place looks amazing, don't you agree?"

Grace nodded. She'd noticed shiny benches, repainted storefronts, jaunty awnings all over the place. There were also several new green spaces and walking paths dusted by fresh snow. "Downtown is gorgeous. Looks brand-new."

"That's because it is, all thanks to J.C. and his Beckett's Run renovation project. This town is lucky to have him around." The other women nodded agreement, and several sang J.C.'s praises, painting him both as a hero and savior.

Grace swiveled back to the women. "You said J.C. is in charge of the Winter Festival?"

"Yep. Doing a bang-up job, too. Even if the volunteers on his committee are letting that poor young man shoulder most of the work, especially with everything else he has going on," Mrs. Brimmer said. The other women nodded agreement." He's a trooper, I tell you. I can't wait to see what he manages to pull off this year. It should be a spectacular…"

But Grace had stopped listening. The wheels turned in her head. A national story. One with a little heart, and a financial twist. She got out of her seat. "I have a call to make. I'll see you all next Tuesday."

She hurried out of the coffee shop, tugging her cell out of her jeans pocket as she did. Just before the door shut she heard Mrs. Brimmer call out, "You left your book behind! You'll never know how it ends!"

Grace let the door shut. She didn't care about the fictional ending created by Austen, not when she could write a new beginning for herself.

The only roadblock? Getting J.C. Carson to cooperate.

J.C. regretted bringing the cookies. And the coffee. He'd led board meetings that accomplished more than this one. Maybe it was the small town atmosphere. Or maybe it was the damned cookies. "Gang, can we get to work? We've got a lot to do and not a lot of time."

Walter Westmoreland, Carla Wilson, Sandra Perkins

and her daughter Anna turned toward J.C.. "Isn't it snacktime?" Sandra asked. "If I don't eat, my blood sugar drops."

"Yeah, and then she can't concentrate," her daughter added. Both women mirrored each other in actions and looks. Red-headed buns, cashmere twinsets, and a complaint gene that often kicked in at the worst possible time. J.C. wondered if that came from the two of them living in such close quarters for so long. Sandra was in her eighties, her daughter only twenty years younger, and a permanent roommate for her long-widowed mother. They did everything together, including this committee.

Walter was only here at Sandra's behest. There'd been an on-again, off-again romance between the two for as long as J.C. could remember. Much to the objections of Anna, who wasn't in the Walter Westmoreland Fan Club.

J.C. could have paid professionals from the outside to come in and handle the entire event, start to finish, but that would have given the Winter Festival a canned feel. The "Most Christmas Spirit" moniker had come about because the magazine liked the town feel of Beckett's Run, the way people pitched in and helped out. If J.C. had come in with his checkbook and his polished experts, he would have eaten away at the very heart of the Beckett's Run Winter Festival. He didn't want to do anything that would hurt the festival's chance of success.

Especially this year. This year mattered more than any in the two hundred previous, at least to J.C.

So he had stepped up as leader and accepted help from the locals. And tried not to grumble too much.

"You have all the cookies you want, my dear," Walter said, handing Sandra a full plate.

"Bring the cookies to the table," J.C. said, "and we can get to work while we eat."

"If I talk while I eat I get indigestion." Walter scowled.

J.C. bit back a sigh. He loved this town, he really did, but there were days… "Okay, a few more minutes. And while you're eating, I was hoping one of you would volunteer for the publicity job. Louise had to step down because her grandson is sick, so I need someone else to head that up."

"I'll do it."

J.C. pivoted toward the familiar voice. Grace Mc-Kinnon stood in the doorway of the community center, her cheeks flushed from the cold. She looked beautiful and cold all at once, her hair up in the familiar pony-tail, and a thick blue jacket turning her curves into a shapeless pouf. Still he knew—oh, he knew—what an amazing body lay beneath that damned coat. He cursed his hormones for reacting when his heart knew to avoid her. "What are you doing here?"

"Volunteering." She put a smile on her face and strode forward. "I heard you needed help, so here I am."

"You? Helping promote Beckett's Run?"

"Of course." She picked up a cookie and took a bite.

"You." It wasn't even a question this time.

"Me." She gave him a grin. "So where do I start?"

"Right here," Sandra said, patting one of the chairs that ringed the table. "We could use another helping hand. J.C. is working us to the bone."

J.C. begged to differ. But he did what his mother had always told him to do—kept his mouth shut until he had something nice to say—and took a seat at the head of the conference table. Grace slipped into the chair of-fered by Sandra, and the rest of the group trudged over

to the table. He called the meeting to order, and started
running down his list of topics.

His mind remained, though, on Grace. Why was she
here? Not just at the meeting, but in town? After she'd
turned eighteen she'd hit the road and ever since avoided
Beckett's Run like the plague. Never much of a fan of
the town to begin with, she'd once told him she'd never
return. She liked the life of freedom that freelancing
gave her. No ties to any one place or person.

It had been the final lynchpin in their relationship.
He'd had to make a choice, and though it had broken his
heart at the time he'd had to face the reality that Grace
would never want the life he did. She hadn't been there
the one day he'd needed her, and that had told him more
than any conversation on the creek ever had. Grace had
been far away, already embarking on her life of adventure—

Leaving him behind as fast as she could.

The familiar hurt from that day resurged in his chest.
Once upon a time he'd thought she cared about him.
Really cared. But when it came right down to it, she
hadn't cared about anyone but herself. Damn. Why did
that still affect him all these years later?

Now she was here, and volunteering for a committee,
for a task that would benefit the town she hated so much.
One that would tie her down, through the celebration
and maybe for a few days afterward with post-publicity.
This, from a woman who wanted no connections? Why?

He wanted to decline her help but had to admit that
having an experienced journalist on his side would be a
boon. He'd been half-assing the publicity himself, along
with Louise Tyler, who meant well but knew little about
media. He'd had a couple meetings with a Boston mar-
keting firm, looking for advice, but all their recom-

mended approaches had felt more New York than small town. Keeping the publicity local was the best and only choice. After all, who knew the town better than those who lived here, who loved this place?

But Grace? She didn't fit either criteria. Maybe this was a mistake. Either way, he didn't have time to bring another person up to speed.

"Okay, so our first big day, as you all know, is the day before Christmas Eve. There'll be festivities all week leading up to that, with the grand finale on the twenty-fourth." J.C. scanned the paper then updated the group on various volunteer activities. Anna and her mother agreed to stay on top of the food donations, while Walter stepped up to coordinate the kick-off parade. Carla, organist at the local Lutheran church, offered to spearhead the musical acts. Across from him, Grace scribbled notes on a slim pad of paper. She asked few questions, but seemed to keep track of everything said.

The meeting began to break up, with Walter and Sandra heading out first, followed closely by Anna. Carla hurried past them to pick up her son from preschool. J.C. gathered up his notes and crossed to the other side of the table.

"I was thinking we should take more advantage of social media," Grace said, her gaze on the notebook, filled with her familiar tight scrawl. "Use them to spread the word to communities outside of ours. And sometimes things like that get picked up by other media outlets. Before you know it, this could go international."

"Good idea. Something I kicked around but haven't had time to do."

Grace tapped her pen against her lower lip. "I was also hoping to profile a few local residents. Those who remember Christmas in years gone by. Maybe some of the ladies from the book club or another resident who has a heartwarming memory or story. If I can make this event have heart, it'll create a connection with the readers."

All business. Which was what J.C. had told himself he wanted. But his mind kept drifting from the project at hand to the woman inches away. A woman he hadn't seen in over a decade, and who was now plugged into the town like a peg in a fencepost.

"Why are you really here?" he asked Grace.

"Because you needed help." She got to her feet, the notebook clutched against her chest like an armor plate. "The ladies at the book club said you've been pretty much single-handedly running this thing for weeks."

"Since when do you help me?"

"We've always been friends, J.C., haven't we?"

Friends. Yes, they'd been friends. And much more for a while. Much, much more. A part of him missed that—the part that clearly had no common sense, because getting involved with Grace McKinnon was like attaching his heart to a runaway train.

He wanted to refuse her help. Wanted to keep her away from him. Wanted to stem the tide of memories that rushed to the forefront every time he saw Grace. He'd thought they were over, that he no longer cared about her. Then she'd roared into town in that impractical car and confirmed what he already knew—

He hadn't forgotten her. Not at all. And the part of him that wanted to keep her far away got overruled by the part that had never been able to resist the allure of the wild rush that was Grace McKinnon. "You're right, I have been handling a lot of this myself. And I can use every bit of help I can get. Ever since the magazine did that story, the simple Christmas festival has mush-roomed into a giant event."

She smiled, and the wattage of her smile hit him hard. "Looks like we'll be working together," Grace said. "I hope you're okay with that."

He took a step closer to her, so close he could see the flecks of gold in her eyes, catch the whiff of that damnable perfume again and feel the slight whisper of her breath on his skin. "I'm okay with it. The question is whether you are."

She lifted her chin to his in that defiant gesture he knew too well. "I am not here to open old doors, J.C., just to get through the holidays."

"And move on again?"

"That's what I do. It's my job."

"No, it's your personality. Never stay too long. Never connect too much. Never think twice about what, or who, you left behind."

She shook her head and looked away. "That's not true."

"Then prove it, Grace, and stay till the end."

"The end of what?"

"Of whatever happens here. Don't run out the door the minute it opens." What the hell was he doing? Challenging her to a date? Picking up where they left off? Maybe more?

Hell, he knew better than that.

She glanced away, and he knew he'd read her right. Grace wasn't here to stay. She never had been, and that brief moment when he'd caught the whiff of her per-fume and been tempted all over again had passed. He'd get through this event, keep it his top priority, and avoid Grace as much as possible. "I appreciate whatever help you can give to the festival." He turned toward the door. "It means a lot to the town."

She laid a hand on his arm. "J.C.?"

He pivoted back, and even though her hand dropped away the imprint of her touch remained, heat on his skin. "Yeah?"

Another smile curved across her face, the smile he had once memorized. There'd been a time when she had smiled at him like that, and his world had spun on its axis. Even now, years later, his heart leapt and filled with hope. *Damn.*

"How about cutting me a break and leading that book club for my grandma? Those ladies really seem to like you," she said.

Disappointment bloomed inside him. When was he going to learn? Grace didn't want or need anyone but herself. Getting close to her again could only lead to disaster, bring him back down the paths he had stepped off a long time ago.

"No can do. I have a job to do, Grace. And so do you." He plucked the paper with the media contacts out of her grasp. "On second thought, I don't need your help. Beckett's Run has always gotten along just fine without you and it will keep on doing that long after you leave. Again."

CHAPTER FOUR

GRACE resisted the urge to march after J.C. and tell him where he could stick his thoughts about her. The man grated on her nerves. Always had.

Well, that wasn't quite true. There'd been a time…

A long time ago. Better forgotten.

She tucked her notepad into her purse and headed out of the community center and into the bright winter sunshine. As she did, she saw J.C. standing across the street, talking on his phone.

Damn, he was a good-looking man. Taller now than she remembered from her teenage years, and stronger, more…masculine. He had an almost predatory leanness about him, a caged panther with tense muscles and unspent energy. Heat unfurled in her belly, reawakening the deepest parts of her. The parts that remembered. Oh, how they remembered J.C. Carson.

And they also remembered the painful breakup. The harsh slammed door on what she'd thought were real feelings.

She thought of the notes in her purse. The article she wanted to write. The short amount of time she had left. To accomplish any of that she needed an inside view of the festival. That would give her access the other reporters didn't have. In order to get inside, though, she needed to convince J.C. she was the right person for the job. His confidence in her was shaky, something she begrudgingly understood. She had never been the kind for staying in one place.

She crossed the street, working a smile to her face. A professional, nice, work-with-me smile. One that she prayed didn't betray any of the riot in her gut. "J.C. Got a minute?"

He nodded, put up a finger, then turned back to the cell. "Shoot me the numbers by the end of the day, Charles. I'll look them over and get back to you." He paused, then his brows knitted with frustration. "Yes, I'll be at those meetings, but I won't be back in the office for good until after the first. The company will be fine until then." Another pause, some more brow-scrunching, then finally J.C. said goodbye and tucked the phone away. "Sorry about that," he said to Grace.

"The pesky day job?"

"You could say that. They're not supposed to be calling me this week. I'm on…vacation."

"You took a vacation here? In the middle of winter? Why not some sandy beach with a blonde and a margarita?"

"I'm not the margarita type."

He didn't answer the blonde part, and Grace caught herself running a hand over her own light locks. Damn him. He kept distracting her. She no longer cared if he preferred blondes or brunettes or if he was married or single.

Didn't care at all.

Then why did she curse silently when she noticed his hands were gloved—and the question about his marital status would have to wait for an answer?

"I wanted to talk to you some more about the event,"

she said. Focus on the story, so she could redeem her career and get the heck out of Beckett's Run before Gram hosted a full-out McKinnon family reunion.

"I told you. I don't need your help."

She propped a fist on her hip. "Don't be stubborn, J.C. Let me help. I'm the expert in this and you know it."

"If I say yes," he said, taking a step closer, "then I have to know that you're going to stick with the job and not leave just because the wind started blowing in another direction."

Was that how he saw her? God, she sounded like her mother. She wasn't like that. At all. Okay, maybe a little. "I'm here until Christmas. Besides, I promised my grandmother, so that means I definitely won't leave."

Although she'd been contemplating doing that very thing, if only to avoid seeing her sisters. J.C. didn't need to know that, though.

"And you'd never break a promise to Gram, would you?" he asked. Implied, unsaid—she would break a promise to him.

"I'm here till Christmas," she repeated. "And since the festival ends on Christmas Eve, that works out perfectly."

His gaze met hers and held for a long moment. "Okay." He reached into his coat pocket and withdrew the list of media contacts, handing them over to her.

"Thanks. You can count on me, J.C."

"Can I?"

They had stopped talking about the festival and publicity and articles a long time ago, if they ever had been. Long-ago hurts popped up like stubborn moles between them. "Yes, J.C., you can. Even I grew up, too." She broke the eye contact and cleared her throat. "Anyway, since we're on a tight time schedule, I wanted to ask you a few questions to help me get a good handle on it for the publicity. Do you have some time to chat?"

He flipped out his watch. She'd expected a fancy designer brand, but J.C.'s wrist sported a plain old watch. "I've got an appointment to get to. I won't be free until later. Can we talk on the phone tonight? Or make an appointment tomorrow?"

She laughed. "Look at you. All scheduled and organized. I bet you even have some tidy little planner to keep track of every minute."

"What's wrong with that?"

"It's not who you are, J.C. You're the guy who would run off in the middle of a hot summer day to take a swim. The guy who ditched school to go watch a drag race. The guy who—"

"I'm not that person anymore, Grace."

"Sure you are. Deep down inside, I'm sure there's a little wild man in you." But her laughter was shaky, the words unsure.

"Teenage foolishness, nothing more. Anyway, I have to get to work."

"Who the hell replaced J.C. Carson?"

"Nobody did, Grace. This is who I always was." Then he turned and left, leaving her wondering if she'd ever really known him at all.

J.C. pulled in front of Grace's grandmother's house and wondered, for the hundredth time, what had prompted him to agree to drive them downtown for Mary's hair appointment. A good chunk of his Grace memories centered around downtown Beckett's Run, which meant just being there meant taking a few steps back in time.

And retreading ground he had no intention of visiting.

But Mary had called him, and asked him to deliver her safely because "you have that S.U.V. and my car is in the shop." Mary had asked him, and J.C. loved Mary enough to say yes, no matter what.

He got out of the truck and started toward the porch. The new snowfall had left a thick coat of white on Mary McKinnon's walk and steps, so he grabbed the shovel by the door and got to work on a little snow removal. The door opened behind him.

"J.C. Carson, what do you think you're doing?"

He turned around and gave Mary a grin. "Just getting into your good graces, Mrs. McKinnon."

She laughed. "You've always been there, young man. I'd say you're angling for some of my homemade fudge."

"Is it fudge baking time again? I had no idea."

She gave him a sure-you-didn't grin, then waved toward the house. "Come on in and I'll give you an extra large helping."

"You're speaking my language, Mrs. McKinnon." J.C. leaned the shovel against the porch wall, then leaned down and bussed a kiss against Mary's cheek. He'd been over at her house so much as a kid he might as well have been a relative. There had been days when she'd felt more like his grandmother than his own grandma. The normalcy of the McKinnon house, the way Mary loved her grandkids with a simple touch, no attached expectations, had been a welcome detour from his own home.

She cupped a hand to his cheek. "You're such a sweet boy, J.C."

He chuckled. "I'd like to think I'm all grown-up now."

She waved a hand in dismissal. "To me, you'll always be a boy. And I never met a man who grew up before the age of seventy." She led the way into the house, where the scents of cinnamon and pine greeted J.C.'s nostrils.

Mary cut a piece of fudge from a pan on the kitchen table, then handed it to him.

He took the sweet treat, raised it to his mouth for a bite, then paused. Grace had descended the stairs, and paused a second to fix her hair in the mirror. He watched the unguarded moment, feeling almost guilty. She raised a hand to the long blond locks, brushing them back from her forehead.

He could count on one hand the number of times he'd seen her hair down, unfettered, loosed from its perpetual ponytail. The first time she'd been twelve, climbing a tree. A branch had snagged the ponytail, and she'd ripped out the elastic and kept on climbing. She'd looked like a wild child, hair a burst of gold around her features, as she clambered from one branch to the next, scaling one lofty perch after another.

The second time she'd been running late for some event or another that slipped his mind now, and she'd forgotten to bring an elastic. He'd been fourteen, and teased her about her model look. She'd slugged him and said he'd never see her like that again. And he didn't, not for years and years.

Until she was seventeen, and he'd asked her to the dance in the park. One of those summer events put on in Beckett's Run and, for J.C., his first official "date" with Grace. That year had been the first one he'd truly noticed her. As a young woman. As someone who made his heart race. Muddled his thoughts. He'd asked her to the dance in a stammering, halting monologue. She'd met him at the entrance to the park in a dress—another rarity for Grace—with her hair a cascade of gold along her shoulders. From that moment on he was a goner.

She pivoted away from the mirror and noticed him standing there, watching her. She reached up a hand to smooth the long locks again, then scowled. "Why are you here?"

"Because your grandmother asked me to drive her downtown."

"*I'm* supposed to go with her."

"That powder puff you're driving is useless on these roads, and we're expected to get more snow tonight. I have an S.U.V. I'm just being practical."

"Be nice to J.C., Grace," Mary added. "He did just shovel our walk."

The scowl edged into a smile. "Trying for brownie points, Mr. Carson?"

He put the fudge on the table, then strode forward. No dress today—a pity—but she had on long sleek black jeans—skinny jeans, he thought they were called—that hugged her thighs, curved over her calves and ended with high-heeled short black boots. A V-necked red sweater emphasized the swell of her breasts, the hour-glass of her waist. "Wouldn't want you to slip and fall," he said.

"And leave you without a publicist again?"

The question drew him back to the present. This wasn't a replay of that dance in the park, nor did he want it to be. It was business, town business, and he would do well to remember that. He had responsibilities, and for-getting them with Grace wasn't in the plan. "Exactly."

She parked a fist on her hip. "I can get through the snow on my own, you know."

He snorted. "In those shoes? I doubt it."

"I can do a lot of things for myself, J.C. I don't need a man taking care of me."

"Oh, I remember that. Very well." Too well. Grace had made it clear she never wanted a commitment, never wanted to be tied down, never wanted to depend on anyone but herself—and especially never wanted anyone to depend on her. The one day when he had needed her—

She'd been gone.

Proving her point to the nth degree.

Why hadn't she been there? Why had she just blown out of town, leaving him to deal by himself? In her eyes he didn't see anything other than the same honest what-you-see-is-what-you-get Grace, which didn't fit the woman who had left him in the dust.

"Fudge?" Mary inserted a platter between the two of them. "A little chocolate makes everything sweeter."

"That it does," J.C. said, selecting a second piece.

Grace took a small one for herself, and took a bite. J.C. told himself not to watch her pink lips close around the treat. Tried not to stare at the tiny dot of chocolate on her upper lip. Tried not to fantasize about kissing her until all traces of chocolate disappeared.

She hadn't changed at all—the comment a second ago reminded him of that fact—and that meant they were still as mismatched as ever. The things that had driven a wedge between them before still existed, and he'd be a fool to ignore those facts.

He cleared his throat. "We better get going."

"Gram, if J.C. is taking you, I don't have to go, too."

"Oh, he's just dropping me off. You have to come, Grace. Who else is going to make sure Jane doesn't turn me into a blue-haired pouf?"

Grace laughed. "Okay, I'll go. But just so you know I'm not exactly fashion-savvy."

Mary insisted on filling a plastic container with fudge for J.C. and making sure he took it with him as a thank-you for shoveling the walk. "I'll make sure someone plows your drive tonight, too, Mrs. McKinnon." He put up a hand. "And don't tell me I don't have to do that.

You're practically my grandma, too, so think of it as your grandson taking care of you. No dessert payment necessary."

"You're so sweet." She smiled, gave him a tender touch and the three of them headed out the door.

At the truck, J.C. helped Mary in, then reached for the back-door handle, but Grace opened it before he could, and swung herself up into the seat without any trouble. He got in on the driver's side, flipping the heat to high before putting the car in gear and heading down the street. Grace sat behind him, bundled up in a thick anorak jacket.

Mary's praise for the town's decorations and the job J.C. was doing filled the space as they made the short, chilly drive to downtown Beckett's Run. J.C. parked in the newly plowed lot that sat between Carol's Diner and the hair salon, and before he'd exited the truck Grace had already opened her door and climbed out.

Clear message—no need to be chivalrous.

Then why did he make sure he got to the salon's door first, to hold it for her? Geez, he was like a schoolboy, and that wasn't who he was. At all.

"Thanks," she said, slipping past him.

The soft notes of her perfume teased at his senses. Once again, the light scent surprised him. He'd never have picked Grace for the sweet type. She was the hard-edged, take-no-crap adventurer he knew as a kid. Of course there'd been a time when he'd seen her as someone else. Someone far more...feminine.

Mary stopped just inside the door of the salon. "Oh, my. I totally forgot."

Grace turned back. "You forgot something, Gram?"

"Tonight's my night to call bingo down at the church. I'll have to skedaddle if I'm going to be there on time."

"What about your hair appointment?"

"Oh, that. Well, I forgot that, too. It's not today. It's tomorrow. Right, Jane?" she called to the hairdresser at the back.

"You're right, Mary. Tomorrow at ten."

"Goodness, I'm getting so old I forget where I'm supposed to be half the time." She bundled her coat again and tugged a scarf over her hair. "Anyway, off to the church!"

"Let me drive you," J.C. said.

"No, no. It's only one block away. You two stay, go to Carol's, get some dinner. I'll catch up with you later. Walter will give me a ride home." Before he could protest, Mary whirled around and out the door, leaving Grace and J.C. alone.

"Well, that was obvious," Grace said, heading back out into the cold. "I've just been stood up and matchmaked by my own grandmother."

J.C. chuckled. "She means well."

"She does. Anyway, thanks, J.C." She started to turn away, but he put out a hand to stop her. A momentary touch, but one that lit a fire in him.

"What about dinner? I'm hungry, and I'm sure you are, too. I'm supposed to be going to my aunt's house for horrible chicken casserole. I'd love to have a reason to miss that."

She cocked her head. "Are you using me to get out of dinner with your family?"

"Absolutely." He grinned. "Do you mind? We could go to Carol's. We're already here."

"I haven't been there in forever. Is Carol still working the counter?"

"Every Tuesday and Thursday. Her granddaughter took over the day-to-day a few years ago, but Carol likes to keep her hands in the pie, so to speak. She says it keeps her out of trouble." He leaned in closer to her, so close she caught the faint scent of his cologne. Dark, musky, male. Tempting. "And they still have the chicken pot pie you love."

"You remember that?"

"How could I forget? It was the only thing you ever ordered."

"I really liked that pie," Grace said, her voice squeaking a bit on the last syllable. Was she talking about pie? Or something else?

"I know you did. It's how we met. Do you remember?"

Her gaze met his blue eyes. Did she remember?

Of course she did. She'd been six, at the diner with her sisters and Gram, a treat to get the girls' minds off the sight of their mother's Buick heading down the street, away from them. Always away.

They'd sat at the counter, Grace, the shortest one, dangling her feet over the stool, shiny new shoes tapping the center pole of the stool. Another family had come in—mom, dad, son, daughter. She heard them telling the hostess they wanted a booth, but the diner was busy and they'd ended up reluctantly at the counter. The dad had complained, loud and long, but the kids had looked happy to have a change of scenery for dinner. The parents took the far end, the kids closest to Grace. She'd noticed the boy, but only as a fidgety body beside her. She'd been focused on jostling for space—and Gram's attention—with her sisters. Then the waitress had brought out a chicken pot pie and both she and J.C. had reached for it at the same time.

He'd given her a shy smile and withdrawn first. "It's yours," he said.

She'd thanked him, then for no reason she could remember except maybe she wanted to avoid her sisters
she'd started talking to the boy. "It's my favorite," she
said.

"Mine, too." Then he threw out a hand, formal, stiff.
"J.C. Carson."

She liked the way he said his name, in one mouthful. Her own tripped over her nervous tongue, but J.C.
just smiled. "Grace," he said, and then, just like he had
the other day, he'd added, "Welcome to Beckett's Run,
Grace."

J.C's father had shushed him and told him to behave.
In an instant the friendliness had dropped from J.C.'s
face and he'd gone stone-cold and still. He hadn't said
another word to her the rest of the night, but when his
chicken pot pie arrived he shot her a grin, then scooped
up a bite almost too big for his mouth.

"J.C., don't make an animal of yourself," his father
had said. "We're in a public place, for God's sake."

"Yes, sir." J.C. dipped his head and the boy she'd met
disappeared again.

She'd run into J.C. again the next day at the park,
and the day after that at the town pool. She'd soon realized there were two J.C.s—the one under his father's
thumb and the one who wanted to wriggle out as fast
as he could.

The latter had been the J.C. she had fallen for. But it
had been the other J.C.—cold, analytical, practical—
who had broken her heart.

They had history. Something she kept having trouble ignoring. She thought of the article she was working on. That was her ticket out of this hellhole and back
to the life she loved. She wasn't going to go back down
Memory Lane with J.C. They'd broken up for a rea-

son, even if she forgot that reason when he looked at her like that.

"That was a long time ago," she said finally. "Pretty much a distant memory now. I'd much rather focus on the present. So if we go to dinner it's to talk about the Christmas celebration."

"Good idea." He led the way the few feet over to the diner, then held the door for her. The diner was crowded, filled with locals looking for a warm meal and a warm place on the chilly winter night.

He cleared his throat. "A booth in the back okay with you? It can get rowdy in here sometimes."

Grace laughed as she followed behind him, weaving their way in and out of the tables and toward the back of the room. "Honey, you haven't seen rowdy until you've been in some seedy bar in Mexico at two in the morning." Then she colored as if she realized she had called him honey. "*That's* rowdy. This is…"

His gaze met hers. "This is what?"

"Safe. Dependable." She mocked a yawn. "Boring."

"Which is exactly why you ran out of here so fast the dust is still settling in your wake?"

"I was never going to live here, J.C. You knew that."

"And where do you live now? Did you settle down in Peoria with two kids and a Labrador?"

"God, no." She pulled out one of the two-sided laminated menus from behind the napkin dispenser and skimmed the offerings. "I have a very small apartment with very little furniture in a very low-rent part of New York, but I'm hardly ever there. I guess you could say I don't really live anywhere." She raised her gaze to his. "What about you? Still living on Merry Street in Beckett's Run? Or did you move to the big city and make your mark on the world?"

"I have a house in the city, and plan on going back there soon. For now, I'm living here, and, yes, back on Merry Street. At my mom's house."

"You're living in Beckett's Run? Why?"

"I have…personal business to attend to here." He left out the specifics. Grace and he were no longer an item, and that meant he didn't need to involve her in his family messes.

Still, a part of him—the part that still remembered long walks down to the creek where they'd chased toads and caught crayfish—missed talking to Grace. She'd been everything his home life had never been—fun, unfettered, spontaneous. Those hot summer days with her had been the highlight of his school vacation. No expectations, no rules. Just some water, mud and a lot of laughter.

That was what he remembered most about those summers. The laughter. The fun. The reckless chances. How long had it been since he'd had days like that?

Forever.

He had grown up, which meant he had responsibilities—one very big one right now in his life—and yearning for what used to be was an exercise in futility.

"I had personal business here, too," Grace said. "Seems no matter how hard we try to escape Beckett's Run, it keeps sucking us back in, huh?"

"Maybe I'll end up settling down here, if my current plan doesn't work out."

"You. Live here." She laughed. "Right. You hated this place as much as I did, J.C."

"I never hated the town. I hated…" He looked away. How had the conversation gone down this road? He was supposed to be here to talk about the town celebration, not about himself. As many times as Grace had pressed when they'd been younger, he'd never told her what it was like to grow up as John Carson's son. J.C. knew Grace had an inkling, but he'd never shared the whole truth. His time with Grace had been a sacred escape, one he'd hated to sully.

"Doesn't matter," he said finally. "All that's in the past. I'm here to work on this Christmas celebration, and help it take Beckett's Run up to the next level."

"Hey, J.C., good to see you again. What can I get you?" A tall woman in a bright white apron clicked out a pen and order pad. Her gaze went from J.C. to Grace. They both ordered chicken pot pies and water.

Once the waitress was gone, Grace's features shifted from inquisitive to serious. She straightened in her seat, dug out the same pad he'd seen before and clicked a pen. "Why is it so important that the festival take Beckett's Run to the next level?"

He segued into business mode, too. "Because the town has been hard hit by the economy lately," he said, speaking slow at first, until he saw her handwriting flying across the page almost as fast as the words left his mouth. "And I think the town could use this economic boost. We aren't on the ocean, so we don't get much of the summer tourism dollars. However, we do have that quintessential New England feel, which is perfect for a holiday celebration. More and more families are looking for destinations for the winter months, and events they can attend with their children. My goal is to get people to visit Beckett's Run when the leaves start to change, then come back throughout the fall and winter months as a family getaway."

She raised her gaze to his. "So it's just about money?"

He bristled. "Of course not."

"Well, then, tell me why again, in a way that doesn't sound like bottom lines and dollars."

He took in a deep breath, and let his gaze wander to the snow falling outside, the townspeople bustling down Main Street on their way to shops, friends, families. There was just something about Christmas that wrapped Beckett's Run in a world of…possibilities. A mask for reality, perhaps, or maybe that lingering hope that stuck with a person long after tragedy had disrupted their dreams. "I want to give that Christmas experience to the people of Beckett's Run, and to those on the outside looking in, to help them…" he paused, thinking of one person in particular who needed this gift more than anyone he knew "…believe in magic again."

A soft smile stole across Grace's face as she wrote his words on the pad. She raised her gaze to his, the smile lingering. "That's perfect. It'll sell the whole world on coming here in the future for Christmas."

He scowled. "I'm not trying to sell the whole world. Well, I am, in a way, but…" He let out a curse and shook his head.

"What? If it's not about the whole world, then what is it about?"

His gaze went to the snow again. "That's personal."

She let out a gust. "Gee, for a minute there I thought I was talking to someone other than J.C. Carson. But clearly I wasn't." She flipped the pad closed and clicked off the pen. "If you want someone who will write something with all the personality of an ad for laundry detergent, then find another publicist. I'm not your girl."

"You never were my girl," he said. He paused, then exhaled. "Sorry. That's the past and we're not going there."

"No, we're not." She bit her lip, and when she did that

he was rocketed back a half dozen years to the Grace he used to know, the wild, untameable spirit who had climbed trees and bucked rules and dreamed of traveling the world. The woman who had once inspired him to do the same, and for a moment he'd been close—so close—to having the dreams he'd wanted. Then reality had smacked J.C. hard and he'd realized responsibilities came with a price.

"I think this was a mistake," she said, as if she'd read his thoughts.

"We're just talking, Grace. Nothing more."

"Nothing?" She leaned forward, elbows propped on the table. "I'd say there's always been something between us."

"There used to be. There isn't anymore." But as he said the words his gaze went to her lips, then to her eyes. Something familiar stirred in his gut.

Something he didn't have time or room in his life for. As far as he was concerned that something had died. And would stay dead.

She was still the same wild child, and he couldn't afford to be that anymore. He'd become the one everyone depended upon to be responsible, grown-up, smart. Responsible men didn't run off with a vagabond writer. Smart men didn't entertain thoughts of taking her to bed. Grown-up men didn't revisit a crazy past.

"You've changed," she said, wagging the pen at him. "It's not just the fancy car and the sudden altruistic nature."

"I grew up, Grace. People tend to do that."

"You're more…uptight. You used to be fun, J.C. Adventurous."

"I'm fun." Though even as he said the words he wondered how true they were. Could he count the occasional ski trip as fun? Two trips in the last five years, both of which had been centered around business, not breaks? Those weren't fun. They were networking. Yeah, he went out with his friends from time to time, and dated off and on, but he wouldn't call anything he'd done since he left Beckett's Run *adventurous*. "It's different when you're an adult. There are…responsibilities."

"Like a wife and kids?"

Was she asking because she cared? Or because she was testing his answers? "No wife." He left off the second answer. He had no good way to answer that question without digging deep into that personal pit that he'd vowed to avoid. "What about you? Still as fun and adventurous as always?" he asked, using her words.

She looked away, then tucked the pad into her purse. "This isn't going to work, J.C. I'm sorry. I'll find you someone else."

He reached for her before she could rise. When their hands connected a familiar charge ran through him, sparking memories, desire, and want for the very thing he could never have. J.C. let go. "Don't run again, Grace."

Fire roared in her eyes, a sudden rush of the old Grace back again. "I'm not running."

"Really? Because last I remember that was your specialty. Every time someone gets close, you speed out of here." Damn. He hadn't meant to say that. What was it about Grace McKinnon? Every time he got around her it was either fireworks or firebombs. He needed to get back on track, back to the subject at hand.

The success of the Beckett's Run Winter Festival.

The waitress dropped off their order, and rather than talk to each other Grace and J.C. dug in. Across from him, Grace took a bite, then paused, a smile on her face. "As good as I remember."

"Some things never change," he said.

"And some things do," she said.

He pushed his pie to the side. "Why don't we start over again? And focus on the event instead of—"

The diner door opened and his mother walked in, an apologetic look on her face. Before J.C. could respond, a three-foot-tall bundle beelined across the restaurant and plowed his four-year-old frame into J.C.'s chest. "I wanna stay with you, not G'ma."

Across from J.C., Grace's brow had raised in a question. J.C. ignored that for now and bent down to Henry's little face. "I'm no fun, buddy. Grandma is the one with the cool toys."

Henry cupped a small hand around his mouth. "But she doesn't like to play trucks. She wants to play Barbie." He grimaced. "I don't like dolls."

J.C. raised his gaze to his mother's. She shrugged, but he could read a hundred emotions flickering in her pale blue eyes. The toys she had pulled from the attic had been mostly her daughter's, and J.C. bet those toys came with a lot of bittersweet memories. His mother's smile faltered.

"I'm sorry," she said, leaning down and placing a hand on Henry's back. "I'm trying, but sometimes it's just…"

"It's okay, Mom. I'll watch him."

She hesitated, sending Grace a distracted hello before returning her attention to J.C. "Are you sure?"

"No problem. I'll be home in a little while, and tuck him into bed, too. Okay?"

Relief flooded her features. "Okay. Thank you, J.C." She said goodbye to Henry, and headed out the door.

When his mother was gone, J.C. tipped Henry's chin toward his own. "Why don't you stay with me, buddy? I'll get the waitress to bring you an ice cream sundae, and then we'll go for a walk in the park after we eat."

"Ice cream? But it's cold outside." Henry giggled. How nice it was to hear that little boy's laugh. J.C. realized he'd do about anything to hear that sound. "Nobody eats ice cream when it's cold."

"Sure they do. It's how all the best snowmen keep their figures." J.C. grinned, then danced a finger on Henry's nose. Henry laughed again. "And you, my little snow buddy, are turning into a snowman right before my eyes."

Henry's eyes widened. "I am?"

"You are. You spend enough time outside to get the nickname of Frosty. All the more reason to keep your hat and gloves on when I take you to the park."

"Are you really going to take me?" Henry's smile flipped into a frown. "You promised and then we didn't go."

Guilt roared through J.C. He hated being the cause of the disappointment in Henry's eyes. But it seemed the more J.C. tried to do the right thing, the more he got pulled in the opposite direction. There were days when it felt like he wasn't doing any single thing well or right. But as he met Henry's eyes again he knew the most important thing to get right was sitting right in front of him. Especially at Christmas. And especially *this* Christmas.

"I know, buddy. I've been working a lot. Sorry. Tonight, for sure, I'll show you all the cool stuff we're setting up for the Winter Festival."

"Okay." Henry nodded, then climbed onto the seat beside J.C., perching on his knees and propping his chin on his hands. He turned toward Grace, and tapped a finger on J.C.'s shoulder. "You're talking to a stranger."

J.C. laughed. "Oh, this is my good friend, Grace. She's not a stranger. She just hasn't been around here lately." He gestured toward Grace, who had watched the whole exchange bemused, curious. "Grace McKinnon, I'd like you to meet Henry. Part-time snowman, full-time troublemaker."

"Hey! I'm not trouble." Henry pouted.

J.C. ruffled his hair. "Nah, you're not at all, pardner."

Grace shook hands with Henry, who gave her back the enthusiastic hand clench of a four-year-old just learning his social graces. "Pleased to meet you, Mr. Henry."

Henry beamed. "Do you like ice cream?"

"More than I like anything." Grace smiled. "Your dad's a big fan of ice cream, too. His favorite is chocolate chip, if I remember right."

"Oh, I'm not…" J.C. put up a hand to correct Grace, then let the same hand rest on Henry's narrow shoulders, like a shield.

"My mommy and daddy went to heaven," Henry supplied, his gaze on his clasped hands. His voice was soft, fragile. "They can't come back for Christmas or my birthday or anything." He heaved a sigh too big for someone so small. "I really miss them. And sometimes I talk to them, 'cept I don't think they hear me, cuz they never talk back."

Grace's hazel eyes filled with sympathy. Her gaze darted to J.C., who gave a long, slow nod. "Oh, God, I'm so sorry. I had no idea."

"*This* is why I'm in Beckett's Run, Grace. And this is why the Winter Festival is so important to me. It's not about money, or fame, or even the town, when you come right down to it. It's about this." He scooped Henry up against him, settling his nephew on his hip. "Come on, buddy. Let's get you that ice cream."

CHAPTER FIVE

J.C...A TEMPORARY father?

Grace sat in the booth at Carol's and watched him prop his nephew onto a stool at the counter, then order the largest ice cream sundae Grace had ever seen. J.C. scooped the little boy back onto one hip, grabbed the ice cream with his free hand, then returned to the table and settled Henry into the booth beside him.

Henry was a slight-framed boy in a red-and-white-striped shirt and dark jeans. He had the same dark brown hair and blue eyes as the Carsons, and Grace could also see J.C.'s sister in Henry's lopsided smile and the cowlick on the back of his head. A small boy with a broken heart. Sympathy filled Grace's heart.

"Now, let's get back to the specifics of the Winter Festival," J.C. said to her while Henry started in on his treat. "I was hoping to go over the publicity plan with you first, then tackle whatever questions you had."

All business. Just the way she liked things. Which kept her from wondering about J.C. and his nephew, and about the man she'd once known becoming a surrogate parent. If she'd been asked to name a hundred things J.C. was doing with his life, that wouldn't have even made it to the list.

She cast a glance in Henry's direction. The little boy

held the spoon in his chocolate-covered fist and scooped vanilla into his mouth, which now had a ring of chocolate that reached all the way to his nose and cheeks. "Are you sure this is a good time?"

"My schedule tomorrow is full. So, yeah, now would be good."

"Okay." She glanced again at Henry, who seemed content with his ice cream.

Grace's experience with kids could be calculated in seconds, not hours. She rarely covered family destinations for the travel magazine, and saw few children at the resorts she did visit. Her grandmother would say Grace was still a big kid herself, but there was something about being around a small child—not even interacting with him, but having him watch her with that steady, assessing, inquisitive gaze—that made Grace nervous.

"For the publicity, I'd like a multi-pronged approach," J.C. said. "Merge social media with interviews with the press, and regular updates for the website. It would be great if we could pick a few key events to focus on. Maybe the snowman-building competition and the ice-carving event."

Grace made several notes on her pad with one hand and took quick bites of pie with the other. "Do you have any food-related events? That way I could send news to the cooking blogs and food publications."

"There's a chili cook-off in the town hall tomorrow night. And an ornament-making event at the community center on…" He paused, pulled out his smartphone and scrolled through it. "Wednesday at two."

"Perfect. Do you have a photographer lined up for any or all of these?"

"Nope. Our last publicist was an all-in-one volunteer. I've been working on getting someone else, even if I have to pay for it, but it's the holidays. A hard time to find anyone. Plus, this is a town event, so people really want a town resident to be involved."

She chuckled. "Well, that eliminates me."

"You're part of this town, Grace."

"Me? Not at all," she scoffed. "I never was."

"You're more a part of this town than you know, Grace. People remember you coming here."

She shook her head. "I was a temporary visitor, and not even that in the last few years."

"There are people here who never forgot you."

She arched a brow. Did he mean himself? Or people in general? Before she could ask, she grabbed the pad of paper and refocused on her goal. "Is there anything else you wanted me to be sure I publicize?"

He leaned forward. "How are you with a camera?"

She shrugged. "Not as good as my sister, but I can do okay."

"Speaking of Hope, how is she?" J.C. asked.

"I…I don't know. I haven't seen her in a while. We're both traveling a lot, you know?" Grace jotted "photos" on her pad, dodging J.C.'s inquisitive gaze. She didn't need to go into her complicated family history, or the last fight she'd had with Hope. Or mention that Hope would be here in town soon. Best to avoid the subject all together. "We'll want to do a live play-by-play for those events on the social networking sites. I can handle that, if you want."

"That would be great. I'm trying to—"

"Do you like horses?" Henry piped up.

"Me?" Grace asked. "Uh, yeah."

J.C.'s phone rang. He mouthed an apology at Grace, then answered the call. He turned slightly away from them, keeping his voice low as he discussed something about a merger. Leaving her to interact with Henry. She dropped her gaze to her notepad and scribbled a few questions to ask J.C.

"Did you ever ride one?" Henry asked, working that chocolate ring around his mouth some more. "I wanna ride one."

Grace nodded, then put down her pen. As long as Henry was talking she wouldn't be able to get much work done. "Yes, I have. A few times."

Henry considered this. "Was it a black horse? I like black horses. They're the coolest."

Grace laughed. "Nope. Brown. No cool horses for me."

Henry turned to J.C. Melting ice cream dripped off Henry's spoon and onto the table. It spread in a pale white circle, running fast for the edge. "Uncle Jace, did you ever ride a horse?"

J.C. paused in the middle of a sentence and turned back to Henry. "Uh...what?"

"Did you ever ride a horse?" More ice cream dripped as his little hand tipped to the right, sending a large clump of vanilla onto the table. It hit with a splash, splattering ice cream onto the table, the salt shaker, and J.C.'s phone.

"I have to call you back." J.C. pressed the end button, then grabbed a few napkins and started mopping at the mess, starting with the ice cream that had landed on the phone's touchscreen. "Henry, you have to be more careful."

The little boy leaned back, away from the dripping mess. "Sorry."

J.C. sighed. "I know you are, buddy. No problem. I'll take care of it." He piled napkins on top of the mess on the table and had started to clean up Henry when his phone started ringing again. Grace could see the tension and stress in the set of J.C.'s shoulders, the shadows under his eyes.

"Go answer the call," Grace said. "I can get this."

J.C. looked at the phone's screen. "You sure? This might take a few minutes."

"That's okay." Though she had never been alone with a child before, so she wasn't so sure about that. So far Henry seemed easy enough. Talk about horses, keep him stocked with ice cream and it would all be fine. She tugged several napkins out from the dispenser and pulled them close by. Just in case.

J.C. cast one more glance at them, then answered the phone and got up from the table. He headed toward the back of the room and the relative quiet and privacy of the hall leading to the restrooms.

Grace cleaned up the rest of the ice cream mess on the table. Henry watched her, the spoon still clutched in his fist. "Hey, you…ah…need to wipe your face." She handed him some napkins.

He swiped at his lower lip, then crumpled the napkins in his hand.

"You're still a mess. Here, try again." Grace gave him another set of napkins from the tabletop dispenser.

The second time Henry scrubbed at his lips and missed the ice cream circle around his lips.

Grace laughed. She'd been the same way when she was a kid. Always messy because of some spill or adventure. "I think you need some help." She dunked a napkin into her water, then leaned forward and swiped at Henry's mouth, then used another wet napkin to wipe off his hand. He watched her work, his blue eyes wide. She wasn't sure if it was because he was scared or curious. "There, all better."

"T'ank you."

"You're welcome." Grace watched Henry finish off the sundae. At least eating kept the kid from talking to her. They'd done okay when it came to horses and ice cream, but what would she say if he asked her something like where babies came from? Or what kind of friend she was to J.C.?

"Want some?" Henry pushed the dish across to her. In five seconds he'd managed to smear ice cream all over his face again.

"Uh, no, thanks," Grace said. What was left in the glass dish had turned into a runny pale mess. "It's all yours."

"My mommy always shared. She said it was…" he thought a second for the right word "…polite."

"It is." Grace watched J.C., who was still deep into his conversation. What was she supposed to say to Henry? How was she supposed to handle this? The kid clearly missed his mother—and Grace, who had known J.C.'s younger sister, Emily, could see why. Emily had been the bubbly one of the two Carson kids. Outgoing, popular, the kind of person who smiled at everyone and never had an enemy. She would have been the kind of mom who made cookies and colored pictures.

And knew what to say when the kid brought up a tough subject.

Grace fiddled with her notes. Henry had stopped eating and was now staring at her, expectant, waiting for her to say something. "I'm…uh…sorry about your mom, kid."

Henry nodded.

"Your uncle J.C. is nice, though."

Henry nodded again.

Grace nudged the ice cream. "You going to finish that?"

Henry shook his head. "My belly's 'sploding."

"'Sploding?"

Henry puffed out his cheeks. "'Sploding."

Grace laughed. "Exploding? Oh, I bet. That's a whole lot of ice cream you ate there." She crossed her hands on the table, and figured if she could get the kid to talk about something else, he wouldn't go back to the subjects she couldn't handle. "So have *you* ever ridden a horse, Henry?"

He shook his head. "At the zoo they have ponies. And, and, I was gonna ride one, but then he made a noise, and it scared me, and I didn't."

"Was it a noise like this?" She let out a long snort sound. Henry nodded, awe on his features at her powers of intuition, or, heck, maybe just her mimicry abilities. She laughed. "The same thing happened to me when I was a little girl. I was so scared I started to cry. Maybe… it was even the same pony."

"It's a scary pony." Henry's eyes were wide, his features serious.

"Nah." Grace waved a hand. "He's just scared of you. That's why he makes all that noise, so he can make himself sound big and scary, instead of showing how worried he is about being around a big boy like you."

Henry laughed. "I'm not big."

"You are to the pony, and that's what scares him. But if you talk to him real sweet, he won't be scared of you."

"Really?"

Grace nodded. "Next time you go to the zoo, just talk nice to the pony first. Introduce yourself. Make a friend."

The happiness and excitement in Henry's features

dimmed. "I don't know when I'm gonna go to the zoo again. My mommy and daddy took me to the zoo lots. My mommy loved the zoo."

And here they were again, back at a subject that Grace had no answer to. She opened her mouth, but was saved from answering by the return of J.C. Thank God.

J.C. slid into the booth and placed the phone on the table. "Thanks."

She shrugged. "No problem."

He lowered his voice and cast a glance at Henry. "It's just been difficult. My mom tries, but she's going through her own stuff, and she's not…there like she needs to be. Anyway, thanks for the help."

Their waitress came by and cleared off the dirty dishes. "Can I get you anything else?" she asked.

"Nothing for me. Though I think we need more napkins." Grace gestured toward the empty dispenser. "J.C.'s a mess when he eats."

The waitress laughed, then laid a hand on J.C.'s shoulder. "I don't know about that." She shot him a smile of familiarity, one that sent an odd quiver of jealousy through Grace, then finished gathering the dishes. "I'll be back with more napkins and a refill of your drinks."

Grace watched her go, and tried not to hate her. Why did Grace care if J.C. had dated the waitress? The man was entitled to a life, and clearly had had one in the years since they'd broken up. She wondered why he hadn't married—after all, he'd seemed so hell-bent on settling down when she'd known him before.

His father had made it clear to her that she was far from the kind of woman J.C. wanted. *"You're a plaything, a distraction. J.C. has no intentions of anything beyond some summer fling with you so stop thinking he's going to ride off into the sunset on some crazy trip."*

In all the years she'd known J.C., she'd also known his father, and though she hadn't seen John Carson very often when she had seen him he'd offered offhand comments about how incompatible she and J.C. were. How the CEO's son would never be out and about with the flighty writer.

Maybe he'd been right. She looked at J.C. now and saw a smart, distinguished, responsible man. Even the way he carried himself screamed dependable. While she was still trekking around the world with a backpack and a passport.

"Seems the sugar high didn't last all that long." J.C. gestured toward Henry, who was curled up in the corner of the booth, his head against the soft vinyl seat, asleep. "You must have worn him out when I was on the phone."

Grace glanced at the little boy, snoring softly. Maybe she'd bored him to death. "All we did was talk about horses and ice cream."

"I appreciate it. More than you know." J.C.'s gaze held honest appreciation and gratitude.

The moment extended between them, a slowly tightening string that went from a simple thank-you to something more. Something fraught with all the unspoken history between them.

Once upon a time Grace had thought she'd run off with J.C. Carson. The two of them would blow out of this town and take on the world, Grace with her words, J.C. with his music. Then he'd changed overnight and ended their relationship without even telling her to her face, rather letting his father do the dirty work. When she'd gone to see him, to get an explanation, he'd been sitting on his porch with another girl, a girl in a frilly dress and white shoes. Grace had left Beckett's Run and never looked back.

Until now.

Damn, that day still stung, even as she told herself it didn't. She wanted to know where the other J.C. had gone, if she truly had been blinded by some crazy infatuation to the person he really was.

"Do you still play guitar?" she asked him, her dinner forgotten, the pie growing cold beside her.

"I used to. Even thought about joining a college band for one semester, but I got too busy and never did. And..." He shrugged. "Lately, I haven't had time."

"And here I thought you'd be the next big rock star."

"Yeah, well, some dreams aren't practical."

"That's the whole point of dreams, isn't it? To let you step out of the practical?"

He scoffed. "I'm as far from being an impractical dreamer as a man can get."

"Oh, I don't know about that. I bet there's some rocker in you still." That was what she was looking for, the J.C. she remembered, the man she had once fallen for. But why did she keep trying to find that side of him? Where could it possibly lead?

"If there ever was some rocker in me still," J.C. said quietly, "then the last few years have erased it completely."

He didn't elaborate, and as much as she wanted to know why she didn't press him. "That's too bad."

"Yeah," he said with a sigh. "It is."

The tension in the string between them tightened even more. Grace sensed J.C. was holding back, yet at the same time it seemed like he wanted to open up, wanted to be that boy sitting beside her on the creek bank.

She could ask, and be that friend for him again. But where would that go? In the end, she was going back to her life, and he to his. Getting close again would be a mistake. So she left the topic of his music alone and returned to the one she was here to focus on.

"Since I helped you with Henry, do you think you could repay me with a little favor?"

He arched a brow. "I know you, Grace. Your favors often get me into trouble. Grounded, or worse."

The words sent a rush of memories through her. The two of them sneaking into the closed high school one summer, just to run in the empty halls, their voices echoing off the tiled floors and walls. Then, another time, climbing the fence at the town pool after hours and taking a late-night swim. Then the day they'd cut roses from the neighbor's garden and presented them in a bouquet to Mary—not knowing the garden party was planning a tour of that garden the next morning. There'd been laughs and adventures, and something new, it seemed, every time they were together.

The memories draped over her shoulders like a blanket, comforting and suffocating all at the same time. Those memories were wrapped up in a town she wanted to forget, a town she couldn't wait to leave.

"Gram's book club is meeting again tomorrow morning," she said, returning to her purpose. Get the story and get out, with minimal personal interaction. "They're trying to wrap up the book discussion before the holiday. Come with me."

"Me? Why?"

"Because you're a good-looking man and you'll distract them from the fact that I didn't read the book."

"You think I'm good-looking?" he said. The question came with a smile, the kind of smile that teased and tempted her all at once. She glanced down, away from that smile. Damn. How did she keep ending up in this place with him?

"J.C., you know you are." She cursed the heat rising in her cheeks. Who was this shy woman? She was never shy. Never caught off guard with a man. She shot him a sarcastic grin. "It's not exactly a newsflash, Mr. Best Smile."

"Those yearbook days are a million years ago." J.C. laughed, then his gaze went to Henry and he sobered. The moment of sexual tension between them eased. "Well, I should probably get him home."

She wanted to ask him why he had stepped in as a parent. Why he was both protective and distant with his nephew. But she didn't. Instead, she glanced down at the pad of paper and refocused on her goal. She picked up the pen. "Before you go, I want to ask you a couple more questions."

"Shoot."

"You said earlier that a lot of why you are doing this Winter Festival is because of your nephew. Were you involved before that? I mean, is this an annual thing for you?"

"I've supported the town festival most years, as well as the town picnic and the summer cookout in the park. But not in as big a way as I'm doing with the Winter Festival this year. Most of my help before was financial. Donations, sponsorships, things like that. I've never been hands-on before, like I am now. In fact, you were right earlier. I used to want to be far from this town and everything it represented. Then that changed." J.C. glanced over at Henry and brushed a lock of dark hair off his nephew's head with a smooth, easy touch. Henry stirred, but didn't wake. "This year, after my sister died, I came back to Beckett's Run. At first just to help with the funeral arrangements. Then I realized my mother needed help with Henry. I thought I'd be here a few weeks at most. At the same time the Winter Festival planning began, and I realized I could be more involved than in years past. I agreed to chair it because..." his gaze again went to his nephew "...this year it's important to me that Christmas is special. Memorable. Fun."

"I understand." J.C. had surprised her yet again. Such a tender, giving thing for him to do, and here she'd been thinking he was doing all this solely to add to the Beckett's Run bottom line. Once again he showed her another side, and it intrigued her. "It must be hard to run your business in Boston and be here at the same time."

"It's challenging, to say the least." At his hip, a continual ding announced emails pouring into his phone as he spoke, all buzzing for attention. "I try to be in both places at once, and of course that's unrealistic." He sighed. "Anyway, after the Winter Festival is done I'm planning on going back to the city and back to running the investment company."

"And what will happen to Henry?"

J.C.'s gaze went to somewhere far off. He let out a long breath. "I don't know."

She could see the weight on J.C's shoulders. The decisions that were in his hands, the grief that still shimmered in his eyes. Her heart went out to him, to the man she used to know. A man she once thought she loved. But then she remembered that he had just said he was going back to the company and leaving town.

"He doesn't want that bohemian lifestyle," John Senior had said to her all those years ago. *"J.C. wants more. He just didn't know how to tell you."*

Well, J.C. had more now, and she was still that bohemian he had rejected. She needed to remember that.

His phone rang again, and he got to his feet, apologizing. "This will only take a second, I swear. If you can watch Henry—"

"No problem. Go ahead."

J.C. headed back to the hallway to talk. The waitress returned with refills for their drinks. She propped a hip against J.C.'s side of the booth and put a proprietorial hand on the back of it, as if claiming the space in his absence. "J.C. never did introduce us. I swear, that man isn't always paying attention."

Grace put out a hand. "Grace McKinnon. I don't live around here. I'm just visiting. I'm Mary McKinnon's granddaughter."

"Oh, my God! I knew you looked familiar, but it's been a long time. I'm Allie Marsh. I lived two streets away from your grandma."

"Allie, of course." Grace could see the girl she'd once known now. She barely remembered Allie, but then again that was probably because Grace had done her level best to forget Beckett's Run—at least most of it. "How are you?"

"Doing good. Still living here." Allie laughed. "I see your grandmother all the time. She comes in every Tuesday night for a piece of Carol's pecan pie. So… what are you doing with the most eligible bachelor in Beckett's Run?" The look that passed through Allie's eyes sat far on the left of friendly or inquisitive. No, she assessed Grace as if Grace was a swarm of locusts invading her land. "Heck, he's probably the most eligible bachelor in all of New England."

"J.C.?" Grace snorted. "I've known him since we were catching crayfish in the creek together. I wouldn't call him the most eligible anything."

Allie shook her head. "Honey, you must be blind or rich, or both."

"Neither." She laughed. "J.C. is still just J.C., right?"

"You have been away from town a *long* time." Allie cast a glance toward the hallway, where J.C. was still talking. "J.C. is a billionaire, or maybe he's a zillionaire by now. Why, next to Andrew Beckett, he's the best thing this town has going for it. Heck, I wouldn't be surprised if they didn't name the town square after him next year, what with all he's done for this place. Cleaning up the place, rebuilding it. He's been a godsend, that's for sure, what with so many residents struggling."

"*J.C.* has?" Grace had assumed the book club ladies had been exaggerating. Looked like she'd been wrong.

"Yup. Paid off some mortgages, bought some houses that were being foreclosed just to rent 'em back to the owners. He's helped businesses, college kids, you name it. He don't talk about it at all, of course, wants to be all anonymous, but believe me, there's no one in Beckett's Run like J.C." She said it with a mixture of admiration and infatuation. She cast a glance over her shoulder at him again. "If you ask me, the woman that lands him is going to be one lucky person. Living in the lap of luxury and waking up to him every morning." She shook her head. "Yummy."

Grace wouldn't call J.C. *yummy.* No, the words for him in her vocabulary tended more toward things like edgy, dangerous, sexy. He still had a way of looking at her and setting her nerves on fire. Of making her forget her sentence halfway through speaking. Of making her heart beat a little faster—okay, a lot faster.

The word *billionaire* lodged in her brain. He'd become the one thing he'd said he didn't want to be—a wealthy executive burning both ends of the candle. The

J.C. she had once fallen for had been determined to shake off his family expectations and become his own man, take his music on the road and go wherever the wind blew. To live the same devil-may-care life she wanted, city to city, no rules, no expectations, no roots holding them back. He couldn't be further from that right now if he tried. Seemed he'd not just stepped into the shoes his father had worn—but also had them custom-made.

If anything reminded her that J.C. was a mistake she didn't need to make, that was it.

Allie slapped the bill on the table, said something about coming back later, then headed off. J.C. returned to the table, paid the check and added a very generous tip. "Sorry about that. I keep getting interrupted."

"No problem." The need to leave, to get far away from J.C.—J.C. the *billionaire*—burned inside her. She gathered up her things and stuffed them in her purse. "We'll catch up later."

He hoisted Henry into his arms. With the sleeping child curled against his chest J.C. looked soft, vulnerable…yummy.

"Did you get all the answers you needed?"

"Yeah, I did." She tore her gaze away from the man she had once thought she knew as well as she knew herself. A man who had been transformed in the years since to a designer-shoe-wearing stranger. "I don't need to know anything else. The picture's crystal clear now."

She walked away, out into the cold winter air. It bit at her lungs, a quick dose of icy reality.

CHAPTER SIX

THE women clucked over him like he was a lost puppy. J.C. shifted in the chair at the coffee shop and wondered what insanity had made him agree to help Grace out with her grandmother's book club.

"We're so glad to have you here, J.C.," Mrs. Brimmel said. "It'll be nice to get the male perspective on Miss Austen."

Miss Watson shushed her. "Pauline, I doubt he read *Persuasion*. Let the poor man go. He'd be much more comfortable with a dartboard than with us old biddies."

He didn't tell her that he wasn't here for the ladies of the Beckett's Run Book Club. He was here for Grace, who had asked a favor of him with those big eyes and that teasing smile he'd never been able to resist.

"She's all wrong for you," his father had said over and over again. *"Flighty, irresponsible. She's going to run out of here one day and break your heart."*

She'd done exactly that, but he kept forgetting that when she smiled at him. She reminded him of the guitar in his closet, the music he used to love, the dreams he used to have. Then reality drew him back to the present, and to the responsibilities that weighed heavy on him.

J.C. had a thousand things on his to-do list, a cell phone that was about to self-combust with emails, texts and calls, all demanding his attention. Even though he knew Grace and he were as different as the proverbial tortoise and the hare, he stayed, watching Grace blush and stammer under the inquisitive glare of the Beckett's Run Book Club.

"Ladies, spending a morning in your company is never uncomfortable," J.C. said. That earned him more twittering from the book club and an eye-roll from Grace. "And I have read *Persuasion*. Several years ago, but I read it."

A collective gasp went up around the room. "You did?"

"You did?" Grace echoed. "Why on earth would you…? I mean, what made you want to?"

He shrugged. "I had a girlfriend in college who needed help with a paper on Austen. At the time I was trying to impress her, so I read the book."

"And how'd that work out?" Grace asked.

"The paper? Or the girlfriend?"

"Oh, the girlfriend, of course," Mrs. Brimmel said. The other book club ladies leaned in, rapt and eager.

"She got an A. And I believe she's now married to an English professor. I bet they talk about Austen every night."

The ladies laughed. J.C. cast a quick glance at Grace, who had a curious look on her face. It couldn't be jealousy, because the Grace he knew had never cared one bit about who he dated or what he did with his personal life. They had their summers, and in between she went off to her life and he went off to his. She'd arrive in town every June and school break, never asking what he'd been up to the months before, and they'd pick up as if they had never been apart.

"And what do you think about a lady's power of persuasion, J.C.?" Miss Watson asked.

"Oh, I think those are like super powers. A beautiful woman can talk a man into most anything."

"Even love?"

"Well, I wouldn't know about that. Seeing as how no one has managed to talk me into that yet." More laughter from the book club.

"You must be playing hard to get," Grace said. "Because, from what I hear, you're the most eligible bachelor this town has ever seen."

"I'm not *playing* hard to get, Grace." His gaze met hers. "At all."

She held his gaze for a long time, then looked away. "I'll let the single women in Beckett's Run know."

He grinned. "Alert the media?"

"I'll do even better than that. I'll send out an all-points bulletin."

"Hmm…that could be trouble," he said.

"Oh, everything about you is trouble, J.C. Carson."

At some point he'd forgotten the presence of the book club. His attention had honed in on Grace, on the way her lips moved when she talked, on that sassy little smile that accompanied every tease, on the way her ponytail danced along the back of her neck, like an invitation for his mouth to do the same.

"I think you're the one who's trouble, Grace McKinnon." Because right now he was having some very troubling thoughts. The kind that could make a man like him, a man who hadn't stepped off the prescribed path of his life in years, take a very serious detour.

"Well, that sounds like persuasion to me," Mrs. Brimmel said. The other ladies laughed, and the spell between J.C. and Grace was broken.

Grace picked up her copy of the novel—no more broken in today than the other day—and thumbed to a random page. "I wanted to get the group's thoughts on the events with Anne's cousin…uh…Mr.…Elliot. In chapter sixteen."

The group went on about their impressions of the book's theories on beauty and social standing, but J.C. wasn't listening. His gaze stayed on Grace, on that tempting flip of hair along her neck, and on the reasons why she seemed to dance closer to him, then jerk away.

Years ago, he'd thought he would marry Grace. Had planned to ask her in that foolish eighteen-year-old way that a boy had of thinking everything would be perfect if he just spent the rest of his days with the right girl. To J.C., Grace had been everything he hadn't been. Wild, adventurous, headstrong. She'd known what she wanted to do and be since she was old enough to hold a pencil, and nothing and no one would dissuade her. She'd ducked curfews and skirted rules, and encouraged him to do the same more than once. She'd turned down a soccer scholarship, opting instead to work her way through college at a school with a better journalism program. She'd started taking solo trips around the world the day she turned eighteen, just herself and a backpack and a pad of paper.

He was supposed to go on that first trip with her, using his guitar to make a living. Even had his bags packed. Then reality had hit, and he'd unpacked the bags, put the guitar in the closet, and gone back to following the path he'd been meant to take, the one he'd bucked until it became clear he could no longer afford that luxury. Grace had left town, without so much as a word, proving to him that her feelings for him were about as deep as a puddle.

A part of him wanted to ask why. Wanted to know how he could have been so wrong about her, so wrong about them. But he didn't. Because no matter what happened, he knew one thing for a fact—

He and Grace would never have that storybook ending, the kind created by Austen.

"Oh, my goodness, would you look at the time?" Mrs. Brimmel said. "We need to get to the Ladies' Tea at church." She turned to Grace. "Will you be with us next time, Grace? When we start *Little Women*? It's another love story, so maybe you might want to bring J.C. along, too." A devilish grin covered her face.

"I'll probably be gone by then," Grace said. "I'm only in town for the holidays."

"What a shame. Beckett's Run sure misses you." The other ladies concurred, dispensed hugs and warm wishes, then headed out of the coffee shop, bundled up like Eskimos.

J.C. checked his messages, read a text from the maintenance man he'd hired to set up several of the displays for the Winter Festival, then crossed to Grace. As much as he'd dreaded going to her grandmother's book club, he'd enjoyed the time away from the demands of the office. The fun of talking about something frivolous. It wasn't the kind of fun he'd had as a kid, but it was a nice departure from his day-to-day. And, most of all, he'd enjoyed seeing Grace. Especially when the ladies of Beckett's Run put her on the spot.

Damn. What was it about her that drew him even when he knew they were all wrong for each other? She was still the headstrong jackrabbit running for the door, and he was now the dependable tortoise, taking the safe and cautious path.

"I have to head over to the park to check on something," he said. "I don't know what you have going on right now, but maybe you want to go with me. You know, check out the inner workings of the festival and everything."

There. He'd clarified it. This wasn't a date, it was work.

"Sure. That sounds like fun."

He chuckled. "I'm just checking on some maintenance issues, so I can't guarantee fun."

"You know me, J.C." That smile winged its way across her face again. "I do guarantee fun."

"Oh, I remember that. Very well."

"Do you? Because it seems to me you're not the same guy I left behind. Now you're the guy with the emails and phone calls and button-down shirts." She skated a finger down the front of his shirt and searing heat raced through his veins.

For a moment he imagined her undoing those buttons, her gaze locked on his and that sexy, sassy smile on her lips. Her hands parting the panels of his shirt, then her skin against his, moving lower, lower—

"Now you're the guy with the emails and phone calls and button-down shirts."

She'd nailed him in a few words. The image constricted his throat, a noose constructed from responsibilities and expectations. Foolishness was what Grace represented. Not responsibility.

"Doesn't mean I'm not fun," he said, his voice quiet, dark.

"Oh, really?" She arched a brow. "So you're still the guy who would dive into a cold lake on the first day of March?"

"Yeah. I am." He wanted to be that guy still, Lord, how he wanted to be. He missed those days. He wanted to forget the ties and the emails and just be J.C., out on another adventure with Grace. Just one more fun time.

Her gaze met his, strong and sure. "Good." She slipped her arm into his and they headed out into the cold. "Then prove it to me."

Grace stood to the side, watching J.C. handle a flurry of issues and problems that could have pushed another man over the edge. Not only had the maintenance man come to him in a panic over a broken-down ride, but so too had two of the construction workers who were assembling the last parts of Santa's Village. J.C. solved each of their problems with fast efficiency and a couple of phone calls. All while his own phone buzzed and rang, a constant blur of activity. Throughout it all he kept his head and stayed focused, which kept those around him calm, too. He had a way of talking to people that calmed them down and got them refocused. Within minutes tempers cooled, and the festival got back on track.

"You handled that great. I'm impressed," she said when he joined her again.

"That was nothing. You should see some of the things I run into at work. Here, it's just a ride or a shed. At work, it's millions of dollars. But in the end the cost doesn't matter. If something is important to people, they want a solution. And I try to provide that."

"You're good at it."

"Thanks."

She leaned against the wall of the Mistletoe Wishes ride and studied him. "But you're not happy."

"Who says I'm not happy?"

"You do. It's in your eyes." She pushed off from the wall and came closer. "I have known you forever, J.C.

Carson, and I know when you're happy and when you're not."

Behind them, music began to play. Happy Christmas songs, a lyrical undertow to the ride. Red and white decorated boats sailed into a dark tunnel on a fake ice road constructed out of shimmery metal. Christmas lights twinkled inside the space, causing a soft glow to spill from the entrance.

"All set," called the maintenance man. "Should work like a dream now. You want to take a ride on it? Try her out?"

J.C. hesitated, his hand on his phone, his gaze going to the steady stream of emails pouring in. More demands for his time and attention. The J.C. he had become was rising to the surface again. She knew she shouldn't care, but she just couldn't—not right now, not for this moment—let him be that man. She may not love J.C. anymore, may not be part of his life now, but, damn it, she refused to let him become the very thing he'd despised.

His father.

John Carson had been a cold, distant man, who rarely cracked a smile and spent his days working, or talking about work. She'd never heard of him taking the family on vacation or going to J.C.'s basketball games or, heck, taking the kids to the park. J.C. had rarely talked about his father, and when he had, it was always around something to do with work. And most of all J.C.'s father had hated Grace and the "distractions" she caused his son. But John wasn't here right now, and J.C. looked like he could use a distraction.

"Anyway, I'll leave her running for a while," the maintenance man said. "Just flip this switch here if you want to try it out. Gotta go look at the lighting for

Santa's Village right now." He headed off to the other side of the park.

"What do you say?" Grace asked. "Want to take a spin?"

J.C. held up the phone. "I really should—"

"Have fun," she whispered, closing the gap by another foot. "Remember? You said you were going to prove it to me."

"Taking a ride is—"

"The first step." She grabbed his hand and pulled him into the tunnel. "So let's do it."

"Grace, I shouldn't—"

"Argue with me. You know I always win." She laughed, then tugged him deeper into the dark space. The boats circled around the track, passing by the boarding dock and into the ebony recesses. She leaned over, flipped the switch, and the next boat chugged to a stop. "Get in, J.C., and let's see how fast we can make this thing go."

He chuckled. "It's set to one speed and one speed only. There's no racing in the tunnel of love. It's meant to go slow and easy." He glanced at her, his blue eyes holding the glint of a tease. "Are you up for that?"

"I'm up for anything," Grace said, and climbed into the boat. But as J.C. sat in the space beside her she realized how confining the small vessel was, how it was meant to bring two lovers close together, to encourage them to embrace. A tunnel of love—the kind of place that meant kissing, touching...falling.

Before she could change her mind the boat jerked to a start and headed down the mechanical path. The movement brought her against J.C. He draped his arm over the back of the seat. "Not much room in here."

"Not much at all. Kind of reminds me of—"

"The Ferris wheel at the summer fair," he said, at the same time she did.

Grace laughed. "That thing was tiny. I don't even know how it called itself a Ferris wheel."

"The whole fair was tiny. But it was fun."

Her gaze met his. In the dark, all she could see was the glimmering reflection of the Christmas lights, dancing in the pools of his eyes. "It was."

"We used to have a lot of fun, Grace."

"We did."

"I miss those days."

"Me, too, J.C." She thought of the trips she'd taken, the destinations she'd stayed in over the course of her career. She'd been all over the world, and nowhere had she laughed as much or enjoyed herself as much as she had during those summers with J.C. Carson.

Letting herself get swept up again, though, would be a foolish mistake. She wasn't staying and she shouldn't act like a woman who was.

J.C. shifted, which brought his leg against hers. Heat raced along her skin and made her pulse thunder. She glanced down at his arm, his thigh, and the urge to touch him became her only thought.

Oh, this was trouble. Big, big trouble. She jerked away and reached for the side of the boat. "Come on, let's check this thing out." Before he could stop her, she leapt out of the boat and onto the platform running alongside them.

"Hey, we're not supposed to be up there."

"You're the boss, J.C. You can do anything you want. Come on—find me." She dashed off into the pretend night, ducking behind one of the dozens of Christmas trees lining the side. Grace crouched down, hiding her body amongst the wide branches of a fake fir.

"This is nuts," he said, but a laugh escaped him anyway.

She heard the sound of his footsteps on the platform, hard at first, then softer, as he snuck among the trees. She shifted to circle to the other side of the fir as J.C. came around to the back. Her foot caught on a tree base, and the fir wobbled, threatening to fall. She caught it, but not before she heard J.C. say, "Got you!"

Grace scrambled to her feet and ran off, laughing as she wove in and out of the trees. The blinking lights cast a golden blanket over the space, illuminating J.C. as he emerged from the faux forest, still laughing. "Give up yet?" she called out.

"Never."

She laughed again, then charged down the back wall. Around them, the Christmas music kept on playing, and the boats kept on moving. The world of Beckett's Run had ceased to exist inside the dark tunnel of the Mistletoe Wishes ride, and a part of Grace wished she could stay here forever, that she could forget the job and family and life waiting for her outside these walls.

She heard a rustle, and before she could move J.C.'s hand curled around her arm. "Got you. And this time I'm not letting go."

"You promise?" She said the words as a joke, but the other Grace, the one who had once believed she and J.C. would be together forever, held her breath and waited for his answer.

"That might not be too practical," he said with a laugh.

"And you are the sensible one." She forced a smile against her disappointment.

"I wasn't always," he said. "Especially when it came to you."

Her breath lodged in her throat again. She wanted to ask what he meant, wanted to know whether he meant that as a good thing or a bad thing, but she couldn't bear to hear the answer. All she wanted right now was this moment, this tiny world of just her and J.C.

And, God help her, she wanted him, too. She always had.

"Oh, Grace," he said, his voice as dark as the tunnel around them, and in those two words she heard the same desire, the same want that pulsed inside her chest. She waited a fraction of a second and then, finally, J.C. did what she had wanted him to do since she'd crashed her car into that snow bank.

He leaned in and kissed her, capturing her mouth with his in a heated electric rush, one made sweeter and hotter by the passing of time, the knowledge of a past lover. Sparks arced in her body, erupted in her brain, overrode her common sense. J.C. captured her face with his hands, a sweet, gentle move that countered the hot demands of his kiss. He made her feel treasured and sexy, all at the same time, and all she wanted right now was more of that.

She leaned into him. Beside them, the boats jerked along on their lazy ride, bumping softly in the quiet, but she didn't care. Her arms circled his back and she pressed him into her, until not a breath of space remained between them. He groaned, and his tongue darted into her mouth, setting off another fire deep in her belly. Her hands went to his hair, burying deep in those dark locks, wanting...

More. Wanting him.

She'd never forgotten what it was like to be touched by J.C. Carson. To be loved by him, to have him take his sweet, slow time kissing her body, touching her skin, igniting her passion. They had learned together, really, the two of them starting out as fumbling teenagers, then daring more and more with each summer, until one summer—

She jerked back so fast she nearly brought the entire row of trees down with her. What was she doing? Going back to those days? Hadn't she learned her lesson before? She and J.C. were no good together, and never would be. Kissing him only made that reality hurt more.

"We can't…we can't do that." Her breath heaved out of her chest, and her body cried foul.

"And what do you think we're doing?"

"Opening a door we shut a long time ago." She turned toward the ride, stepped into the nearest boat, and reached for the handle to the dock on the other side. J.C. followed, reaching for her arm.

"You're running again, Grace."

"I'm not." She'd never run from him. That was what he didn't understand. She'd only done what he had told her to do all those years ago—she'd left without him. His father had said J.C. would be happier, and she would be, too. She told herself he'd been right. "I'm just not… staying."

"That's the same thing."

She pivoted back to him as the hurt she'd felt that day years and years ago surged to the surface. *We had plans,* she wanted to scream at him. *You were supposed to be there forever. To be the one I could depend on. Always. And you let me down.* "You would know, J.C."

Then she headed out of the tunnel, and back into the cold winter sunshine.

CHAPTER SEVEN

J.C. WALKED through the door of his mother's house, hoping this time would be different. But no smells of dinner cooking greeted him. No scent of pine cleanser stung his nose. There was only the same scene as the day before and all the days before that—the soft undertow of the television playing yet another sappy movie that had gone direct to video. On the living room floor, Henry played with a set of toy blocks, building something that could have been a house, a castle or a gorilla enclosure.

Henry scrambled to his feet and plowed into J.C. "Uncle Jace! Look what I made!"

J.C. followed his nephew into the living room and marveled over the bright creation. "That's a great… house," he said.

"It's not a house. It's a rocket!" Henry jerked up the tower and started running around the room, making *vroom-vroom* sounds.

"Henry, please keep it down. Grandma is trying to watch her show."

His mother had never even taken her eyes off the television when she spoke. Henry nodded, then sat on the carpet and went back to building. J.C. crossed to the seat in front of his mother.

Grace's words from earlier came back to him. She'd

accused him of never having any fun, and she was right. But what she didn't understand was the enormous pressure and responsibility that lay on J.C.'s shoulders. First the business, then his widowed mother, and now his orphaned nephew. There were days when J.C. felt like he might bow to the weight of all that, but he knew he couldn't. Because if he did, people would get hurt. He was the rock they all stood upon, and a rock never crumbled.

Then what was that in the tunnel today? his mind asked.

A moment of insanity. He'd let himself get swept up in the game and lost track of the end result. For a moment he'd been eighteen again, Grace hot and soft in his arms, the world some far off thing.

Then she'd broken away and done what Grace always did—left.

Which was exactly what Grace was going to do after Christmas, too. Right now J.C. needed stability and predictability in his life—*that* was who he was, what people needed him to be. Grace was as far from those adjectives as she was from the moon.

He turned his attention back to his mother. "Hey, Mom, what's for dinner?"

"Sandwiches."

"I'm going to have to get that printed on the menu here, we have it so often." J.C. gave her a grin. "Come on, Mom, let's go make something. You love to cook."

"I used to. Not now." She thumbed the volume on the remote.

J.C. got to his feet, and started for the door, to do what he had done for weeks now—let it go and put off the hard discussions for another day. Then he glanced at his nephew and knew it could wait no longer. The holidays were here, and soon J.C. had to make a decision about staying in Beckett's Run or going back to Boston.

J.C. worried that if he returned to Boston his grieving mother would withdraw even further, which would hurt Henry. J.C. pivoted back. "Henry, can you do me a favor? Can you go in your room and draw a picture of a horse for Grace? She'd really like that."

"Yup! I'll draw the horsey from the zoo. Grace is scared of him too cuz he sneezes funny." Henry dashed off, enthused and excited.

When he was gone, J.C. stood in front of the television. His mother let out a sigh of exasperation. "Mom, we need to talk."

"I'm watching my show."

"You're always watching your show. I think you should watch your grandson." Before her daughter's death Anne Carson had been an engaged grandmother, who saw Henry daily and took him to the park and the playground. Since her daughter's fatal car accident Anne had barely acknowledged Henry.

"He's fine."

"He's not," J.C. countered. "He wants a grandmother who interacts with him. He wants something other than sandwiches for dinner. He wants you to look at his rocket and tell him it's the best rocket you've ever seen." Things his mother used to do with J.C. when he was little. She'd been the one who had encouraged him, paid for his music lessons out of her pin money. She'd been the one who had dipped Easter eggs with J.C. and his sister, who had camped out in the living room on summer afternoons. Before J.C.'s sister died, his mother had been the one who kept the family together. Now it seemed all she did was fall apart a little more each day.

"I do that for Henry." She tried to peer around J.C. but he remained where he was.

"No, you don't. You know it, and I know it, and poor Henry does, too. He needs you, Mom. Just like…" J.C. swallowed hard, then went on, "I used to when I was his age."

All those unspoken memories hung in the air. The tough, demanding, cold father, tempered by Anne's warm heart, tender touches. J.C. often wondered how he and his sister would have turned out if they hadn't had their mother to ease their difficult childhoods. He knew Anne had loved John, loved him with a fierceness that J.C. envied. The few times J.C. had seen his father vulnerable had been with his wife, as if she was the only one he could let down his guard around.

It took a moment, but his mother finally raised her gaze to his. "I'm trying, J.C. I really am."

"I know you are, but you're not helping yourself or him by watching these shows every day. It's Christmas, Mom. Your favorite time of year and you haven't even wanted to put up the tree yet."

"It's a lot of work and—"

"And that's an excuse. I told you I'd help. Hell, I'll do the whole thing if you want."

"I'm just not in the mood for the holiday." Her gaze went to the far wall, past him, into moments that had come and gone long ago. When she didn't say anything J.C. shifted away from the television with a sigh. He'd tried.

"Don't worry about it," he said. "I'll do it this weekend."

This was what Grace didn't know, or see, or understand, when she pushed him to be that wild kid he'd once been. That kid had grown up and had people who would fall apart if he didn't keep it together.

J.C.'s mother got to her feet and stood before him. "You're always taking care of me. It should be the other way around."

"I don't mind. Think of it as payback for doing my laundry when I was younger."

That brought a spark of life to his mother's eyes, and for the first time in a while J.C. began to hope that things would change. "And you had a lot of laundry for one little boy."

He shrugged. "Being a boy is a messy business."

She glanced at the space where Henry had been just a while earlier. "I see a lot of you in him. The way he looks at the world, the way he loves to create, to build. He's a bit impetuous, too, like you used to be."

J.C. didn't think about his creative, impetuous sides. One of these days Henry would grow up too and those things would be pushed to the side. The thought saddened J.C.

"Henry's a good kid." Already J.C. had gotten used to seeing his nephew every day. He hated the thought of moving back to Boston. He'd asked his mother several times about moving into his Boston house, but she'd refused. She loved Beckett's Run, always had, and didn't want to leave.

"He is a good kid. And…he deserves more than this. You're right, J.C." His mother nodded, and in that gesture, J.C. saw her turn a corner, one that took her a step away from her grief. "Maybe we can string some lights or something this week."

"That would be great." It was a start, and for J.C. that was enough. He took his mother's hand and met her eyes. "If it wasn't for you, Mom, we wouldn't have had a Christmas. You made this house a home, even on the days when it felt like..." He let his voice trail off instead of saying the words.

"A prison?" she supplied. Anne's features softened. She cupped his jaw. "Your father was a hard man. I'm sorry for that."

J.C. didn't want to talk about his father, who had passed away four years ago. That was a past he had put behind him, a past he intended to keep there. Choices had been made, paths had been taken that couldn't be undone now.

He thought of that kiss he'd shared with Grace, and wondered for the first time in a long while where he would be if he and Grace had worked out. If they had done what they'd planned and run off into the sunset, him with his guitar, her with her pen. Would they still be happy all these years later? Or would they have learned a life without expectations was as empty as a bag of air?

It didn't matter. Then, and now, J.C. couldn't afford to take off on a whim. That weight sat heavy on J.C.'s shoulders, even as he wanted to delay Henry's leap into being a grown-up as long as possible. Maybe find a way to bring out the kid in Henry, and in the process find a bit of the kid in himself, without forgetting the main task—to take care of his family.

"Don't apologize, Mom. We did okay. And now we have a chance to do even better for Henry. We're all he's got, and he deserves the best Christmas ever."

Tears shimmered in Anne's eyes. She nodded. "You're right." Then she covered his hand with her own. "The tree's in the attic. Why don't you go bring it down? And I'll start dinner."

* * *

Grace had spent the better part of the night tossing and turning, wondering about J.C. and then cursing herself for caring. So he was taking care of his sister's son. So he seemed…different. So he had kissed her.

And her body had responded the same as always, with fire.

Didn't mean she was going to open that door again. She was here to get a story, restore her career and get the hell out of Beckett's Run. Hopefully without running into any other members of her family.

Gram had gone to church, leaving Grace a note on the kitchen table beside a basket of blueberry muffins. Grace slathered butter on one, popped a big bite in her mouth, then ran down her notes from the day before. She tapped her pencil against the pad.

Nothing she had so far contained that hook she needed. That unique spin. Everything about the Beckett's Run Winter Festival in her notes fit the definition of cliché. Small-town Christmas celebration, lots of mistletoe and greenery, a great tourist stop for a family to while away a weekend. She'd done a hundred stories like this, and for years that had been the foundation she built her career upon. But that wasn't the kind of story that was going to bring her career back from the dead. Or get her editor to give her a second chance.

She needed something more. Something like…

"I want to give that Christmas experience to the people of Beckett's Run, and to those on the outside looking in, to help them believe in magic again."

She stared at J.C.'s words, then thought of him with his nephew. People believing in magic. People like Henry.

Henry, a vulnerable, hopeful little boy, with big blue eyes and a trembling smile, who had lost both his parents at a time of year meant for families and hope. The kind of story people connected with, remembered.

A quiver of hesitation ran through her. This was J.C.'s nephew. Someone who was practically family. The last thing J.C. wanted, she was sure, was to have his personal life in the media.

She thought again of her editor's words. *Washed-up. Lost your touch.*

Maybe she had stumbled, but she hadn't lost it entirely. She still knew a good story when she saw one, and this was a good story. She could already see how she would shift the coverage of the Winter Festival to what came from a child's eye level. It would be whimsical and bittersweet, the kind of article people shared with their friends. The kind of article that careers—or renewed careers—were built upon. Surely J.C. would see that—and trust her to write a heartwarming, non-exploitative piece.

"You need to put your heart into your stories. Then the reader will laugh and cry right along with you."

That was what this story would be. She knew it, deep in her gut. Steve had told her to show that she cared in her writing, and she realized that after just a couple days she did care about Henry, and that fueled her to want to do a good job with his story.

She had her story. Now to make J.C. agree.

Grace ran upstairs, showered and changed into jeans and a V-neck white tee, then pulled on a thick green sweater. She swiped on a minimum of make-up, swung her hair into a ponytail, then tugged on some boots and headed out the door. She cursed herself for not getting J.C.'s phone number but figured in a town as small as Beckett's Run he wouldn't be that hard to find. She could have called his mother's house, but knowing J.C.

he was undoubtedly out and about, working on another task for the Winter Festival.

Her car fishtailed on the slick roads as she turned onto Main. She slowed, pulling into the parking lot of the drugstore. Rick Anderson, the pharmacist, had lived in town longer than anyone, and knew more about the goings-on than a high-tech satellite. If anyone knew where to find J.C., it was Rick.

But that wasn't who she encountered when she stepped through the glass doors. Grace drew up short when she saw a familiar figure with short blonde hair standing by the Christmas candy display. She blinked. Was she seeing things? "Mom? What are you doing here?"

Lydia McKinnon—though she hadn't been a McKinnon for many years—reached forward and drew her youngest daughter into a hug. The scent of her perfume and fresh snow filled Grace's nostrils. The hug comforted and suffocated all at the same time. "Oh, my God, Grace! Mary said you were in town."

Grace drew back. "Gram? When did you talk to her?"

"This morning. I called her when I was almost to town. She invited me for dinner tomorrow night so we could catch up." Her mother hugged her again. "Oh, I'm so excited to see you!"

Gram, always trying to create a happy ending in a family that had never been anything close to happy. Grace stepped out of the embrace before she got too used to it. Chances were, her mother was on her way *through* town, and on to something else, and would be gone before the table was set. "I didn't know you were coming to town."

"Well, neither did I, but then I was talking to Hope and Faith—"

"You talked to them? When?"

"I've always talked to them, and I would talk to you all the time, too, if anyone could pin you down, you globetrotter." Lydia smiled. "Anyway, the other day your sisters and I were talking about all the wonderful things happening in their lives, and I just wanted to come here and see them and have a perfect family holiday."

Wonderful things happening in Hope and Faith's lives? Hurt bloomed in Grace's chest. Her sisters hadn't called her and told her a thing. Had the three McKinnon girls really drifted that far apart that good news couldn't be shared?

Or had Grace been the one to pull back? Over the years her sisters had called and emailed and texted, but Grace, always busy with the next assignment, another plane to catch, had vowed to catch up later. Later had never come.

"The girls are on their way into town," her mother went on, "and should be here before Christmas Day." Lydia clasped her hands together. "I'm so excited to have us all together again. I have so many plans, Grace. It's going to be an amazing holiday."

"That's great, Mom," Grace said. She didn't add that she knew her mother well and doubted Lydia would hang around town long enough for the holiday to arrive. There'd be another man, another adventure, something to drag Lydia away—or rather something that Lydia allowed to drag her away from her family. There'd be no amazing holiday. Just another disappointment to add to the list.

"Listen, let's get a bite to eat. I haven't seen you in forever." Lydia smiled. "So let's get some lunch and catch up."

"I can't. I have things to do today. But maybe later."

Lydia's face fell, and for a moment Grace wanted to apologize, to say *Yes, sure, let's get burgers and act like nothing ever changed.* But she didn't.

"Okay. You have my cell, right?"

"Yeah. I'll call. I promise." Grace gave her mother a fast hug, then turned and exited the drugstore. It wasn't until she got back to her car that she'd realized that she'd left without the one thing she needed—information.

She sat in her car and let out a long sigh. What was it about seeing her mother that set her on edge? Five seconds into seeing her and Grace wanted to run for the hills. She tugged out her cell, scrolled through the contacts, then paused, her finger over the name. Finally, she pressed the button and waited for the call to go through.

"You've reached Hope McKinnon." Hope's voice exploded in a breathless rush in her voicemail message. "I can't come to the phone right now, because I'm…" a giggle—from *Hope*, of all people—then another rush of breath "…busy, but I promise to return your call soon."

The excitement and happiness in Hope's words drew Grace up short. The last time they'd talked they'd been fighting about Hope helping Grace out with an article. The nightmarish Fiji article, the one from where it had all gone so far downhill that now her editor had sent her on a required vacation, or rather a forced leave of absence. Now Hope sounded as joyous as a kid at an amusement park.

"Hey, it's Grace. Gram said you were coming to Beckett's Run and I wanted to give you a heads-up, in case she didn't already tell you. Mom's here. For as long as Mom will stay. Maybe she'll be gone by the time you arrive, or maybe she'll stay. Who knows with her? Anyway….I just wanted to let you know."

Grace hung up the phone and put it back in her

pocket. She thought of calling Faith, then stopped. She didn't need her sisters to reinforce what she already knew—that having their mother here wouldn't end well. It never did, and Grace wasn't about to get her hopes up now.

Instead she put the car in gear and headed down the street. She didn't know where she was going to stop until she made the last turn and ended up parked alongside the town park. She turned off the car and got out, slipping on her gloves as a gust of winter's chill raced down her spine.

The festival preparations were nearly done, from what she could see. The entire Beckett's Run park had been decorated in red, green and white. Pine swags looped between oversized wreaths hanging on the streetlights, while a mini Christmas village anchored the center of the park. To the right, the pond had been changed into an ice skating rink, where dozens of people circled, their breath forming frosty clouds. Santa's Village dominated the eastern side of the park, complete with a mini-toy factory and a place for the big guy to take appointments and hear Christmas wishes. Reindeer pranced inside a wooden pen located beside a smaller green building labeled "Elf Shop."

"Too much?"

Grace whirled around at the sound of J.C.'s deep voice behind her. When she saw him her heart stuttered, and her mind flashed back to that hot kiss in the dark tunnel of the Mistletoe Wishes ride. An apt name, if people only knew. Damn, that man could kiss. And damn her hormones for wanting him to do it again. Right here. Right now.

"It's Christmas. There's no such thing as too much, if you ask my grandmother."

He chuckled. "Wait till you see the swimming swans and leaping lords we booked."

"You didn't?"

"No, but I have to admit I considered it."

She chuckled. "You always did like to do things in a huge, memorable way, J.C."

"Not me."

"Oh, really?" She leaned back against a tree and crossed her arms over her chest. "Remember the town picnic? When you sang 'Happy Birthday' to me from the roof of the gazebo?"

"That was…an anomaly."

"And the time you caught the biggest fish in the annual fish derby?"

"Beginner's luck."

"Maybe, but no one else tossed their fish back and dove in after it."

"It was a hot day."

She shook her head. "I don't get you. You used to be so…spontaneous, J.C. Now you're all serious and grown-up. It's as if that person you used to be never existed."

"That's the key, Grace. I grew up."

He took a step closer, winnowing the space between them to mere inches. The winter cold disappeared, replaced by a heat that raced through her veins, sped up her heart.

"We both did."

She laughed and looked away. She wouldn't call herself a grown-up—at least not entirely grown-up. "I don't know about that."

He put a finger under her jaw and turned her face until she was looking at him again. He had the bluest eyes. The kind of eyes that stayed in a girl's memory…

forever. She'd never forgotten him, no matter how many times she told herself otherwise. J.C. Carson had always lingered in the back of her memory, a shadow she couldn't shake. Not that she'd tried very hard.

Maybe it was because he was her first—first everything. First real friend, first boyfriend, first lover. Hadn't she read once that a girl always compared every man in her life to her first? That was all it was. Not that J.C. had been special or amazing or anything like that.

Because he'd also been her first heartbreak.

She needed to remember that more than anything else.

"You are very, very grown-up, Grace." His thumb traced her lower lip, slow, easy.

Okay, remembering that last fact was a little harder than she thought. She took in a sharp breath, her gaze locked on his. She knew she should step away. Should stop this before it went…wherever it might go. But she didn't. Because the part that remembered all those other firsts kept winning out. "It's all an act."

"No, it's not." His gaze dropped to her lips. "You may fool others, but I know you."

"And what do you know?"

"That we keep dancing around this subject."

"What subject?"

"This one." He leaned in and kissed her again, this time slower, sweeter. Her resistance faded in the wake of his tender touch, and she leaned into him, her hands going to his hair, pulling him closer. It was wonderful and amazing and as memorable as their first kiss.

No, it was better. After that kiss in the tunnel and this one now she had stopped telling herself that her memories were flawed, that she had built up J.C. in her mind to be a better lover than he'd been in reality.

Because he was amazing, in person and in memory. J.C. was everything she'd remembered—and more. He touched her exactly the way she liked to be touched. Kissed her exactly the way she liked to be kissed. It was as if he had opened the book of Grace and memorized every page.

She knew, oh, she knew, that he was an incredible, tender, giving lover who could send her soaring and bring her back to earth with a gentle touch, a whisper in her ear. And she wanted, oh, how she wanted to take him to her bed.

That was the whole problem. What she wanted and what she knew she should do.

She jerked away from him and her hormones screamed in protest. "We keep doing this. And we can't. Going back to where we were before. That would be a mistake." She inhaled, held the breath, then let it out in one long, slow exhale, letting sanity replace the desire. "A huge mistake."

"A mistake we've made before." His gaze sought hers, then he nodded, and the serious, grown-up J.C. returned. "But you're right."

"Good. I'm glad you agree." Though being right didn't have the satisfaction she'd expected. She ignored the disappointment in her chest and took a step back. "So, let's concentrate on why we're really here. The festival." She reached into her inside pocket and withdrew her notebook and pen. "I wanted to talk to you some more about it."

If the new direction in their relationship bothered him, J.C. didn't show it. Part of Grace hated that about J.C. How he could throw up a wall and keep part of himself hidden from her. There'd been a time when she'd thought she knew everything there was to know about J.C.

She'd been wrong.

These last few days had proved that. Every time she thought she saw the old J.C., the one she had first met in that diner over a chicken pot pie, this other one, the one he'd vowed he'd never be, rose to the surface. If she was smart she'd stop trying to figure out why and concentrate on her career.

"You know, I don't feel like talking about work right now. In fact, I don't feel like working at all. I'm ready to have some fun," he said, and the serious J.C. disappeared. His grin quirked up on one side in the way she remembered, the way it had the day they had run through the high school, the day he'd jumped in that icy pond. "Meet me back here in an hour. And wear some snow pants."

CHAPTER EIGHT

HENRY stood at the top of the hill, bundled up like a giant marshmallow. His snowsuit covered him from head to toe, and every time he moved he had the jerky movements of a robot, not a little boy. But happiness radiated from his features, and laughter spilled from him in a steady stream.

And J.C. felt like he could breathe for the first time in a month.

His mother wasn't a hundred percent involved with Henry yet, but she had made the first attempts at setting up for the holiday season, and when J.C. had left today there'd been a roast in the slow cooker. One step at a time, he told himself, and it would all be okay. Henry's mood was brighter, his smile bigger. He had that magic look in his eyes, the one that radiated from children at Christmas. The very look J.C. had worked so hard and so long to bring to his nephew.

Grace made her way up the snowy hill, looking both sexy and practical in a thick blue winter coat and matching snow pants. The boots she wore—zebra patterns that came nearly to her knee and had a thick faux-fur top—were all Grace. Quirky, yet fun.

"Sledding? *That's* what you want me to do?"

"Yep."

She cast a dubious glance at the long wooden sled in J.C.'s hands. "Well, if I'm going, you're going."

"I'm no good at sledding. Not exactly my area of expertise."

"One little accident, J.C. And it was years ago. I'm sure you've improved your driving abilities since then."

Henry tugged on J.C.'s sleeve. "Are we gonna go, Uncle Jace?"

J.C. had invited Grace along so that she would do this, and he could get back to work. Maybe make a few phone calls while Grace and Henry rode the slopes. He hadn't expected to be part of it himself. As much as he wanted to, he had details of a merger breathing down his neck, with lawyers, accountants and other suits all waiting on his responses. Carson Investments needed some attention, too, even as the snowy hill and Henry's big blue eyes beckoned. He didn't have time for fun or sledding or anything but work. "Sorry, buddy, no can do. Grace is going to take you down the hill."

Henry pouted. "I want you to go, too."

"That's two votes for J.C. to go," Grace said, then waved at the sled. "You're not chickening out, are you?"

The challenge in her voice awakened something inside him. Something he hadn't listened to in a long, long time. Something that reminded him of who he'd used to be...before.

Before the emails and board meetings, the to-do lists and the power suits. He could take one ride, and just for a minute forget all those things. The part of him that had pretended for a little while on those hot summer days that his father wasn't waiting at home with lists and chores and extra homework for J.C. to do. For those moments J.C. could just...*be*. The urge to do that called like music, rising in his chest.

The snow began to fall around him, light flakes kissing against his coat, his face. *Just...be,* it seemed to whisper. *Just...be.*

"Okay, let's do this." J.C. grinned, then brought the toboggan to the top of the hill, cemented himself on the front, then turned to Henry. "Climb on, buddy."

Henry clambered onto the sled and put his arms around his uncle's waist, sure, trusting. J.C. looked back at Grace. "And now you, milady."

She laughed, and when her gaze met his he knew she was thinking of another winter, another sledding trip. She'd been sixteen, visiting over Christmas break. Their first kiss had been shared on this very hill, after they'd skidded off the path and into a snow bank, ending up in a tangle of arms and legs. He'd looked at her and for the first time really seen her, as a woman, not as a girl or a friend.

And from that moment on things had never been the same.

"Are you sure I can trust your steering? Last time we did this I ended up buried under the snow and..." she lowered her voice "...you."

"I remember." Every single second.

"Me, too." She smiled, a soft, secret smile that seemed meant only for him.

Henry looked from one to the other. "Are we gonna go?"

J.C. chuckled and ruffled the boy's hair. "Yep. Right now." Then he looked at Grace. "Are you ready?"

"As ready as I'll ever be."

"Trust me, Grace," he said, and wondered if he was still talking about downhill rides. She climbed on behind Henry, propping her legs onto J.C.'s, forming a human sandwich of protection for the little boy. J.C.

looked down at those zebra boots draped over his thighs, making his thoughts veer for a moment from blankets of snow to blankets on a bed, then he drew himself back to the present, took the controls of the sled, shouted back a quick "Let's go!" then pushed off.

The sled rushed down the hill, past the families tromping back up, past the thick green pine trees that fronted the woods on one side of the park. Cold air frosted J.C.'s face, burned in his lungs. He hunkered down, using the controls to keep the toboggan heading for the soft flat space at the base of the hill. And then, just as fast as it began, the ride was over and the sled was sliding to a stop.

Henry clambered off. "That was fun! I want to do it again!"

His nephew was right. The whole ride had been fun. A break from the demands and expectations of his life. Inside his pocket his cell phone buzzed with a missed call. J.C.'s hand went to the cell, then he stopped and let the call go to voicemail. A flicker of guilt, but he ignored it. He could take this time and the world would not stop spinning.

"You got it, Henry." J.C. got to his feet, then put out a hand to help Grace rise. But she had already stood, and didn't need his help. "You want to go again?"

"When have I ever said no to a fast ride?" She laughed and he realized how much he had missed that sound. "And thanks for not hitting that snow bank."

"I told you to trust me."

"I know. And you know how good I am at trusting people." Her eyes danced with merriment.

"Oh, I know." His gaze met hers, then he turned away and bent down to his nephew. "Want a ride on my shoulders, little guy?"

"Sure!" Henry put out his arms and J.C. hoisted him up. Grace grabbed the sled and the three of them made their way back up the hill, looking for all appearances like any other family in the Beckett's Run park. At the top, J.C. lowered Henry to the ground, then let out a breath.

"I've been spending too much time behind a desk." He stretched out the kinks in his back. Like a reminder his phone began to ring again, and the guilt rang louder in his head.

Grace pressed a hand to his before he could answer the call. "Let's race," Grace whispered in his ear. "And for just a second pretend we have wings."

Just for a second. He muted the phone, then bent down, set the sled in place and repeated the actions of earlier, climbing on the front, then waiting for Henry to settle his small frame in the middle. Grace got on the back again, and those damned zebra boots reappeared on his thighs, like a visual representation of her challenge to race.

He shoved off, and as they rushed down the hill a second time he thought how right she was. How, for the few seconds it took to go from the top to the bottom, it seemed as if they *had* taken flight. Behind him, Henry laughed and squeezed J.C.'s waist tight. Grace's legs pressed against his thighs. Too soon, the sled came to a stop and they climbed off. A flush filled Grace's cheeks, brightened her eyes.

When he'd asked for her help he'd thought it would be a good idea. A way to help Henry deal with his grief and find the spirit of Christmas again. After all, J.C. wouldn't be called the fun one in the family, at least not anymore, and his grieving mother had trouble finding ways to keep her rambunctious grandchild busy.

Of everyone he knew, Grace was the one person who embodied fun. She reminded him of who he'd used to be—before his life had changed.

Except being with her kept opening those doors he'd done a good job shutting a long time ago. The things that had broken them apart still existed, and no amount of sledding or laughter could leap that fence.

"Again?" Henry asked.

J.C.'s phone buzzed. Persistent, demanding, and angry about being ignored earlier. He fished it out of his pocket, and glanced at the Caller ID. His C.O.O., Charles, who had already left three voicemails. He couldn't put this off forever. That was the trouble with reality—it inserted itself at the worst possible time. "How about you go with Grace?"

"Okay." Henry slipped his little hand into Grace's. "Are you a good driver?"

Grace bent down to his level. "The best. You ready?"

Henry nodded, and the two of them climbed on the sled and took off. J.C. answered the call, but his gaze and attention stayed on Grace and Henry. On the way they laughed as they careened down the hill, on the happiness on Henry's face and on the way he hung tight to Grace, then jumped up and down with excitement when the sled came to a stop.

"J.C.? You listening?"

"Oh, yeah." Then he realized he hadn't heard a word his C.O.O. had said. He turned away from the sledding hill and faced the pond instead, filled with ice skaters circling the frozen water. "What did you say again?"

On the other end of the phone, Charles went on about the state of the company's finances. He reviewed the information about the upcoming acquisition, something that J.C. had been excited about—

Before.

Before he'd moved back to Beckett's Run. Before he'd stepped in as a surrogate parent to Henry. Before Grace McKinnon came back into his life.

"Let me call you back later. Email me the numbers and I'll take a look at them."

"But—"

"I'll call you. Don't worry so much." J.C. said good-bye, then hung up the phone. Before he even tucked the cell back in his pocket it started ringing again. By the time he finished the conversation with his accountant, his lawyer was beeping in. Grace and Henry had reached the top of the hill and taken one more ride to the bottom before J.C. disentangled himself from his phone. A half dozen voicemails still waited for him, and emails flooded his phone's inbox in a steady stream.

"Uncle Jace, are you coming?" Henry asked. "Grace's gonna drive again! She goes really fast!"

J.C. arched a brow in Grace's direction.

"Not too fast," Grace said. "Come on, Mr. Over-achiever. Play hooky with us a while longer."

"I can't." He thought of all the messages he'd ignored this afternoon already. He couldn't keep letting his business flounder without him. He had a responsibility, and ignoring it wouldn't make it disappear. He hated that he was going to have to disappoint his nephew. "Henry, we need to go home now."

Henry's face fell, and the happiness that had radiated from him just a second ago evaporated. "Okay."

No argument. No begging to stay. Nothing but a solemn agreement. That broke J.C.'s heart. Stoic Henry, trying so hard to be good.

"If it's okay with you," Grace said, "I'll stay here

with Henry awhile longer, then meet you back at your mom's house."

"Are you sure?"

"Yup." She glanced down at Henry. "We're getting along okay, aren't we, kid?"

Henry nodded. "Uh-huh. Grace isn't a stranger, Uncle Jace. She's my friend, too."

J.C. chuckled. "I think you're right, buddy."

Grace offering to take Henry was something J.C. would never have expected to hear. Grace had surprised him—a lot—in the last few days. Still, he hesitated. "How are you going to get over to my mom's? It's too far to walk. And you'll never fit the sled in that clown car of yours."

"We'll be fine, J.C.," Grace said.

"Please, Uncle Jace?"

He glanced down at Henry, big blue eyes filled with tentative hope. J.C. let out a sigh. Two against one. "Okay, you guys stay, but take my truck instead and I'll drive your car."

"You. Drive my sportscar."

"I can handle a sportscar."

"Oh, I know you can. In the past. I just wondered if you remembered how to drive one," she teased.

He remembered. Too well. The tiny little sportscar he'd borrowed from his cousin Mike, hoping to impress Grace on their first "real" date. They'd hung out a thousand times over those summers she spent at her grandmother's house, but after that kiss in the snow when they'd been teenagers the easy friendship they'd had became layered with a new kind of tension, an attack of nerves every time he got within ten feet of her. He'd borrowed the car, and picked her up at Mary's house, then headed for Carol's. "I was a cautious driver."

"If you'd gone any slower they would have arrested you for blocking traffic." She grinned. "I thought it was…cute."

"Cute?" He arched a brow. "You know guys hate to be called *cute*."

"Yeah, I know." The smile that crossed her face held a sassy edge. "And it was cute. Very. Cute."

He chuckled. "You are a stubborn woman, Grace McKinnon."

Her features sobered and her eyes met his. "Some people say stubbornness is a plus, not a minus."

"Very true." He thought of his own career, his path to success. Part of it had been tenacity. As if reminding him of that very fact, his phone began to vibrate again. He cursed the timing, then took out his keys and put them into Grace's palm. "Take care of him."

"You know I will." She fished her own keys out of the depths of her bulky coat, then gave them to him. "And take care of my car."

He lingered a while longer, watching Grace and Henry climb onto the sled for the tenth time, then zip down the hill, weaving past the others that crowded the slope. Then he turned and walked away, back to the life he was born to lead.

A life he hated with every ounce of his being.

CHAPTER NINE

By the fifteenth trip up the hill, Henry had had enough. Grace gathered up the sled and turned toward the parking lot. "Ready to go back to your grandmother's?"

"Uh-huh." Henry slipped his little mitten-covered hand into Grace's.

She paused a second. Then let her own hand curl around his. The way he walked with her, trusted her, seemed so natural. Which was weird, because if there was one person on this planet who had no intentions of being a motherly type it was her. She'd never considered having children of her own, figuring that she hadn't learned much about parenting from her mostly absent parents, so she had no business thinking she could do a better job. And there had yet to be a man—

Okay, there'd been one. For a short window of time when she'd been eighteen she'd considered becoming Mrs. J.C. Carson, traveling the world for a long time, and eventually settling down somewhere.

But in the years since J.C. she hadn't met anyone who made her want to settle down, put up that white picket fence and a swing on the porch. As she walked along, slowing her pace to match Henry's shorter, boot clad strides, she wondered if maybe she'd missed out on something by steering off the marriage and children path.

Once at J.C.'s car, Grace struggled with the booster seat in the back. Henry climbed in and pointed out where the seatbelt fit and how to click it in. Kid had more mothering skills than she did, for goodness' sake. A clear sign she shouldn't be fooling with thoughts of being a mother herself. She stowed the sled in back, then drove a good five miles under the speed limit all the way over to J.C.'s mother's house.

She hesitated in the drive. The last time she'd been here she'd seen J.C. with another girl. His father's words had still been ringing in her ears. *"He doesn't want someone like you. If you really care about him, then go your own way and let him have his life."*

She couldn't sit in the driveway forever, so she sucked in a breath, got out of the car, and helped Henry out. No one answered the door. Henry danced from foot to foot beside her. "Grace?" He tugged at her sleeve. "I gotta pee."

"Your grandma's not home. Do you think she went to the store?"

Henry shrugged. "She goes to church a lot."

"Oh." Well, that could mean that J.C.'s mom would be back in five minutes—or an hour. Grace had no idea. In the meantime, Henry was wriggling and squirming, and the temperature outside was dropping. "Let's go to my grandmother's house. It's just around the corner. And I'll call your uncle and tell him where you are. Okay?"

When Grace arrived at her grandmother's house with Henry in tow she thought Mary might just explode with joy. "Oh, what a precious little boy! Come here, come here, let's get you some hot chocolate and cookies and—"

"Gram," Grace interrupted, laughing. Leave it to her grandmother to start with dessert. "He needs to pee. Then you can stuff him full again."

Henry slipped his hand into Grace's. Oh, no. She knew what that meant. He wanted her to take him to the bathroom. She looked down at him. Surely he knew what to do and how to do it? "Uh...here's the bathroom," Grace said, leading him to the small room off the main hallway. Thankfully, Henry went inside the room and shut the door. She waited outside, just to be sure he didn't, like, fall in or something.

The doorbell rang, and through the oval of glass Grace saw J.C.'s face. Relief flooded her and she pulled the door open. "You got my message?"

"Yep. Thanks for stepping in and taking care of him. I didn't expect my mother would go out. Again."

Something in the way J.C. said that told Grace a lot more lurked under the surface. More worry, more stress, more secrets. She waited for him to tell her, to open up, even though she knew it was a fruitless wait.

J.C. proved to be the same man as always. The one who kept up the walls around his personal life and kept his emotions tucked in tight. She'd thought on the hill today she'd seen the J.C. she remembered, but she'd been wrong. It made her wonder how well she had ever really known him if he kept so much of himself hidden. He'd rarely opened up about his family life, something she hadn't noticed until after they were over and she'd realized she'd been doing all the talking over the years. Was it because J.C. didn't have anything to say or share? Or didn't he trust her enough to tell her about his feelings, his fears?

Or did he think she would judge him if he did? The glimpses she'd had of his life had painted a sad picture.

J.C. striving for his father's approval as a child and falling short time and time again. John Carson had had few kind words for anyone, most of all his family.

"So tell me the truth. Did you put the pedal to the metal with my car?" She gave him a grin.

"Of course not," J.C. said, then a smile flashed across his face. "I waited until I was on the outskirts of town."

She laughed. "Glad to hear you aren't completely a button-down guy."

Instead of responding, J.C. turned away and rapped on the bathroom door. "Henry, you ready?"

The little boy emerged from the bathroom, soapy hands dripping on the carpet. J.C. laughed, then took him back to finish hand washing. When he was done, Henry pointed down the hall toward the kitchen. "She's gonna make me cookies and hot chalk."

J.C. chuckled. "Hot chocolate, you mean?"

"Mommy called it hot chalk. Cuz the stuff on top is white."

"Oh, yeah. It is." J.C.'s face tightened. He cast a glance at Grace, and she sent him a smile of sympathy.

These little moments, the ones when the loss of Henry's parents returned, almost broke Grace's heart. She barely knew the boy, but she knew how much J.C. had loved his effervescent sister. The absence of her in their lives had to be an intolerable blow.

It also reminded her of the article she wanted to write. Handled correctly, Henry's story could touch a lot of hearts.

"My grandma makes the best hot chalk in the world, Henry," Grace said. "If you hurry into the kitchen, I bet she'll let you help her."

"Okay!" He dashed down the hall and rounded the corner.

Grace heard Mary exclaim, and knew Henry would be in good, if overindulgent hands for the next few minutes. J.C. started to follow, but Grace put a hand on his arm. "Wait a second. I wanted to ask you for a favor."

"What kind of favor?" he asked.

She took a deep breath. "I wanted to profile you and your nephew for my article. I think it adds a human piece to what would otherwise be just an ordinary—"

"No."

"You didn't even hear me out."

"Doesn't matter. I don't want my family and my personal life splattered all over some magazine."

Just like that. Without even letting her finish. "Is that what you think I'd do? Create some invasive harsh piece that takes advantage of you?"

He studied her for a long moment. "No. I don't."

"Then trust me and let me interview you two. Or, better yet, just let me spend time with the two of you and write up an article from that. Nothing formal, nothing stuffy. Just an uncle and his nephew taking in the Christmas magic."

"You want to use my family's tragedy to advance your career?"

She swallowed hard against the truth. "It will also help you get the kind of publicity you want for the festival."

"I have TV crews and reporters are all over the place here, plus the pieces you're writing and the social media you've been implementing. There'll be plenty of PR."

"Yes, but it'll be the kind of articles that talk about the reindeer and the swimming swans." She gave him a smile, but he didn't return the gesture. "Not the kind that touches people's hearts and makes them seek out Beckett's Run because..." She thought of the ice skaters she'd seen earlier today at the park. The Winslows, making a slow circle of the pond, holding hands, laughing with each other. Harriet had had one arm linked with Bert's, her free hand resting on top. She had kept glancing up at him with adoration. Contentment. "Because it's a place for second chances."

"Is that what you're here for, Grace?"

She drew herself up. "We're not talking about me. We're talking about you and Henry."

He shook his head. "Still the same Grace. Avoiding the personal subjects."

"My job is to focus on the other stories that are here, not on myself." She paused, then let out a sigh. How could she be mad at him for not opening up when she did the same thing? "Okay, you're right. I am here for a second chance. My career…well, it hasn't been going so well lately, and I really need a story that will help find my groove again. For me, this isn't just about promoting Beckett's Run, J.C. It's about what I'll be doing after I leave here. And how, hopefully, I'll be able to carve out a new niche. Something that has more depth than just another piece about another hotel in another country."

He considered her for a long moment. "Fine. I'll help you find your story. One that *doesn't* focus on my nephew. I'm sure we can find another heartwarming happily-ever-after for you to use. Deal?"

It wasn't what she wanted, but maybe she could do the same with another story. She could see the protectiveness for his family in his eyes, and couldn't argue with that. "Okay." He turned to go, but she put a hand on his arm. "It's probably not my place to ask, and I wouldn't say a thing if we weren't friends—"

"Friends? Is that what we are?"

"We always have been, haven't we?"

"I'd say we want way past friends a long time ago."

The words, low, dark, sent a rush of heat through her veins. A slideshow of images of her and J.C. in his bedroom one hot summer night while his parents were away at some company event in the city. The window open, a soft breeze drifting over Grace's bare skin as J.C. made his way from the top of her head to the bottom of her feet, kissing, touching, loving every inch of her. And then, when he'd entered her, the stars had exploded in her head and she had thought in that moment that she knew what perfection felt like.

"But in the end we came back to being friends," she said. Because she wanted to believe that. Wanted to believe that hot summer night could be forgotten and they could turn back the clock.

Even if it had never gone that far from her memory, and standing here, in close quarters with J.C., it was all she could do not to think about being in his bed. His arms. His life.

God, she missed him. In a hundred ways that went beyond a bedroom. But J.C. wanted everything she didn't—corporate life, putting down roots, working nine to five—and that meant they could never be together. Hadn't his father made that clear to her? J.C. would never love a vagabond like her. Yet a part of her heard Henry's laughter in the kitchen and Gram's soft murmurs of encouragement and she wondered if roots were such a bad thing after all.

"Anyway, as a friend," she said, pushing the words forward before her thoughts brimmed to the surface, "I wanted to say I know this has to be a hard time for you, with Henry and everything, after the loss of your sister. And…" She took his hand in hers. It felt so familiar, so right. "I'm sorry."

"Thanks."

"Your sister was an amazing person. A force to be reckoned with." She grinned.

"That she was. She'll be missed. More than I can say."

Sorrow filled his eyes again, and Grace wished she could take the pain away. She wished she and J.C. could go back to those lazy summer afternoons by the creek when the biggest worry they had was being home in time for supper. When they'd while away an entire afternoon, doing nothing but catching minnows and eating crackers and listening to the frogs calling to each other.

"I heard what you said about your mom. Is she okay?"

"She's fine. She's just had a hard time after the loss of my sister and sometimes she just…unplugs. It's getting better but it's going to take time." He let out a long breath. "Anyway, it's nothing you need to worry about. I can handle it."

"And run a business from afar. And watch over Henry. And plan a major event for the town. You're super, J.C., but you're not Superman."

He chuckled. "Lately, I'm not so sure I'm either."

"I know you, J.C. You tend to take everything on your shoulders. It's okay to let your mom do more. To expect more out of the people around you. To ask for help, or, heck, admit you can't do it all."

He shook his head. "That's not going to happen."

"I think—"

His features hardened. "Grace, you don't know my life. You don't even really know me anymore. So don't tell me what to do." Then he headed down the hall and into the kitchen.

She stood in the hall for a long time. He was right. She didn't know this grown-up, serious J.C., this billionaire who had become the town hero. Maybe she had never really known the J.C. by the creek, either. And she needed to remember that every time she let the memory of one summer night cloud her thinking.

Two days later, J.C. had to admit Grace knew her stuff. The publicity machine was in full swing, and she had the social media thing down to a tee. She'd covered the snowflake-decorating contest with a quirky, fun story that had gotten picked up by the wire services. That brought more interest in the Santa lookalike contest, and the attendance numbers for other festival events promised to rise. Every hotel in the tri-county area was booked for Christmas Eve with out-of-towners.

They'd had hundreds of visitors from the surrounding area, which had beefed up tourism dollars and created an actual traffic jam in downtown Beckett's Run for the first time that anyone could remember.

The town was abuzz with anticipation for the big event on Christmas Eve, and the out of town media had stepped up their coverage. He'd seen several pieces on the Boston news channels, and even something on the Rhode Island stations. He'd had a call from the *Today* show, and an email from another morning show producer.

Grace had done it all with barely a phone call to him, leaving him free to work. He'd finished the merger in record time, which had taken the stress out of his C.O.O.'s voice.

J.C. knew he should be grateful. It was why he'd asked Grace to be part of the team, after all. And he was—

Sort of.

But he had to admit he had missed seeing her and talking to her. After the disagreement at her grandmother's house Grace had told him she needed to do some work and left him and Henry alone with her grandmother to enjoy the hot chocolate. In the days since she'd kept her distance.

All the while the kisses they'd shared kept springing to the surface, a determined memory demanding he reckon with the implications.

He still found her attractive. He still wondered about her. And he still wanted her. Even though he knew nothing had changed between them—she was still the girl who would rather run than tackle the tough issues, and he was still the guy who would stay and stick it out—he still wanted to kiss her again. And more.

Instead he watched the magic building around him— the sets going up, the events being organized, the decorations being hung—and cursed the workload that kept him busy most of the day. He wanted to get his hands dirty and get right in there, rather than run back and forth to Boston to sit in on yet another meeting. J.C. let out a sigh and dialed the office, turning away from the view before him so he could concentrate.

"I can't believe you pulled that merger off, J.C.," said his C.O.O. when he answered. "In record time, no less. I know everyone's happy to have the holiday off."

"You still heading to Cancún with the wife and kids?"

Charles sighed. "Nah, I'm putting that on hold. My wife's so mad, I'm sure the only thing I'm getting for Christmas is a lump of coal and the cold shoulder."

"You should go," J.C. said. He knew Charles had been planning this vacation for months. It was supposed to be a second honeymoon of sorts for the couple. "I've got this under control."

"J.C., you have enough on your plate. You need someone here in the city to—"

"The company won't fall apart if we both are out of the office at the same time."

"It'll be hurt by our combined absence, and you know it. The last time we were both gone—"

"You worry too much. It'll be fine. Go on your trip." Charles started to interrupt and J.C. cut him off. "That's an order. Life's too short to spend it in an office."

"Is that the same J.C. talking? The one who works more hours than the entire company combined?"

"Hey, it's Christmas. Take this as a gift and run with it."

"Okay, okay. You just made my wife happy, J.C." Charles chuckled, then sobered. "But when we get back in the office—"

"The work will be there." And it would. As it had been the week before, and the ones before that, and all the years since J.C. had taken over his father's company and made it bigger and better than his father could have ever dreamed. But in the process he had become the very thing he'd never wanted to be—a corporate, suit-wearing workaholic who barely had time for his family. His time in Beckett's Run was coming to an end, and J.C. knew as well as he knew the sun would rise that once he went back to Boston he'd be working dawn to dusk, and barely, if ever, see Henry. He thought of the merger he'd just completed—one that would combine his company with another similar in size, giving J.C. an even larger empire to command.

It was what he had worked hard to achieve, but a part of him wondered why. He'd started off filling his father's shoes out of necessity, then growing the company to ensure futures for those who worked for him, and then, at some point, he had found the business becoming a wayward animal that needed constant tending. One he wasn't so sure he wanted to tend anymore.

Life's too short to spend it in an office. His own words, yet he hadn't taken that advice either. He couldn't call the few weeks he'd been in Beckett's Run a break from the office. Given the way his phone remained tethered to his hand and ear, he hadn't really stepped out of the office at all—merely relocated it.

He thought of the day he'd gone sledding with Grace and Henry. That had been fun—real, honest-to-goodness fun. He wanted more days like that. More days when the office was a distant memory. When he thought about music, or enjoyed the bright sun, or played hooky in the middle of the day. But walking away, or selling, meant hurting those who worked for him, and those who depended upon him, and he couldn't do that.

Grace's words came back to him. *"I bet there's a rocker in you still."*

Maybe, but he hadn't picked up a guitar in so long he wasn't so sure he could remember "Smoke on the Water," never mind anything more complicated. He hadn't even brought his guitar to Beckett's Run—and it used to be the one thing permanently attached to him. He'd told Grace dreams like that weren't practical.

That was the word his father had used over and over again. *"Be practical, J.C. Where would you go with a career in music? Nowhere but the unemployment line."*

Maybe so, but would he be happier? Or would he be just as dissatisfied with his days, and wondering if there was more to life than just existing?

He hung up the phone and leaned against a tree as a winter storm started kicking up around him. He watched the snow fall for a long, long time. He remembered the bright laughter of Henry, followed by the teasing voice of Grace.

And when he did he realized what he wanted.

CHAPTER TEN

THE park buzzed with activity. Grace had her pen and pad of paper ready, and had brought along a tape recorder, too, to capture as many comments as she could. Beside her, people were getting ready for the Beckett's Run Winter Festival Snowman Shuffle, one of the last kick-off events scheduled before the big day-long party on Christmas Eve. Two dozen competitors were lined up by piles of snow, ready for some serious snowman building.

She knew she should be focusing on the competition, and on her job, but she found herself looking for J.C. Beside her, Henry danced with excitement. "Can I go watch?"

"Sure." She followed along with Henry, to stand beside the competitors. J.C. was across the park, talking to the construction crew as they assembled a few last-minute items. Christmas Eve was tomorrow, and anticipation rang in the air.

She had yet to get her story. J.C. had introduced her to several Beckett's Run residents with heartwarming tales, but none of them had her mind whirring like Henry's. Thus far she had honored J.C.'s wishes and not probed when it came to his nephew, but her gut told her the real story was right beside her. She needed to talk to Henry some more, and find the angle that would work the best. She watched him gazing at the snowmen with longing, and decided an activity would be the easiest way to get Henry to talk.

"Hey, let's build our own snowman," she said to Henry. "Want to?"

"I'm a good snowman-maker," Henry said. "Uncle Jace says so. He helped me make one 'fore, when the snow was up to here." He put a hand against his chest. "It was a big snowman."

"I bet."

Every time she learned something else about J.C. it surprised her. He was the kind of guy who built snowmen with his nephew and told him stories at night and tucked him into bed. Yes, he worked an insane amount of hours—she had yet to see him without that phone of his, tending to company issues around the clock—but he made time for the littlest person in his life. That didn't jive with the unemotional man she kept seeing in him.

Had she misjudged J.C. all these years?

Instead of thinking about J.C., she bent over and started rolling a small snowball through a pile of snow until it became big enough for a base. Henry joined her, pushing the giant ball around in a circle, then running off to create a second one. Grace let him handle the head of the snowman all by himself, then reached out for the third ball.

"I wanna put it on," Henry said. "P'ease?"

"Uh…okay." Grace bent down and hoisted Henry up. The little boy weighed almost nothing in her arms. He nestled the last snowball on top.

The two of them stood back and admired their handiwork. Henry slipped his little hand into Grace's. She was beginning to get used to the feel of his hand in hers, holding secure and strong, despite his size. "My mommy liked snowmen."

"Did you build one with her?"

Henry nodded. "We named him Earl. Cuz he looked like a king."

Grace laughed. "That sounds like a perfect name." She bent down beside him and started shaping some snow into an arm for the snowman. "What was your mommy like?"

"She was really nice. She liked to watch cartoons with me." As if a plug had been pulled, Henry started talking in a non-stop chatter about his mother and father while they gathered snow and packed it onto the snowman. As their icy creation took shape, so too did the conversation. Henry talked about the way his mother had made macaroni and cheese, and how his father had told him Santa was always watching to make sure Henry was being good, and how angels could fly. It was a conversation that went in ten different directions, then back again, in the way that kids had of circling a point.

Grace heard the longing in Henry's voice and found herself relating. Her parents hadn't died when she'd been little, but they both had been gone so much—after the divorce her father had rarely come by and her mother was always off on one adventure or another—but it was still a loss. Most of her Christmas and summer memories were centered around her grandmother, and her sisters.

And J.C. Carson.

She saw so much of him in this chatty little boy who talked about wanting to be a veterinarian, or maybe a fireman, and definitely a magician when he grew up. She saw J.C. in the way Henry suddenly decided their snowman needed a big head of hair, and she hoisted him up to let him pat snow in a fluffy pile on top. She saw J.C. in the way Henry stood back and put his chin on his hand and assessed the snowman, deciding one arm was too big and one was too little.

And as she and Henry talked about Christmas and Santa and miracles Grace found her story. She could feel it taking shape in her mind, could hear the words she would later put on paper. It wasn't the kind of article she normally wrote, so she wasn't sure how her current editor, Paul, would react. It was the kind of thing she'd tried to write—and failed to do well—during the brief time she'd tried to get a job at *Social Issues*.

Was she up to this challenge? A quiver ran through her.

She glanced over at Henry, at the hope and worry in his little features, and decided she was. He had the kind of story that could touch hearts, and for a writer there was no greater goal to achieve. She could do this. She had to do this.

"Great snowman."

Grace whirled around at the sound of J.C.'s voice. Every time she saw him her heart skipped a beat and she forgot to breathe. He still affected her, even after all these years, and she couldn't decide if that was a curse or a blessing, or a little of both. "Thanks. It's all Henry's doing. He was the brains behind it."

Henry beamed. "I gave him hair, Uncle Jace. Like you!"

J.C. chuckled. "Hair? That's creative as heck, buddy. I'd say that one should take first place."

"Can I go down the snow slide?" Henry asked, pointing across the park. Earlier that day a crew had packed snow onto the kiddie slide and children of all ages—and in thick pairs of snowpants—were riding down and into a cushion of soft snow at the bottom.

"Sure. Just be careful."

But Henry had already run off, and J.C.'s words fell on deaf ears. J.C. laughed. "That kid is so wound up for Christmas. It's all I can do to get him to go to bed at night."

"I remember someone else who used to get excited about Christmas." She gave him a little elbow nudge.

"You couldn't mean me." He grinned. "Okay, maybe when I was little. But Christmas was the one holiday my mother did up huge, and it was impossible not to get excited."

"Gram loves Christmas, too. I think she made the holiday big because she knew us girls were often here instead of with our mom. The few holidays my sisters and I did spend with our mom were always full of last-minute kind of things, like running out to the drug-store on Christmas morning because she forgot to fill the stockings or didn't have any food in the house. She would concoct some grand scheme for a holiday cele-bration, then get distracted by something like knitting us all sweaters, and end up almost missing the holiday altogether." Grace swiped a handful of snow off the back of a park bench and let the flakes tumble to the ground. "I guess that's why I've never been really big on the holiday. Or any holiday."

"Head off the disappointment before it happens?"

"Something like that."

"I can relate," he said quietly. "Is that why you've avoided Beckett's Run the last few years?"

How had this conversation got turned to her so fast? She bristled at the implication that she'd been avoiding the town only because of the holiday connection. Didn't he remember how it had ended? Or had he put his own spin on history, painting her as the villain? "It wasn't just about ditching Christmas, J.C. There was more to it than that and you know it."

"You ran out of here, Grace, and you never looked back."

She whirled around to face him. "Is that what you think happened? That I wasn't hurt by what you did? That I just went on my merry way and forgot everything that happened?"

"Hurt by what I did?" He raised a brow. "You're the one who left, Grace, without a word."

"Because you told me to go." She shook her head. How could he possibly not understand? Not see? Had so many years passed that he had forgotten? Or was he truly that cold? "When I got that call—"

"What call?"

"The one you had your father make. You couldn't even tell me in person, J.C." She shook her head and cursed the tears that sprang to her eyes. She was over this, really over it.

Then why did the pain rear its head again, as fresh as the day it happened?

"Just forget it." She turned to go, but J.C. grabbed her arm and spun her back into him.

"I never told anyone to call you, Grace," he said. "I thought you left because I didn't show up to leave on our trip. I came to your grandmother's house the next day to talk to you and tell you what had happened but you were already gone. *You* were the one who wasn't there for me, so don't go blaming it on some fictional call."

"What do you mean, I wasn't there for you? What happened?"

"Don't you know?"

She shook her head. She'd left town fast and never looked back. She'd stopped in a couple times for day visits with her grandmother, but never stayed long enough to talk to anyone else in Beckett's Run. She'd flitted in and out of this town because every time she turned a corner, something reminded her of what she had lost. And the one topic that had been *verboten* on all her visits had been J.C. Carson, so if something had happened she would have been blind and deaf to it. Had she run too fast?

"Know what?"

"My father had a heart attack that day. I didn't show up because my mother rushed him to the hospital and I had to stay home and watch my sister."

His father had had a heart attack? Remorse filled her chest and she reached for him. Even through the thick fabric of her gloves and his winter coat she could feel the tenseness in him. J.C. had always been like this—an island unto himself—and now was no different. Maybe his withdrawal stemmed from anger at her for letting him down. She wished she could go back in time and redo that afternoon, because no one should go through something like that alone. "I had no idea, J.C. None at all."

"You really didn't know?"

She shook her head. "I would have been there. You know that."

"All these years I thought you left because you didn't want to deal with it."

Was that how he saw her? As a woman who ran at the first moment of need by a friend or loved one? "I would have stayed, J.C. If I had known." She drew in a deep breath and went on. "In fact, I came by your house before I left town. I was going to talk to you about the call. But then I saw you talking to some girl and—"

"Girl?" He paused a second, thinking back. "That was my cousin, Grace. My aunt came in from out of town to help out around the house, and I was talking to my cousin. Because my best friend was gone."

"Your best friend?"

"You."

She'd been his best friend, and he had been hers, all those years ago. That was a bond that would always remain, she realized, no matter how far she went away or how much water went under the J.C./Grace bridge. The friendship was a rock they could each stand on, and that gave her comfort. For a moment she was back there in those bright summer days with J.C. smiling at her, the two of them full of hopes and dreams, talking about everything and nothing. "I'm sorry."

"It's okay, Grace. I understand now. And, really, it was years and years ago."

"I still wish I could do it over." She let out a long breath, watching the air form a frosty cloud in front of her. "Why would your father do that? If he didn't like us being together, fine, tell me that. But why lie and say the message was from you?"

J.C.'s gaze went to Henry, who was twenty feet away, laughing with the other children as they took turns sliding down the slide. Around them, the activity of the Winter Festival hummed, people working like bees in a hive to ready everything for the next night. "He thought you distracted me."

"Me? From what?"

"From my 'destiny.'" J.C. put air quotes around the last word. "To run the company and take care of the family. He saw me getting off track when I ran off with you and did all those crazy things we did, and he kept trying to rein me back in. But I didn't want to do that. Then he heard about our plan to run off, and I guess that was the last straw. I never thought he'd go that far." J.C. let out a curse and shook his head. "I'm sorry, Grace."

"It's not your fault. You didn't even know." She reached for his arm again, and this time felt an easing in the tension in him. He turned to her, his gaze seeking forgiveness and a way back to that bridge between them. "I should have known you wouldn't do that. I should have trusted you."

It was a conversation they should have had a long time ago. One they might have had that day if she hadn't misinterpreted the entire situation. But she'd been acting on hurt, and running had been easier than dealing. Wasn't it always? She'd become her mother, in many ways, dashing away at the first sign of conflict.

But just the thought of staying put, of taking that kind of risk, made her throat close. She took risks in her job—ziplining, bungee-jumping, water-skiing—but not in her emotions.

"Maybe you would have hung around for a couple days, but then you would have gotten that itch to run and you would have hit the road," he said, honesty in his eyes. "It's what you do, Grace. Even when someone needs you."

Hurt tinted the color of his words. All these years she had thought she was the one who had been betrayed and let down, never knowing that he had felt the same way. Her leaving at such a critical time in his life must have seemed like a slap in the face. "I would have stayed a while, yes. And once everything was taken care of, and your father was better, we could have gone on our trip.

Pursued those dreams. Both of us wanted to leave this town, remember?"

"That was a foolish dream. And it was a good thing it never happened."

"What do you mean, a good thing? You wanted to leave as much as me. You ended up still here and working in an office all day. That's the opposite of what you always said you wanted."

"It didn't matter what I wanted, Grace. Don't you understand that? My family needed me and I had to be there. My father was sick for years. I started college, and worked after school and on breaks with him, learning the business from the inside out, trying to keep it afloat so my family could pay the bills and the people who worked for him could pay theirs. People depended on me, Grace. I couldn't just up and leave for some pipedream."

The words hit her like a slap. "That 'pipedream' used to be important to you."

"So was taking care of my family." It had started snowing, and a light dusting of flakes coated J.C.'s hair, his shoulders. "The day after I graduated from college my father died. I stepped into his shoes. And I never left them."

"But…why? You never wanted that life. You never wanted to be tied to that company. To him." The relationship between father and son had been acrimonious at best. Even if J.C. had rarely talked about it, that much Grace had been able to discern from the few times she'd seen them together, and the way his father had looked at her, like mud sullying his son.

"Because people were depending on me. People who needed that paycheck every two weeks. Which meant they needed a Carson to be there every day. Over the years, the company has gotten huge, and now it's like a runaway train that requires me to constantly be on board."

He sounded stressed, overwhelmed. Not at all like the J.C. she used to know. "So sell the company, move on. Live your own life."

"It's not that simple, Grace. I can't just shed it like a winter coat."

"Of course you can. Why do you have to stay and make it bigger and badder? What are you trying to prove?"

He scowled. "I'm not trying to prove anything."

"Well, you did prove one thing. That you're afraid to take that leap into the unknown. To just pick up and go and leave everything behind." She leaned in closer to him. "Is it because you're afraid, J.C.? Afraid of being on your own? Afraid of failing?"

"Says the expert at never getting tied down. You're the one who's afraid, Grace. Not me."

"I've climbed mountains and stood on the edge of volcanoes, J.C. I'm not scared of anything."

He closed the gap between them and put a finger under her chin. "You are terrified of staying in one place. You are terrified of settling down. And, most of all, you are terrified of giving away your heart."

She shook her head. "I already did that. With you. A long time ago. But we'd never work out, would we? You're still going to want to stay here and I'm still going to want to go."

"What is so wrong with staying here?"

She looked around the park. Happy laughter flowed from the people like water out of a spigot. Christmas music piped in from a hidden sound system carried on the air. There was a spirit of hope, of family, of wonder everywhere around her.

"I've learned that nothing lasts, J.C. Especially the things you depend on most."

Then she turned and left, clutching her notepad to her chest. It was her ticket out of this town, and she refused to let it go.

Lights blinked, ornaments gleamed. J.C. came home from working on the festival to find the tree decorated and his mother and Henry standing before it, admiring their work. Henry was beaming, and J.C.'s mother looked tired but happy for the first time in a long time.

"Uncle Jace! We gots the tree up! And the socks! And presents!" Henry grabbed J.C.'s hand and dragged him around the living room, pointing out all the activity of the past afternoon.

"It looks great," J.C. said, raising his gaze to his mother's. "Really great."

"Thank you."

The two words were about a lot more than a compliment, and when his mother reached for his hand and gave it a squeeze J.C. knew it was going to be okay. They'd all been on a long and painful road, but at last they were finally heading into the sun.

"Henry and I are going to make some sugar cookies after dinner," his mother went on. "Want to help?"

"Maybe later. I have a dinner invitation."

His mother arched a brow. "With Grace?"

"Grace's grandmother. She wanted to thank me for having her driveway plowed. Whether Grace will be there or not…" He shrugged. "Who knows?"

"Did you guys have a fight?"

"We talked about some things we should have talked about a long time ago."

The conversation still stewed in his mind. All these years he and Grace had gone without speaking because of a misunderstanding. No, not a misunderstanding—

An interference.

Resentment rose in J.C.'s chest. After all he had done for his father, for the family company. John couldn't have let his son have that one relationship? Of course if J.C. had stayed with Grace he would have left Beckett's Run and never worked at the company. Never been there for his mother, and now Henry.

"All these years I thought Grace left without me," he said. "Turns out there was a lot more to the story than that."

"Henry?" J.C.'s mother said, bending to talk to her grandson. "Would you like to watch a Santa movie until dinner's ready?"

"The one with the reindeer? I love that one!" Henry clambered onto the sofa and waited while the movie was loaded and started.

J.C.'s mother gestured toward the kitchen. The two of them went into the other room, and while his mother started boiling some water and mixing up a quick spaghetti sauce J.C. took a seat at the table. "I knew about the call," his mother said.

"You did?"

She nodded. "When he was in the hospital, your father told me what he did. By then Grace was already gone and you were working at the company, and I didn't say anything because..." She let out a long breath. "I didn't want to rock the boat. It was always easier to keep the peace than to go to war."

That had been his mother's job. To soothe the waters, mend the broken fences. He wondered if she'd been happy married to his father, or if she'd stayed because of the kids. It was too late now to ask such questions, and a part of J.C. didn't want to know the answers anyway. His mother had been widowed for several years now, and before the death of her daughter she'd been active, living a new life. Traveling, taking music lessons, indulging her only grandchild. She had worked part-time at the library, even though J.C. provided her with a generous monthly stipend.

She'd kept the peace, and for that J.C. was grateful. His mother had been the true rock of this family, even if she didn't realize it. He crossed to her and gave her a warm hug. "It's okay, Mom. I understand why you did it."

She turned in his arms. Tears brimmed in her eyes. "Do you?"

He nodded. "Your number one concern was your children, and that's what a mom is supposed to worry about. Dad was hard on us—"

"Especially on you."

"But I guess in the end he wanted the same thing. The best for us." J.C. let out a long breath and stepped back, leaning his weight on the counter. "I wouldn't agree with his methods, but I see the why now. And after working his job for several years, I can also understand why he was so short with people at the end of the day. Being the boss is tougher than it looks."

"In some ways, I wish you'd never taken over the company," his mother said. "You should have gone on that trip with Grace, J.C. I should have encouraged you. Packed your bags for you. Instead, you stayed and you helped the family and put everything you wanted on hold."

"If I'd really wanted to go, Mom, I would have," he said, realizing that truth for the first time. He could have easily walked out the door all those years ago and headed off with Grace. Or, heck, left at any time. But he never had. "I think a part of me wanted to work at the company. To prove I could do it."

"To prove you were better than what he said."

J.C. shrugged, as if that didn't matter, but he knew there was a part of him that had always wanted his father to acknowledge the job his son had done. To stop criticizing and compliment. Just once.

"He was proud of you. He just never said it."

J.C. dropped into a chair again. "He had plenty to say, Mom. None of it was ever good."

His mother put down the spoon in her hand and came over to the table. She sat down across from J.C. and covered his hand with her own. "Your father was a hard man. Never one to admit a weakness or, even worse, show one. But he loved you, even if he didn't always tell you the way he should. And even if he made a few mistakes in trying to protect you. He said all that to Grace because he thought he was protecting you."

"Protecting me?"

"He didn't want to see you get hurt. Not by Grace, but by the world. He knew that if you went out there into the great unknown with your guitar you'd risk rejection and disappointment. And he didn't want that for you. He wanted you to go into the family business because he knew you'd do well there."

"And he could control the outcome."

"Maybe. I think it was more that he wanted to be there, as much as possible, to guide you and watch over you. He worried about you and your sister's futures. He wanted to be sure you'd be okay long after he was gone."

She squeezed his fingers and a soft smile stole across her face. "And you, my dear son, are more than okay. You have far surpassed anything your father or I ever dreamed of for you."

"Financially, yes. But personally..." He let out a breath and looked away. "I gave up a lot when I took over that company."

"You have a chance now to have what you missed," his mother said. "Don't let your life keep passing you by."

"Someone has to run the company, Mom. And take care of Henry. And—"

"And you can ask for help. Henry will be fine here with me. And the company will be fine if you step down and let someone else take over. You've made your money, J.C., you've proved your point."

"It's not that easy, Mom, to walk away."

"Yes, it is." Her words held firm conviction. "What are you afraid of?"

"I'm not afraid of anything."

Hadn't he had the same conversation with Grace today? She'd accused him of being afraid and he'd turned it around on her. Maybe he'd been wrong all these years. Maybe Grace wasn't the fleeing jackrabbit.

Maybe he was.

His mother patted his hand, then got to her feet and reached for the spoon again. "Then go after what you want, J.C. It's Christmas. A time for miracles and hope. And new beginnings."

She pressed a kiss to his temple, as if he was six all over again and about to head off for his first day of school.

And maybe, J.C. thought as he got to his feet and reached for his coat, he was. He was heading off for his first day of something new—something he had denied himself for a long, long time. Maybe his mother was right and it was time for him to do the very things the detour into the company had put on hold—

Risk rejection and disappointment.

CHAPTER ELEVEN

THE doorbell rang just before dinner. Grace finished fixing her hair, then headed for the stairs. Gram hadn't mentioned anything about company for dinner, and as far as Grace knew her sisters weren't due to arrive until tomorrow, Christmas Eve.

There had been two dinners with her mother this past week. The meals had been strained and short—both times, Grace had used her work on the festival as an excuse to leave early. It wasn't that she didn't love her mother, it was that she was tired of believing in change that would never come.

Her mother kept talking about how she'd settled down now. Was planning on buying a house, planting a garden. Grace wanted to believe her mother was different, but past history was a cruel teacher and Grace had learned her lessons well, as had her sisters.

Soon she'd be back at work and would be able to put off seeing her family for another year. She thought of the article she had written after building the snowman with Henry. She had yet to send the email, because for the first time in forever she was nervous. Not just about whether the editor would love the piece as much as she did, but because somewhere in the writing her view of the article had shifted.

It was no longer about saving her career. It was about sharing a piece of her heart. She had opened up a vein to her soul on the page, and what mattered now was that people connected with that. Whether she got a job at *Social Issues*—or, heck, anywhere after this—was no longer important.

The doorbell rang again. Gram called out, "Coming! Just a second."

Grace paused at the top of the stairs while Gram opened the door, and as if conjured up by Grace's thoughts Lydia stepped into the house.

Followed by Greg McKinnon.

Grace stared at her parents—divorced, remarried, divorced again—standing together with wide smiles on their faces. "Hi, Grace. Hi, Mary," Lydia said. "And… well, surprise."

Surprise didn't even begin to describe it. Grace couldn't find a word to say.

Her grandmother stepped forward first, drawing her son into a hug, then reaching out and giving her former daughter-in-law one, too. "So good to see both of you."

Grace stayed where she was, processing the sight in the foyer. Her parents together again? When had this happened?

Lydia reached for Greg's hand and held it tight. She smiled at Gram. "Thank you for inviting us for dinner."

"You invited them for dinner?" Grace said, descending halfway down the stairs.

Gram nodded. "Your mom said your dad was flying in today, and I thought what better way to start bringing the family together than at dinner tonight?"

"I'm so glad you did, Mom." Greg looked over at Lydia and smiled, then raised his gaze to his daughter.

"I know this is a surprise, honey, but we didn't want to say anything until we were sure."

"Sure? About what?"

He grinned. "Well, your mother and I have been talking over the last few weeks, mostly by phone, a few times in person."

Mom blushed—actually blushed. "Several times in person."

"Anyway," her father went on, "when we realized you girls would all be here in town at the same time, well, we thought we'd make it official and come for Christmas, too."

"Make what official?" Grace said. She had yet to leave her perch on the stairs, as if she was half in the room and half out of it.

"We're back together. For good."

The words seemed to ring in the hall. An excited avalanche of questions and good wishes followed, led by Gram. Grace stayed on the stairs, and wondered how her sisters would take this twist when they arrived tomorrow. Chances were good that Hope, the leader, would take it in stride and be the first one to congratulate everyone. Faith, who had been fathered by another man between the McKinnon marriages, had always held onto a little guilt that she might have been the reason for the marriages' demise, and would be the most reticent, though she'd be her usual warm self around their parents. They'd all congratulate and offer best wishes, and support this new twist, Grace was sure.

But Grace knew better. Her parents were as different as oil and water, and had never been meant to share a roof. This reunion would be lucky to last as long as the wrapping paper on the presents.

She was tired of people not facing the truth. Of thinking some fantasy was going to come about just because they wanted it to. The reality was simple—some people weren't meant to be together and wishing otherwise didn't make it better.

"What's changed?" Grace asked. The conversation came to a halt and all eyes turned to her. "Because, last I checked, the two of you were the same people as always, albeit a little older. And that means you'll get together, honeymoon for a few weeks or a few months, and then, *wham*, end up hating each other again. At least there aren't any little kids to catch in the crossfire this time."

Lydia crossed to her daughter. Behind her, Gram gave Grace a look that asked her to tame her thoughts. But Grace didn't want to gloss over this. She didn't want to put on some happy family holiday event, knowing that as soon as the New Year rolled around the fiction would fade.

"We're older and wiser now, Grace," Lydia said. "We—"

"Don't tell me that, Mom. You haven't changed. You're still everywhere but with us. And Dad's still working a million hours, and waiting for you to come back."

"I'm here now," Lydia said. "With all of you. And so is your father."

"It's a little late for that, don't you think?" Grace hurried down the stairs, grabbed her coat from the hook by the door and pulled open the front door. She stepped out into the cold, even as her mother protested that this time was different.

Grace ignored the words. She'd heard them before.

J.C. found Grace sitting on the porch, bundled in her coat, and watching her breath form puffy clouds in the cold air. The sky held the promise of snow, and the tart crispness of winter. It was going to be a white Christmas, which seemed to add that extra element of magic to the holiday and the Winter Festival. Right now, with Grace sitting there so quiet and sad, the festival was far from his mind. He put the flowers in his hands on the porch and sat down next to Grace.

She gave him a wry grin. "No matter where I go in this town, you pop up like a dandelion."

"It's a small town."

"Not that small."

"True." He gestured toward her. "You look upset."

"My parents are here. And my sisters are on their way." She waved a wide circle. "All one big happy family for the holidays."

"That's good." He caught the arch of her brow. "Isn't it?"

She shrugged. "You know my family. We've never been happy. My parents were separated or fighting more than they were together, and my sisters and I...well, we've never quite gotten along."

"Why?"

Such a simple question, but as Grace considered it she realized the answer was far from easy. Why *hadn't* the three McKinnon girls stayed close? It would have seemed, given the way their mother was always leaving, that they would have banded together more, and stayed that way. There'd been years when they'd been inseparable, but as they'd gotten older the gulf had widened. "I don't know. Sibling rivalry, I guess."

"Want to talk about it?"

"No." She bit her lip. "Yes. But..."

"But what?"

She pivoted to face him. "What are we, J.C.? Friends? More? Old flames?"

He grinned. "How about D.—all of the above?"

"That's not an answer."

"If you don't like the answer, ask a different question."

She let out a gust. "You are a frustrating man."

"Me? I'm easy. Some would even say nice."

"Some?" She arched a brow.

"Well, only a few opinions really matter." He gave her another grin, then sobered. "Come on, Grace. Lean on me for a little bit."

She bit her lip and considered him. The hood of her coat shielded most of her face from the cold, and from his view. "I've always done that. The trouble is, you've never done it with me." An icy breeze ruffled the flowers in their paper wrapper. Cars passed by on the street, tires crunching on the snowy road. Grace let out a long breath. "All the years I've known you, J.C., you've barely opened up about your life or your family. Most of what I know I figured out on my own after seeing you with your parents."

He leaned forward, bracing his elbows on his knees. The cold skated down his back, lifting the back of his jacket. "You don't understand, Grace, how hard it is for me. I didn't grow up in a house where we wore our emotions on our sleeves. In fact, showing any emotion at all…" He let out a gust. "Well, it was a sign of weakness. A strongly discouraged weakness."

"And yet you wanted me to be the one to pour my heart out to you." She raised one shoulder, let it drop. "That's not a friendship, J.C., or, heck, even a relationship."

She was right. He hated it, but she was right. All

these years they'd had a one-sided relationship where he listened and she talked and he never reciprocated. At the time it had seemed easier. If he didn't talk about it, it didn't exist—or, more, it couldn't hurt him. His father's distance, the constant judgment, the ridiculous expectations. Would telling Grace have helped alleviate some of that stress and tension? Made his childhood an easier row to hoe?

He couldn't go on keeping his emotions locked up tight. Where had that gotten him?

The answer came like a punch to the gut.

"I've turned into my father."

Grace didn't say anything. She didn't have to. Her silence was agreement enough.

"I vowed all my life to not be like him, and yet here I am, working at his desk, spending my life in the same office and cutting myself off from the people around me." He let out a curse. The change had come on him so gradually he'd never noticed. The only difference was that he didn't have any children in the mix. Well, he hadn't had any children. But now there was Henry, and as soon as J.C. returned to Boston, to his daily schedule, he knew the job would suck up his time. Henry would be the loser in that equation. "That's not what I wanted."

"You aren't like him, J.C. You're here, in town, with your mom and Henry. You're—"

"Half the time I'm here I'm working. Hell, two-thirds of the time. That's not being with my mother or Henry or you. That's being..." J.C. let out a long breath, and with it, the truth "...him."

"Then stop doing that," Grace said. "If you don't like your life, change it, J.C."

"My mother told me almost the same thing." J.C. shook his head. "That's easier said than done. The company is counting on me. My family is counting on me. Heck, this whole town is counting on me. I can't let those people down."

"You could always do what I do and hop on the next plane out of here."

He grinned. "That's not funny. Okay, maybe it is. I can just see the headlines now if I did that."

A part of him wanted to take Grace up on the offer. Head to Logan Airport, plunk down his credit card and book the first available flight to anywhere. Leave his cell phone behind and just be somewhere no one knew him or wanted anything from him. A good idea in abstract but not in reality. The company would be plunged into chaos if the C.E.O. disappeared, and poor Henry and J.C.'s mother would be left adrift.

"How did you do it?" he asked her.

"Do what? Take off for destinations unknown?" She shrugged. "It's scary, especially when you're traveling solo. That first trip, when I left Beckett's Run, was the most terrifying. I'd never really traveled, and never left the state of Massachusetts. But I knew that if I could handle that, I could handle anything."

"And now? Still ready to hop on the next plane?"

"A part of me always is," she said. "When I stay in one place too long, I get…antsy."

"And are you antsy now?"

"There you go again, turning the conversation into a Grace confessional." She gave him a smile, one that said she wasn't going to answer the question. "We're not talking about me, remember?"

"Old habits die hard," he said with a grin, then he sobered. "You're right, though, about me. I'm sorry for not opening up to you. I should have done that all along. Maybe then we could have avoided what happened that last day, because you would have known that I would never have had my father call you like that."

She interlaced her fingers and wrapped her arms around her knees, drawing her body in tight. "I think a part of me did know that, but I was so hurt I refused to admit it."

"From now on, I swear—" he crossed his heart "—to tell you all my deepest, darkest thoughts."

She laughed. "That could lead down some very dangerous paths."

"Yes, it could." His hand reached for hers. She uncoiled herself and shifted toward him, her eyes wide. When they touched, the familiar electric charge ran through him and desire rushed through his veins. Damn, he wanted her. Not just physically, but in every way. How could he have ever let this woman out of his life?

"Would that be so bad? If we went down those dangerous paths?" he asked.

She held his gaze for a long time, and he wondered if she was thinking of those lazy summer days by the creek, or their long walks through the park, or these last few days, when it seemed like something had been rekindled.

Finally, she released his hand with a sigh, and he realized her thoughts weren't on the same road as his. "I don't know, J.C. I look at my parents and I think anyone would be crazy to get married. They've been on again and off again as often as a light switch. They get married, divorced, date, marry, divorce. Then they realize all the reasons they broke up and they have a huge fight and it's over again." She bit her lip, and sadness washed over her eyes. "My parents couldn't keep it together because they wanted totally different things out of their lives. My father is the worker and my mother is the hummingbird, flitting from thing to thing."

Now he saw what she was trying to say. This was a part of why Grace kept pushing him away. "You think we're like that."

"We're exactly like them. I can't repeat that, J.C. I've seen firsthand how that yo-yoing can destroy people. Not just them, but me and my sisters. We never knew which way was up or who would be in the living room when we got up in the morning. My parents loved each other, but that wasn't enough."

"That doesn't mean we'd end up the same way, Grace."

Why wouldn't she trust him? Why wouldn't she take that risk? Every time he thought she'd changed—and he'd thought that a hundred times over the last few days when he'd seen her with Henry and working on the festival—she came right back to this familiar refrain.

"Yeah, we would." Resignation filled her features, and he knew the battle was lost before it even began. "I've known you a long time, J.C., but I only realized today that I've been the one doing all the talking. You kept so much of yourself from me. You keep telling me that I'm the one running, but you are, too, J.C. Running and hiding behind this wall you have up between you and the rest of the world. It's still there, even if you say it isn't anymore. You want me to trust, to take a chance, and yet…you don't do either."

"I do trust you."

"No, you don't." She reached into her coat and pulled out a sheaf of papers. "Remember I told you I wanted to write a story about Henry? And you told me not to?"

"I didn't want you to do that because—" He cut off his words before he said something he'd regret.

"Because you didn't trust me to do it right. To not turn your nephew and your family's loss into some sensationalized piece. That, right there, *that's* the problem. You know me, J.C., and yet you don't trust me. Is that about me? Or you?"

"Grace—"

She pressed the papers into his hand, cutting off his words. "Read that. Please." Then she got to her feet and buttoned her coat around her neck. "And see if I was as self-serving as you thought I was."

"I never said that."

A sad smile flitted across her face. "You never had to." She took a step off the porch.

"Where are you going?"

Her gaze went to the street, then the town beyond, and finally to the horizon. "Anywhere but here."

"Don't go. It's almost Christmas." He reached for her. He could see her pulling back emotionally, and soon, he knew, she'd get on a plane and be a hundred, a thousand miles from him. And he'd have lost her again. "At least stay for the holiday. Beckett's Run is a wonderful place—one of those towns that just sort of wraps around you if you let it, Grace."

She shook her head. "I don't belong in this small town life, J.C. It doesn't matter what day of the year it is."

"How do you know that? You can't find out what you have or what you truly want if you keep leaving, Grace."

But she had already headed down the stairs and off into the gathering storm.

Grace walked for hours, traversing the town that she knew so well she could map it in her sleep. Then she returned to Gram's house—to a quiet, dark home. Everyone had left and Gram had gone to bed early. In typical Gram style she'd left a note and a plate of dinner on the counter for Grace.

> *Missed you at dinner, but saved you some chicken*
> *and dumplings. Get a good night's sleep, Grace,*
> *dear. Everything looks better in the morning.*
> *Love,*
> *Gram*

Grace took the plate and the note up to her room. She considered her backpack, sitting by the door, packed and ready to go. She could leave tonight and be on an airplane headed to some island somewhere before the sun came up.

Then she thought about what J.C. had said about how she was always running. For the first time in her life the thought of getting on the road again exhausted her. She was tired of being afraid of staying, of taking personal risks.

Tomorrow she would decide. For now she didn't want to deal with any of that. Didn't want to make a decision any more complicated than what pajamas to wear tonight.

But she did make one decision. She set up her laptop, sent out a single email, ate her dinner and then crawled into the bed she had slept in a good portion of her life and fell into a deep, dreamless sleep.

When the morning dawned, the smell of fresh coffee dragged Grace out of bed and down to the kitchen. She didn't check her email first. Coffee before disappointment, she decided.

She had just poured a cup when her oldest sister came into the room, a little sleep-rumpled. Grace reached for a second cup and filled it with hot coffee. Her sister had blue eyes and blonde hair, her features tempered by a wisdom and intelligence that came from being the one they'd all relied upon and turned to when their parents were gone. Or, at least, they used to turn to. The days since either Grace or Faith had done that were long past.

Grace knew she shouldn't be surprised to see Hope— Gram had only mentioned a thousand times that the other McKinnon sisters were coming for the holiday— but she was. Grace loved Hope and Faith, and missed seeing them, but over the years the three of them had drifted apart. They'd gone their own ways, maybe more used to not having connections than building them. Some days she wondered if it was too late to rebuild the closeness they'd had when they were little. Maybe they'd all grown up a little, or rather a lot, and instead of having a relationship where one sister was the substitute mom they could all have more equal footing. Friendship.

"Hey," Hope said, a slight smile on her face. "Where's Gram?"

"Hey, yourself." Grace handed her sister the cup. "Gram's helping out with one of the events today. She went to bed early. I got in late..." She let the words trail off, not wanting to explain everything that had happened in the last few days, or the muddle of emotions running through her.

"I heard you. That board on the porch, remember?" Hope grinned and the shared memory, the common secret, connected them for a moment. "It always did cause you trouble. With J.C. then, too, if I remember right."

J.C. The last person she wanted to think about today. She'd left him with her article, and with a lot of hard questions, and he had yet to contact her. Not so much as a text message. Had she made a mistake?

Instead of dwelling on what couldn't be undone, she

changed the subject. "There's a lot to do to get ready for today. I need to be out the door soon." She paused, the mug warm against her hands and the sight of her sister warm in her heart. It had been a long time, too long, and Grace wondered how she could have let all those months build up. Her sisters used to be her anchor, the two people in the world she knew she could always depend upon. When had she let that go? And why? "It's good to see you, Hope."

"Really?" Hope sat down at the table. "After our last talk…"

Grace waved a hand. The argument no longer mattered. At the time, Grace had blamed Hope for the failure of her own career, which wasn't fair. At all. Grace had been her own undoing, and after last night she began to understand why. She hadn't been pouring her heart into her stories. She'd been running from emotion on the page as surely as she ran from emotion in her own life. Until she'd met Henry and finally opened up.

"It doesn't matter now. It was good for me to come back. To see Gram. To…" Grace let the sentence run off. *Had* it been good to be here? To reopen old doors? Like the ones with J.C.?

Because right now his silence hurt. A lot. She'd started falling for him all over again, and Grace suspected this time the leaving would be ten times harder than when she'd been eighteen.

She forced a smile to her face. "Anyway, how was ranch life?" she asked Hope. "Gram said you were taking pictures for some therapy-type place?"

Hope blushed, and then began to tell Grace about the therapeutic riding facility she'd been working at. When Grace asked if that was all that was making her blush, Hope hesitated. "I thought you had to skedaddle?" she said.

Grace was tired of running. Of not being there for her family, her friends, and most of all for herself. Where had it gotten her? Nowhere but on another plane, to another destination, none of which filled her like these moments in Gram's kitchen.

"Beckett's Run is a wonderful place—one of those towns that just sort of wraps around you if you let it, Grace."

J.C.'s words rang in her head. What did it say about this town that it was the one place she returned to over and over again? The only place that drew her back? Grace dropped into a chair opposite her sister. "I can manage a few minutes."

Hope's gaze met hers and the moment extended between them. One filled with forgiveness, connection, love. And just like that the years melted away and the sisters became sisters again, as if they were little all over again, twin beds pushed together, whispered secrets exchanged long after the light had been turned off.

"The guy that owns the place...Blake...I kind of got involved."

As Hope talked about Blake, and falling in love with the sexy rancher, Grace listened and smiled and—

Envied her sister.

Hope had done it. She'd leapt off that cliff and dove headfirst into the murky waters of love. A world that came without guarantees, or even so much as a promise of happy forever. It was a risk and, looking at the happiness radiating from every pore of her older sister, a risk worth taking.

At the end of the conversation Grace embraced her sister, then told her to bring her camera to the festival.

An idea brewed in Grace's head. One that came with a little risk—

And hopefully a lot of reward.

CHAPTER TWELVE

J.C. STOOD in the park and admired his handiwork. Well, his and about a dozen other people's. The entire park had been converted into a winter wonderland, and people from Beckett's Run and several surrounding towns were walking from section to section, enjoying the steaming hot cocoa, the crisp-fried dough, the ornament-decorating stations. The Winter Festival was a success, and with the last events finishing up tonight he finally felt like he could relax. Breathe. Think.

He had a lot of decisions to make in the coming days. One he needed to make right now, he thought, as his gaze caught on a familiar figure in a dark blue coat standing by the pond. His heart leapt and his pulse raced, and all he could think about was getting to Grace as fast as possible. He wove his way through the crowd, answering the questions that others peppered him with, and accepting thanks from the townspeople, until he finally reached the pond. Ice skaters circled the space, some hand-in-hand, some solo. Grace stood on the sidelines, her arms wrapped around herself.

For a second he watched her, admiring the graceful curve of her neck, the slight smile playing on her lips. Damn, she was a beautiful woman. She teased him and tempted him, and made him think about all the things he had put on hold for so long.

He'd dated women over the years, but none had stuck in his mind or heart like Grace McKinnon. Just the thought of her leaving made a pain rise in his chest. But if she stayed, what could he offer her?

An instant family with Henry, and a husband who worked an insane amount of hours? That would never make Grace happy. She had made it clear she didn't want to be tied down. The best he could do was let her go, and let her find her happiness on the road.

But not quite yet. Not without telling her what he had come here to say and taking one more chance. He had missed that chance all those years ago, and he refused to let it happen again.

He crossed to her. "You came."

She turned to him and a wider smile crossed her lips. "Had to see how it turned out. It looks wonderful. You did an amazing job."

"Thanks. I owe a lot to you. Our attendance is up twentyfold. Maybe even more."

"I didn't do much."

"You did a lot, Grace." And she had. Her publicity efforts had spawned a ton of media interest, and a serious boost in revenue for the town. Business owners had been thanking him all day, gratitude and relief on their faces at the increase in their daily totals. He could only hope the effect lingered, and that people returned for next year's Winter Festival. Beckett's Run would never become a major city or a top destination, which was just fine with J.C. and probably most everyone in town, but it would be nice to see the town get its due share of the tourism pie.

"Did Henry enjoy the parade?"

J.C. chuckled. "He loved it. Sat on my shoulders and watched every single second of it. At the end, Santa gave him a little wave and that just made Henry's day. He's at my mom's right now, helping with some chores, because he wants to be extra good before Santa arrives."

Grace smiled. "He's an adorable kid. I'm glad to see he's enjoying Christmas."

"He deserves it." J.C. let out a long breath and thought of all Henry had been through and the strides his nephew had made in the last few weeks. They weren't out of the woods yet, but it was a start, a good one, and J.C. was glad he had been a part of it. "It's the least I can do."

She put a hand on his arm, let it linger for a second. "You're a good man, J.C."

He scoffed. "I don't know about that. I think I'm working on being a good man."

She shook her head. "You always were a good man. Everything you've done in your life, you've done with the best intentions. You took care of your family, and even this town, because you cared. There's nothing wrong with that."

He wanted to protest, but he saw the earnestness in her face, and for the first time in his life let the compliment fill him with a sense of accomplishment. "Thanks, Grace. That means a lot."

It meant more than he could say. He was still working on that opening up thing.

She shrugged, as if it was no big deal. "Anyway, I better take a walk around the festival. I need to write up a post-publicity piece."

"Wait. I wanted to talk to you about that article on Henry." He reached into his coat and withdrew the typed pages she had given him yesterday. They were a bit wrinkled from his many readings, last night and again this morning. "It was…amazing. Hell, it even brought a tear to my eye. You captured him perfectly, and brought the whole thing full circle with the story about making the snowman."

"Thanks." A blush filled her cheeks.

"I had no idea you could write like this, Grace. I mean, I've read some of your articles—"

"You've read my travel articles?"

He smiled at her. "You don't really think I forgot all about you when we broke up, did you? Of course I read your articles. I'd pick up magazines all the time and look for your name in the bylines. The people in the bookstore must have thought I had some kind of travel bug, given how many I bought. It was my way of making sure you were okay, I guess."

"As long as I'm water-skiing in Florida, or shopping the outdoor markets in Indonesia, I must be fine?" She smiled, clearly touched that he'd done that.

"Something like that." He reached up and brushed a lock of hair off her forehead. "I never forgot you. I tried, but you're a pretty unforgettable woman, Grace McKinnon."

"J.C.—"

"Don't." He put a finger on her lips. "Don't tell me not to say this. Don't tell me you don't want to hear it. And don't leave before I finish." He lowered his hand and decided if he didn't tell her this now he may never get another chance. All week he'd wanted to take this risk, to open his heart to her. If she still left at the end, at least he would know he had told her how he felt— how he'd always felt. Even before he spoke, he could see the familiar fear in her eyes, the urge to bolt. "I have never forgotten you. Never found anyone who is like you. And I don't want you to leave. Not today, not tomorrow, not ever."

"We can't—"

"Don't." He grinned to soften the admonishment. "I woke up this morning and realized, after reading your article, that there's only one thing I want to give Henry, and myself, for Christmas this year." He exhaled the breath in his chest, and with it the words that would change his future. Put him on the path he had foregone many years ago. "I'm selling the company and I'm staying here."

Before his first cup of coffee J.C. had called the owner of the company that was expecting to merge with Carson Investments and offered the other man the opportunity to play out the merger in reverse, with the other company bringing Carson Investments under its wing. They'd hashed out the details, and a tentative offer was in place. It was done, and though this decision would have ripples throughout Carson Investments, J.C. knew it was the right move. A long-overdue move, at that.

Grace blinked. "You're…what?"

"Moving back to Beckett's Run. For good. I've made my money. I've proved my point. Now I want a life. And I want one right here, where my family is, where my heart is." He grabbed her hands with his own and held tight. "I know you want to leave, Grace. I see it in the fear in your eyes and the way you're only half here. But I'm asking you to reconsider. Stay here with me in Beckett's Run and let's take that journey we planned all those years ago."

"Back then we were going to ride off into the sunset and go where the wind took us."

"The wind brought us both back here at the same time this year. I don't think that's a coincidence. I think it's a sign that we have a second chance, and we'd be fools not to take it."

She searched his face. Doubt and questions knotted her brows, drew lines in her forehead. "What are you saying, J.C.?"

"I'm saying I love you and I always have. I want you to stay, Grace. I want you to take a chance."

She was already backing up, already letting go. "I can't, J.C. My career takes me all over the world and—"

"That's an excuse. You can still be a travel writer. You can still go to Bali and Cancún and all those places. But when you are done come home to me, to Beckett's Run."

"What if it doesn't work out? What if we do this with the best intentions and we end up breaking up? What if we have children caught in that? Kids like Henry, who don't need any more hurt in their lives?"

"Are you saying that because you don't love me, too, or because you're afraid of turning out like your parents?"

Beside them, the skaters continued in their endless circle, skates whispering softly on the ice. A light dusting of snow began to fall, the sun catching each flake and making it sparkle.

"I'm exactly like my mother, J.C.," Grace said. "I can't settle down. I can't stay. Even the thought of doing that scares me to death. So I know that even if I say yes to you right now, I'm going to get antsy and I'm going to leave again someday."

"Why did you write that article about Henry?" he asked.

She shook her head at the change in topic. "What?"

"Just tell me. Why did you write that article?"

"Because I knew his story would touch people's hearts."

"I've read what you write, Grace, and it's nothing like that. I mean, your articles are good, but they aren't the kind that tackle deeper issues like this one did. So why this story? Why now?"

She let out a breath, and though she didn't come any closer she didn't move any farther away, either. "When I was in Russia a few years ago I met this little girl. It was early winter, and it was so cold. She didn't even have a coat, and yet she was standing on the street corner, trying to sell newspapers to feed her family. I bought a paper, took her to a store to buy a coat and fed her every day that I was there. She moved me, J.C., and I decided I wanted to write a story that would make people notice little girls like that. And do something about it. So I wrote that story and I sent it off to my college professor, who's the editor at *Social Issues,* the kind of magazine that covers those things. He rejected it."

"Why? You're a fabulous writer."

"I have what it takes to write about the best hotel for your honeymoon, or some hidden getaway in Costa Rica, but when it comes to the stories that matter I'm not good enough. The editor said it was because I didn't put my heart into it. I tried to do it with this article on Henry, because this time it mattered to me. More than whether my career would be there tomorrow. But I don't know if I accomplished that." She raised her gaze to his and tears shimmered in her eyes. "That's why my articles don't move people, and that's why I don't stay, J.C. If I did, I'd have to put my heart into this place, and my heart's been broken so many times that I just can't do that anymore."

Grace McKinnon, abandoned and left dozens and

dozens of times as a little girl. The youngest of the McKinnons, and the one most affected by their mother's frequent departures. He'd always thought of her as the strong one, the one who seemed to have it together the best. When really that had all been a front. "You're not afraid of counting on other people, Grace," he said gently. "You're afraid of other people counting on you."

She opened her mouth to argue, shut it again.

"If you don't hang around, if you don't put down roots, no one is going to expect you to step up to the plate. To be the leader." He shook his head and gave her a smile. Grace, a woman so good at reading and writing about other people, couldn't see the stories in herself. "What you don't understand is that you have been the leader forever. You were the one who took all the chances, who encouraged me to step outside the boundaries. You gave me the childhood and teen years I never would have had, and you taught me to take risks."

"All I did was get in a lot of trouble, J.C. I didn't do anything else."

"You took off on an around-the-world trip by yourself at eighteen. Who does that? You're the bravest woman I know, Grace, and yet you don't see it. I wish you would." He reached up and cupped her jaw, and met the eyes that he loved so much. "I wish you'd take a chance on loving me. Because I've taken that chance on you." Then he pressed a tender, easy kiss to her mouth, praying it wouldn't be their last kiss. "Come back to the festival tonight. There's something I want you to see. I'll be in the gazebo around seven."

"J.C., I don't think I'm staying for the rest of the festival. I need to get back on the road and on to my next assignment."

He let his hand drop away. "You already have your

next destination, Grace. It offers everything you've ever been looking for. And then some."

If Grace had been hoping for peace, she didn't get it. She parked in front of Gram's house, walked inside the door, and was swamped by a flurry of hugs and good wishes from her sisters. Hope and Faith sandwiched her between them, giggling and talking as if no time at all had passed since the three had seen each other, while Gram stood to the side with two men Grace didn't recognize. Their parents were also there, also standing to the side, chatting with the men.

The whole family. Together for the holiday. Grace wanted to run back out the door, but she couldn't—not with everyone between her and the outside. She thought of the backpack upstairs, packed, ready to go.

Then she thought of J.C.'s words. He loved her. *Loved* her.

How long had she waited to hear that? And now that she had all she wanted to do was run in the opposite direction. Because her heart was beating too loud and too fast to think about anything else.

"It's about time you got home," Hope said. "We've been waiting for *hours*."

Grace pushed a smile to her face. "Sorry. Got tied up at the Winter Festival."

"We were afraid you were going to run out of here before Christmas. It wouldn't be a proper holiday without you, too, Grace." Faith gave her sister a quick, tight hug.

Grace returned the warm embrace and vowed that, no matter what, she'd be sure to keep in better contact with her sisters. For too long they'd been flung all over the world—England, Canada, Australia—and it was time the McKinnon sisters banded together and stayed that way.

"And now that we have so much news to share, you have to stay."

"News? What news?"

"We're getting married!" Hope and Faith exclaimed at the same time.

They dragged over the two men, introducing them as Blake and Marcus, their new fiancés. Hope and Faith talked over each other, rushing to tell all about the rancher who had stolen Hope's heart and the Earl who had Faith blushing.

"That's wonderful," Grace said, drawing each of her sisters into a hug. That feeling of envy raised itself in her chest again.

J.C. had asked her to stay, to start a life with him here in Beckett's Run. She could be celebrating with her sisters if only she'd take a chance. She felt torn in two, her heart and mind warring for two different courses of action.

"That's all really wonderful," she repeated to Hope and Faith, then turned to Blake and Marcus. Given the way they were beaming at her sisters, she had no doubt the two men were in love, and determined to give Hope and Faith happy futures. She was happy for her sisters, who deserved that happy ending.

What about you? her mind whispered.

Grace tried to breathe, but her throat suddenly felt tight, her chest seemed as if a twenty-pound weight sat on her heart, and she turned away, grabbing the newel post like a lifeline. "I have a…a deadline to meet. Let me just run upstairs and get this emailed out, and I'll be back to catch up with all of you soon. Okay?"

"Sure, sure," Faith said. "We'll be here for a few days. We have lots of time to catch up."

Grace hurried up the stairs. She dashed into her room, shut the door and lay down on the bed. Her heart raced, her breath whistled in and out of her chest, and her mind raced. What *was* all this? She was never this discombobulated or scattered.

A knock sounded on her door. Grace scrambled to her feet, reaching for her backpack to feign the work she'd used as an excuse, but Gram entered the room first.

"You doing okay, kiddo?"

"I'm fine. Just…busy." The closed laptop and empty desk belied the statement.

"Too busy to spend time with your sisters?"

"I will…later."

Gram crossed the room and came to sit on the corner of the bed. "Honey, I know it's hard for you. In fact, I think sometimes it's hardest on you out of all them. Hope was the oldest and she kind of took charge. That gave her something to do, something to focus on when your mom would leave. Faith was in the middle and, oh, such a vocal girl about everything. But you, my sweet, dear, Grace, you were the youngest. The one who got forgotten sometimes."

Grace shook her head, but her eyes burned all the same. "It was okay."

"No, it wasn't. And I think you put up walls and distance because that keeps you from getting hurt. Going on trips, staying too busy for family get-togethers, and jetting off at the last minute are all walls, just a different kind." Gram cupped Grace's face in soft hands. "Sometimes you just have to take a chance, Grace, and love other people. And stay still long enough for them to love you."

"I just… It's hard for me." She bit her lip and willed the tears to stop. They didn't listen. "I understand why Mom did it. I think she was scared. Scared of falling in love, scared of being hurt."

Gram considered that for a moment. Her wise light blue eyes were filled with kindness and understanding when they met Grace's. "I think you're right. But I also think this time your mom and dad are going to make it work. I've listened to them and watched them together. After losing each other the second time, I think they finally changed and grew up. Realized what's important and how much they love each other. How much work it takes to keep that together."

"And how scary it is to fall in love with someone?" There. That was what had her throat tight and her breath caught. The fear of falling in love. With J.C.

"Exactly," Gram said. "Did you know your grandfather had to ask me four times to marry him?"

"Four times? You never told me that."

"Oh, he was a stubborn one. Good thing, too, because he turned out to be more stubborn than me. I didn't want to settle down and get married, which in my day was a crime against nature and society." She chuckled. "I was afraid that if I got married it would make me give up my freedom. I'm like you. I want to make my own rules, decide my own fate. It took me a while to realize that loving someone, and being loved back, gives you more freedom than anything else in this world."

"How's that?"

A soft smile stole across Gram's face, and Grace could see her reaching back in her memory for the man who had been with her most of her life. Even now, with him dead and buried for many years, her love was evident and strong. "Their love becomes the gust of wind beneath you. It helps you soar higher. Your grandfather encouraged me in every crazy idea I ever had. And, you know, your father did that with your mother, too. He wanted her to find herself, and it took some time but she did. Now look at them."

They *had* looked happy this week, Grace realized. Happier than she could ever remember seeing them. She thought of her sisters, and how each of them seemed to have become more themselves with the men they loved by their sides. If she took that chance, would she find the same thing?

She glanced at the backpack. Battered and worn by all her travel, all her destinations. She'd been all over the world, and in the end she'd come right back to the beginning. A sign, J.C. had called it. A sign of what?

"Anyway, I've said my piece." Mary gave her granddaughter a hug, then drew back. "It's Christmas Eve, and after dinner we're all heading over to the festival. One big happy family. Exactly what you asked Santa to bring you every Christmas, my sweet granddaughter. You finally have what you wanted. Now, come enjoy it."

The Monday Morning Carp Club sent J.C. a wave as he passed them on his way through the park. The dance was in full swing at the pole barn set up outside of Santa's Village, and the rest of the park was filled with visitors trying out the enticing sweets and rides. He glanced at the Mistletoe Wishes ride as he passed, and felt a pang.

Grace.

She'd taken off out of the park after their conversation earlier today, and hadn't returned. He had tried calling her a couple times, but his calls went straight to voicemail. Because she was on a plane somewhere? Or because she didn't want to talk to him? Either way, the answer wasn't one he wanted.

He saw his mother and Henry coming toward him, Henry's little legs pumping fast to keep up with his grandmother's longer strides. Both of them were smiling and walking hand in hand. Henry released his grandmother's hand and dashed toward J.C., who bent down, put out his arms and scooped up his nephew. J.C. knew as long as he lived he'd never get tired of doing that, or get tired of feeling Henry snuggle into him with a joyous hug.

"Uncle Jace!" Henry said, drawing back. "We saw Santa! And he says he's coming to my house tonight! He says I've been a good boy!"

J.C. ruffled Henry's hair. "You have indeed. I think Santa's going to bring you lots of gifts."

"Spoil him rotten, you mean," his mother added, and shot her son a teasing smile. "Hopefully Santa didn't make any more toy store runs today."

"Maybe just one." J.C. grinned, then released Henry. He reached for the item in his mother's hands. "Thanks for bringing this. I'm surprised you found it."

"That attic is full of all kinds of forgotten things," she said. "I also got out some of your toys from when you were a kid. Henry prefers those to the ones his mom had, as any boy would. I should have done that a long time ago." She sighed. "I guess I was just trying to bring her back."

J.C.'s chest grew tight. He missed his sister, too, and the loss seemed to sting more as the holiday neared. "She's in every smile Henry gives us, Mom. And in every laugh. She's right there, right with us. All the time."

His mother came to stand beside him and watched her

grandson talking to some other children. A proud smile stole across her face. "You're right. I raised a pretty smart son, didn't I?"

His gaze scanned the park. But nowhere did he see a familiar blonde ponytail. "I guess so. Right now, I don't feel so smart."

His mother patted his arm. "She'll be here. I know she will. I'm going to go grab Henry and get a seat. I'll talk to you later, son. Good luck." She pressed a kiss to his cheek, then headed toward the gazebo.

J.C. stood a while longer in the cold, while snow dusted his head and shoulders. People milled about him, but he paid them no mind. Across the way he saw committee volunteers Walter and Sandra walking arm in arm, and he envied them their moment of romance.

His phone dinged with a reminder of the hour. Seven o'clock. And Grace wasn't here.

J.C. let out a breath, then headed toward the gazebo and the tent erected over it, put in place earlier today to create an indoor space in the outdoors, a shelter against the cold. His shoes crunched on the snow, and to his ears the sound seemed to echo. He peeled back the clear paneled entrance to the tent, headed down the aisle past the assembled townspeople, sending a wave to the Beckett's Run Book Club as well as his mother and Henry, then climbed up the stairs and took a seat in the center of the gazebo.

"I'd like to welcome you all to the Beckett's Run Winter Festival," he said into the microphone. "I hope you've all had a great time."

A collective cheer went up from the crowd, followed by a burst of applause.

"Thank you. But I couldn't have done this without the help of many fabulous volunteers. And now—"

The panel peeled back again. A blonde stepped into the tent.

Hope McKinnon, followed by a brunette. Faith McKinnon. Two men joined the women, then Grace's parents, and finally her grandmother, Mary. The panel slid shut again. The hope in J.C.'s chest died. He cleared his throat and swallowed hard against the disappointment. He couldn't do this.

"Anyway, I know you all were expecting a performance tonight," he said, his hand lighting on the case beside him, "but—"

The panel opened again. Grace stepped into the tent and raised her gaze to his. A moment passed, then a smile winged across her face and hope took flight in J.C.'s chest again.

"But I'll delay it no longer," he said.

He undid the clips on the side of the case and withdrew the wooden acoustic guitar inside. It wasn't the top-of-the-line electric guitar that he'd taken with him to college, which sat in a closet gathering dust in his Boston home, but rather the first guitar he'd ever owned—a gift from Santa when J.C. was ten years old. The same guitar he'd used to bring on those trips to the creek. In the quiet of lazy summer days he used to played songs for Grace while the crickets chirped and the birds added a melody.

Now Grace walked down the aisle and took a seat in the front row, between her grandmother and his mother. Henry climbed down off his seat and into Grace's lap, leaning back against her chest. She hesitated only a second, then wrapped an arm around him and leaned down to whisper in his ear. He grinned, then nodded and settled in to listen.

J.C. strummed a note, paused as a moment of panic flooded him, then let out a breath, closed his eyes and started playing again. The haunting melody from an old song came back to him with each note, and before long he had added his voice, too. It had been years since he'd played in front of any kind of audience—and never had he played in front of anyone in Beckett's Run, except for Grace—but the song came easily after a while, and as people began to move along to the beat he relaxed and let the music carry him forward.

When he was done, the audience erupted into applause. J.C. got to his feet, did a comical bow, then introduced the next musical act before leaving the stage.

When he got down the stairs, Henry started toward him, but J.C.'s mom held her grandson back and told him to wait a bit. Grace's family got to their feet and greeted him, and though he returned the friendly words, and gave hugs to Hope, Faith, Mary and Lydia, his attention stayed on Grace.

"I think we need to make some room," Hope said to Faith. "For Grace's happy ending."

The two sisters laughed, then stepped aside, leaving a direct path from J.C. to Grace. As he closed the distance between them everyone else in the room dropped away. He saw, heard, noticed nothing but the way her eyes lit up as he approached. Her hair was down tonight, dancing around her shoulders and tempting him to come closer, to touch the silk tresses. His fingers flexed at his side. Damn, he wanted her.

"Thanks for coming," he said. As far as lame opening lines went, that one had to be at the top of the list. For only the second time in his life he was nervous around Grace. As if he was sixteen again and about to ask her on a date.

"I recognize that guitar," she said. "In fact, I remember it very well."

He grinned. "I hoped you would."

"And the song. You used to sing that to me."

He nodded, and in her face he saw she was thinking of those summer days, too. Back when they had thought there was nothing outside the little world they had carved out for themselves. "I never sang it for anyone else before today."

"Really? Why?"

"You're not the only one afraid of risk," he said with a smile. "You know the real reason I didn't go on that trip with you? I was afraid of failing. Of taking that risk and proving my father right. That I'd never make it with my music and I'd end up pumping gas at a gas station for a living. So I kept my music just between you and me. But I don't want to do that anymore. I'm not looking to make a career out of this, or to have a hit record, or anything other than just enjoy playing. I don't care about being the next big thing; all I care about is showing you that I'm serious."

"Serious about what?"

"About taking more risks from here on out." He leaned the guitar against a nearby chair, then took a step forward, closer to her. She stayed where she was, which J.C. took as a good sign. A very good sign. "If you want to leave Beckett's Run, Grace, and travel the world, I'm ready to go with you. To take that chance on the unknown. I don't want to lose you, and if that means leaving here, then so be it."

"I don't want you to do that," she said, sending a glance in Henry's direction. The little boy clung tight to his grandmother's hand, watching the exchange. Grace sent him a smile, and Henry returned the gesture. "I don't want you to do that at all."

J.C. sighed. His heart sank. He'd expected her to say

anything but that. "Okay. Well, thanks for coming to the show, and thanks for helping with the festival." He turned to go, but before he could take a single step she put a hand on his arm and stopped him.

"I don't want you to do that because I want you to stay right here and raise Henry and help this town get back on its feet, and…" she took a deep breath and let it out with a smile "…be with me."

"Be with you?"

She nodded, and now the smile widened, lit up her eyes. "I'm not going anywhere. I'm staying right here in Beckett's Run, with you and Henry and my grandmother. I love you, too, J.C., and I always have. I never told you before, and I should have, a long time ago, because you are my first and only love, J.C. Carson, and I can't imagine being with anyone else."

"Oh, Grace, I love you, too." Joy threatened to explode inside him. He met her gaze with his own. In her eyes he saw the reflection of his own heart. She did love him, and the thought filled him with a happiness he had never known before. "I've realized in the last few days that it doesn't matter how much money I make, or how much I achieve, if I'm alone at the end of the day. I want to begin and end my day the same way every time. With my best friend."

She grinned. "Is that what we are, J.C.? Best friends?"

He closed the gap between them and placed his hands on her waist. "I think we're best friends. And a lot more."

"A *hell* of a lot more," she emphasized, then leaned in and kissed him. A light, easy kiss, that lasted barely a second before she drew back. "I don't want to run anymore. I don't want another stamp in my passport. I want to stay right here with you and build a home."

"Doesn't that scare you?"

She laughed. "It terrifies me. But I'm the girl who traveled the world by myself. I'm pretty sure I can handle a white picket fence and a dog in the yard."

He chuckled. "I think I can handle that, too. Though I have to admit my mowing skills are pretty much nonexistent."

"Then we'll get goats." She laughed again, a light, merry sound, then leaned into him again. "And you know I don't care if the lawn is perfect or the dinners get burned or the paint starts to peel. That kind of thing has never mattered to me."

"Me either." He drew her even closer to him, then gave her a long, sweet kiss. Behind him, he heard the excited, happy chatter of their families. He drew back. "But what about traveling the world? Writing?"

"Turns out you were right about that article on Henry. The editor at *Social Issues* loved it. He wants me to write more pieces like that. Now you've said it's okay, he's going to run it in the next issue, and I asked my sister Hope to take some pictures of Henry to go with it."

J.C. had seen Hope's work. He couldn't think of a better accompaniment to Grace's powerful words. "That's awesome. Maybe someone else who has lost a loved one will read it and find comfort."

She nodded. "You know, when I wrote that story, I thought I was writing it for other people. So they would read it and remember the true meaning of Christmas."

"And what is that?"

"That family trumps any present in the world. It's the one thing Santa can't bring, a store can't sell, but you can create yourself." She glanced over at her family, all standing on the sidelines, watching her with smiles on their faces. "When I wrote that article, I realized what was different about this one, as opposed to the one about the girl in Russia. I put my heart into it, J.C., because I opened my heart. To Henry. To you. To this town. And when I thought about leaving again…" She let out a long breath, "I just couldn't go. I love it here. It's the same as it was when I was a little girl, and probably will be when I'm an old lady, and that's what I love the most about Beckett's Run. You can depend on the book club to meet on Tuesdays and the diner to serve chicken pot pie. I'll probably have to travel some to research articles, but in the end…" she grabbed his hand, giving it a slight squeeze "…I'll always come home to Beckett's Run."

"To me."

She nodded. "To us."

God, he loved hearing those words. He didn't think he'd ever tire of hearing Grace saying she wanted to be with him. "Does this mean you want to take that journey with me? Because I have the riskiest trip of all planned."

She cocked her head. "What's riskier than skydiving in Malta and scuba diving in Australia?"

"Marrying me." He gave her a grin, and took her other hand. For a man who usually prepped and planned, this was one time when J.C. hadn't done either. Another step outside the lines for him. He had a feeling he'd be doing a lot more of that in the months and years to come, and it felt good. Liberating. "I know I'm not doing this right, and I don't even have a ring—"

"You're doing this exactly right, J.C.," she said softly. "You're asking me to marry you in front of everyone who loves us."

Someone cleared their throat behind him, and he heard the soft murmur of anticipation from the crowd assembled in the tent. "Not to mention in front of the whole town."

She laughed. "I couldn't think of a better audience." Then she surged into his arms and a smile broke across her face. "Yes, J.C. Yes, I'll marry you."

And as J.C. leaned in to kiss his soon-to-be-wife, the woman he had loved since that first bite of chicken pot pie, he heard Walter behind him mutter, "It's about time," while the rest of Grace's family and J.C.'s family sent up a collective cheer and loud congratulations.

He kissed Grace for a long, long time, and even when the kiss ended he held on to her. She leaned against his chest, and J.C. thought how right and perfect that felt, and always had.

The book club ladies came over to offer their best wishes. "I'm so glad you're staying in Beckett's Run," Pauline Brimmer said to Grace. "You can be a part of the book club every week now."

Grace put up a hand. "Oh, I don't know about—"

Pauline cut her off with a dismissing wave. "Don't forget, we're reading *Little Women*. I think you're going to love the ending. The last scene with Jo and Mr. Laurence is just so…" she put a hand to her chest and sighed "…romantic."

Grace looked up at J.C., at the man she had loved for as long as she could remember, and shook her head. "I don't need to read it. I already know how the story ends. They got married, settled in the perfect small town, and, most of all, they lived happily ever after."

Then she took J.C.'s hand and headed out into the falling snow as Christmas Eve came to an end and a new beginning began.

* * * * *

Sparkling Christmas kisses!

Bryony's daughter, Lizzie, wants was a *dad* for Christmas and Bryony's determined to fulfil this Christmas wish. But when every date ends in disaster, Bryony fears she'll need a miracle. But she only needs a man for Christmas, not for love…right?

Unlike Bryony, the last thing Helen needs is a man! In her eyes, all men are *Trouble*! Of course, it doesn't help that as soon as she arrives in the snow-covered mountains, she meets Mr Tall, Dark and Handsome *Trouble*!

www.millsandboon.co.uk

1112/MB391

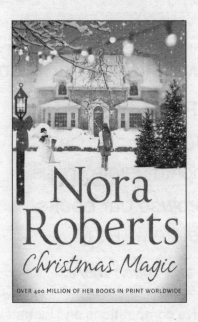

Have Your Say

You've just finished your book.
So what did you think?

We'd love to hear your thoughts on our
'Have your say' online panel
www.millsandboon.co.uk/haveyoursay

- 🌹 Easy to use
- 🌹 Short questionnaire
- 🌹 Chance to win Mills & Boon® goodies

The World of Mills & Boon®

There's a Mills & Boon® series that's perfect for you. We publish ten series and, with new titles every month, you never have to wait long for your favourite to come along.

Blaze®

Scorching hot, sexy reads
4 new stories every month

By Request

Relive the romance with the best of the best
9 new stories every month

Cherish™

Romance to melt the heart every time
12 new stories every month

Desire™

Passionate and dramatic love stories
8 new stories every month